# The Faking of the President

## NINETEEN STORIES OF WHITE HOUSE NOIR

# The Faking of the President

## NINETEEN STORIES OF WHITE HOUSE NOIR

EDITED BY

## Peter Carlaftes

THREE ROOMS PRESS

New York, NY

*The Faking of the President: Nineteen Stories of White House Noir*
EDITED BY Peter Carlaftes

© 2020 by Three Rooms Press

ISBN 978-1-941110-89-8 (trade paperback)
ISBN 978-1-941110-90-4 (ebook)
Library of Congress Control Number: 2019953538
TRP-081

Publication date: April 21, 2020

First Edition

COVER ILLUSTRATIONS:
John S. Paul
www.johnpaulpaintings.com

COVER AND BOOK DESIGN:
KG Design International
www.katgeorges.com

DISTRIBUTED BY:
PGW/Ingram
www.pgw.com

Three Rooms Press
New York, NY
www.threeroomspress.com
info@threeroomspress.com

# TABLE OF CONTENTS

# THE MAKING OF AN ANTHOLOGY
## A FOREWORD BY PETER CARLAFTES

I'D ALWAYS ADMIRED THEODORE WHITE's factual account of the 1960 election, *The Making of the President*. The book set a journalistic standard and enlightened the reading public. Then Idealism gave way to Paranoia, and on November 9, 2016, our galaxy was sucked into an Orange Hole. There were some pit stops along the way—Reaganomics, Sexual Misconduct, Forever War. Now, three impeachment processes later, comes *The Faking of the President: Nineteen Stories of White House Noir.*

CITIZENS OF THE WORLD—
WE COME TO EXPOSE ABSOLUTE POWER, NOT TO PRAISE IT.

*"The dangers of a concentration of all power
in the general government of a confederacy so vast as ours
are too obvious to be disregarded."*
—FRANKLIN PIERCE, *14th U.S. President,
from his inaugural address on March 4, 1853.*

These are some of the leanest years for Democracy in America. And *The Faking of the President* is a creative act of resistance. Each brilliant author reveals how the corrupt nature of power overrides commitment and who, by any means, develops the boldest course of action has eyes on an eternal legacy of glory. And the means right here is noir.

The nineteen stories in this anthology give full regard to the dangers imposed upon the people by our duplicitous leaders and their abuse of the executive branch. Take for instance—the first story in this collection, Alison Gaylin's "Burning Love," a Nixon/Elvis love story that doesn't end well. But for which king? Turn the page now. Why wait for long-winded explanations? You'll be laughing right through it and the next tale penned by Angel Luis Colón, which involves squirrels on the White House lawn who may (or may not) like Ike.

Still haven't jumped ahead yet? Okay—you've forced me to continue.

While the Oval Office has been home to very little diversity, namely *one* African-American (Barack Obama makes a surprise appearance in my story "But One Life to Give") and *one* Catholic (JFK is taken for a ride in Alex Segura's "The Camelot Complex"), *The Faking of the President* was conceived to showcase a very diverse cast of writers, with many thanks to the inestimably talented Gary Phillips. In 2017, Gary edited the Three Rooms Press release *The Obama Inheritance: Fifteen Stories of Conspiracy Noir*, which won the Anthony Award for Best Anthology in 2018. That volume—a companion book to the *The Faking of the President*—featured a few of the same writers you'll find here, including Christopher Chambers (writing here on James Madison) and Danny Gardner (Abe Lincoln), who have both created fascinating tales of lore featuring the Underground Railroad with evil personified by the likes of Francis Scott Key and John Wilkes Booth, respectively. Gary himself has crafted "Y2 Effin' K" for *The Faking of . . .*, which finds Bill Clinton searching for a son born out of wedlock.

And while the US of A has yet to have a woman hold the highest office, women have been equally important to the making of *The Faking of . . .* Take Mary Anna Evans's "All Big Men Are Dreamers." Not only is the country being run by

Woodrow Wilson's second wife when he is taken down for the count by a stroke, no one has a clue who she really is. Two brilliant WOC jump into the fray as Abby L. Vandiver digs into the legacy of LBJ in the fantastical "Reckless Disregard" and Nikki Dolson goes up against Ronnie and Nancy in the moody "Services Rendered." Both S. J. Rozan and Kate Flora (who was also in *The Obama Inheritance*) tackle FDR—with S. J. offering an epistolary admonishment from Eleanor Roosevelt, and Kate exploring the reaches of Huey Long's South.

Greg Herren takes a different tack in "The Dreadful Scott Decision"—where a doctoral student hopes to achieve academic recognition by proving beyond a doubt the sexual orientation of President James Buchanan. One story after another exposes the "unknown": S. A. Cosby takes Bush Sr. far out of his comfort zone; Adam Lance Garcia puts Andrew Jackson in the line of fire; Erica Wright makes sure Teddy keeps it all in the family; Travis Richardson speculates on what would have happened if Gore had been elected; Eric Beetner gives Gore and Bush Jr. an alternative way to settle the score; and Sarah M. Chen takes us into the not-so-distant-future where we find the President is . . . Mike Pence *(egads!)*.

Now you have all nineteen tales laid out before you. Turn the page. *The Faking of the President*—a literary coup d'etat—awaits. Enjoy!

The revolution will remain in print.

*—Peter Carlaftes*

# The
# Faking
# of the
# President

# BURNING LOVE
## BY ALISON GAYLIN

*"I have done an in-depth study of drug abuse and Communist brainwashing techniques and I am right in the middle of the whole thing where I can and will do the most good. I would love to meet you just to say hello if you're not too busy."*

—ELVIS PRESLEY, *in a letter to Richard M. Nixon, 1970*

\* \* \*

SEVEN YEARS LATER

"G'morning, Mr. President."

Elvis says it as soon as Dick picks up the phone, before he's even able to choke down the last spoonful of cottage cheese and ketchup and get a goddamn hello out of his mouth. He's like that, Elvis. Quick on the draw. Impatient with the formalities. Dick only met him once before, and he hardly ever thinks of that time. But he had noticed it then, too—the way he'd grabbed his hand and shook it so fast, the secret service guys were reaching for their guns. Dick remembers feeling sorry for that entourage of his because it had to be hard, keeping up with a whirlwind like The King. More than once, Dick had seen those poor Memphis Mafia bastards get their asses handed to them for being too slow in fulfilling his requests (*"Where's my Fresca, Sonny? Didn't I ask for a Fresca fifteen seconds ago? I'd bet the President would like a can too. I shouldn't have to tell you that, Charlie. What the fuck is wrong with you, man? Am I the only one who* THINKS *around here?"*).

Elvis had impressed Dick as a man who knew what he wanted and wanted it yesterday. A good quality for a leader, and one that had reminded him of himself—though Dick would sooner be tarred and feathered than wear a dress shirt unbuttoned that far down the belly.

*Mr. President,* Dick thinks. What a damn kind thing to call him. It's August 6, 1977. Three years to the day after the Commies and Jews forced him out of office. Outside of David Frost (and Dick is pretty sure that limey motherfucker was being sarcastic), nobody calls him *Mr. President* anymore—and that includes Pat, no matter how much he begs her to. "Hiya, Elvis."

"Mr. President, I'd appreciate it if you called me FEDERAL AGENT PRESLEY."

*Christ on a crutch. Forgot all about that.* "FEDERAL AGENT PRESLEY, of course. Thank you for your service."

"It's a lifetime appointment, right?"

"Yes, siree. Lifetime. Longer, even, if you want it to be." Dick can feel the sweat beading up on his forehead, his pulse starting to race. It's not just The King. All celebrities make him nervous—especially the rock n' rollers. The hep cats. A few seconds with one of those guys, and it's the Kennedy debacle all over again. He still turns red thinking about that time he got mauled by Sammy Davis Jr.

Elvis is saying something about the peanut farmer honoring his FEDERAL FIELD MARSHAL title, but Dick's having trouble focusing. All he can think is, *Why is he calling me?*

Dick hasn't talked to The King in seven years. He barely remembers most of what was said during that meeting, but as he recalls, they had said goodbye on a cordial note. *No unpaid debts, right? Right?*

Elvis had contacted him in the first place because he wanted to be a FEDERAL DRUG ENFORCEMENT MARSHAL and SPECIAL AGENT FIRST CLASS, and even though Dick had no idea what any of that meant, he'd gotten Rose Mary to make up a certificate. She special-ordered a shiny badge, too—sort of like those plastic wings the commercial airline pilots used to give Tricia and Julie when they were little. Nice souvenirs. Of course, the girls never called those pilots out of the blue while they were eating their breakfasts, demanding to be called captain. . .

Presley's talking about Las Vegas now, how it's the only place he truly feels at home anymore. "I know I'm a Southern boy at heart, Mr. President. But Vegas . . . I gotta get back there. It's something else. It's special, but I don't need to tell you that, do I?"

Dick says, "Pat and I saw Wayne Newton play there once. Great little town."

For several seconds, Presley goes quiet. If Dick didn't hear him breathing into the phone, he'd have thought the call had disconnected. "You don't remember."

"Huh?"

"Vegas, Mr. President." He says it again, very softly. "Vegas."

Dick clears his throat. His cheeks feel hot. Twin beads of sweat trickle down his rib cage, and he tries telling himself it's the celebrity thing again. How famous people are semi-delusional because they live in their own world, everybody treating them like royalty and telling them they're right all the time, and that's why they make him so nervous. He's a man of logic, after all—a meat and potatoes guy, when people like Elvis, the hep cats, they're all granola and moonbeams and utter nonsense. But there's more to it than that. *Vegas.* The tone in Elvis's voice. It stirs something in him, the faintest hint of an emotion he can barely remember experiencing, of tiny, bright dots, and a warmth welling in his chest, a sea of lights and a landscape of hope. . .

"Mr. President, I need to talk to you."

Dick shakes the image from his brain. "Go ahead," he says.

"No, I mean in person."

"El . . . FEDERAL AGENT PRESLEY, uh . . . My plate's kinda full right now. I've got to go over the proofs for my memoir, and Pat's cousin's visiting so I don't think I can get out to Memphis—"

"Mr. President."

"I'm awfully sorry but—"

"*Brother.*"

"Yes," Dick says. He can barely speak.

"I'm here in San Clemente."

He grips the receiver, his hand starting to shake. He feels as though he might cry, because he remembers now. The twinkling lights, the racing of his heart. All of it. Every mind-blowing second. *Brother.* "You're . . . here?"

"Staying at the Sea Horse. Just about five minutes from your pad, if I tell the limo driver to gun it."

A thousand questions roam through Dick's mind, and he stares at the receiver as though he expects it to answer all of them. "Okay," he says. "I guess I'll see you in a few."

\* \* \*

ELVIS LOOKS LIKE SHIT. THERE'S no denying it. Whereas he was a powerful specimen seven years ago, he's easily got another hundred pounds on him, pretty much all of it relegated to his face and gut. Dick's read about him in the *National Enquirer,* The King's heartbreaking physical decline. He knows about the heavy drinking and the pill binges and the peanut butter and bacon sandwiches, and he's seen the pictures of him, sweating into his white jumpsuit, pale and bloated, a hair's breadth away from collapse. But as Kissinger once told him, facts don't matter, as long as they're not looking you in the eye.

Dick can't get himself to look Elvis in the eye as they sit in the sunroom of La Casa Pacifica, untouched glasses of iced tea in front of them, but that's for different reasons. He remembers now.

Actually, he's never forgotten that night—only compartmentalized it so he could go on with his life. And with Elvis sitting right here, breathing the same air as him, it's busting out of its compartment and filling the room. *Brother.*

"Where is the Memphis Mafia?" Dick says it partly to make conversation, partly to drown out Presley's labored breathing and his own intrusive thoughts. "You never go anywhere without those guys."

"I left them back home," Elvis says. "Nobody knows about this trip except for my pilot. And he thinks I just flew out here to work on my tan."

Dick clears his throat. "Why the secrecy?" he says. But he can't get himself to play dumb anymore. "Don't answer that. I know."

Of course he knows. He knew it seven years ago, when he shooed the secret service out of the room, and he and Elvis had counted to five before placing the tabs of acid on their tongues—grade A stuff, the best of the best, straight from the CIA. Before Elvis's visit, Dick had never even thought about doing drugs of any kind, let alone that hippie garbage. But then they'd gotten to talking, Presley explaining to him how the Beatles and their ilk had been brainwashing America's youth—these foreign freaks, feeding the kids acid, urging them to tune in and turn on and distrust authority. It was shameful, really. Then he'd suggested they try it themselves.

*"How are you supposed to get inside the mind of a bank robber if you've never even held a gun?"*

The thing with being President of the United States is, you can get your hands on anything you want. All it takes is a phone call—and someone to make the call for you so those hands of yours stay clean. Dick's phone caller of choice was Bebe Rebozo. He had called Bebe and boom. Two tabs of acid delivered by a spook with a big leather briefcase and an ask-no-questions look on his face.

"You remember," Elvis says. "Thank God."

"Yes."

He casts a meaningful glance at the secret service agents standing by the door, and Dick says, "You mind giving us a minute, guys?"

Once they leave, Elvis says, "I haven't been the same since then," and the memories fly at Dick like bats.

"Me neither."

"I can't sing like I used to. I can't sleep. I try to spend time with Ginger and my little girl, but it feels like a lie. All of it. I've been trying to escape with pills and food and booze and the TV, but when I wake up in the morning, it's always the same. It's always you, Dick. I'm empty without you."

"Elvis . . . "

"We're only strong together. You know that. We need each other to survive. The acid told us the truth. You said it, man. You said it back then. 'I see the light,' you said. I finally know where I belong and that's with—"

"Elvis."

"And the thing is, I know you feel the same now. I can see it in your eyes. It's why you're sweating like that. Lord, your hands are shaking. Let me hold you and keep you warm."

"*Stop!*" Dick grips the edge of the table. His head swims. His vision is blurry, his mouth dry. For a few seconds, he's worried he might throw up, or faint, or something else unbefitting a former President of the United States. *I can't afford this*, he thinks. Because he can't. He can't. He absolutely cannot. "Look," he says. "I've got a memoir coming out next year."

"Okay."

"And some of the guys in the party, they're talking to me again. Telling me I got a raw deal from the liberal media. They think I deserve a second chance, and I do, Elvis. Nobody deserves a comeback more than me."

"That stuff isn't important."

"Not important? Are you kidding me? Governor Reagan's talking about running for president, and he asked me to be his advisor. This is big stuff."

"Not as big as destiny."

"What the hell is wrong with you?"

"Run away with me. We can go to Vegas. Live in Caesars. They love me there."

"Jesus, keep it down. You want the guys outside to think we're a couple of fairies?"

"We're bigger than that and you know it. We're *brothers*, Dick. *The acid told us the truth.*"

Dick's muscles tense up. He can actually feel the blood rushing through his veins, the roiling, burning emotion. "*I don't give a fuck about the truth!*" It comes out a bleat. He closes his eyes, feeling Elvis's big mitt of a hand on his. He wants to push it away, but he's too weak. *I'm not weak. I'm not.* "Please," he says, once he catches his breath. "Just try and forget me."

Elvis stands up. As unhealthy as he's become, he's still formidable once he reaches his full height. "I'll never forget," Elvis says. "With or without you, I'm telling the world."

"What?"

"I listened to the David Frost interview. You never mentioned me, but you can rest assured. I won't do you that disservice."

"What are you talking about?"

"You said you're writing a memoir. Well guess what? I'm writing one too."

Dick rises to his feet. He slams his hand on the table so hard it stings, and when he speaks, it's loud enough to shake the walls. "*Elvis! You can't do that!*"

But Elvis is calm. "Sure, I can, Dick," he says, as the secret service men hurry back into the room, hands at their holsters. "I'm The King. I can do anything."

* * *

ONCE ELVIS LEAVES, DICK EXCUSES himself from the sunroom and heads into his private library. "I, uh, need to look at some notes for the memoir," he tells his detail. "I'll only be a minute." Then he locks the door behind him, starts a crackling fire in the marble fireplace and gets to work.

Maybe it wasn't as bad as he remembers. He could explain it away, the acid trip at least. His food could have been spiked. He could blame one of those Memphis Mafia losers—Sonny or Charlie or Red—all those grown men with dogs' names. He wouldn't put it past a single one of them to drug the Commander-in-Chief's rumaki.

If that didn't work, he could blame Commie spies or the Democrats or . . . Hell, he could blame Elvis himself. The pill-popping. The bloat. *All you have to do is look at him to know he's a deeply troubled man . . .*

What bothers him more than what he took that night, though, is what he said. But maybe he's just remembering things wrong. It all could have been in his head, those crazy ideas.

Dick is down on the floor now, unlocking the bottom drawer in his desk and searching through his tape library until he finds it. December 21, 1970. Four days before Christmas. The one day of his life that he'd spent with The King. He places the tape into the reel-to-reel and turns up the volume, grateful for the soundproof walls.

He listens to the start of the meeting, the formal introductions and the presentation of the badge, then fast-forwards to the hour and 45-minute mark, the sound of his own voice, pained and squeaky from the onset of the drug . . .

*"They're right. The kids. The hippies. War is nothing more than a money-making enterprise. We could have called off Vietnam five years ago, but the thing was . . . "*

He fast forwards again.

*". . . and you know something about Alger Hiss. He was smarter than me. That's what I really hated. That's why I went after him. I don't give a damn about Communism, Elvis. Hell, there are parts of it I actually like. For instance . . ."*

And again.

"*. . . sometimes when I get bored, I call Hoover over here, and we listen in on John and Yoko and let me tell you . . . *"

Jesus, why couldn't he stop talking? Dick wasn't normally wasn't like this, was he? Sure, some of it was the drug, but it was so much more the companionship. He'd never quite understood the phrase "kindred spirits" until he'd dropped LSD with The King and looked into his eyes. It was like looking at a younger, better version of himself, and all he wanted to do was talk to this person, spill all his secrets. Tell him the truth.

"You're like the son I never had," he'd said just before Elvis had invited him into his private plane. And the response . . . It's still so clear in Dick's mind he has no need for the tape.

"*No man, listen. I had a twin. His name was Jessie, and he was still-born, and I feel like my whole life, I've been missing him, hurting for him, needing him . . . You're that twin, Mr. President. My brother. My long-lost Jessie. I love you.*"

"My brother," Dick whispers. He fast forwards to the very end of the recording. The three-hour mark, when they'd left the White House together in the dark of night and climbed into the helicopter that took them to Elvis's private plane and they'd set out for Vegas, just the two of them, no secret service, no hangers-on. Elvis, clutching both Dick's hands in his own, telling him over and over that it was okay, he understood, that he would always and forever understand . . . *My soul brother.*

Dick presses play. All he can hear is the sound of his own sobs.

"I love you," he says gently. "But I can't have you ruining my comeback."

Dick removes the tape from the reel-to-reel recorder and unspools it. He cuts it up with scissors and throws it into the fire, vowing never to think on Elvis, to long for him, again.

Then he picks up the phone, presses his private line, and dials the one number he knows by heart. "Bebe," Dick says. "I need you to do me a favor."

\* \* \*

Ten Days Later

"It's done," Bebe says.

"How?"

"It's probably best we don't know the details, Dick. But my guy says it's untraceable, and it'll look like a heart attack."

Dick looks at the clock. It's 3:00 a.m. Pat is sleeping next to him. Her chest is rising and falling as though nothing has happened and he envies her that. In a few hours, the world will wake up. The King will be dead. Everyone will know.

"Thanks, Bebe." Dick hangs up the phone and stares at the ceiling, the dark of the room heavy on him. For one last time, he allows himself to remember it—Las Vegas through the private plane's windows just before dawn, the lights spread out beneath the wings like sequins on a black velvet cape. He remembers Elvis's face close to his, the sweetness of his breath and the softness of his lips as they shared that one, gentle kiss. *My brother. My soul brother.*

Most of all, he remembers a feeling he'll never have again, no matter how long he lives: the thrill. The soaring hope that comes from knowing that now, at long last, you're no longer alone.

# IS THIS TOMORROW
## BY ANGEL LUIS COLÓN

LOOKING OUT OVER THE SOUTH White House lawn, Navy Lieutenant William Crowe noticed the pristinely manicured green pockmarked all over with tiny holes. He dug his hands into his pants pockets and then jerked them out, deciding to cross them behind him instead as he stiffened his back.

"Squirrels?" William asked.

President Eisenhower grunted. "Squirrels. Darn things are driving me insane." He held a putter in his hand and pointed at the far end of the green. "This entire patch was installed by the PGA, you understand that? This is where I relax, where I take my mind off the reds and the coloreds. But these squirrels, which Frank and the boys in Secret Service won't simply shoot, are going to be the end of me. Imagine that, son: squirrels. Not an assassin or a bomb, but a rodent." He raised his putter into the air. "They're even stealing my tees. Got poor Daisy riled up beyond belief. I've had to keep her in the kitchen all week and you've seen that dog; it's no indoor dog."

William didn't say he agreed with that assessment for fear of angering the Commander-in-Chief. They'd explained the situation before he arrived, but Eisenhower insisted on relaying the issue in person. The newly installed putting green was being ransacked by squirrels on the hunt for acorns and other treats.

"I swear it got worse once they finished. As if we've been invaded," The President said. He paced back and forth. William heard Eisenhower wasn't the type to swear, but he could tell the man was on the verge of breaking. His face was flushed, teeth bared. These rodents were driving the man past the edge. He understood the feeling. The weight of the free world on one's shoulders and these little bastards were pecking away at what little sanity the man had left.

"They told me you solved that starling problem over in Jersey?" Eisenhower continued pacing. He slowly swung his putter in a wide arc. "You used a radio?"

William nodded. "Something like that, sir. We found that hearing other birds in distress kept them away. Saved us a big headache. Things were nesting just about everywhere before we implemented the solution. Haven't heard a peep since then."

Eisenhower kicked at a small hole in his green and glowered. "You think you can get something out here? Maybe do the same thing?"

"I'll need to talk with some people, but I think we might be able to repeat the process. I have heard of squirrels making noises to warn others of predators. Maybe we can isolate that sound and play it over your putting green here, sir. Keep them away and isolated to a specific spot on the grounds."

"I'd rather we just shoot the things." The President sighed. "Very well. I have meetings with Mr. Falwell. You have free reign to do as needed to get this solved. Just try to maintain the integrity of the green, please."

"Absolutely sir. We'll get this sorted out immediately."

"I certainly hope so," Eisenhower said, "I'm going to go insane if this isn't fixed soon."

\* \* \*

"THEY AIN'T MAKING ANY NOISE," one of the sergeants tasked with recording the squirrels said as he burst into the office. "We're shaking the cages, making all sorts of ruckus and not a damn peep."

William looked up from his paperwork. "How many did you bring in?"

The sergeant shrugged. "Maybe five?"

"Get more. I'm sure the President would be all right if we collected them either way. We can set them loose far from the putting green as a preventative measure in case we don't collect the sounds we need." William rubbed his temples. "We'll have to increase efforts to get a useable recording. Maybe I can help."

The sergeant crossed his arms. "What else can you possibly do?"

"There have to be some enhanced methods." William stood and grimaced. "We're not the leaders of the free world because we're bad at getting the results we need when we need them, right? Do what needs to be done. The longer we take, the more likely the President is going to harass the Senate to pass a law requiring the Secret Service shoot anything that wanders around that lawn on four legs."

"What if we kill the damn things?"

"Then we're doing our jobs still, right?" That was cruel. William crossed his arms. "I'm sorry. We're not here to be exterminators and I'm getting frustrated. Do the best you can." William stood and collected his jacket and hat. He was running late for an appointment and needed to hurry across town.

"I'll be back soon," he said.

\* \* \*

"HOW IS WORK GOING?" WILLIAM's father, David sat across from him. The man was spritely for his age. Walked everywhere. This was their monthly dinner, an event formerly attended by both his mother and father, but David was now a widower. Nothing about that fresh pain showed on his face. The man was impenetrable.

William smiled tightly. "I've got an assignment straight from the Commander-In-Chief. Slow going, but I think we should be able to find a resolution." He shifted in his seat and picked at the remaining french fries on his plate. "Still, I think this should lead to bigger and better things."

David gave his son a nod. It was as good as a smile when it came to the man. He served his country for a shorter time than William, but he held his son's pursuits in the highest regard. "Well, then you're doing the right things. Before long, they'll have you running the whole show."

"Maybe." William motioned to his father's half-eaten plate. "Not hungry?"

"Ah, well. The neighbors keep force-feeding me. The widow from down the way, Eleanor, has a habit of popping around with a new pie every other day." He winced. "Afraid I'm going to get a little rounder if she doesn't stop."

"Worse fates than taking up a little more space after a lifetime of doing your best, Pa."

The men sat quietly a moment. Things were still awkward between them not for any issues but because William's mother, Mary, was the one to instigate conversation and maintain the rhythm. Without her, they were out of beat—a horn section consisting only of tubas and no sheet music.

"Excuse me." A man walked over with a hand extended. "William Crowe, correct? Navy man?" He was a dumpy looking man. Almost an unkempt clone of the President himself.

William stood and shook the man's hand. "Yes sir, and you are?"

"Richard Neuberger." The name was familiar. As was the face.

William shook Neuberger's hand. "I'm sorry. Have we met before?"

Neuberger smiled joylessly. "Yes, I'm a Senator from Oregon. We've probably walked past one another once or twice over at the White House." He turned to David and extended a hand. "Richard Neuberger."

David stayed seated but offered a hand with a congenial smile. "David Crowe."

William remained standing. "Well, sir, is there anything I can help you with? Any business I'm unaware of?"

"Well, I happened to be eating here and I caught a glimpse of you. I'd been hoping to speak at some point regarding your assignment with the squirrels." Neuberger's eyes lingered on a booth where two broad-chested men were clearing the check. The men stood and left without acknowledging the Senator. "I have a few concerns regarding the treatment of the animals in question. I know the President has been disturbed by them, but I worry about any extreme measures that could be taken."

"Oh, sir, I understand the concerns. I've worked similar cases, and we've often reached very measured and safe solutions. We have no intention of hurting any animals."

"And what of moving them? I've been told that a team of men were collecting squirrels. I'm of the hope none will be displaced." Neuberger puffed up a little. This seemed to be a cause of true concern to him.

William found it strange to be having a conversation like this, but entertaining politicians was often the easiest way to make them go away without a repeat visit. "Well, sir, I can assure you we are not displacing or killing any of the animals, we're simply trying to record some sounds to play as a measure of preventative practice. See, animals listen to each other and if we can have one of our fine, furry friends just state for the record that the President's putting green is a privileged zone, then we'll be able to sort everything out."

"On the record?" Neuberger's eyebrows raised high enough to make the man look as if he'd grown in height.

"Apologies, a bad joke. We're simply going to record sounds that would make other squirrels avoid the area."

"Ah, well then." Neuberger smiled. "I'm happy to hear that. I must be off. Please feel free to let my office know if you need any help. We Oregonians are a little more suited to dealing with the outdoors than our Commander-in-Chief might be." He nodded to David. "You both have a great evening."

When the Senator was gone and William was seated again, David shifted in his seat and frowned. "What was that about?"

"I have no idea."

"Squirrels?"

"Yes. Similar job to the starling issue last year. My reputation preceded me."

"Well, I'm sure this is another good step."

"Hopefully," William said.

"You sound unsure."

"Well, concerned now, really."

"How come?"

William leaned forward and lowered his voice. "Well, Pa, as far as I knew only I, my team, and the President knew about this assignment. I have no idea why anyone, a senator at that, would be at all concerned about this."

"Does it matter?"

"Maybe. I'm not sure. These kinds of things, Pa, they have a habit of going places one would rarely expect in a place like DC."

"Just get the job done and you can be back on your way. Don't worry too much."

William nodded. "Sure. Sure. Absolutely," he lied. Something wasn't right and he hoped he could finish the job without finding out what it was.

\* \* \*

"Where did you find this one?" William motioned to the squirrel with the pointed ears in a cage at the left side of the table. The cages were now stacked on top of each other, each housing the same type of grey squirrel. This one, though, was reddish and a little larger than the others.

The sergeant on duty looked up from his magazine. "I'm not

sure. Think he came in with original haul." He lifted a notepad and read it. "We haven't tried to get a response from him yet."

"Why not?"

The sergeant shrugged. "I assume it's an oversight."

William stared at the squirrel. It looked at William with fleeting interest before curling up and going to sleep. William slipped on a pair of gloves for bite protection—no telling if the squirrel was rabid—and slowly opened its cage. The squirrel opened its eyes but didn't move. It didn't react to William's touch either. William transferred it into a testing cage with a jury-rigged recording device attached. The testing cage was purposely narrow and squat to prevent the squirrels from having any room to move. There were a few tiny holes just large enough to fit pencils through. The thought here would be the squirrel's natural desire to move freely mixed with being bothered by the poking from the pencils would be enough to illicit an audible response.

William set up his furry friend and it sat calmly in the cramped space. It watched him intently as he gathered his pencils and turned on the recorder.

"Test twenty-three," William spoke into a recorder. "Subject is different species of squirrel than the normal kind on White House lawn. I'm hoping this will not be a disqualifying factor as I do not believe it should make any sounds that would be different than the other subjects." He slid a pencil through a hole and gently prodded the squirrel. "First attempt at aggravation. I'll increase intensity every two tries."

The squirrel reacted to the poking by gnawing at the pencil. William maneuvered it out of reach and then tried again.

"Come on," he said as he jabbed the pencil into the cage again, "Squeak for me. Let's finish this." He rotated the pencil inside the cell and managed to catch the squirrel below its abdomen right above its testicles.

"b`lyad`!" a voice in the room said.

William turned to see if anyone was coming. Seeing nobody, he assumed it was simply someone elsewhere in the building. He poked the squirrel one more time.

"b`lyad'!" It was the squirrel.

William leaned over and stared at the furry prisoner with wide eyes. "Was that Russian?"

\* \* \*

"PLAY IT AGAIN," UNDERSECRETARY OF State Smith said. He eyed the red squirrel in its cage.

William pressed the button on his recorder.

"b`lyad'!" The voice was high-pitched and tinny.

The Undersecretary narrowed his eyes. "That's definitely Russian." He paced back and forth. "And this happened when you poked it?"

"Yes sir." William nodded. "I went directly to you. Figured you would be the best man to confirm. I think it cursed at me?"

"Oh, it absolutely swore. That's for sure." Smith scoffed. "Crowe, I've seen things I'll have to take to my grave. Subterfuge that has gone above and beyond bizarre, but this? This is something I have never witnessed or honestly could have expected. A talking squirrel and one that speaks Russian? For God's sake, its fur is even red." Smith took a deep breath. "Any sign that the others speak too?"

"No sir." William motioned to the other squirrels. "They barely made a sound that was entirely usable. This fella, though, he's repeated that swear word every single time I've approached him."

"It's a breach then. They're clearly on the White House property with a mission." Smith pointed his chin to the squirrel. "I'd ask your men to round up as many as possible and get to work repeating your experiment until we identify all potential spies."

"Spies?" William shook his head. "How?"

"The squirrel spoke Russian, Crowe. He told you, in Russian, to fuck off. It was vindictive and responsive to you poking at it with a pencil. It might not be smart, but it's certainly smarter than the average squirrel and clearly flying its banner for Khrushchev. Son of a bitch is barely running things for a year and this is his first little game. Unbelievable." Smith raised a hand. "Keep this quiet. Maintain exclusive access to the subjects. Collect them, confirm, and eliminate."

William was exhausted and overwhelmed. "Eliminate? All of them?"

"Just the reds. The others, go and take them off the property. That should please Ike well enough."

Smith placed his hands on a desk and lowered his head. "This feels far too complicated. They're only squirrels, Mr. Smith. It's not like these are red-blooded communist spies."

"Commie spies, nonetheless, Crowe." Smith stepped towards him and puffed his chest. "Unless you're feeling empathetic simply because they look like something Mr. Disney would put up on a theater screen."

William shook his head. "No, no. I'm sorry. It's simply bizarre and I am tired."

"Then go home and get rest. Get started tomorrow. I want this resolved by week's end."

"Yes sir."

Smith stomped off to do whatever it was the Undersecretary had to do. William felt regret at calling the man. While his knowledge of Soviet spy craft was probably informing a wise course of action, it still felt like an overreaction. The squirrel simply let out a blue word in another language. For all William knew, the damn thing was hand raised by an immigrant. Perhaps it was above average intelligence. Something like a parrot—simply repeating a phrase it would mutter to delight a pack of drunk Russkies at the end of a long day of work.

A cadre of communist squirrel spies? Thinking the words in that sequence nearly gave him an aneurysm, but William wondered, was that far-fetched? He knew people working on mind altering substances that could topple entire governments, weapons built to obliterate cities with a simple press of a button. How unlikely could this gambit be? Like Smith said, a new leader would dip their toes in the water first before diving into the Cold War. Talking, spying squirrels were indeed silly and slightly lunatic, but perhaps lunatic enough to work. The rodents plagued the President daily and knew where he'd be spending his time. It all lined up perfectly.

Still, even amid furry Russian spies, William needed sleep. He packed everything up, secured the squirrel cages—double padlock for the red one—and effortlessly secured a car back to the apartment he'd been provided during his time working in DC. William sunk into the upholstery in the back of the car and he immediately fell asleep.

He opened his eyes and the car was stopped. William jerked up and looked out the window. They were under a bridge and the river was in view. The driver was gone, but the car's engine idled.

"Hello?" William called out. "Is everything OK?"

The rear driver-side door swung open and Senator Neuberger slid in. In his right hand: a pistol. On his left shoulder: a squirrel identical to the red one William knew he locked away securely. The squirrel remained stone still on its perch, its eyes flashing in the darkness.

Neuberger raised the gun and held it between William's eyes. "Why would you do something as stupid as bring Smith into this?" he asked quietly, "Why would you go and do that?" Neuberger's voice was drained of the jovial bounce it had at the diner. It sounded like he was reading—poorly.

William raised his hands and watched the squirrel. "Any reason I should believe this is the Senator speaking?" It was a long shot, but his day was already bizarre. Taking the next leap in logic felt like the obvious thing to do.

"You mustn't remove any of the wildlife from the property. Do you understand me? Crowe look at me not him," Neuberger swung the gun back and forth. "There is no more need to talk to anyone about what happened or what you found."

There were a million questions bouncing around William's aching skull. For one, why? Why something so ridiculous and elaborate? Why something that would attract the attention of the Commander in Chief almost immediately? Couldn't the Russians use something less obvious? Perhaps roaches or actual human spies?

Neuberger leaned forward a little, his chin dipping down. "I know that look in your eye," he rasped, "I assure you; it's all going to be worth it. We are going to lead the world into a better place. It will take time, but one day you will be happy this is how it all happened."

"Are you going to kill me then?"

"Absolutely not. You're on Ike's radar. Like I said, release the squirrels. Give them a recording of whatever you have on hand and move on. Keep your head low and we will all be fine. Even that father of yours. Can't imagine he needs more on his plate, what with losing your mom. I don't think he could stand any further stresses, do you?"

William's cheeks flushed and he bit his tongue, but the anger wouldn't subside. The anger at the threat. The anger at himself for taking such an idiotic job to begin with—he could have easily recommended an associate to solve this problem. The anger at this scheme to infiltrate his government with woodland creatures. And it was the squirrels wasn't it? Neuberger wasn't all there. His eyes were glazed over. The gun wavered a bit. It was the damnable furry bastard perched on his shoulder that was focused, stiff, and intent on this action.

So, William took the chance. He swung a haymaker fueled with patriotic intention, expecting Neuberger to turn as he telegraphed the move, but as he felt fur brush against his knuckles and heard the loud and alarming chirp of terror, William realized the punch connected with the wrong target. The squirrel, flung from its perch, landed on its back and remained stiff. Neuberger also remained stiff, his eyes wide and his nose bleeding. William scrambled away and his back met the passenger side door. There was no appropriate response. Neuberger's hand slowly dropped to his side and remained still, staring wistfully right through William.

No time to waste then, William thought as he turned and flung the car door open. He stumbled out of the vehicle and saw the body of his driver only a few feet away. He crouched to check the man's pulse and was relieved to feel a heartbeat and noticed the rise and fall of the man's chest. The driver was alive and that was good enough for William. He needed to find a phone booth or someone to help him. There wasn't much hope under the shadow of the bridge, so William ran towards the street to find something or someone nearby.

Within a quarter mile, he found a phone booth and ducked in, spinning around to see if he was followed. He dug into his pockets for change and quickly dialed Undersecretary Smith. He had to warn him about what happened—that a United States Senator was not only compromised, but that this little circus act was far darker than he imagined.

"Hello?" Smith's voice was groggy.

"Undersecretary Smith, it's William Crowe. Look, please just listen to me. This Russian thing. It's worse than we thought. I was attacked by a Senator under their control, sir."

"Under their control? How?" Smith asked.

"I don't know. He had a squirrel on his shoulder, and he seemed wrong. Like he wasn't fully in control."

"Are you safe?"

"Now I am. I think."

"Where are you?"

"I'm not sure. I haven't spotted a street sign, but they brought me." William craned his neck to view the bridge under streetlights. "Maybe the Douglass? I can't tell."

Smith cleared his throat. "Stay where you are. I'll have a car find you. We'll meet at the White House. This insanity has gone too far. We need to inform the President and his cabinet immediately. If this is as far-reaching as it sounds, we may need to go to war over it." He scoffed. "A war over squirrels. It sounds like something from the pulps. Stay safe, Crowe. We'll see each other soon."

"Yes sir." William hung up the phone. He turned to lean against the side of the booth and slowly slid down into a sitting position. He needed to get back to the White House. He understood the line Russia crossed with this effort, but the end of the world because of squirrels? He never in a million years imagined things to be this manic. William rubbed his eyes and shot back up to his feet with a jolt: his father. Neuberger's threat could still hold true.

Making the phone call with the last of his pocket change, William said a silent prayer and nearly yelped when his father picked up. "Pa," he said, "I'm sorry. I know it's late. Is everything OK?"

"Everything's fine," David said, "What about you? You sound a little shaken."

"No. No." William turned in place to see if his car was arriving. "Working late. I realized I'd forgotten to give a call."

"Well, that's nice of you. At the risk of sounding rude, I have company over."

Company? Did Neuberger send someone over?

"Sorry, Pa. Who is there?"

"Eleanor again. More pie." David chuckled softly. "I'll need to let out my pants at this rate. We're enjoying some coffee. Playing with her strange little pet."

"That's nice. I'll let you go, Pa."

"Well thanks for calling. Remind me to have her over next time you're here. If only to discuss shared interests between the two of you considering the work you've been doing."

William's heart dropped a little. "What shared interests?"

"The squirrels, William. This thing, my how well-trained it is. Simply sits on her shoulder and chitters away for acorns. Very amusing."

"That sounds very interesting, Pa. I'll be sure to remind you." William wanted to scream, but he worried any sign of distress would get his father killed. "I'll call you tomorrow."

"Have a good night."

"You too." William hung up the phone and punched the number pad enough times to draw blood. He had to stop this. Had to gather any information they had, work with Smith and the cabinet, and prevent the rest of the world from burning in a nuclear holocaust before it was too late. It would be difficult. Eisenhower didn't surround himself with many war hawks, but the men he did have weren't shy about maintaining their conviction. If this threat felt large enough, they would take decisive action before Russia further cemented their plans. This wasn't his job, though. He wasn't hired to help solve a crisis like this. He was hired to help preserve a putting green.

\* \* \*

WILLIAM CHECKED THE TIME. IT was almost 6 hours since he'd left the White House when the car brought him back. The sun was making its presence known in the horizon and the birds began to sing as he walked towards the staff entrance near the South Lawn. He stopped a moment to look at the putting green and saw a few grey squirrels running around. They stopped every couple of moments to sit on their haunches and sniff the air, desperate to find a source of food.

There were no agents at the entrance, but William heard voices as he walked inside. He made a beeline straight to the Oval. Nodding to the secret service agents posted outside the door.

"William Crowe," he produced his credentials, "I believe I'm expected."

The agents opened the door for William, and he stepped past the threshold only to stop cold.

Inside, the President, his cabinet, and some other advisors—Falwell included—all turned to greet him. Each man with a red squirrel perched on his shoulder.

It was too late.

"Crowe," Undersecretary Smith turned to him. He too was taken. "So glad you can finally join us."

William stepped backwards into the waiting grasp of the secret service agents. Why were they doing this without the squirrels perched on their shoulders?

Smith grimaced. "I understand your worry, but I assure you this is not what we thought it was. See, our friends here mean to help us. They mean to stop the menace that intended to use them for harm." He turned to look at his controller. "We just needed to listen. Now I know everything will be fine. All of America is slowly coming to know that as we speak."

An invasion. That's what this was. Even if there was a kernel of truth to Smith's—if it was Smith speaking—little explanation, it meant nothing. Nobody in this room was exercising free will. They were overtaken and serving some other power.

William turned his attention to a large map on the President's desk. Multiple pins were stuck to allied nations.

"There will be peace in our time," Eisenhower spoke, "If you can believe it." He shook his head. "And to think I was worried about something as silly as a putting green. I commend your help, though, Lieutenant Crowe. I understand this is a challenging position to be in, but," The President raised a hand, "We're certain we can help to allay some of the worry, right Smith?"

"Certainly," Smith said as he motioned to one of the secret service agents.

They were going to take him next, William concluded. Never. He swiftly drove his elbow into the closest agent's midsection and made a break for it. His path to the exit was blocked by others with squirrels on their shoulders; one man held a squirrel intended for William, so instead he headed to his working space. Perhaps he could find a firearm or at least hole up for a little while before finding another solution. The recordings, William thought, there were some recordings he could use against these monsters. A means to repel them. That was his key out of this mess. He could use his expertise to stop things before they truly escalated.

Hastening his pace down the hallways, William made it to his working area. The door was locked, but he had his key—which worked, thankfully—and he made it inside. He locked the door and turned on all the lights. Inside, all the cages that were once filled stood empty, doors swung open or entirely torn off. All of William's notes were gone, but his recording equipment was still on his desk. He checked to see if he still had tapes and checked his files for other recordings. If he could find something close to a warning call, perhaps he could convince these squirrels to leave.

"We eliminated all of your recordings," a voice behind him said. It felt faraway. Not exactly behind him, but closer to the floor. There was a hint of an accent in the voice too. European?

William turned around and saw the first red squirrel perched on a tabletop. It sniffed the air, tail twitching back and forth. "You know English?" he asked.

"I know many languages." The squirrel stood on its hind legs and watched William. "You seem uneasy. Did they not explain to you that everything will be fine? That we will solve all the problems you humans keep creating? Sure, this investigation of yours has forced us to hasten the plan, but the plan will work nonetheless."

William was locked in the room with a talking squirrel. There was no more time to make sense of these things or to interrogate it. Instead, William grabbed his recorder and swung it at the rodent, but it was too fast. It bounded to the side, off the wall, and onto William's shoulder. He felt its heft and his arms went slack. The recorder clattered on the floor, the little lid that secured the tapes breaking off.

"This is a shame," the squirrel said, "I prefer not to compel any-one to our cause, but you all are always so insistent on fighting against those you consider your inferiors, no? Khrushchev learned that lesson as well." The squirrel's nose twitched as it sniffed at William. "But you are smart. You will help from now on. Make the world better for all, not just yourselves."

William felt the urge to walk, so he did. He walked out of his office, back through the hallways, and back into the Oval. His head felt light. As if he'd had a couple of beers too many. It was a pleasant feeling, an optimistic feeling—even if he felt the insatia-ble urge for peanuts.

Within, the men with their squirrels turned to greet him. Undersecretary Smith gave him a hearty pat on the back. The secret service agents closed the doors to the Oval and President Eisenhower cleared his throat.

"So, let us pick up where we left off," he said, "The country of Vietnam . . . "

# Y2 EFFIN' K
## BY GARY PHILLIPS

Jazz mellow on the speakers, he piloted the dull-colored, purposely dented Crown Victoria on the 110 Freeway North, traversing the downtown exchange to get to the 10 West. To his right he could see the new sports complex was almost finished. He recalled the Lakers would be moving from Inglewood, where they played now at the Forum, and taking up residence in this brand-new modernistic venue. He also fondly remembered a particular trip out here in '82, as a then-obscure ex-southern governor who found himself, through a friend, at the Forum Club with California cool waitresses in short togas, the liquor and more flowing way too liberally. Always able to moderate his drinking, he'd had his wits about him when he was invited into the inner sanctum of the club, Jerry's Room, named for the team's owner. In there partying of a more libidinous nature took place.

Shaking off the memory of that night, damned if he could recall the name of this new sports arena being built. The Office Depot Depot? The Osco Center? No those weren't right. A guy who was touting his New Markets Tour should probably be better informed on what companies were doing what.

Momentarily he allowed his attention to shift again and float along the notes as Sonny Rollins laid down his rendition of "Cabin in the Sky" to where only Sonny could take it on the sax. He shook his head in envy and awe. How could any one human being get a mechanical instrument to do that? The saxophone was just a funny-shaped tube and a series of valves and yet under the masterful control of Rollins, it was if he blew the breath of angels through the thing. Man. What would his life have been if he could blow like that? He'd wanted to lay on that cat a Medal of Freedom but his advisors had warned such would be seen as too self-serving given he was known to riff a Rollins lick or two when he was wailing. "Y'all are being short-sighted," he'd told them but they'd prevailed. On the CD played as he resumed other considerations.

Negotiating around a slower station wagon to make the lane change for the 10, a thinly disguised President William Jefferson Clinton reflected how the visit to Watts had gone, ending less than an hour ago. This was the tail end of his four-day cross-country trek designed to highlight areas of chronic poverty and under-development, evident especially in these places during the boom of the last decade. He'd started in Appalachia and finished here, a formal roundtable at the community college and impromptu one-on-one talks all part of the effort. Of course, he'd encouraged the young folks who showed up to stick to their studies and do the right thing, but they and he knew that was just so much window dressing. Pretty words, if not backed by real policies or initiatives, were easily blown away by the harsh winds of want. That was why he was so pleased he'd been able to announce his Youth Opportunity Movement, backed by the Department of Labor. That tough little bastard Bob Reich might be gone, but various initiatives he'd set in motion were now seeing fruition. Clinton couldn't help but enjoy that it made him look good.

Still, he wasn't so taken with his own generated flash that he didn't notice the protestors outside the sealed-off campus with their placards demanding living wage jobs. He understood deindustrialization had hit the Southland hard like it had the Rust Belt. He drove past the Crenshaw exit and, taking a look in his rearview mirror, got into lane 4 from the center lane. He took the Washington Boulevard slash Fairfax Avenue exit and took the left at the bottom of the ramp to continue west on Washington Boulevard. He could have stayed on the freeway to take the 405 south, but Clinton knew from experience that the best way to spot a tail was on the street, and not heading straight toward your destination. You stopped, reversed course, and backtracked. Years of philandering had taught him well.

He almost laughed out loud. For all his chasing poontang, what had it got him but a few moments of illicit pleasure coupled with being haunted by his antics years down the line? Gennifer Flowers damn near derailed his candidacy and the price Hillary extracted for not divorcing his conniving ass, "Who-wee," he muttered softly. And then there was the Starr report and the impeachment hell he'd been dragged through. Yeah, it depends on what "is," "is." *Christallmighty, what had been wrong with him*, he assessed, shaking his head. Hell of a thing to change your spots at this stage of life. But at least his sneaking off this afternoon was for a good reason.

Even with his customary precaution, it wasn't long before he'd reached his destination, a Spanish Revival fourplex on a leafy street nestled along the western edge of Culver City. He pulled to the curb and, setting the parking brake, sat there for several beats, the transmission in neutral. His face too was in neutral as several scenarios played out in his mind. Finally he exhaled and, shutting the engine off, got out of the vehicle, adjusting the baseball cap on his recently trimmed greyed hair. In the near distance was a bluff upon which he could see the silhouettes of earth-movers and bulldozers at rest. From what he'd been told, the rise and the flatlands beyond, after a series of court battles between various factions including environmentalists, were to be mixed-use development as well as preservation of the wetlands.

He noted his more immediate surroundings—across the street there was an older woman in a quilted housecoat watering her lawn, a cigarette dangling from her thin lips. Down the block on his side were a man and woman dressed as if there were on their way to church. They were black and the woman had a valise and the man, in a snazzy fedora, had what Clinton presumed were Watchtowers in his hand as they decidedly gave off a Jehovah's Witness vibe even at this distance. With his sunglasses on, he went along the walkway and up the short flight of stairs to one of the two apartments on the second story.

He knocked and heard feet moving across the hardwood floor on the other side. The door opened inward to a pleasant-faced black woman who Clinton knew was past seventy but looked like she was no more than fifty. She and her late daughter had legitimately been mistaken for sisters many times in the past.

"Professor," he said to her as he leaned in to give her a quick hug and kiss on the cheek.

"Bill," she answered warmly, stepping aside to let him in after they disengaged. As he did, she closed the heavy wooden door behind him.

"How's retirement treating you?" he asked as the two stood on an oval rug of Yoruba design. African, Caribbean, and South Seas masks and such decorated the walls and mantle. These had been obtained in the lands they originated in by the professor. The effect was not overwhelming but gave off a comforting cocoon-like aspect of hearth and homestead.

"Working on my book."

"Oh, that's wonderful, Maylene. I'll be gone by then but you know I'll do something to promote it. The foundation should be up and running so we can put on the dog." He thickened his drawl effectively.

"I appreciate that of course." Maylene Finley, PhD, social anthropologist, removed her thin glasses and pointed a stem toward a short hallway. "He's back there."

Clinton hesitated. "Did he say anything about the records I sent him last month?"

She smiled thinly. "He said he kind of liked the Ella and Dizzy ones. But he hasn't traded in his Will Smith. He did though appreciate your letter with them."

"He say that?"

"Even I remember being a teenager, Bill," she chided. "Of course he didn't say that."

"Wouldn't want that," he smiled, already moving past the dining room table. He got to the closed bedroom door and used the middle knuckle of his finger to knock softly on it.

"Come in," said a voice.

Clinton opened the door to see his 15-year-old son Alex Finley stretched out on his bed, his back against the headboard. On his lap was the Macintosh PowerBook the president had sent him, weeks before its official release, a few months ago. On the wall over his orderly arranged desk was a poster, a down-angle shot of Shaq O'Neal in full force dunking the ball in his massive hand. Clinton stood frozen in the doorway taking this in. The boy, the teenager, had grown since he'd seen him last summer.

"How are you, Alex?"

"Good to see you." The kid made no move to unlimber his lithe form from his current position.

Clinton touched his shoulder and sat on the end of the bed. "Working on anything in particular?"

The golden hued youngster, in jeans and a loose Lakers' colors tank top with Kobe Bryant's number 8 on it, stopped tapping away on the keys. His jawline and cheek structure looked like his father at that age. The similarity was particularly noticeable when he smiled. His copper-colored eyes fixed on the President of the United States.

"The Russians have hacked us, father."

"What do you mean?"

"They slipped in a virus in several municipalities to affect I'm not sure what yet. Though if I were to guess, I'd say vote tabulations." He turned the PowerBook so as to give Clinton a look at the screen as he opened a new window on the machine. "These emails went out to people in charge of elections in a few states." He clicked one of the emails, opening a message. Clinton leaned in, having left his reading glasses back at his hotel room.

The president said, "I know this official in Atlanta."

"I know, I saw her on the news with you. That's why I picked this one."

The message was supposedly from Clinton's Council on Year 2000 Conversion. He knew this hadn't come from that body as the message requested passwords and so forth.

"I traced this and the others from out of the country."

"To Moscow?"

"St. Petersburg. They're gathering addresses and phone numbers and more about voters and whatnot."

Clinton said gravely, "I don't think this is Yeltsin's doing."

"Wouldn't this have to come from the top?"

"Maybe. But this strikes me as the work of his prime minister, the one in line to replace him."

"Who's that?"

"A guy named Putin. Slippery devil used to be their spy chief. From the reports I've read about him, this is very much in line with his type of operation."

The door to the bedroom was ajar and the phone could be heard ringing. The young man's grandmother picked up the handset.

"Hello?" After a moment she said, "He can't come to the phone right now, he has company . . . no, it's not another girl . . . yes. I'll tell him." She hung up the instrument and poked her head in. "That was one of your little friends. Georgette. Isn't she a senior?"

The younger Finley flashed even teeth. "You're hilarious, grandma."

"I know," she said, withdrawing.

"Alex, come on. What with all the hullabaloo and hand wringing over Y2K, we've been monitoring our computer systems."

"But you didn't know about this."

"You can believe I'll have this looked into."

Clinton worried the young man was too serious for his age but then again, wasn't it better he was some sort of nerd than not attentive to his studies? But this thing with the girl calling him. He was awfully good-looking.

"Are you dating?"

The teen cocked an eyebrow at his old man, looking up from his monitor screen. "You gonna give me the talk? Uncle Ned handled that . . . years ago."

Ned Finley was Maylene's younger half-brother. He was something of a shady character, into who knew what. It irritated him imagining how that went. "Safety first is all I'm saying, son."

"Yeah, I got that. You ain't out to be no secret grandfather." The kid stared at his screen.

*Bad enough I'm a secret father*, Clinton mused. Hands on his knees, he added, "I'm sorry to be rushed, but--"

"I know, next time it'll be different."

"You're too damn quick for a guy your age."

"Didn't they say that about you back when?"

He rose. "Smartass."

That got a rueful smile.

"We should go."

The young man worked his keyboard. "This is not a joke, Mr. President. I think these sneaks are a test. The real deal might come after New Year's when everybody's let their guard down."

"I'm not blowing you off. I'll have it looked into.

"I hope you mean the NSA. They've got eyes and ears on the Russians."

The kid was sharp, he reflected proudly. "Programmers have been reviewing millions of lines of computer code for months, you know."

"Yeah, I hear you, but sometimes you gotta come in the back door, know what I'm sayin'?"

"You ready?"

"You got the flowers?"

"In the car."

He got off the bed, Clinton regarding his sturdy frame. His shoulders were planed, his jaw Dick Tracy chiseled, and he knew sooner than later he best have a Come to Jesus talk with the lad so he wouldn't repeat his mistakes chasing tail. The triad of ministers currently providing him weekly counseling and prayer sessions weren't just for show. He'd taken their administrations to heart. Alex changed out of his top and into a T-shirt. Clinton placed a hand on his son's shoulder.

"I want you to know, I'm very happy to see you."

Alex Finley nodded curtly and like side-stepping an opponent on the hardwood, managed to slip out from the grasp of his father and place his closed PowerBook on his desk all in a seemingly effortless motion. And as if materializing from the atoms invisibly whirling about him, he now held a bunched-up Raiders hooded sweatshirt in his hand.

"Let's do this," the teenager said.

Clinton opened his mouth hoping for weighty words to penetrate Alex's defenses but a loud knock on the front door froze them in his throat.

"Grandma's got this," his son whispered. The young man closed the door some but left it ajar enough for the two of them to hear. Clinton stood at his back.

"Hello, I'm Richard and this is Elaine."

"Hello," said the grandmother politely.

"We'd like to share the good news with you," said a voice.

"Thank you," Maylene Finley said. "But I've got to get back to what I was doing."

"Maybe when we're around next week you'll have time to talk?"

"Could be."

Clinton assumed it was the Jehovah's Witnesses he'd seen earlier laying one of their tracts on her.

The door closed and the two stepped into view. "Better wait a minute or two until they get further along," the older Finley advised. "Up close one of them might recognize you."

"Most of them Witnesses don't vote," the president quipped.

"They watch TV."

"What does fame feel like?" Alex asked his old man.

"A burden. You figure when you make the NBA it'll be all glitter and glamour?"

"That boy is going to MIT or he ain't going nowhere," his grandma said, country in her voice as well.

"Yes ma'am," Clinton agreed.

Alex looked balefully at both of them.

"You sure you don't want to come with us?" Clinton said to the older Finley.

"It's better you two have this time together," she answered. "I always have my time with her."

"Very true, Maylene." He put his cap back and looking at his growing son, gestured toward the door. "Shall we?"

The youth led the way and the two descended the enclosed stairwell upon exiting the apartment. Reaching the ground floor, Clinton scanned the street, frowning. Did somebody actually ask those Jehovah's Witnesses inside? They were not around now. Well it took all kinds. They fell in step as they headed for his car. Unlocking the passenger side door, Clinton and his son gaped. Popping up from the street side of the vehicle was Richard, the male half of the proselytizing duo just heard at the Finley doorstep. He looked to be in his late forties and his thick, trimmed mustache lifted at the edges as he smiled like a third-grade teacher welcoming his returning students after winter break. Clinton expected him to say he recognized him but the man continued to smile while he extended his hand. There was no *Watchtower* in it.

"Damn, they found you," Alex uttered.

Clinton remained calm and depressed a stem on his wristwatch, a heavy-looking chrome Breitling Transocean Chrono.

The teacher's hand and arm undulated sideways then up and down as if he were imitating a cobra about to strike. Out came the end of a tube in his sport coat sleeve followed by a puff of air.

"Get down," Clinton was already yelling, grabbing his son. Over their heads flew a small translucent dart. Its needle sunk into the trunk of a palm tree, crackling with an electrical charge.

"Where's the woman?" the president muttered. His son instinctively started toward the vehicle's rear end. But Clinton tapped his arm, indicating they should head toward the nearer front end. Acting counter-intuitively was the way to go. This mantra had been his North Star throughout his political career.

Sure enough, as they rounded the closer end, the school teacher was creeping toward the rear. Another dart whistled through the air, this one nicking a ducking Alex along his shoulder blade. But the dart hadn't plunged in too far and Clinton removed it from the fabric of the warm up jacket. The woman charged them from the gap between the fourplex and the single-family house next door over a shared expanse of lawn. She aimed an odd-looking gun at them.

The one calling himself Richard whipped his arm around at Alex but the younger man moved quick. Coming in under the other's strike like Sugar Ray Leonard, he knocked the arm aside and punched. He also stepped in tight, entangling the fake. He cussed and it wasn't in English.

*Russian*, Clinton recognized. He instinctively held his breath as Elaine released a plume of gas at him from her gun. He swatted at this with his cap as he closed the gap between them. He inhaled some of the stuff, but he was determined not to succumb. Though it bothered his fifty plus years of manly sensibilities, he pounded a fist on her jaw. He reminded himself he was protecting his boy. But the demurely dressed woman fooled him. Her kung fu defense aptly deflected the blow. In turn she lashed out with her own punch, which he did not see coming until she smacked him hard. This staggered the president, but he was heartened to see his son was doing better. Richard was on his butt. He didn't brag it, but clearly Alex had been keeping up with his jiu-jitsu, which he'd been doing since he was little. School Teacher tried to rise and Alex clocked him with the side of his Converse sneaker.

Elaine ripped away the lower portion of her dress, exposing runner's shorts underneath as she kicked at Clinton. But this time he was ready and, while he was struck, he'd managed to ward off the brunt of the assault. Taking his cue from Alex, he went in close intending to rip the gas gun from her hand. But she boxed him back, sending him sprawling toward the rear of his car.

"I gotta get grandma." Alex tore off toward the fourplex.

Richard jumped from the roof of the Crown Victoria he'd hopped on and landed on the younger man. Elaine moved in on Clinton who was hunched over, hands on the trunk like a drunk being arrested, a bruise purpling on his cheek. She lunged at him, the trunk lid sprang up, slamming her chin viciously. Clinton had unlocked the trunk using his remote and lifted it as fast as he could. She was momentarily dazed and he ran to his son as the young man and Richard grappled on the ground. Clinton struck the older man in the back of the head twice with his fist and got his son out from under the stunned man and to his feet.

"Let's go, there might be others."

"We can't leave grandma."

"We aren't, Alex. I signaled her, she's out of the apartment."

The kid glared at him even as they began to jog away.

"She's fine, believe me. We've planned for contingencies. Secret Service is on its way, but we have to stay mobile until they get here."

They were running toward the end of the block and rounded the corner and down that street toward the main thoroughfare. Overhead a plane rose, its engines thunderous in the sky as it took off from nearby LAX. Alex was pointing toward a neighborhood market opposite where they stood, separated by an expanse of roadway. Alex's words were momentarily drowned out by the jet.

" . . . behind there," Clinton heard. He shook his head in the affirmative and the two navigated their way across the lanes of traffic heading north and south, accompanied by honking and the screech of several sets of brakes. The president had a hand on his son's elbow but it was soon apparent to him he was holding the lad back and not helping him.

"Don't worry about me," he told Alex who had his hand up signaling an oncoming bobtail truck to slow. "You just keep going."

"We got this, old man," the kid said. Now he was cupping his father's elbow.

Despite the threat of immediate danger Clinton chuckled and together they managed to make it to the other side. He was breathing harder than he cared to when they did but he had to keep up as Alex was still moving, heading around the side of the Stop & Shop market. He followed and in back was a small parking lot bordered by a cyclone fence.

"That's the wetlands?" he said, referring to the terrain behind the fencing to his left.

"Yeah. All this land used to be owned by that crazy rich guy you sent me that book about. He was scared of germs and shit. The one with the big goofy plane."

"Howard Hughes."

"Right, him. Come on." He ran toward the fence and for a moment Clinton was worried the kid had been reading too many Flash comic books and expected to rip through the fencing with his super speed. His hand out before him like a running back stiff arming his opponent, he pushed the fence in at that section and revealed a slit in the links.

"You and your buddies come over here?' Clinton asked as he slipped through, Alex ahead of him. *Smoking Mary Jane with girls and hoping to cop a feel,* he imagined but didn't voice—at least not now.

"Great place to get my head on straight, feel me?"

They crashed through some brush and were now on a dirt path that wended through a lush terrain of trees, tall grasses, and assorted shrubbery. They were in the midst of a variety of flora including sagebrush, California poppies, and Mexican elderberry. A waterway was before them as well.

"That's Ballona Creek," his son said, indicating the water. The algae was so thick and luminescent green, it seemed like you could walk across the surface.

There were ducks floating and diving in the algae covered water as well as prowling about reed covered islands. This instant immersion into a marsh, reminiscent of the ones he'd been hunting in back home in Hope, had Clinton nostalgic and impressed this type of environment also appealed to his city-boy son His watch buzzed and he flipped the face open to reveal a wire mesh screen.

"Eagle we're in route," said a disembodied voice. "Pride Leader is safe and secure."

"Copy that. Home in. But Bear Cub and I are not going to be stationary. He's the primary target they want." It wouldn't make them come any faster, but it warmed him that his smart son had figured out what the Russkies were up to.

"Understood."

He shut the watch face, his son looking on. "Can I get one of those? That's fly."

"We'll see, youngster." They went on. "I'm figuring we better get off this path." He was looking out onto the body of water. "How deep is it out there?"

His son hunched a shoulder while he showed his displeasure at where this line of questioning was going.

A scuffle in the dirt had both whipping around, tensed. The newcomer appeared to be a jogger but that didn't make it so. They separated to either side of the path and the runner went past, huffing in her workout.

"This here crick takes us to the ocean?"

"I suppose so."

Clinton was wading in. "Time's a'wasting." A duck quacked its annoyance at this invasion.

"Aw come on, man." Horrified, the teenager glared at his shoes.

From behind his son came a swish as a projectile tore through the bushes. Before Clinton could yell a warning, the teenager reacted. He went flat as a grey studded sphere the size of a tennis ball shot over his head. Landing several feet away, it burst and emitted a sparkling lavender cloud like the gas gun had. A seagull happened to be swooping low at that moment and after it passed through the purple haze, fell to the earth immediately; breathing but out.

Clinton was rushing back to shore, his arm extended, pressing another button on his fancy watch. Out from it shot a thin silvery cable headed by what looked like a tiny barbed hammerhead. This struck the supposed Richard emerging from the brush holding what looked to be a mini bazooka, bringing it up toward Alex. The barb struck the pretend Jehovah's Witness and he was rocked with voltage, shaking and trembling in place as yellow-white sparks burst around him. Alex finished off the schoolteacher-looking individual with a right cross that sent him limp to the ground.

"Not the only one using electrical doohickeys," Clinton said, the cable retracting.

"I've got to get one of those," his son repeated about the gadget-laden wristwatch. The two went into the water and started across to one of the small islands.

"We gonna hide out there?" Alex asked.

"We don't have to stay low for too long. Just enough to wait for the cavalry." On they waded, then he said, "It hasn't escaped my attention you seem to be taking this all in stride."

"Yeah, well a lot of my life hasn't been normal."

"Wise beyond your years," Clinton mumbled as they got

out of the water, neon green slime on their clothes. "Let's get further in."

They entered the tall stand of reeds and grass, startled as a bird flew out of the tufts before them. Further in Clinton held up a hand signaling a halt.

"What?" His son whispered.

"Disturbance in the water," he said just as quietly.

"A duck probably," he whispered back.

"Bigger," the president knew, tugging on his son's sleeve to crouch down as he did so. He was certain the movement had been ahead of them, someone who'd come into the reserve from another direction. Could this be the female partner or reinforcements or both? If so, how many? Whatever, they had to be kept at bay if not overcome.

"Let me show you something," he said in his son's ear, deftly indicating another aspect of the watch. "Now you try it, only don't depress the button."

As he mimicked his father's instructions, the younger man asked, "What's going on?"

"It's you they want," the president declared.

"Huh?"

Clinton wasn't able to answer as yet another projectile came whistling at the two out of the green. This time it was a weighted meteor chain favored by martial artists. The links wrapped around Clinton's throat and he was dragged over from his crouched down position.

Alex went to help his father as another meteor chain was deployed. This wrapped around the teenager's upper body and he too was pulled from his feet. Out stepped the supposed Elaine, now in her athletic gear accompanied by a second woman, muscular and dressed in form-fitting leather replete with zippers and thigh high boots. A red star glistened on one side of the fierce woman's upper torso and she looked to be from Khazakhstan, of mixed Asian and white heritage. Her hair was jet black and straight. She was reminiscent of women Clinton had encountered on a trip to that region a few years ago.

"Good work, Comrade Novabraxa," Elaine said to the larger woman.

Novabraxa made a guttural sound, tugging on the chain around Alex Finley.

"Up," Elaine commanded, and the shackled father and son stood.

"My people are converging on this place," the President of the United States said.

"We know," Novabraxa said in flawless English.

Like the deluge of numerous birds in flight, the quiet whoosh of wings had them looking up.

"Son of a bitch," Clinton swore. An aircraft right out of that show he used to watch on Saturday nights while sipping a bourbon in the governor's mansion, *Airwolf* was hovering into view. Its deep red coloring almost black.

"Damn" his son muttered.

"Your spies didn't know about this," the one called Elaine gloated. "The Crimson Hawk would be the English translation. Some secrets remain secrets until they must be revealed, President Clinton."

The technologically-advanced jet copter took up position overhead on whisper mode. Down came a rope ladder.

"No funny business or we cripple the boy. It's his brain we want, not his body. Your capture," she added meaning Clinton, "is an added benefit." Elaine produced an old-fashioned Tokarev pistol and pointed the weapon at Alex. "Where's the watch?"

"You better give it to her," he said to Alex.

The teenager hesitated.

"Please, son," Clinton urged.

The kid opened his hand, the watch on his palm. The big women took it and crushed it under her boot heel.

Gun trained on his son, the chain was removed from Clinton's throat.

"I'll go up first to keep an eye on them from above," Novabraxa said.

"Good," Elaine answered.

The leather-clad woman effortlessly ascended the twisty rope ladder.

"Now you." Elaine tapped the barrel of the gun against the younger man.

His hand on a rung, a burst of automatic fire rattled from nearby, sending ducks squawking. Everyone hunched down, heads turning each way. Alex grinned at his frowning father.

"I'll drop you like a bad habit," boomed a voice from the reeds. "Leave baby boy be and get the hell out of here."

Elaine made to threaten the youngster but another round of fire sent bullets vip-vipping into the dirt at her feet.

"I'll blow your goddamn feet off, lady. I ain't playing." Stepping into view was a middle-aged black man with a low top fade haircut and a salt and pepper Fu Manchu mustache. He was dressed in slightly flared slacks, dingo boots with buckles, a jean jacket, and a ribbed turtleneck. He looked to have stepped out of a Sears catalog page featuring men's wear circa 1977. He also had a Thompson sub-machine gun in hand that had to be World War II vintage. There was a second magazine taped to the one inserted in the weapon.

Novabraxa swore in Russian, slashing her meteor chain at the man who'd stepped from the past. As fast as she was, he was faster. He blew the links of the chain apart, the top portion falling away impotently.

"Eagle," came another voice over a megaphone.

"Over here," Clinton called out.

"Y'all better get to gettin'," the machine gunner grinned.

Even as Elaine began to clamber up the ladder, the futuristic looking helicopter engaged its jet engine and, arcing away from the wetlands, zoomed off. Several male and female Secret Service agents spilled onto the small island or were on a raft. Some had their guns out. One of them, a thick-necked individual gazed at the retreating Crimson Hawk as he spoke into a walkie-talkie.

"We'll intercept that fancy chopper," he said, taking the walkie-talkie from in front of his mouth.

"Thank you, Ned," Clinton said to the machine gunner.

Ned Finley nodded. "Anything for my nephew."

Thick neck said to him, "That's an illegal weapon, sir."

Finley glared at the agent.

Clinton said. "I think, just as I was never here and this incident never took place, Pete, you never saw this pea-shooter."

"Yes, sir," thick neck Pete said.

"Now as you all have this under control, me and this young man have a very important appointment to keep." With that Clinton got into the raft followed by his son. Taking up the paddle, he sat toward the rear and the two set off down Ballona Creek amid the quacking ducks and tall grasses swaying in the gentle wind.

"Just to be clear, I ain't Jim to your Huck," his son said.

"Never crossed my mind," Clinton said, laughing and paddling.

\* \* \*

ALEX FINLEY HAD TEXTED HIS uncle there was trouble and his general location on the Nokia phone he'd given him. Back in D.C., Bill Clinton had Richard Clarke, National Coordinator for Security, Infrastructure Protection, and Counter-terrorism for the National Security Council look into the matters to which his son had alerted him. Eventually a confidential report he read indicated the Council felt it had ID'd and neutralized the computer invasion efforts. Though there was concern that the then Soviets had put in place sleeper agents in areas throughout the country who the incoming Russian president might activate. Palm Beach County in Florida was one of the specified locations.

# ARTICLE 77
## BY ERIC BEETNER

"AND AS THIS ELECTION DRAGS on for another day with, frankly, no end in sight, Florida officials assure the American public they are doing everything possible to expedite this recount. Public sentiment seems to have reached a breaking point, however, with voters all across America expressing frustration and impatience."

Secret Service Agent William Boone pressed the power button on the remote and the screen in the situation room went dark. The half dozen screens surrounding the main video monitor still displayed real time maps of global positions and blinked with red and green icons of major military installations the world over, but everyone in the room ignored them and focused on Boone.

"Gentlemen," he said, then nodded at the two women in the room, "and ladies, the time has come for us to do something."

Around the table sat the players in this game. Vice President Al Gore sat next to his wife, Tipper, with his running mate, Joe Lieberman, on her side. Across the table from them sat GOP nominee George W. Bush next to his wife, Laura, and his running mate, Dick Cheney. Behind each candidate was another Secret Service agent and behind Boone stood two more.

Boone continued. "Those idiots down in Florida are being so . . ." he searched for the word. ". . . damn Floridian. It's like watching that team that always loses to the Harlem Globetrotters."

"So what do we do?" Al Gore asked.

"I thought the Supremes were taking care of it," said Bush.

Gore scoffed. "You mean the court or the girl group?"

"Either way," Boone interrupted before things got out of hand again. "We need a quick solution or we risk losing the confidence of the American voter."

Cheney snorted. "I think that ship has sailed."

Gore turned to him and said, "Aren't you the one who said the voters are sheep and need a shepherd with a good, strong stick?"

"Not on the record." Cheney smiled with half of his mouth.

Boone again regained control of the room. "Agent Turley has found a small provision that could offer a solution to this." He turned over his shoulder to one of the men standing stoically against the wall. "Eddie, why don't you show them what you've found."

Turley stepped forward and carried with him a small bundle of yellowed parchments in his white-gloved hands. He cleared his throat.

"The Founding Fathers did provide for this outcome in a situation where a contest is too close to call or is otherwise undecided in a timely fashion. Article 77."

He turned to the third page of the parchments in his hands. The sheets crinkled and scraped against each other like sandpaper.

"This is direct from the Library of Congress," he explained. "This statute was written in the fall of 1787."

Everyone in the room nodded along, impressed with such a foundational document.

"We have, of course, never had cause to use it before," Turley said. "Or at least not that is documented."

He gave a glance to Boone who waved him to continue.

"It's written a little confusingly but the idea of it is that if a contest is left undecided for more than a week, the matter shall be settled, and I'll use their word here, by 'fisticuffs.'"

He was met by blank stares from the men in the room. Turley held up the page and pointed to the word—in the text, written in slightly smudged ink with wide loops of cursive in the double f's.

"A fistfight?" Gore said.

Turley nodded.

Boone stepped in to clarify. "It is to be conducted out of the public eye and known only to the parties involved."

"So Al and I are supposed to fight each other?" Bush asked.

"Well," said Turley while pointing out the word—again. "Yes."

"This is ridiculous," Cheney said. "Why not pistols at dawn?"

"I bet you'd like that, wouldn't you, Dick?" Gore said. "You and your precious second amendment."

"You're damn right I would. I'd like to shoot you in the face with a goddamn shotgun." He pounded on the table. "And I've damn well done it before."

"Gentlemen," Boone said, holding out calming hands over the table. "A situation like this undecided election leads to vitriol and bad blood, which is exactly why this statute was written. To provide a definitive and swift end to the dispute like men, or at least a 1787 version of men."

"Don't fool yourself," Cheney said. "Those fellas were still wearing powdered wigs and silk stockings."

"In any event," Boone said, "the founders left this here for us and it has been decided that now is the time to use it."

"If we haven't used it in two hundred years," Bush said, "why use it now?"

"It's the year 2000, George," Gore said. "The country is 224 years old."

"You know damn well what I meant."

"I know you're no good at math."

Boone had lost his patience. "Gentlemen, please."

Lieberman cleared his throat and said, "Well personally I think that—"

Bush, Gore, and Cheney all together said, "Shut up, Joe."

Lieberman sank into his chair and remained quiet.

"If we want this to end," Boone said, "we have here a legally binding process with which to achieve an outcome this very afternoon so the American people can start to move beyond this election and into the next administration."

"I won't do it," Gore said. "It's beneath the office of the presidency."

"I won't either," said Bush. "I say we let the Supremes decide."

Gore began humming—under his breath.

Boone ran a hand over his face, exhausted. Turley shuffled his papers back in order.

Boone let out a long sigh. "Well then, it seems we're at an impasse. I suggest we—"

"I'll do it."

Everyone turned to the voice. Sheepishly, Tipper raised her hand. "I'll do it. I'll fight."

With slack jaws and dumbfounded expressions, the men all began to admonish Mrs. Gore with why they thought it was a bad idea.

"I will too."

Again the room fell silent and now all eyes turned to Laura. She leveled her steely gaze at Tipper. "I'll fight."

* * *

TWO LEVELS BELOW THE WHITE HOUSE, directly beneath the bowling alley everyone knew about, was a seldom-used room built in the late fifties. Originally installed as a bomb shelter, it was converted over to a workout room during the Reagan years when a more substantial fallout bunker was constructed to appease Ronnie's paranoia that the Russians had it out for him. According to White House records during all eight years of the Clinton administration it was only used twice for exercise.

The room was nearly empty. A heavy bag hung in one corner and a low rack of dumbbells sat gathering dust in the other corner.

The Secret Service agents led the group into the room.

Al Gore walked closely behind his wife. "You don't need to do this," he said.

"Well, clearly you're not going to," she said. Al hung his head and slunk back a step behind her.

George Bush walked behind his wife, Laura, but it was Cheney who did the talking.

"What you're gonna want to do is go for the ankles. Get her off balance and get her on the ground and then you've got her. If she gives you the opening, a swift kick in the baby maker is always a good way to go."

"Laura," George said. "I don't feel right having you fight in my place."

She stopped and fixed her husband with a cold stare. "Your daddy isn't here to do it for you so I guess we have no other choice."

She turned and kept walking. Cheney put an arm around her shoulder. "Now, when you've got her down, go for the eyes."

Agent Boone moved to the center of the room. "Okay. Since all parties have agreed to terms, the winner will, by proxy, be declared the winner of the 2000 presidential election and be appointed the forty-third President of the United States."

He motioned to the door. "We're joined now by Secretary of State Madeline Albright and House Speaker Dennis Hastert as witnesses. They've been briefed on Article 77 and have agreed to the same terms the candidates have."

Albright and Hastert entered the room and stood against the wall. An agent closed the door behind them and the heavy, six-inch steel blast door slammed with the resounding metal-on-metal clap of a prison gate.

Tipper swallowed hard and flexed her fingers. Laura let out a sharp breath and slapped a fist into her palm.

"Ladies," Boone said. "In Article 77 there are no provisions on the type of combat required so we'll leave it up to you what _ boundaries we should set. If I could suggest—"

"Fuck boundaries," Laura said. She stared across the room at Tipper who met her gaze with a less-than-confident look.

Al set a hand on his wife's shoulder. "Tip, you don't have to—"

"Agreed," she said. "Fuck boundaries."

Boone looked to the two candidates who each gave a shrug of acceptance.

"Then we can commence whenever you're ready."

"Rings off," Laura said. "Agreed?"

Tipper said, "Agreed," and slipped off her wedding rings, handing them to Al.

Cheney clapped his hands together once. "Hooo boy, this is gonna be a hoot."

* * *

SECRETARY ALBRIGHT STEPPED BEHIND Al Gore and set a hand on his shoulder. "She'll do fine," she said.

"I don't know," Al said. "She's not a fighter."

"She's a woman in politics. Trust me, she knows how to fight."

Speaker Hastert stood beside Bush. "This sure is a new one."

"Laura knows her way around a scrap, I'll give her that."

"Texas versus Tennessee. I'm keen to see how this turns out and I don't think I need to remind you how important this is to the party at large. Four more years of this agenda is—"

"I get it, Dennis. Can we just focus here? My wife is about to throw hands."

Hastert stepped away and gave Cheney a look and a shrug.

"Stay back and shut up, Hastert," Cheney said. "This isn't your wrestling team and they aren't young boys so this shouldn't interest you at all."

Red-faced, the speaker moved to stand against the wall behind his fellow party members.

Boone stepped into the middle of the room.

"I'll act as referee and if I call the fight, you both need to respect the call. Agreed?"

Both women nodded, as did their husbands.

"Get on with it," Cheney said. He had bloodlust in his eyes like he was seeing an extra-rare steak being brought to his table, the plate sloshing with pink juices. "I don't see why we aren't allowing any weaponry. This is a nation with the world's largest fighting force. We live by our weapons. Besides, it might hurry this thing up a bit."

"Dick," George said. "Not now, okay? Show some respect for Article 77."

"If we're gonna bring respect into it, this fight is going to be shit." With a pout on his face, Cheney took a step back toward the wall with his arms crossed over his chest.

Boone raised his hand above his head, then brought it down sharply. "Begin."

Laura came out of her corner like a greyhound at the track. Tipper saw her charging across the room and ran the other way.

"Don't be a pussy," Cheney barked.

"You got this, Tip," Albright said.

Tipper found her footing and put her hands up in a boxing stance. Laura lifted her hands too and they met an arm's length apart, each dancing on the balls of their feet, waiting for an opening.

Al called out across the room, "George, we don't have to do this. If you concede, we can stop this craziness. You know full well those butterfly ballots were deceptive. And if you go by the popular vote then—"

Laura launched a haymaker with her right hand and caught Tipper on the shoulder. Luckily, the pads of her pantsuit deflected much of the blow, but the fight was on.

Both women moved forward and tangled into a clinch. Laura raked her foot along Tipper's leg, trying to knock her off balance.

Tipper gave several short punches to Laura's midsection, but she didn't have enough arm behind them to do any damage.

Laura pushed off and swung another right that caught Tipper high on the cheekbone. The crack drew an audible gasp from everyone in the room. Tipper stumbled backward and Laura grabbed her right hand in her left.

"Don't go knuckle against bone like that," George cautioned. "You'll break a finger."

"I think I just did."

"Use the heel of your hand," he said, demonstrating with a few smacks to his own palm.

A short streak of blood slashed across Tipper's open cheek. She charged forward and shoved with both hands against Laura, knocking her back. Laura tripped over her own feet and tumbled to the floor.

"Hey, no pushing," George said. "Boxing rules."

"We never said that," Al said.

"It's a fight, god dammit," Cheney said. "Back alley rules. Now get to it. We already got blood, let's see some more."

Laura stood and rushed Tipper. She got hold of Tipper's jacket and spun her, flinging her off into the heavy bag that walloped Tipper like a heavyweight fighter and sent her to the ground. She immediately scrambled to her knees, but Laura was on her. Laura pulled her up by the back of her pantsuit jacket and landed a kick to her abdomen. Tipper coughed out all the air in her lungs and fell flat to the ground.

Laura stood over Tipper, reached down and flipped her over on her back. Laura could smell the blood again. She smiled down at Tipper and reveled in her bloody cheek, the gasping for air. Tipper kicked out with her feet and swept Laura's legs out from under her. She landed on her tailbone with a smack.

A cheer rose up from the Democratic side of the room.

"That's it, Tip," Albright said. "Sweep the leg."

Lieberman said, "Hey, like—"

Al and Madeline both said, "Shut up, Joe."

Tipper climbed up on all fours and sucked in air. Laura, stunned, sat up and shook the fog from her head. Tipper lifted a hand off the mat and swung out, catching Laura across the chin with her knuckles.

The Democrats cheered again.

"Quiet down, you pinkos," Cheney said. "Remember when you celebrated too early on election night?"

"Clam it, Dick," Lieberman said.

"You don't tell me to clam it." Cheney took off at a moderate trot around the edge of the room, bushing past Hastert and shoving him into the wall. He reached Joe Lieberman and socked him in the stomach. Lieberman bent forward and let out an anguished sound like a cat getting its tail stepped on. With Joe bent forward, Cheney ripped the yarmulke off his head, balled the black circle of fabric in his hand. Eyes shut and mouth open in a pained O, Joe did nothing to stop Cheney shoving the yarmulke into his mouth and punching an uppercut to close his jaw with a sharp crack.

"Mr. Cheney, please!" Boone shouted. "This is between the ladies."

Cheney waved him away. "Aww, bunk!" But he walked back around the room to his side next to George.

The women were standing again, circling for position. Laura took a swing but Tipper dodged it. Tipper tried out a right hook, but Laura leaned back and it swished impotently through the air.

Tipper shucked out of her pantsuit jacket. She bounced on the balls of her feet, skipping left, then right. Trying to be unpredictable.

Laura kept eyes locked on her prey like a missile tracker. She watched Tipper's eyes. It might take time, but they would give her away.

"You know I play drums, right?" Tipper said. She got a blank stare from Laura. "Well, I'm about to beat your ass."

Tipper rushed. Laura swung but Tipper ducked her head so Laura's fist bounced off the crown of her head. Laura yelped in pain as her knuckles took another beating. Tipper crashed into her opponent with a tackle right from the playbook of the '85 Chicago Bears. They drove into the floor as a two-headed beast. Tipper wormed her fingers into Laura's hair and began pulling.

With their backs to the wall watching the action, the two Secret Service agents behind Gore and Lieberman silently handed a twenty dollar bill from one to the other, winnings from a bet about who would start the hair pulling first.

Tipper slammed Laura's head against the floor once, twice, three times. Laura swung her arms wildly, connecting only with Tipper's shoulders. She bucked her hips, lifted Tipper off the floor, but Mrs. Gore rode it out like a pro rider hanging for his eight seconds.

Laura gave an open-handed slap across Tipper's already split cheek. The blood flowed fresh, but Tipper didn't let go. Laura slapped her again. Tipper bounced Laura's head off the floor again.

"What is this, a cat fight?" Cheney shouted. "Christ, if my Liz was in there she'd whip both of your asses like a Mother Superior at a Catholic school. Damn, Laura, go for the eyes!"

Laura didn't have to be asked twice. She dug a thumb into Tipper's right eye. Tipper screamed and rolled off. Clutching at her face.

"That's against the rules," Al shouted.

"There are no rules," George said.

"But this is a nation of laws."

"Not after election night. It's goddamn anarchy, baby! Nobody knows who's running this country. Anything goes." George pumped his fist and howled like a fan at a college football game. He hadn't had this much energy pumping through his veins since his cocaine days.

Behind Boone, the door opened. He turned away from the scene in front of him to see the first lady standing there.

"Mrs. Clinton. I'm sorry, but you can't be here right now."

Hilary peered over his shoulder at the room. Her face was a pinched knot of confusion and concern.

"What's going on here?"

Turley held up the parchment in his white-gloved hands. "Article 77," he said.

"Article what?"

Turley pointed to the word. "Fisticuffs," he said.

Boone blocked the doorway. Behind him, Mrs. Gore had stood up and she and Laura were stalking each other again, though more slowly now, panting like two bulls in the final stages of a bullfight.

"I'm so sorry, ma'am. It should be over soon."

Mrs. Clinton looked past him. "Madeline, what is all this?"

"Democracy in action," Albright said.

Mrs. Clinton gave a last look around the room and a disapproving scowl. She turned, but not before palming a fifty dollar bill and handing it to Boone. "I got fifty on Laura."

Boone closed the door and locked it this time.

* * *

Tipper launched across the room with a guttural screech in her throat. Her hands out in front of her like talons on a raptor. Her pink-painted nails raked slashes across Laura's cheeks. Blooms of red sprouted. Tipper was a ball of flying fists, flailing hair, and wild tribal noises.

Laura fought back. She reached out and stopped Tipper's right hand as it swooped in for another swipe at her face. Laura bent the fingers back until she heard pops. Tendons detaching. Bones dislocating.

The pitch of Tipper's wailing went up.

A knee dug into Laura's belly. Lucky for her, they weren't planning on more kids. As hard as the hit was, she wouldn't have been surprised if the twins felt it back in Texas.

Laura shot out a straight arm and put a tight fist into Tipper's left breast.

Al saw it and winced, thinking—

One after the other they traded blows. Blood flowed from noses. Rib bones cracked. Hair was pulled, eyes gouged, fingers fish-hooked into mouths. One of Tipper's teeth swung tenuously close to falling out, like a hanging chad on a Florida ballot.

Panting, bleeding, swelling, they stood facing off, the future of the United States hanging in the humid air between them. An obscure rule from the forefathers brought the two women to a place of feral rage. For pride, for country, for their husbands they fought.

Tipper swayed on her feet, one eye nearly swollen shut. The fingers of her right hand were a broken, tangled mess.

Laura tasted her own blood flowing freely from her nose. At least three ribs on her right side were cracked. She faced down her enemy. Out of moves, her hands decimated by the fight, she tilted forward and drove her skull toward Tipper.

Mrs. Gore was too slow. Laura's forehead crashed into Tipper's nose with a crunch of shattering bones and cartilage. Tipper went down and Laura followed. Once on the ground, Laura straddled her and began punching the ruined nose with the heel of her hand. Tipper raised no hand in defense. Cheney sounded like a bull in heat as he cheered on the carnage. George was frenzied like hour seven of an all night coke binge.

Al covered his eyes.

Boone raised a hand over his head. "That's it!" He stepped in and four Secret Service agents followed him. They pulled Laura Bush off Tipper. She still thrashed like a shark out of water as the men pulled her to a neutral corner.

Tipper lay there, choking on her own blood. Al knelt by her side. He leaned into her ear where only she could hear him. "I am so going to divorce you for this."

Boone shook his head, incredulous at the brutality he'd witnessed.

"We have a winner. Mrs. Bush, as proxy for her husband, has won. The presidency is yours, sir."

Cheney raised his arms in victory. "Yes! I win!"

"He meant me, Dick," George said.

"Yeah, yeah, whatever."

"According to Article 77," Boone said, "this election is officially over."

\* \* \*

GEORGE W. BUSH STEPPED TO the middle of the room. The two Secret Service agents lifted Mrs. Gore to the corner and radioed for a medic. George extended a hand to Al Gore.

"At least it's over, right?"

Al regarded the hand, seemed like he wasn't going to take it. "You promise to do a good job?"

"I'll work hard for the American people."

"I know you have it in you, George. Please don't let the people down."

Gore took the hand and shook.

"Don't worry, by this time next year I bet nobody even remembers all this mess. By November . . . no, even earlier. By October or September 2001, this country will be healed and on its way to a brighter future than ever. You'll see, Al. Nothing but blue skies ahead."

# ALL BIG MEN ARE DREAMERS
## BY MARY ANNA EVANS

*"We grow great by dreams. All big men are dreamers."*

—WOODROW WILSON

I CANNOT DENY MY PLEASURE in seeing Mrs. Wilson after being so long parted. She is not my patient, although her husband has been in my care throughout his presidential term, yet my medical training drives me to assess her health and well-being. A physician is never not a physician.

Her silk skirt, cerulean blue, rustles as she hurries down the White House's center hall to greet me at the top of the stairs, and the soles of her tiny shoes clatter against the old wooden floor. "Doctor, I am so pleased you could join me. The president and I have sorely missed your companionship during our time abroad, especially Woodrow. You are far more than a physician to him. If any man needs friends in this troubled world, it is my husband."

I know, and Clara herself knows, that she understates the case. While I trust that Wilson cares for me as a friend, it was as a physician that he needed me most during his long sojourn in Europe negotiating an end to the World War. I failed him.

His health, always precarious, had struck fear in my heart in the months before duty took the two of them away. He suffered terrible headaches that I was powerless to treat. There were times when his face went suddenly white, as if deprived of blood, and I could only guess as to whether his brain was sufficiently suffused. Judging by his extreme fatigue and recurring neuritis, I had feared the advent of apoplexy at any moment. I knew that if this man crumbled, humanity might well destroy itself. I confess that I soothed my guilt over being too old to fight by imagining that I was doing my part by keeping him alive.

Imagine my dread when my own health stood in the way of my accompanying him to negotiate the treaty that would end the war, once and for all. Had I been ambulatory, I could not have been moved from his side. I would have risked apoplexy for myself to keep him alive. Instead, I was unable to travel for the most mortifying of reasons, severe and uncontrollable dysentery and vomiting. My patient, upon whom the world depended, sailed into the Atlantic under the care of a doctor who knew nothing of him beyond my extensive notes. And, of course, the testimony of his loving and solicitous wife.

A full day has passed since their return, and I cannot express how anxious I am to see how well the president weathered the journey. Ever mindful of propriety in the company of the elegant Mrs. Wilson, I hesitate to ask after him outright, but she anticipates my desire.

"My husband is resting after so many days aboard ship, but he has expressed his wish to see you soon."

She opens her mouth to say more, then closes it. Ever socially adept, she has managed without words, and with only the hint of a gesture, to convey that all is not right with Woodrow Wilson.

I am not surprised. I have been reduced to assessing my patient through newspaper photos, indistinct and grainy, and what I have seen does not leave me sanguine about his condition. In some images I saw a familiar face that would have seemed unchanged to others, but which was twisted ever so slightly on its right side to my worried eyes. I saw scarves around his neck in weather too warm for scarves, and I tried to discern whether the right jaw beneath them sagged. His familiar wire *pince-nez* was replaced by a pair of sun cheaters with heavy tortoiseshell frames, and their darkened lenses frustrated any attempt of mine to discern the state of his pupils. Most concerning was the sling that supported his right arm. News reports said that he had slipped on a wet deck while aboard ship, fracturing his wrist, but I viewed him through a physician's eyes and I was not so certain. A sling does more than support a broken arm. It can just as easily camouflage a paralyzed one.

Mrs. Wilson—Clara—sees my expression and says, "Let us take our tea in the East Sitting Hall."

We are standing at the top of the stairs and must walk away from the bedchamber where I presume Wilson is resting and away from his adjacent office. Though the world does not know this, Clara has long assisted the president in that office with such tasks as decrypting messages and encrypting their replies. To be truthful, only I know the extent of her involvement in our country's affairs. Several members of the cabinet suspect her of being a meddling wife, but even they would be shocked by her wide-ranging influence. Certain housekeeping staff may wonder about the things they see, but they are a closemouthed lot. They are well-aware that this is crucial to their continued employment.

"Would you choose something for the gramophone?"

From this deceptively ordinary question, I surmise that, though we cannot be behind closed doors for propriety's sake, Clara would like to speak without fear of eavesdroppers. My heart quickens in concern for the president. I attempt to slow it by reflecting that she would have ushered me directly to his sickbed if the situation were dire.

I sink into my accustomed chair, and she pours my tea. Her graceful hands are lovely against the old china. How many times have we met thus, playing an extended game of chess that pits the nation's—and indeed the world's—interests against the well-being of a man we both love?

I allow myself to look at her with a physician's trained scrutiny. I am gratified to see that she looks well. In itself, this is an accomplishment for a woman in middle years who has recently ended a long journey with a man of not-dependable health. Upon further thought, I will say that "well" is not the right word for her appearance. She looks splendid. There is color in her fair cheeks, and she moves with the particular grace of a healthy woman. The skin of her face and hands is remarkably unlined and unblemished for a woman in her forties. If there is gray in her golden hair, it is not apparent, not even to a man whose training drives him to observe physical details that a gentleman should perhaps neglect when viewing a lady. Along those lines, I am finding it difficult to ignore the ankles revealed by her modishly short skirt, cut to the mid-calf. They are so finely modeled that I believe I could encircle them with a single hand.

I do not wait for her to slice the cake before I speak. "I have watched your trip through newspaper photos. I trust that his broken arm is healed and that all other things are well with him."

She deflects my implied question and says, "We were careful with the photographers. They saw him at his best."

"I saw no photos of the president climbing stairs for far too long, but I was relieved in recent weeks to see him do so again."

She wields the cake knife like a Turkish scimitar, dismembering the cake and serving us each a slice. "Did you see photos of him eating? They were few. There were days when he was incapable of connecting his utensils with his mouth. When he is in that condition, I must feed him."

I take a bite of the cake, as if to prove with my fork that I am more of a man than her husband. "Am I right to presume that he has been ill again but is improving?"

She dislikes direct questions. I know this, but still I ask them.

"The trip was a success," she says, and it is not an answer. "The United States has negotiated a treaty that establishes our victory and divides the spoils of war. It recognizes the sacrifices made by Russia to achieve victory. It restores national borders into a configuration that gives some hope for long-term stability. And yet it does not crush the Germans so completely that we can expect them to burst out of their borders again in twenty years."

My eyebrows rise despite themselves. This policy reflects her opinions far more closely than it does her husband's. In particular, Wilson's prejudice against the Bolsheviks has been strong since the recent uprising that overthrew the Tsars and placed the Reds in power.

Who would have expected a genteel widow to marry into the White House and bend world affairs to her own will within a span of five years? My admiration for Clara Andrews Avery Wilson rises, and it was already considerable. She was, in fact, on my arm at the moment Woodrow Wilson saw her and decided that she must be his wife.

Had I considered the danger of being put into competition with the President of the United States, I would have endeavored to keep her to myself until our courtship reached my desired endpoint, which was most emphatically marriage. I was besotted and, truth be told, I still am.

But, alas, I made a strategic error. I attempted to sway her heart with my reflected importance as the president's friend and physician. I even live in the White House, a fact that I wished her to know as I presumed it would be a point in my favor. I invited her to a formal reception at the executive mansion, knowing the impression that the gilded entry hall of the great old house can give. As if it were destiny, the president himself stood directly in view at the instant we were ushered through the door. Edith Bolling, the woman he was intently courting, was beside him, so perhaps I can be excused for failing to foresee the speed with which he would convince my Clara to take Edith's place. And who could fail to love

Clara, sheathed as she was that night in a lilac gown, her shoulders wrapped in a wisp of aubergine chiffon that obscured but did not conceal her flawless décolletage? She was installed in the White House as Mrs. Woodrow Wilson within six months.

And so I have watched five years of their happiness and am still watching, as I live a lonely bachelor's life in my third-floor quarters. Should I be ashamed that I have survived those years by drinking up the scant drops of friendship and camaraderie that a woman in her position can appropriately dole out to an unmarried man? Perhaps I should, but I am who I am.

"Foreboding grips me, and I cannot sleep," she says. "He loses grip on reality and this symptom is not new. Do you know that we spent the afternoon before our departure discussing the furniture here in the executive residence? 'Perhaps the mauve chair is best in the Yellow Room, alongside the green davenport,' he said to me as he dragged chair after chair into the room, emptying all of the other chambers on this floor."

I see faint scuff marks leading from the chair underneath me, a double line that extends across the wooden floor and into the central hall. I do not ever need confirmation of her truthfulness, but these scuffs provide it anyway.

She wrings a handkerchief between her fingers. "Oliver, he was desperately agitated and stayed that way until he had arranged an array of chairs precisely around the room's oval floor, measuring the distance between them with a ruler."

"Quite disturbing behavior," I say, reveling in the fact that she has called me by my given name.

"An hour later, he grew quite frantic to see that the mauve chair was next to the green davenport. He shifted chairs until I feared he would collapse. He would only rest when he was comfortable in his mind about the chairs' arrangement."

"I never saw the Yellow Room in that state."

"That is because he rose from resting with no memory of what he'd done. He walked past the Yellow Room, stopped in his tracks, and asked, 'What on earth has happened here? Ring for Adam and have him put things right.' Ever since then, his mind is . . . not dependable. You saw in the newspaper how I cling to his side in public. I guide. I suggest. When he is asked a question, I whisper the answer in his ear. Woodrow has not spoken for himself in quite some time."

I feel my own face grow pale. I have seen many physical symptoms pointing to disease in the vasculature of the president's brain, but this was my first evidence of any effect on his mental functions.

"Oh, my dear. You have been through so much."

She nods and refills my teacup.

My memories of the past year take on a new shape. So many afternoons, the two of us met here for tea, pretending to be old friends in conversation while we plotted ways to lighten the president's burden. She learned to decrypt his messages. I learned to summarize the blizzard of information that necessarily falls on a president at war. And I learned to be content with fragments of stolen time with the woman I loved as we labored to save the man she loved. I loved him, too, or I would have prayed for a fit of apoplexy that would widow her and give me another chance.

"I had no idea it was so bad, Clara. Why didn't you tell me?"

"I needed your help, but I couldn't bear to draw you into conspiracy. You'll never know how much your notes on his correspondence helped me navigate the war to a close. I will need you as I map a future for us all."

The teacup slips in my hand and I am embarrassed to see tea sloshed across my lap. As I attempt to digest her suggestion—no, it was a statement—that she has served as *de facto* president during wartime, she dabs her handkerchief at the damp tea stains. I am not unaware that her ministrations have crossed the line between friendship and impropriety. I am no gentleman, because I do not urge her to let me dry my own trousers.

"I am so relieved to be back home with you," she says. "Your kind assistance makes my husband's illness bearable. You have no idea what my time away has been like. No one can know what my husband has become."

I try to imagine her traveling for half a year beside a man who looks like her husband but is no more, and my heart breaks.

She looks up and bravery is spread across her face. "While we were abroad, I grew expert in managing him. When he was amiable, I led him by the elbow where he needed to go. I guided his conversations, allowing him to make no commitments on the spot, and then we retired to our quarters where I buried myself in mountains of written communication without your help in filtering it. When he was not amiable, I made excuses for his absence. Nobody is unaware of the burden that the American president carries, so these absences were tolerated. And yet my husband was not carrying that burden. I was. I am proud of the treaty that was negotiated, but it was none of my husband's doing."

I seize the hands that are still dabbing at my thighs. "This is not your burden and it will break you. No woman was meant to carry such a load. You must tell the Cabinet. The vice president would not be my choice as Commander-in-Chief but, with competent advisors, he will suffice until next year's elections."

She pulls away and stands, very straight, and her anger is evident. "I *have* carried the load and I have *not* broken. How dare you suggest that our incompetent vice-president is better suited to lead than the woman who negotiated the Treaty of Versailles?"

I leap to my feet, unable to sit in the presence of a woman. And, I suppose, I am unwilling to sit in the presence of the leader of my country.

There is steel in her voice as she says, "And I will see that treaty ratified."

I find myself explaining that the political situation makes this highly unlikely. I also say that this would be true even if the president were himself. This comes perilously close to ending my dream of winning her favor. I don't recall placing my hands on her shoulders, but they are there.

She shakes them off. "You are correct. If the president were himself, the treaty would die in the Senate. But I am in charge now, and I have leverage that he does not."

Worried now that the strain has affected Clara's faculties, I murmur solicitously. "I'm sure you do. But—"

"But what? Are you saying that I, a woman, cannot possibly have the ear of Prime Minister Lloyd George? Of Clemenceau? Of Orlando? How do you think I have spent the past months? Playing bridge-whist with the wives of great men? More to the point, when one speaks of treaty ratification, do you think that I haven't spent the five years of my marriage studying the weaknesses of each of our senators? My husband is above exploiting their vices to secure their votes, but I am not."

The word "five" rattles in my head. "What purpose did studying the senators serve before the president's health began to fail? Five years ago, you couldn't have known that you would ever need that information."

And now she is laughing at me. "Ambition cannot be understood by those who do not feel it." Seeing that she insults me, she pats the almost-dry tea stain on my thigh.

"You are a fine physician, dear Oliver, but can you honestly say that you have ever aspired to more?"

I do not need to answer. She knows me. I am beginning to suspect, however, that I do not know her.

"You hoped to gain influence from the moment you married him?"

"My naïve friend, I had that hope long before I married him, but shall we stop calling it something it is not? I did not seek influence. I chased a dream of power, and now I have it."

I am too stunned to speak and, apparently, my face is an open book.

She laughs. "I see that you remain ignorant of a salient fact. I have known Woodrow Wilson for many, many years, long before you believed you were introducing us."

"How?" I ask. And then I happen on the better question, when one is speaking of a personal relationship with a man who was married throughout any period that could possibly be described with the words "many, many years." This better question has but a single word. "When?"

"Surely you recall his propensity for traveling alone, with his wife's blessing, to Bermuda, the Lake District, the Caribbean. He claimed that he spent his time bicycling and playing Canfield solitaire, but those were lies. Ellen knew it, but she was the kind of wife who pours her life into her husband's happiness. During those journeys, he sought escape with me, and I helped her make him happy. Somewhere in this house are my letters to him, years of them. I certainly still possess every letter he ever wrote to me."

I try to remember what she gave as her reason for moving from Bermuda to Washington, but I cannot. I only remember seeing her for the first time, golden hair glinting in the light as she so prettily apologized for bumping into me on the sidewalk outside my club. Within a week, we began a most proper courtship. Within three weeks, I escorted her into the White House and lost her to Wilson. Within six months, she was the wife of my patient, who could justifiably be called the most important man in the world.

I study her face, lovely as the crescent moon, and ask myself, "Who is this person? How can I not know her after all this time?" I have long prided myself on my powers of observation. I am a fool.

"I had planned to wait a decent period after poor Ellen's death to write him and suggest that we no longer needed to hide our feelings," she says, shaking her head at her own naiveté.

"Imagine my shock when I learned that he was near to marrying another woman before the wife whom he honestly loved was cold in the ground. That was perhaps my only misstep, underestimating his need for womanly companionship . . . underestimating how much he needed *me*. I traveled here, believing that he would be mine again once our eyes met. And I was not mistaken. My superiors did not believe I could do it, but I proved them wrong. I have proven many people wrong."

"Superiors?" I hate myself for the weakness in my voice.

"At that time, I was still in the employ of the German government."

I do not believe her. I cannot believe her. My incredulity shows on my regrettably readable face, because she says just one word.

"*Ja.*"

In that single syllable, I hear the relaxed and natural accent of a native speaker.

"You are a German spy?" Hearing myself and hating my timidity, I revise my question to a statement. "You are a German spy."

"Hardly. Defeated nations do not have the capacity to maintain a corps of spies. They certainly do not have the money. I was, however, a spy for Germany before the war and during most of it, until they ran out of money."

"But you said 'many years.' Wilson was likely still at Princeton most of that time. Why would the Germans put the president of a university under surveillance?"

"They were resistant, but I made the case that many of America's future political and financial leaders come through Princeton. Woodrow could act as a single point of contact. It was nonsense. He would never have agreed to it, but my argument that he could connect us to the American ruling class convinced them to let me be his paramour. He was only in Bermuda for a few weeks of any year, leaving me ample time to attend to the princes and prime ministers that my superiors preferred. Yet, of all the men whom I was paid to cultivate, I only cared whether one of them lived or died. I tell you these things so that you will help me save him."

Alarm makes my voice tremble. "Save him? You have said that his mind is failing, but you have also led me to believe that his physical difficulties are minimal enough that even Lloyd George and Clemenceau were oblivious to them."

"Spies are facile liars. Woodrow is at death's door."

I think of the photos published daily during his absence. I remember an image of Woodrow, arm in a sling but still sprightly, strolling with Clara down the Champs-Élysées. There was another image of Woodrow and Clara in intent conversation with Clemenceau and Lloyd George. And another as he and Clara climbed a gangplank onto the *George Washington* for the trip home. He could, of course, have suffered an apoplectic fit aboard ship, but I have seen, this very day, a photo of him striding down the same gangplank onto American soil, followed by an array of travel trunks carrying Clara's fine wardrobe, Woodrow's restrained one, and the considerable load of gifts they received from foreign dignitaries. Beside him walked the woman for whom I longed with all of myself.

Unless he has been struck down this very day, Woodrow Wilson cannot be at death's door.

"I see that my subterfuge has been successful." Why does she smile?

I look at her, uncomprehending.

"My husband lost the use of his right arm the night before we sailed for Europe. He was then still ambulatory but only intermittently coherent. I knew that the world would soon be without his fine mind and leadership, and I knew that this was not the time for us to lose Woodrow Wilson. Within the day, I set a long-laid plan in motion. I have hoped for five years that I would never have to implement it, but here we are. First, it was necessary to remove you from the equation."

I have never realized that my face was so hilarious but, once again, she laughs at me. Then I understand. "That was no ordinary case of dysentery. It well-nigh killed me."

"I was confident that it would not, although a less-than-fatal dose of arsenic will make one wish for death. I needed to be free of your solicitous eyes."

"You found a better doctor in France, one who restored his capacities after such a severe episode? You found someone who transformed him into a spry man who twirls his cane as he walks? I have never heard that such a thing is possible."

"It is not. But it is possible, I have learned, to hire an actor to impersonate one of the world's most famous men, especially when one has an entire country's resources at one's disposal. It was no small feat to find an actor with sufficient skill who also closely resembled my husband, but I still have capable foreign associates. No one knows Woodrow's mannerisms better than I do, so such an actor could have no better coach."

And now I see that Wilson's dark glasses had not hidden dilated pupils or a drooping eyelid. They had hidden an unfamiliar set of eyes, enabling an impostor to step into the life of the man wearing the glasses. Their heavy frames, so unlike his customary *pince-nez*, had served to further obscure his face, as had the unseasonable scarf that he had worn far longer than the temperature had required.

The president had never before traveled to the other side of the Atlantic, and he had never met the dignitaries who waited for him there. It would not have been difficult for an actor who looked like Wilson's newspaper photographs to fool them. And, if Clara's tale of being a paramour to men of power was to be believed, they very well might have known her. Why would they doubt that the man at her side was truly her husband?

"Why did you tie the actor's arm in a sling?"

"I had tied poor Woodrow's paralyzed arm up and wrapped his face with a scarf before we arrived in France. Camouflaged thus, I was able to get him to our quarters where the actor was waiting. Praise God for the telegrams and ciphers that brought him to my aid. Some days passed during which I managed my husband in public as I have told you—guiding him, monitoring his conversations, and hiding his lack of capability with a fork—but my false Woodrow soon rose to the occasion. He affected a broken arm so that no one could accuse him of a miraculous and unbelievable cure. In the early days, he even held his mouth in a slight twist to mimic my husband's face during his last public appearance. Over time, he relaxed it, as if a spasm was slowly easing. He really is quite talented."

"Where is this actor?" I ask.

She rises, beckoning for me to follow. "Let me take you to him."

My shoes clatter on the hall floor and I remember the sumptuous carpets that Ellen Wilson had used in the private residence. "Did you take up the rugs so that no one could approach you without being heard?"

"My Oliver is gullible, but he is not without intelligence. Yes. I took up the carpets so that I could monitor traffic on this hall. When one works as a foreign agent, one becomes acutely aware of the need to remain far from curious ears."

"But you are not still a foreign agent. You said that the Germans no longer have the money to pay you."

"Indeed. But the Bolsheviks have recently stolen the incredible wealth of the Tsars and they do."

I stop dead still in the middle of the hall, and my eyes turn involuntarily to my left, peering through the elegant Yellow Room and through its window. Outside, there are people who know none of this. I wish myself among them.

"You are working for the Reds."

"Not as of today. I have negotiated a treaty that is more than favorable to their interests, and there is honor among spies. The Russians' gratitude for this gift easily buys my freedom. What is more, they cannot touch me even if they are insufficiently grateful. I serve as *de facto* Commander-in-Chief of the forces that just won the greatest of wars. It matters not one whit that I must operate from the shadows. I am the most powerful person in the world. I no longer need to feed myself by selling trifling secrets. Or myself."

We reach the room that she shares with the president and I hover outside its door. Even knowing what she is, I cannot bring myself to step into a woman's bedchamber.

"Don't be silly, Oliver. We will not be alone in a room with a bed in it."

She opens the door, and the man stretched out on the bed is almost my dear friend.

In physicality, the impostor is strikingly like the president, with the same height and lean musculature. I suspect that his hair is not naturally so gray, but it is dyed to the same shade as Woodrow's. The lantern jaw, the high forehead, the jug ears—they are all as much like my friend's features as it is possible to be.

He props himself up on his elbows and says, "Hello, Doctor." His speech when not performing as the American president has the flavor of Moscow.

I look from him to her. "You believe that you can keep up this charade until the election."

"No. I believe that this faux Woodrow will easily win re-election for a third term. Imagine his flair on a whistle-stop tour."

"Third term?"

"It is only custom for presidents to be limited to two terms. The recent war was sufficient disruption to justify a third term for the man who led us through it. And when the nation's tolerance for his extended tenure is done, I will run in his place."

Now it is my turn to laugh at her. "You? You cannot even vote."

"As the *de facto* president, I can have women's suffrage passed within months. Eligibility for public office will come with it. It will take a bit longer, but I can also undo the wrongs my husband did to other races before his doppelganger's next term is done. Imagine how many grateful voters these actions will generate."

I may be too feeble-minded to see though the lies of the woman at my side, but I can count. Those grateful voters would have the power to change everything.

"There will be an amendment ensuring equal rights for all within a decade, and I will see it passed. When you've been forced to live in the shadows as long as I have, you are disgusted by the very idea of leaving other people there."

The man who looks so much like Woodrow Wilson clears his throat. I look at him and he cautions me in his pronounced Russian accent. "Do not turn your back on her, Doctor. She is quite single-minded in her aims."

"Where is the real Woodrow? Have you killed him?" I can think of no safe way to replace the president with a double except to destroy the man whose very existence threatens to expose the lie. Was my friend buried in an unmarked French grave? Was he dumped overboard during the long sea journey?

"He is quite alive, I assure you, and this is the problem that you will help me solve."

"I must speak to him."

"You can try. He is very unlikely to answer you."

She opens a door leading from the president's bedchamber into his dressing room. There, in a bed that nearly fills the small, windowless space, lies the physical shell of the President of the United States of America.

He is motionless, gray. Apoplexy has twisted his face far beyond the subtle bend affected by the actor lying behind me. His right cheek droops so severely that spittle escapes his mouth. His right arm and leg lie in a position too awkward for a healthy person to endure. I only know that he lives because his chest rises and falls.

I am thunderstruck to see tears on Clara's face. She has been so fearless, so triumphant, until this point.

"Can you help him?"

I have never seen a man so far gone regain use of his body, nor have I ever seen one regain his faculties. The remedies available to me—warm baths, passive exercises, massages—are laughable for a patient so debilitated.

"Please help him, Oliver."

"How did you get him here?"

"The crowned heads of Europe showered us with gifts, some of them quite large. It was no great trick to load Woodrow into a pine box and wheel him past the reporters and their cameras. We have cooperative servants, most of whom were also Russian agents until very recently. The reporters were quite satisfied to get photographs of Alexei here."

The voice behind me says, "I do my utmost to please."

She still has her gaze fixed on the motionless president. "The pine box had an unfortunate resemblance to a coffin."

She turns her cornflower blue eyes on me and I cannot help asking the most terrible question a wife can be asked. "Why didn't you kill him?"

Tears gather on her thick lashes as she says, "It has occurred to me. My Bolshevik friends have for some time provided me drugs to control him—soporifics, hypnotics, and the like. You know his stubbornness. Subduing him was my only path to power."

I know that the president's spells of near-apoplexy date to his youth, so she did not cause his underlying illness, but I feel ill myself when I consider the effects of her drugs on his failing circulatory system.

I find that I cannot soften my words for her feminine ears. "You have done this. It would be a mercy to kill him now. Why do you risk the power you desired so much by keeping him alive?"

"Because I love him."

I close my eyes to shut out the sight of him. No human soul would wish to live this way. I have at my disposal drugs that would painlessly end his suffering, but I know that they will stay locked in my cabinets. Because I too love him. If I must fail in bringing him back from the brink of death, so be it, but I must try.

"I will do my best for him, Clara. Do not expect much."

And now her arms are around me and I find that I believe her torrent of tears. I believe the warmth of her arms as they encircle my chest and shake with her sobs. As a general practice, it is wise to disbelieve the words of a spy who has betrayed your country to two sovereign nations, but I am not wise where Clara is concerned.

Her voice cracks from weeping, but her words flow quickly, easily. "I need you, Oliver. Unknowingly, you have helped me run the entire country. Help me now that there are no secrets between us." As if to seal the deal, she whispers, "When he is gone, I will be yours for the rest of our lives."

I know how likely it is that she lies. Realizing that I am no more in control of my destiny than a mouse choosing between a cheese-baited trap and a stalking tomcat, I lower my face to kiss the top of her head.

Of their own accord, my lips form the words, "Whatever you want. I'll do whatever you want."

We embrace within an arm's length of her husband's bed, but he is beyond hearing. Tomorrow, I will begin efforts to rehabilitate his broken body, but I know how little the water cure will accomplish. Still, I am bound to try.

I made a promise to Clara.

# RECKLESS DISREGARD
## BY ABBY L. VANDIVER

SHE WAS DANGEROUS. BIG AMBITIONS. Little caution.

And she had the ear of a big, powerful man.

A sultry honey blonde. Blue-eyed and tall. She could captivate any room she graced with her presence. Tonight, as always, she'd captivated him.

Only now it was getting late. He needed to get home to his wife.

And she her husband.

"Do you have to go, Lyndon?"

"Bird's waiting for me," he said. He sat with a cigarette hanging from his lip, buttoning up his white shirt.

The light in the room was dim. A bed, a chair filled the space. The light blue carpet made it cozy.

"Is this the way you're going to treat me when you become president?"

"Darlin', I'm gonna always treat you good."

She slipped out of bed and walked over to him. Sitting on his lap, she pulled the cigarette from his lips and took a drag.

"You got it all worked out?" she asked. "Are we going to be able to help others? Make our dreams come true?"

"We are," he said, happy to have a woman with his same motivations. Even if she wasn't his wife.

"And are we doing it like we talked about?"

"You know it." He snuggled his head down into the crease of her neck, her perfume drawing him in to her. He ran his hand down her back, the cool silk of her gown riling him. "I'm going to become the President. We'll get that Great Society plan we've been talking about rolling. Civil Rights for the Negro. Help for the elderly."

"How are you going to do it?" His words excited her. She wanted more. She'd asked before, but he hadn't said exactly. "You know, become president."

"Just because you put the bug in my ear, Sweetie, doesn't mean you get all the details."

She chuckled. "But you've got it all worked out?"

"Sure do," he said lowering his voice and stroking her back. He wondered if he shouldn't stay a little longer. "I've always been known as a man who had a plan."

She leaned in and whispered in his ear. "Tell me your plan."

He gently pushed her off his lap, taking back his cigarette. She stood over him.

"You'll find out soon enough," he said looking up at her. "Might just need your help in part of it."

"Which part?" He felt the warmth of her breathy words on his neck.

"Helping me clear the path."

She pulled away and looked into his brown eyes. "Are you saying what I think you're saying?"

"Usually you can read my mind. Know just what I want. What I'm thinking."

She smiled. "Just didn't know you'd think that way."

"Sugar, you're gonna learn a lot of things about me. You'd better get ready for this ride. It's gonna be a wild one."

Bending forward, she dragged a finger down the side of his face to his mouth, planting a kiss where her fingertip had landed.

"He's well liked," she said. "Might have some people mad at you."

He tilted his head to the side and squinted one eye. Speaking through tight lips, he held onto the cigarette in his mouth, the smoke curling up into his eye. "They all hate him. Frank Sinatra and his mafia thugs. The CIA for getting them involved in Operation Oink Oink down there in Cuba. I'll be doing them a favor."

She laughed.

He took his cigarette out of his mouth and blew out smoke. "I know what I'm doing."

"Hope so," she said and sauntered back over to the bed. She got in and pulled the covers over her. "Sometimes," she patted the bed next to her. "you get to moving too quickly. Everything can't be accomplished in a day."

"I do things how they suit me. And they always work out fine." He stood up and unbuttoned the shirt he'd just fastened. "This country needs me and my brand of doing things. Can't nobody run it better than me."

"Tell me all about it, Landslide Lyndon." Her voice was low and teasing.

"Better listen up," he said, nodding.

"Any threat to your rise to power . . . " she said, a nearly unseen smile curling up her lips.

"Had better get out of the way," he finished her sentence.

Lightning crackled as it hit the ground, bright enough to penetrate the sheer curtains covering the bedroom window. It lit up the room just as he climbed back into bed with Mrs. Glass.

\* \* \*

SHE HURRIED OVER TO THE phone and picked up the receiver. She'd been standing at the window waiting for him to come home. Maybe he was calling to say he was on his way.

"Hello," she said, tugging the clip-on earring from her earlobe and holding it in her hand.

"I've sent him home."

"I was just watching out for him," she said. "Thank you for calling."

"You needn't be so nice. I've just been with your husband. Doesn't that concern you in the least?"

"Have you forgotten? I sent him to you." Her voice was even. Calm. Nice. "What concerns me, Mrs. Glass, is him making it home before this frightening storm that's brewing rips the top off his convertible."

Lady Bird placed the receiver back into the cradle and hurried back to the window. She wanted to be there when he pulled up in the driveway.

She was quiet about his affairs, his obsessiveness. She shut her eyes, hand placed over heart and shook her head. His irrepressible ego and deep-rooted insecurities were going to bring them troubled days. She knew it and so did he.

She also knew that these "secret" rendezvous she indulged quieted his desires and often calmed his temper. But as of late they had seemed to fuel his ambitions.

She hoped after his night out, he'd be calm enough to talk about this plan of his.

The one he thought she knew nothing about.

* * *

THE HIGH-SPEED UNDERGROUND RAIL SLOWED as it pulled up in front of the entryway to the three-level, subterranean building. Alfred pushed his black horn-rimmed glasses on his face and blew his nose into his handkerchief as he waited for the train to come to a complete stop. The first time he'd ever called out sick, he'd been called in to the branch he oversaw because of an emergency.

The first time there'd ever been an emergency.

The ride was much smoother and more efficient now that the tunnels were finished. Boring through new rock as other agencies were placed throughout the catacombs of the bureau system had been quite tedious.

He glanced at the glass front, the revolving doors rotating as people came in and out. He wiped the sweat from his brow with that same handkerchief and headed down the forty steps to the front door. Met with nods from others, the robust pedestrian traffic would dwindle by the time he made it to his lower level agency's office.

HRI, as it was referred to in agency-speak, was a one-man operation. As he entered the elevator, readying to speak with the two men who'd substituted for him, he realized that might have been the cause of the current problem.

Alfred stepped off the elevator and walked down the long hallway. There were no other offices on his end of the third level, just white walls and linoleum floors. He stared straight ahead at the door as he approached. From the exterior it seemed fine.

Inside, he knew, was a different story.

His bureau job didn't take much shepherding. Some forecasting calculations. Adjustments here and there. A keen eye for small details and an unadulterated knowledge of history. Mostly, he observed. Still, his department ranked high in importance alongside the other agencies. And he often admitted, holding back his abundance of pride, there was no other bureau like it.

HRI, the Bureau of History Repeats Itself, had its nuances, but for the most part was a straight-forward operation.

It had become known early on that throughout the centuries, humankind didn't change. Humans' ambitions and thought processes were nearly immutable. Invariably things were going to go the same way. It had then been determined that a push in a different direction could create an entirely new outcome and set history on a different course. The bad that intertwined their movement through Eros didn't have to be hurled through time on an endless loop of reputation.

The next time around things could be better.

And at some point, the history that was repeated, would be worth repeating.

From his office Alfred could monitor when things were going along a path that hadn't worked out so well in the history of human-kind. And he could change them. Sort of. As long as he stayed within the confines of the articles that governed the bureaus.

That was Alfred's job. He was good at it and didn't question the why of it. He'd often wondered, however, why his bureau wasn't called: EBHDNRI—the Bureau of Ensuring Bad History Does Not Repeat Itself.

He surmised it was because it would have been too many letters.

The world above their secret underground installation had been divided into sections. Segregation of democracies and republics, as they had termed them, made it easier to control repeated occurrences. To ensure a different—and hopefully bet-ter—outcome, it was his job to program some things to happen, or allow events to occur that were borne out of the consequences of peoples' actions and their environment.

*What could be so hard about that?*

There was, once in a blue moon, the "I didn't see that com-ing" factor to consider. The one where things happened that couldn't have been known ahead of time. But that was a rare occurrence because the algorithms of his mainframe were good at foreseeing hiccups.

"Tell me again what happened?" Alfred pressed palms together, bringing them up to his face, he rested his lips on his fingertips. If his higher power hadn't been a mainframe, some might have thought he was praying.

(He would later note that the people in the affected sector might need to do just that.)

Alfred hadn't taken his seat behind his glass and acrylic desk more than ten minutes and he already knew the disastrous conse-quences of what he was hearing.

The two men who'd been sent to cover his bureau while he was out on sick leave were trying to explain. Checking his clipboard for accuracy as he spoke, Brewster appeared to be the one in charge.

The other, Coleman, followed along. Both, Alfred determined, were responsible for the debacle and would face the consequences.

"There was an alert that came through." Brewster pointed at the board through the glass wall that made up one side of Alfred's office. "At first, it was all green—"

"As it should be," Coleman noted.

"Yes. Yes." Brewster nodded. "But then . . . *Boushhh!*" His balled fists, held up in front of his face, opened when he made the sound then he stretched his fingers and wiggled them.

Coleman, just seconds behind him, made the same motion and sound.

"It started flashing yellow and red," Brewster said finishing his description.

"And buzzing," Coleman added.

"Buzzing." Brewster nodded.

Their assignment in his absence, Alfred was sure, had to be to watch the board. The operative word, he wanted to emphasize, was "watch."

Each dressed in a black tunic, their uniform, and badge, hanging around their neck on a lanyard, signified their limited access and apparently, in Alfred's opinion, their limited intellectual abilities.

"It's a modular spectrum pulsater utilizing a matrix patching system." Alfred liked calling things by their correct name.

Both stared across the desk at Alfred. Eyes blinking, trying to process what he'd said to them.

"Continue," he instructed, waving a hand.

Brewster cleared his throat. "We knew that meant a historical recurrence calculation was needed."

"That would have been correct," Alfred said.

"It worked out so well the last time," Brewster said. "An action was called for with a nearly identical historical precedence. The previous time it was a civil war needed to achieve the goal. It obtained the sought-after freedom one marginalized segment required but came with a horrific loss of life and brutal disagreement. Now again those people were in the same dire straits."

"Eureka!" Coleman said.

"Yes. Yes." Brewster nodded. "Eureka! We found we had the perfect historical occurrence to replay." His nose shot up in the air, he sat a little straighter in his seat. He was rather proud of what he'd done.

"Nothing is supposed to happen the same way," Alfred said. "At least that is the goal of *this* department."

"Well of course not." Brewster frowned, unable to understand why Alfred didn't know he knew that. "We programmed it not to be a civil war like before. No war this time, in fact. A few protests and unofficial murders. And this time the new president, ascending due to the current Commander-in-Chief's suffering a gunshot to the head-"

"Insufferable weapons," Coleman interjected.

"Yes. Yes." Brewster nodded his agreement, but he hurried to get back to the point he was making. "This Johnson won't be impeached!" A wide grin swept across his face.

"Yes, but to have both of them serve in the Senate, the house, as vice president and president." Alfred was shaking his head. "Both last named Johnson. Both born in '08 . . .

"A century apart," Coleman noted. "Born a century apart. Years they call 1808 and 1908."

Further explanation of their reasoning seemed to excite the pair even more.

"It just isn't how it's done," Alfred said, wanting to quash their delight. After all, if some harm hadn't happened, he wouldn't have been summoned.

"But you must see that it was ingenious!" Brewster said. "The two of us," he turned to look at Coleman, "with our limited knowledge of your mechanisms—"

"The pulsating matrixes." Coleman wiggled his fingers toward the glass wall.

"Yes. Yes. The pulsating . . . matrix patches. With them we created a plan that was nothing less than ingenious. Something that you may want to take note of. No long mathematical equations, plotted outputs, calculated functions. We took a historical situation—a segment of the populations' rights denied—and duplicated it for the same situation one hundred years later."

"There is supposed to be a similarity. Yes." Alfred nodded. "A *small* similarity," Alfred said. "You have to be creative, though. We want to give a push in another direction, not the same one."

"Did you not hear what we said?" Brewster asked, his brow furrowing even more. "We made changes. This Johnson won't be impeached. There will be no civil war."

Alfred fingered the dark granite paperweight on his desk, not commenting on what he really thought.

Coleman shook his head, his eyes fluttering. "I told you."

"Told me what?" Brewster turned, stiff necked, to look at his cohort. "We agreed to it all. We both agreed it was ingenious."

"If it is so ingenious, why am I here?" Alfred asked.

"Well," Brewster cleared his throat. "There has been a hiccup, nothing related to us duplicating the Johnson Effect mind you."

"What pray tell is it?"

"It seems that this Johnson," Brewster glanced down at the clipboard, "first name Lyndon, second name Baines, has decided to take the matter into his own hands. He will be the one responsible for his predecessor's demise."

\* \* \*

"Who put this bug in your ear?" The black-haired man sat near the window, the sweat on his face telling how nervous he was.

"I agree, this is a lot to pull off. A lot," the other man said.

Three men sat in the study of Johnson's Stonewall, Texas ranch. One was the current vice president, owner of the ranch and idea conjurer. The others: one a former VP, and currently unknown to the people in this sector, soon to take on the role of president himself.

Only, he'd admit at some point, he wouldn't kill to do it.

The third one: the governor of the great state where they'd convened.

"This here fellow has been to Cuba and they turned him around," Johnson said. "He's been to Russia and they did the same thing." He pointed to the tall blonde sitting in the corner. A risky move to bring her into his home, but Vice President Johnson needed backup. "She knows him. She'll tell you we won't have to *make* this guy do anything. He wants to do this."

The other two men in the room looked her way. She sat, stylish and aloof. She lit her cigarette and gave no more than a demure nod. That satisfied the vice president, but not anyone else.

"He's a Communist for Pete's sake." The former VP turned his gaze from the window. He knew his country didn't take on as allies the very people who, for the last decade, they had railed against.

"All the better to use him," Johnson roared. "He ain't one of us. No consequences. No backlash. No traitors."

"Seems like we're the only traitors." The governor got up and started pacing the floor.

"It is *us* that's hiring him," the former VP said, his voice cracking with the words. "Having him do our bidding." He shook his head. "Seems like the definition of the word traitor to me."

The one pacing nodded. "We're doing the killing."

The one by the window blew out a breath. "Just come right out and say it, Lyndon. Why don't you just come out and say it?"

"And what about if he talks?" the governor asked. "He kills the president and then tells everyone who got him to do it."

"We shut him up," Johnson said.

"Kill him, too?" The governor abruptly stopped his pacing.

"We can't get into bed with Commie rednecks," the former VP countered. "We're already at a face-off with the Soviet Union with this Cold War. Even when I served as VP for President

Eisenhower, we couldn't get a handle on it. It's scaring the bejesus outta everybody and now you want to use them to get to our president!"

"Our president?" Johnson looked over at the man sitting at the window.

"Whether you like it or not. Whether you change that fact or not. Right now, that's who he is."

"Look. We're not using *them*," Johnson raised a hand to the heavens. "By God, I'd die before I see those Communists come here and devalue and erase the very ideals our nation was built on." He thumped a hand to his chest. "I am the man who will pass the Civil Rights Act. That's what I'm about."

"I don't know," the man at the window said.

"I do!" Johnson squawked. "We are just using a person that aligns his beliefs with them. We are not aligning anything, I repeat, anything, with him or them."

"And there's a difference?" the former VP asked.

"What's to stop them if you're using them in this plan of yours?" The governor interjected. "What is to stop them from holding this over your head? Using it against you if you do become the president?"

"Not if, Governor. When."

"When," the governor spat out the correction. He just needed an answer and he stared at Johnson until he got one.

"John. Big gains come from big plans," Johnson replied. "I need to be president. I was born to be president. I can't keep getting close and no cigar."

"Landslide Lyndon," one said and the others chuckled, including Mrs. Glass who'd been sitting quietly in the corner.

Lyndon Johnson won the senate by eighty-seven votes and got the seat. He'd been teased by others referring to the small victory as a landslide. But he hadn't even gotten close to winning in the democratic primary. for the position he sought after now. The President of the United States.

"Yeah, you SOBs can laugh. But I don't need any votes now. I'm already vice president. There's only one thing standing in my way."

"It's a big thing." The man by the window coughed and chugged down his drink. "It's the killing of the most powerful man in the world."

"Lyndon, dear." Johnson's wife stuck her head in the room. "I was told you needed me?"

"No, Bird. We're talking business. Something over your head."

"I'm just out here," she pointed over your shoulder. "If you do."

She shut the door and Johnson looked at his cohorts. "I don't know what to do with that one."

Mrs. Glass spoke for the first time. "One thing I wouldn't do is underestimate her."

* * *

HE'D SEEN A LOT IN his tenure in the Bureau. Wars and traitors. Coups and dictators. But not in this place. Not in this sector. Here, they had started a new country. An idealistic one. They had fought and given their lives, passed resolutions, built and defended a framework free of interference from other sovereignties for it.

After he'd been briefed and Brewster and Coleman left, Alfred had checked the database, the programming data and all addendums and deletions. He'd gotten up to speed and now was taking notes in real time. Well, in their time.

It was a mess.

Too much of a mess for him to make any sort of adjustments to send this course on a different path.

For the most part he'd have to see how it played out. It would definitely set a precedent. A new crack in history that would at some point, in some way—perhaps miniscule, perhaps not—play out again.

There wasn't much he could do about it now.

He had, for precautionary as well as punitive measures, sent Brewster and Coleman to another bureau to be debriefed and reassessed. A top-secret arm of the agency system, no one knew for sure what they did, or even what their initials abbreviated. But what Alfred did know was that they were effective.

Alfred, upon learning what the two had been up to, hadn't ever been fully able to quite grasp what they'd been thinking. They'd created a total disaster. For no ungodly reason, they'd set into motion another disastrous course to achieve a cause that was this time on a path to a non-violent resolution.

Not being able to change what they'd done, Alfred's only hope was that the people in the Bureau of WTF would be able to rehabilitate them.

* * *

JOHNSON STOOD NOSE-TO-NOSE WITH THE Secretary of Defense, Robert McNamara. His kind of bullying. Up close and personal.

"We've got no choice," LBJ said, his mouth tight, his jowls shaking. "I am the president. I am going to win this fight against Communist insurgency. And I already have the support of Congress."

"That resolution they passed on August 7, the Tonkin Gulf Resolution, doesn't give you carte blanche to escalate this situation and put troops on the ground," McNamara said stepping back from the President but still standing his ground. "You have to get approval from Congress for war."

"I've already got it. A broad mandate to do what I want," he said, laying on thick his Texan accent. "Do you know what the domino effect is, Bob?"

"Of course I do—"

"It means," Johnson said without giving the Secretary time to answer, "that those Commies will invade all of Asia. They will fall to Communism, then Europe will, and then they'll try to bring their brand of politics right here to us. Is that what you want?"

"That's not what I'm saying-"

"We've got to contain this. I need somebody who'll go in there that'll kill some of them. Win this thing."

Secretary McNamara rubbed his fingers across his brow. "I have a few people I can talk to and see what we can do."

"See what we can do! Those Viet Cong attacked our ships in international waters. Unprovoked!" The President dropped down in his seat behind his desk. "This is going to give me another heart attack."

His defense secretary retreated from the Oval Office, tail between his legs. The two men left in the room, having forged an unbreakable bond with him through their actions, caught his eye.

"What?" Johnson asked.

"I just don't know about you going to war over there." John Connally had managed to keep his governorship in the state of Texas even after that fateful November day in Dallas.

"Governor Connally, it's the only way for it to be done," Johnson said.

Nixon shook his head. "This is because of what happened. What we did. Our country is going down the toilet because of what we did."

"What are you talking about, Dick?" Johnson asked. Weary, he held his head up with one hand. "You need to focus on what is going on right now."

"We were all at the ranch when the plan was hatched," Nixon said, still fixated on what he considered the igniting factor. "We were all in Dallas the day it happened. All of us gave the thumbs up. All of us watched it be put into motion."

"I never agreed to get shot," John said, he rubbed his knee where the bullet had lodged.

"What does that have to do with this?" Johnson said, his anger ramping up.

"We invited foreign interference and now we have to fight to keep those we let in from attacking us and taking over. That same foreign entity."

"No one is taking over!" Johnson shouted.

"Your escalation of Vietnam has taken over," Nixon said. "All because you're afraid of what we did."

"Look. It was one man," Johnson said. "Oswald was one man. He is not going to ruin my presidency. My legacy. He has nothing to do with this." Johnson slammed his hand down on the desk. "I don't want to hear it. I just want to know what to do about this. I don't want to be the president remembered for this war!"

"Oswald was one man but with a big movement behind him," Connally said. "One that is now trying to take over South Vietnam and according to you, take over the world if we don't stop them."

"What am I supposed to do? I don't know how to win this," Johnson said.

"I think it's my time," Nixon said. He'd been sitting on that couch contemplating. "You can't run again, Lyndon, not with what the Communists have on you. Not with you having used them as your patsy.

"They don't have anything," Johnson said. "That nitwit didn't live long enough to tell anything he knew."

"Thanks to Ruby," Connally said.

"Here's to Ruby," Nixon said. He lifted his glass then downed the rest of the whiskey in his tumbler. Swallowing hard, he nodded at Johnson. "I'm going to have to take over from here. Lyndon, you can't run. But you can help me. I'll put a stop to this war, you have my word on it. But you have to give this up. Blame it on what we did. And maybe, someday, we'll all pay for it. You, just happen to be paying for it now."

"Jesus!" Johnson said and dropped his head onto the desk.

Nixon looked at Governor Connally. "John, you've got a place in my administration. Long as you became a Republican like God intended you to be. And you," he looked at the current president, "will always be a friend. A good one. One whose secrets I will take with me to my grave."

"It's all of our secret, Dick," John said. "And let's hope when it comes to our time to pay, it won't be as bad as Lyndon's."

\* \* \*

AT THE SAME TIME THE lights starting flashing orange on his console—a new, rather frightening sight—Alfred's desktop modular communicator rang. The digital display showed it was a department that he'd rarely dealt with.

"Alfred speaking," he said.

"This is Matheson from the Bureau of WBP."

"How may I help you?" Alfred asked.

"We've had an anomaly come up in our registrar. Never seen it before." He cleared his throat. "Thought we'd check with you to see if you have any unusual activity."

"Your anomaly may be due to a rift in history. A new course of action taken that will have ramifications in the future of the population of Section 1492." Alfred knew that must be what Matheson wanted to clarify.

"Yes, it is. One specifically dealing with this agency."

"Tell me about it."

"Well," Matheson started. "This new one that has popped up seems to be following a rogue path. Nothing seen before."

"Never before?" Alfred questioned that. He knew it was the Johnson Effect, as he'd termed it when he logged it into his archival system. He'd made the notation that it had torn the fabric of what history in the sector had been built on, although he knew he'd never forget it, and he planned on never being sick again. There'd never again be a need for substitution.

He was just amazed the ramifications had manifested so quickly.

Matheson chuckled. "You got me there. Actually, we had seen it. An earlier ideation."

"Ahh," Alfred nodded in confirmation.

"We called over to your office," Matheson continued, "and were reassured that everything was as it should be. Is it still?"

"Wasn't me who gave you that conformation," Alfred said. "And yes, it is something that is off the beaten path. The same thing is happening right now."

"Now? As in their time or ours?"

"Theirs."

"Oh. I see. So, what should we expect? Speaking of course out of my own curiosity. We here at the Bureau of Would Be President only monitor. I know you have the ability to change things."

"Not change, steer. Nudge."

"Uh-huh."

"This time, however, things were given a push and I'm afraid there's no coming back," Alfred said. "Future events based on these historical manifestations, like the one that is lighting up my system, as I'm sure it's doing yours, won't be pleasant. If I were a betting man, which I'm not, I'd put money that the history Section 1492 is weaving now is what your algorithms are showing."

"I see," he said his voice far off as if distracted. "I do see . . . I queued up their current time, just so I could get a better picture. Hope you don't mind?"

"Not at all," Alfred said.

"And I do see that the next Would Be, as we call them, has difficulties to say the least. Doesn't look like he'll make it all eight years."

"Really?

"Yes."

"Interesting," Alfred said. "But I don't believe, according to history, that one will be caused by what the current, uhm 'Would Be,'" he included the other department's lingo, "has done. Too soon. This accumulation of power based on the interference of other sections will have to simmer awhile I believe. At least based on my observations."

"I understand," Matheson said. "And I can see what you mean. I'd bet, if I too were a betting man, that the Would Be who has just hit, might be what you're speaking of. Would, say, sixty or so years cause the manifestation brought about by your aberration?"

"Possibly," Alfred said. "I think it could show in that amount of time."

"Ha!" Matheson said. "I think this might be it then!" He sounded delighted. "This Would Be is going to be a doozy. That must have been a sizeable occurrence to set a precedent so huge."

"It was."

"That sector will be in for one bumpy ride," Matheson said.

Alfred coughed into his handkerchief. "I can just imagine."

* * *

"You have a reckless disregard for limits, Lyndon." Lady Bird had come into the bedroom where he was resting. He'd worn himself out the day before. "The sanctity of marriage. The commitment to values. About power."

"I don't have much of anything anymore. I just want to make sure my legacy is what I wanted it to be."

"You set your legacy in stone the very day you became Jack Kennedy's vice president." She slid a pack of cigarettes across the snack tray in front of him.

"How is that?" he asked.

"The Russians were a bad choice to use to kill Jack."

He looked up at her. Without saying anything he tore open the pack of cigarettes and lit one.

She watched him without saying a word.

"I didn't kill John Kennedy," he finally said, blowing out the smoke. He looked at the cigarette. "You know the doctor said these things were going to kill me."

"I wouldn't worry too much about that." She smiled. Her voice calm and low.

"No?"

She shook her head.

"What makes you think that I had anything to do with John's death?" He went back to that.

"I'm your wife. It's the same way I know about all the things you've done. But this time everyone will find out."

"I had the Chief Justice stop all the fuss over who killed him long ago. No one knows. Not the truth."

"Jackie knows."

He pulled the cigarette from his lips and picked a piece of tobacco from it. "She doesn't know anything."

Lady Bird raised an eyebrow.

"Well, it's nothing to be done about it now, Bird. What's done is done."

"You used the assets of a foreign power to get what you wanted, Lyndon. That may not come back to get you, because you'll be long dead. But it's not something the leaders of this country would do."

"You'd be surprised what the desire of power can do to a man," he said. "Who they'll call on to get what they want."

"The next one might not be as smart as you, huh?"

"Probably won't," he said. "But he couldn't fall any harder."

"The true domino effect is the effect power had on you," his wife said. "But you're right, when you live high, Lyndon, you can always bet that when it's over, you'll come crashing down."

# 999 POINTS OF LIGHT
BY S. A. COSBY

ALLEN SIPPED HIS COFFEE AS he sat in the window of Smitty's Diner on H street, D.C.'s Chinatown. The traffic passed by the window at a snail's pace in the late October rain. Allen checked his watch. He was going to give Gary five more minutes then he would pay his bill, head over to the exercise facility in the D.C. Secret Service headquarters, and do something constructive with his one day off this week.

"How is it you look younger now than you did in college?" a raspy voice asked. Allen raised his head and Gary Tunstall was standing in front of him. His old college roommate was looking a little worse for wear. His long brown hair was streaked with gray. His deep blue eyes were rimmed in red. A road map of broken veins wound its way across his nose and across his cheeks. He had on a worn leather jacket over a plaid lumberjack's shirt and chinos so thin they seemed to shine at the knees.

"What can I say? Black don't crack," Allen said. Gary laughed. It came out sharp and high-pitched. He cut off the laugh so abruptly that it startled Allen. A few awkward seconds ticked by as Gary stood near Allen's table rubbing his forefingers against his thumbs.

"You want to sit down, Gary?" Allen asked.

"Oh yeah," Gary said. He slid into the booth opposite Allen and motioned for the waitress. He slipped his hand inside his jacket and Allen stiffened until he saw Gary remove a flask from his inner pocket. The waitress poured him some coffee. He eschewed sugar or cream and instead added whiskey.

"Do you want some coffee with your whiskey?" Allen asked. Gary blinked. He seemed to realize he was still pouring from his flask and stopped. He screwed the cap back on and placed it back in his jacket.

"Just a little something to fight the chill," Gary said. He took a long swig from his cup. Allen noticed his hands were trembling but said nothing.

"What's it been, seven years?" Gary asked.

"Eight," Allen said.

"Allen Jefferson. Star running back for the Maryland Terrapins. I never pegged you for an establishment man. How does all that work anyway? Do you have to say you're a Republican if the president is a Republican?" Gary asked.

"It's not a political job, Gary. That was always your thing," Allen said.

"Yeah but last I heard you had graduated with a degree in accounting. It's a long jump from crunching numbers to punching protestors in the face," Gary said.

Allen took out a dollar and put it on the table.

"I agreed to meet with you because you said that you had some information pertinent to the safety of President Bush. I agreed to meet with you as a courtesy, Gary. I don't spend my days punching people in the face or stomping on the necks of activists. I used to arrest counterfeiters and now I protect the president. Regardless if he's a Republican or a Democrat or a member of the Bull Moose party," Allen said. Gary smiled and for the first time Allen thought he looked like the Gary from their dorm days. The bright, funny philosophy major with the Mensa-level IQ.

"So, you did pay attention in political science class," Gary said. Allen sighed.

"I'm going," he said. He stood.

"Timberwolf," Gary said. Allen swiveled his head to the right.

"What did you say?"

"Timberwolf. The Secret Services code name for George Herbert Walker Bush, right?" Gary said. Allen sat back down.

"How the fuck do you know that?" he asked. His voice was a low bark. Gary finished off his coffee.

"After college I went out to San Francisco to join a self-sustained community. I wanted to get off the grid, man. Create a life for myself that didn't diminish the planet or force me to conform to the standard Western civilization bullshit."

"Gary, how did you find out—" Allen started to say but Gary cut him off.

"I met some folks out there in Silicon Valley. People who were using the tools of our technological imperialism to tear down the foundations of that imperialism."

"Gary, under the law I could detain you right now just for knowing that code word. So, listen to me when I tell you this: you have five seconds to cut the shit and the philosophical double talk and tell me exactly why you asked to meet with me." Allen said harshly. The waitress glanced at them. Allen put on his best unthreatening smile. She went back to counting her tips.

"Did you know Bush was shot down during the war? Spent four hours on a life raft in the South Pacific. He was rescued by a submarine. He then spent a month on the submarine helping to rescue other pilots. Some of the pilots he didn't rescue were captured and had their livers eaten by their captors. Supposedly," Gary said.

"Gary, I don't need a history lesson. We were cool in college. You were one of the few white boys who didn't assume I was an Affirmative Action pity case. But that only goes so far. Explain yourself. Now. Or I'm going to arrest you," Allen said. Gary locked eyes with him.

"What if I told you that Bush being shot down wasn't a random act of fate? What if I told you that when he was rescued, he didn't spend a month on a submarine but instead was taken to a special center where he was given psychotropic drugs and subjected to hundreds of hours of psychological manipulation and hypnotic suggestions?" Gary said. He never broke eye contact with Allen. Allen licked his lips.

"Gary, I can tell you've had some hard times. I get it. Look I don't know how you found out what you found out, but I tell you what I'm going to do. I'm not going to arrest you. I'm going to go back to my office and write a report. But I won't file it for twenty-four hours. Get out of D.C., Gary. Get some help," Allen said.

"Have you ever heard of the Bilderberg Group?" Gary asked.

"Yes. It's a bunch of rich businessmen who meet every few years to count their money."

"That's not all they do. How about the Bohemian Club?"

"Yes, it's a private club in California."

"And the Illuminati?"

Allen rolled his eyes.

"The Illuminati doesn't exist. I'm going, Gary. Twenty-four hours."

"Listen to me, dammit!" Gary screamed as he slammed his fist on the table. The other patrons turned and stared at them.

"Gary, calm down," Allen said softly.

"You don't get it, Allen. It doesn't matter what name they go by. These guys, these guys control everything. I know people who have cracked the computers of Lehman Brothers, JPMorgan, Halliburton, General Dynamics, the Pentagon—"

"Gary, Jesus, man . . . "

"They are all in on this. For years they've been manipulating us. Indoctrinating us. Herding us like sheep toward an inevitable slaughterhouse. War. Famine. Death on a biblical scale. They control presidents, prime ministers, crime lords. All to further their agenda," Gary babbled. Allen saw tears running down his face. He grabbed Gary's wrists and squeezed them tight.

"Hey. Hey, we're gonna go over to the hospital and get you some help, man," Allen said. Gary snatched his arms back and put his hands to his face.

"Don't you get it? There is no help! The game isn't rigged. There isn't even a fucking game. They've been building to this for YEARS!"

"Everything all right over here?" the waitress asked.

"We're fine, ma'am," Allen said. She walked away but shot him a look over her shoulder.

"I don't even know why I'm talking to you, Allen. They are everywhere and they control every fucking thing. But you . . . you are close to the president. And you're the best of us. Always have been."

Allen rubbed his temple. Gary was obviously a very sick man.

"And how do you know I'm not a part of this Bohemian Club Illuminati Bilderberg Group?" Gary swallowed hard.

"Because these bastards are not just obnoxious members of the bourgeoisie, they are also racist as hell."

"Okay. Well, great catching up, Gary, but I gotta go," Allen said. He stood again.

"There are seven words. If you say these seven words to Bush it will break his indoctrination. I mean, it's supposed to. 'Green, Time, Neutral, Texas, Lira, Blood, Cord.' Say those seven words in that exact sequence and it should break his mental blocks. Maybe then he won't plunge us into a never-ending war. They tried to start in Panama but that didn't have enough juice."

"Goodbye, Gary," Allen said.

"I'll be dead in a week, Allen. Remember the sequence. Remember the sequence!" Gary yelled as Allen headed for the street.

That night, after working out at the Secret Service exercise facility and a post workout beer at his local bar, Allen collapsed on his couch and turned on his television. The flickering azure light and the delicate ambient sounds would sing him the single man's lullaby until he drifted off to sleep. Just as his eyelids began to fall, he heard a report that slapped him in the face and had him sitting up ramrod straight.

"Yes, Diane, a tragedy here today on H Street. A homeless man was run over by a garbage truck right in front of Smitty's Diner. Witnesses say the man slipped or was pushed into the street where he was struck by a D.C. Metro sanitation truck. The dead man has been identified as Gary Tunstall. Apparently, Mr. Tunstall had been homeless for a number of years," The blonde talking head said from a remote near Smitty's Diner.

Allen stared at the television. His psychology professor used to quote Shakespeare when someone asked about the nature of coincidence. Peering over the top of his glasses, he would intone, "'Trifles light as air are to the jealous confirmations strong as proofs of holy writ.'"

In other words, if you want to believe something bad enough, you will. Just because he had met with Gary and Gary had spun some fanciful tale of a New World Order and conspiracies didn't mean his death had anything to do with said conspiracies. Did it?

Sleep didn't come easy to Allen that night and when it finally arrived it was as slick and slippery as the rain-soaked concrete outside his window.

A week later Allen was a part of the security detail at Camp David. President Bush, the first lady, the vice president and his wife, along with the House minority leader, were taking a short break before continuing negotiations with the Democrat-controlled House and Senate. Allen had spent his whole career around white people who always seemed shocked that he was intelligent, articulate, and actually skilled at his chosen profession. The Bushes were no different. A sort of lazy, uninspired racism that was so subtle they probably thought it was just cultural dissonance.

Allen was posted outside the den where the president and the vice president were having a casual discussion over a few cups of cider. Allen's partner on this detail, Chuck Bethany, was down in the kitchen ostensibly getting a sandwich but was in reality flirting with the new cook. Allen sat in his straight-backed chair with the wire from his earpiece trailing down to the transmitter in the left interior pocket of his blazer. His Smith & Wesson .357 Magnum was in a shoulder holster on his right side. Everyone in the Service had heard the story of a prospective agent who had put his earpiece in the ear that was on the same side as his sidearm and how he had become hopelessly entangled during a training exercise.

The door to the den opened and the vice president entered the hall. A sandy-haired man with a faraway befuddlement that never seemed to leave his face, the veep always struck Allen as a man just happy to be here. He had his own detail, but the two teams worked together seamlessly at Camp David. The vice president passed him on his way to the bathroom without saying a word. Allen was used to it by now, but that didn't mean it didn't stick in his craw.

The vice president had left the door open and Allen could see Timberwolf sitting at his desk in a gray cardigan and white button-down shirt. In stark contrast to the vice president, the current president always reminded Allen of a man on a blind date—not really sure if he wants to stay or if he wants to go because the person across the table has turned out to be less exciting and more neurotic than they had originally let on.

"Son, could you do me a favor and close that door? The draft in here is a doozy," the president said.

*I'm a college-educated, duly-sworn Federal officer, not the fucking butler,* Allen thought before rising from his chair and walking over to the door. The vice president would be back in less than ninety seconds. Timberwolf could've just waited a minute and a half. Could've but wouldn't.

Allen walked over to door, grabbed the handle, and paused.

"Mr. President, can I ask you a question?" Allen said. The old man folded his hands over his thin chest and leaned back in his chair. It didn't squeak. The first lady had thrown a fit about a squeaky door once so the staff had oiled every spring hinge and hasp within an inch of its life.

"Sure, son. Shoot. Wait, poor choice of words." The old man smiled.

"What was it like being shot down?" Allen asked. The smile faltered. Timberwolf's eyes seemed to dull.

"Every day since it happened, I've asked myself why I was spared and so many other men died. I used to think it was because God had a special purpose for me. Now . . . well some days I don't know," he said wistfully. Allen nodded and started to close the door. Then on a whim, for no other reason than to quiet his own restless fears, he whispered seven words.

"Green, Time, Neutral, Texas, Lira, Blood, Cord."

He said the words in one long, low breath. As the door rushed to meet the jamb, he heard a wet cough. The cough became a strangled groan. Allen opened the door and saw the president rise from his chair and walk to far corner of the den. He pressed his narrow head into the corner and continued emitting a strange, phlegmatic cry.

Allen entered the room.

"Mr. President, Mr. President, are you all right, sir?"

You were taught from your first day of training to give the men who lived at 1600 Pennsylvania Avenue considerable room and leeway. Each new occupant of that address had their own set of idiosyncrasies and quirks. Move too quickly to intercede when they were in the privacy of their own home was to court disaster and a transfer to the fraud detail in Juneau, Alaska.

This didn't seem like a new quirk to Allen. It seemed like a stroke or a mental breakdown or both. He moved quickly toward the president but before he could reach him, he felt a sharp blow from behind. It felt like a hammer had slammed into the small of his back. He went down to one knee and half-turned just in time to see a leather-loafer-clad foot barreling straight toward his face.

Allen leaned back until his head was nearly parallel with his ankles. The kick whistled over him with deadly intent. He kicked his own legs out from under him and performed what his trainer referred to as a kip-up to get back to his feet.

As soon as he did, the vice president advanced on him, his feet kicking and striking with murderous precision. Allen blocked and parried as many kicks as he could as he tried to grab his gun from its holster.

The vice president executed a vicious spinning crescent kick that slammed into his ribs, expertly placed in the exact space left unprotected by his bulletproof vest. Allen fell back against the edge of the president's desk. Instinctively he reached behind and grabbed for something to use to defend himself. His hand landed on the cup of cider. Allen tossed the cup and its contents at the vice president. The hot cider slowed down his assault, but only for a moment. That was all Allen needed. He grabbed his gun and aimed it at the sweater-clad, second-most powerful man in the country.

"Freeze!" Allen screamed. The veep stopped and held up his hands. He was barely breathing hard.

"All agents, Timberwolf has been trapped. I repeat Timberwolf has been trapped." Allen said as he touched his earpiece.

"What is going on here?"

The first lady was standing in the doorway dressed in a voluminous robe and a pair of sensible slippers. Allen turned his head. He was going to tell her to step back and stay out of the way, but before he could the vice president executed an inside crescent kick and knocked his gun out of his hand. As it clattered across the floor, the vice president aimed a punch at Allen's head. Allen slipped the punch and slammed an uppercut into the vice president's chin. He outweighed the man by forty pounds and the laws of physics were on his side. The vice president left the ground then landed in a heap at Allen's feet.

The President was still in corner bumping against the wall like windup toy that had lost its way. Allen bent over to retrieve his gun.

"No, no, no," the first lady said. She was holding a small chrome pistol in her frail right hand.

"I always told them they were making a mistake. They wanted a failsafe in case George was compromised. I told them the only failsafe we needed was a high-power rifle with a night scope."

"You're a part of this?" Allen asked incredulously.

"You're not," the first lady said.

She shot Allen in the left cheek. The bullet exploded out the back of his head, leaving a crimson Rorschach test all over the wall behind him. Chuck came running up the hall but stopped short as he saw Allen slide to the floor. The first lady put her gun back in her pocket.

"Can you see that Dan gets a nice shot of something strong and comforting when he wakes up? I'll call the men in black to readjust George," the first lady said.

"Of course, ma'am. *Ouroboros Infinitum.*"

"*Ouroboros Infinitum.*"

# THE DREADFUL SCOTT DECISION
BY GREG HERREN

THE CHEAP WHISKEY TASTED LIKE flavored turpentine, burning so intensely as it went down it felt like it was leaving scorch marks in its wake. Scott Devinney was just high enough from the joint he was smoking to consider that a plus—a sign that he was still alive no matter how numb he felt.

He was sitting in the dark in his cheap apartment near campus, streaming the panel he'd been on at the presidential historians' conference at UCLA the previous weekend. It had aired live on a PBS network in Los Angeles—it took him a while to figure out how to access it, and now that he was watching it was even *worse* than he feared. He'd always suspected Pulitzer prize-winning historian Andrew Dickey was a homophobe; his behavior on the panel proved it without question.

Alas, Scott allowed Dickey to get under his skin. He wasn't proud of that, and his doctoral advisor, Dr. Keysha Wells-Caldwell—also head of the department at UC–San Felice—wasn't happy, either.

He wasn't about to apologize to Andrew Dickey, though. He'd die first.

"You have no proof!" Dickey wagged his finger at Scott on the computer screen, his face reddened and his voice raising. "Just like the activists who try to claim Lincoln was gay without proof, there is no proof Buchanan was, either, no matter how bad you want him to be!"

He sighed and closed the window. He didn't need to watch himself screaming in rage, embarrassing himself and the university in the process.

Which was what Keysha really cared about.

*He's right, you know,* her email had said. *It's just a theory without proof. Slurs from political rivals aren't proof—just like a hundred years from now historians can't use "but her emails" as proof Secretary Clinton was corrupt.*

Maybe she's right, he thought as he picked up the plastic bottle of whiskey—who even knew whiskey came in plastic bottles?—and filled his glass again, taking another hit off the joint. But if I don't make the case for Buchanan being gay . . . what will be my thesis? That, somehow, he wasn't the worst president?

He laughed bitterly. He couldn't make that case. Buchanan's record as president spoke for itself. The whole point of the thesis was that James Buchanan, fifteenth president and the man who served before Lincoln, had been a bad president because of his secret preference for other men; that his long-time "housemate" Rufus King, a slave-owner from Alabama, used Buchanan's love for him to sway him into becoming a Southern sympathizer.

He could—and did—make that case eloquently. The problem was he couldn't definitively prove Buchanan was gay and his relationship with King went any deeper than friendship.

Without that proof, his thesis was significantly weakened, defending it was next to impossible, and Buchanan was just another White House mediocrity.

Just not up for the job, unable to read the mood of the country, fervently pro-slavery and a conniver in the equally horrific *Dred Scott v. Sanford* decision, perhaps the man most directly responsible for the outbreak of civil war.

Scott always felt that was unfair—who was up to the task of bringing the divided country back together without war?

Keysha wanted him to change his thesis, had tried to talk him out of it from the beginning.

But he was so certain, always so certain, that the proof was out there, somewhere. He'd combed through archives, read scores of diaries and letters from contemporaries, certain he'd find the corroborating information.

Buchanan couldn't have gone through his entire life without leaving some evidence behind.

His phone chimed the new email sound.

He sighed and clicked open his web browser, and there it was.

His salvation.

ANN COLEMAN'S LETTERS was the subject line of the email, the return email address someone he didn't recognize: hreed57@gmail.com

*Ann Coleman's letters?*

He felt a rush of adrenaline so intense he had to grip the arms of his desk chair with his sweating palms.

The Coleman letters!

*No, it couldn't be.*

The record showed that the Coleman letters were burned when the former president died in 1866. All that remained of them was the ribbon with which they'd been tied together and the wrapper, on which Buchanan's own handwriting stated clearly the letters were to be destroyed, unread, in the event of his death. Underneath his handwriting was a note that the letters had been burned per instructions, with the signatures of the executors beneath that.

That ribbon and wrapper were on display at Buchanan's home, Wheatland, which was now a museum.

Could it be possible? After all this time?

*The goddamned Coleman fucking letters!*

Ann Caroline Coleman, the young woman whom all historians used as proof of Buchanan's heterosexuality. They were engaged briefly, and she died shortly after breaking things off with him. Buchanan allegedly swore he'd never love another, and thus remained a bachelor until the day he died.

Because such Dickensian vows were normal in the nineteenth century.

Most historians, determined to erase any possibility of his homosexuality from the record (as historians have always tried to erase any trace of 'deviance' and 'sodomy' from the historical record), pushed the idea that his tragic romance with young Ann Coleman and her early death resulted in a vow to never marry as long as he lived.

As romantic and lovely as the story sounded, Scott was positive it was just another piece of American mythology, like George Washington's cherry tree and Lincoln's rail splitting. It couldn't be true—at least, not the story as told. While there was certainly enough evidence to support his courtship of her, and the marriage proposal—that was to be expected. He was of marrying age, and that's what men did in those times. They married, had a family, raised children . . . but that didn't mean they didn't, couldn't, have relations with other men.

Ann Coleman was the only woman there was any record of him showing any attention to. Her refusal to marry him was because of his "moral failings"—that statement was the key, wasn't it?

He was so sure he was right.

But he couldn't find the evidence. His letters to and from his long-time roommate—Rufus King—were mostly destroyed; the ones that survived showed the two men were affectionate and close, but homophobic scholars dismissed that as simply the effusive writing style of the time.

They would, he often thought in despair, only be satisfied if he could find pornographic daguerreotypes of Buchanan in bed with another man.

All of these thoughts rushed through his muddled head as he stared at his email inbox.

It was probably nothing, he decided, just someone writing to him *about* the letters.

He clicked it open. There was an attachment.

Mr. Devinney:

I saw you on a panel show discussion the other day and thought to myself, maybe you are, after all this time, the right person to talk to about something my family has been keeping quiet for a very long time.

I am the last living descendant of George Coleman, whose youngest daughter was the Ann Coleman whom President Buchanan apparently loved, according to legend. Over the years, we in our family have kept a great secret—one that no one outside of the family has been allowed to suspect or know. Why we have kept this secret all these many years I can't say—it really doesn't make sense, especially now that I'm dying. Originally, the secret was kept to hide our shame, I think—our shame at the humiliating circumstances in which a member of our family died.

The historical record claims that after his death, the former President insisted that his executors destroy his letters from Ann that he had kept all those years, pining away for her and condemned by his love for her to die a bachelor.

As I watched you on my television, the rudeness and impertinence with which you were treated by the others on the panel for daring to presume that even a bad president like Buchanan might have been gay, I made up my mind. My only son died from AIDS twenty years ago, he was a gay man and listening to those horrible men dismiss the very notion of Buchanan's sexuality not being oriented towards women was like watching my son die all over again.

When he was dying, the former President wrote to my ancestor, Ann's brother, and asked him to come see him.

Buchanan gave those letters back to my family, to do with as we pleased. We chose to keep them secret over the decades and centuries since. But now . . . now I think it is time they are made public.

I have attached a scan of one of the letters.

If you are interested in them, please reply to this email and we can make arrangements.

Sincerely,
Harriet Coleman Reed

He stared at the computer screen, his heart pounding.

It was . . . it was almost too good to be true.

He clicked on the attachment, which was a PDF of a yellowed brittle page, with elegant handwriting. It was hard to read—the scan wasn't a high enough of a resolution to view larger so he could actually read the letter—but he could read the signature at the bottom plainly enough.

*Ann Caroline Coleman.*

He clicked on the *reply* button, wrote a quick response and hit *send*.

If he had a dollar for every time someone had asked him *why James Buchanan* since he entered grad school at UC–San Felice, he'd never have to work another day in his life. He wouldn't need the PhD he was working towards (the same PhD that made his mother roll her eyes and use air quotes whenever she talked about it, the usual supportive self she'd been his entire life) nor would he be worried about eventually scoring tenure at the University of California–San Felice. His future would, indeed, be secured.

A few weeks later he was pulling his battered old Honda Civic into the driveway of a decaying old house up in the mountains near Rocky Beach, about an hour or so up the coast from San Felice. Never once had the question of what Harriet Coleman Reed wanted in exchange for the letters come up. He suspected, feared, that she might want money; the value of the letters was inestimable.

The long friendship and close living quarters with Senator Rufus King of Alabama certainly played a role in Buchanan's opinions on slavery and emancipation.

But now that his car was bumping along the dirt driveway and he could see that the yard was overgrown and the house itself was dilapidated and in need of repair, he became more certain the old woman would want some money for her prize.

Her emails implied she was most interested in correcting the historical record. "It's time for the world to know the truth," she'd said in her last email. He knew he shouldn't get his hopes up before reading them, and there was also the authentication process to get through . . . but wouldn't she have asked about money before he drove up there?

He pulled up alongside the house and turned off his engine. An ancient Chevrolet was parked back by the dilapidated barn, the field beyond dead, fallow and barren. A tawny cat blinked at him from the back corner of the house as he got out of the car; it yawned and vanished in an instant. The steps to the porch moaned and groaned beneath his feet as he climbed them. The peeling front door opened before he could raise his hand to knock.

"Ah, Mr. Devinney, a few minutes early," the old woman at the door clucked, her wrinkled and tired looking face creasing into a smile. Her white hair was pulled back tightly into a severe bun, pulling the face of her skin tighter.

He wondered how far her skin would drop if she loosened the bun.

Her blue eyes behind the wire-rimmed glasses were sharp, though, as she stepped aside so he could enter the dark interior of the house. She was very short, barely five feet tall if he had to guess, and thin. Her shoulders hunched forward and her body seemed shapeless under the folds of the enormous dark blue housedress. She led him into a darkened living room. The curtains were closed, the only light cast by yellow candle-shaped bulbs in a chandelier hanging from the ceiling. Every available surface seemed to be covered with knick-knacks of some kind, most of it tourist garbage collected, apparently, over the course of a lifetime: plastic snow globes depicting various sites throughout the country, polished sea shells, little brass replicas of the Statue of Liberty, the Brooklyn Bridge, Mount Rushmore, and various other pieces of Americana. The wallpaper was faded and water-stained in places; yellowish-brown water stains marred the dusty ceiling. An enormous, ancient television console was shoved against one wall. He sat down on the couch—the cushions were covered in plastic that squeaked under his jeans.

She sat down in a rocking chair and crossed her legs at the ankles. "It's time, I think, for the letters to be made public."

He tried not to let his emotions show on his face. It was all he could do not to snatch them out of her hands and run for the front door.

"You have a lovely home," he replied politely, forcing his eyes up to meet hers. *Don't let her know how important they are to you.*

She snorted. "It's a dump. Flattery isn't going to get you these letters, Mr. Devinney."

"Scott," he replied automatically, the way he did whenever someone called him Mr. Devinney. He forced another smile onto his face. "Please, call me Scott, Mrs. Reed."

"How much do you think the letters are worth?"

"Well, that's hard to quantify." He broadened his smile despite the sinking feeling in his heart.

"I should think the letters proving that our nation had a homosexual president would be worth a great deal to a great many people." She smiled back at him. "For different reasons, of course. But make no mistake, they have value." She nodded. "If I simply gave these to you, you'd make a fortune using them to write a book. And what about the poor widow woman who gave them to you? Doesn't she deserve something for helping make you famous?"

His voice sounded a million miles away. "What do you want, Mrs. Reed?"

The smile was predatory; he could see that now. She gestured around her. "I'm an old woman, Mr.—Scott. I don't need much. But compensation is certainly necessary, don't you think?" Her voice was taunting now. "I did my own homework on you. The Google is a useful tool. Your goal is to become the leading expert on James Buchanan, and prove he was a gay man, right?" She leaned forward, her eyes glistening. "You'll become famous, won't you? And won't your book be a bestseller? You'll get that PhD and tenure and be set for life, won't you, Scott? And what about the poor old woman who gave them to you? Doesn't she deserve something?"

"I don't have any money," Scott replied slowly, trying not to let the panic he was feeling show in his voice. He saw his dreams beginning to slip away.

If she sold the letters, took them to auction, he'd eventually be able to have access to them—maybe. And maybe he'd still be able to write his dissertation, sell it to a publisher, and ride the wave of success she was describing.

But the novelty, the surprise, wouldn't be there.

He'd dreamed of it, of course, ever since she'd emailed him the first time. The talk shows, the major announcements, the release of the letters, the morning shows on the networks, interviews with the major publications, invitations to speak at historical conferences—and of course, the inevitable pushbacks from homophobes in both academia and the general public, which would only bring more publicity.

No, it was all contingent on *him* bringing the letters to the public, along with the announcement of the book to come.

He'd taken her bait, and now she was of course going to make demands.

It had been too good to be true.

"I could, of course, just burn them," the old woman went on, a nasty smile on her face. "That's what was supposed to happen to them in the first place, you know. He left behind a packet of blank paper, wrapped up with the ribbon and the instructions to burn them, so everyone would think the letters had been destroyed, so no one would look for them. He didn't want anyone to know the truth. He assumed my ancestors would want them destroyed as much as he did." She laughed. "Instead we held on to them. I could have just burned them, and you'd have never known they'd survived all these years."

He had so many questions, but he couldn't think of anything besides making sure he had the letters with him when he left. To come so close . . .

"But you didn't." Scott heard himself saying, his voice sounding like it belonged to someone else and was coming from a far distance. "You kept them for years. Why do something with them now?"

She pushed herself to her feet and grabbed a cane with a dragon's head on the tip. She used the cane to hobble over to the fireplace, where she pulled back the screen and poked at the fire with the poker. She hobbled back to her chair, sitting down with a sigh of relief and peered at him. "When I saw you on that television panel, talking about Buchanan so passionately, so convinced you were right, I remembered the letters and knew how important they'd be to you. I thought, that young man is the perfect man to sell the letters to, after all this time." She closed her eyes and exhaled. "I want to get some money for them, does that make me such an awful person? I'm old, I've struggled, I'm struggling now. Medicare doesn't pay for everything, you know, and the taxes on this house, and my social security . . . ." Her voice trailed off. "They're the only thing I have of value."

"I don't have any money."

She nodded her head. "Then I'm sorry, Scott, you can't have the letters."

"Can I at least see them?"

She shook her head. "I don't think that would be wise."

"If you're not going to let me have them, you could at least let me see them. I drove for several hours to get here." He held up his hands. "Maybe I can get some money together—"

She pushed herself up to her feet again. She gestured to the rolltop desk sitting pushed up against the wall. "If you open the rolltop, you'll find them sitting on the desk."

He moved so quickly he surprised himself. He pushed the rolltop up—it squeaked and squealed and complained a little bit as he did—and there they were. A stack of yellowed, brittle paper, with ink browned and dried with age scattered across them with a florid, elaborate script. He picked up the one on top delicately, carefully, the page crumbling slightly on the edges. The letters belonged under glass, in a temperature-controlled vault to preserve them. It was a wonder they'd lasted as long as they had, without being placed in proper storage.

*My dear Mr. Buchanan* was written directly beneath a date: 23 February 1817.

"Why did she break off the engagement?" he heard himself asking. The letter felt hot in his hands. He'd never wanted to own anything more in his entire life. Thoughts raced through his head: *I have good credit, I could take out a loan to make a down payment, I can write a proposal and get a lot of money for the advance maybe, I could give her some of that I have to have these letters I can't leave this house without them.*

"I haven't read them," the old woman replied. "I don't need to know what they say."

He scanned down the page. The letter said nothing, simply talked about her day and how much she appreciated his attentions, how much she was looking forward to being Mrs. Buchanan, like the one she'd scanned and sent him. He turned the stack of pages over and picked up the last one.

*Mr. Buchanan,* it opened.

Jackpot, he thought. The lack of a fond salutation was the key.

*It is with great difficulty that I find myself writing to you. I am returning the ring with the lovely sapphire stone in it that I cherished so much as a memento and token of your love, of our future together. But I cannot, as a moral woman and a devoted follower of our Lord Jesus Christ, marry a man capable of such sin, such moral weakness, and spend the rest of my life loving such a man and making a family with him. I had thought all my dreams of marriage and motherhood were coming true when you asked me to be your wife. But I know now that my happiness very much depends on my returning your ring and calling off our engagement.*

*You have been nothing but kind to me, and a gentleman, and it breaks my heart to know that the tender feelings you have shown me were not coming from a pure heart, from the proper feelings of love and passion that a man should have for a woman. No, you were trying to deceive me, to get me to fall in love with you and commit myself to a marriage that would make me nothing but wretched, that would leave me feeling unloved, unwanted, and not a full woman.*

*I had noted before your close friendship with Mr. Robinson. It is indeed the talk of our town, what good friends and how much love you have for each other. You have told me many times that such talk is vile slander, impugning both your character and that of Mr. Robinson; scurrilous stories told by those who wish you harm, for reasons of jealousy or revenge or spite. I chose to believe your defenses out of my deep love and respect for you.*

*But I cannot deny the evidence of my own eyes, Mr. Buchanan. I have no desire to hear any more of your lies, your defenses, your denials of your unnatural desires. I cannot risk my own immortal soul by serving as a mere subterfuge, to be the screen behind which you hide your unnatural desires to lay with men the way a man is supposed to lie with a woman. I cannot welcome you to my marriage bed knowing you come to it from the arms of another man. I saw the two of you in a loving embrace, I saw you cover his face with tender kisses, I saw the love for each other you share on each of your faces. I cannot deny the evidence of my own eyes, Mr. Buchanan. I would not believe the calumnies of others had I not seen it with mine own eyes.*

*I will tell no one the true reason why I no longer wish to marry you, Mr. Buchanan. Wounded as I am by your artifices and your lies, I do have some tender feelings for you still. I do not wish you ill, Mr. Buchanan. I shall pray for you to renounce your sin every day until the day I die. The door to Heaven and the love of our Lord still remain open to you.*

*In return, I must insist that you never see or speak to me again.*

*Sincerely,*
*Ann Coleman*

His heart was pounding. It was practically an eyewitness account!

But who was this Mr. Robinson? He'd never read anything about a relationship between Buchanan and a Mr. Robinson.

It didn't matter. This was proof, and he could find Mr. Robinson in records. He was the reason she refused to marry Buchanan, that was all that mattered, and she had seen them in a lover's embrace.

He couldn't leave without the letters.

He couldn't.

He set the letter back down and turned back to Mrs. Reed.

She was back at the fireplace, poking at the burning wood with the brass poke.

Her back was to him.

He was across the room in three steps, grabbing her cane and raising it up over her head before she knew he was there. She turned and looked back at him, fear in her eyes at last, and he brought the dragon's head down on her head before she could even scream. There was a horrible crunching sound. He brought the dragon's head down again and she fell backwards into the fire without much of a sound.

Horrified, he stepped back, watching as the flames spread to her clothes, as her skin began to crackle and burn. Her hair was aflame, and now the fire was spreading to the rug in front of the fireplace.

He grabbed the stack of letters and ran for the front door.

He sat in his car, watching as the flames spread through the living room through the windows.

*I killed her. I killed her and stole the letters.*

He glanced at them on the car seat beside him.

Tenure. Fame. Fortune.

The flames were now licking at the windows of the living room.

He started the car, took a deep breath, and backed down the long driveway.

*She lives in the middle of nowhere,* he thought as he reached the county road, and turned the car around to head back home, *it'll be hours before anyone notices the fire or calls for help.*

He'd be long gone by then.

She was still alive when he left.

It wasn't a lie, was it?

He shifted the car into drive and headed home.

He'd eventually forget the sound of her screaming.

# THE GREAT COMPROMISE OF 1901
## BY ERICA WRIGHT

THE BODY LOOKED AS FRESH as the day a .30-caliber ball cartridge entered its right abdomen, rupturing the small appendix, nicking the pancreas, and exploding out the back. Remarkably, no bones were broken by the bullet's journey, though the victim's subsequent fall did shatter three ribs, which had to be repaired before being wrapped—like the rest of the skeleton—in thread. Of course, that was easy enough. There's a joke that the Colonel wrote himself in a little notebook, typically kept for supply inventory and specimen dimensions. How do you skin a huntsman? Trigger-finger first.

The Colonel stepped away from the neck to survey his progress. To be sure, working with feathers and furs was easier, but he'd tanned the skin first. He hoped that the wax and arsenic solution created some stability, as well. And to think, only a few months earlier, he despaired that he'd ever do more than ducks. Most importantly, the body was upright again, could be swirling a brandy and holding court at a salon. Well, aside from the nudity, of course, though the Colonel had tied an apron across the genitalia, which had mostly been recreated from clay anyway. Artistic license and such. It was hardly improper and would be covered by a sturdy fabric, he imagined.

Most people think that taxidermy requires a butcher knife, something ghastly and rigid. But a small, flexible blade does the best work. And the Colonel kept a set of them sharpened at all times should a request come tapping at the inconspicuous door on Wallach Street. Thankfully, this subject has been frozen rather than salted, making it easy to scrape off all the meat and blood. And he'd been a lean man, rendering the question of fat almost negligible. Yes, indeed, the Colonel considered himself lucky. He hummed a little as he considered the empty sockets, deciding that he'd make a special trip for the glass eyes. Nothing on hand quite suited the senator from Colorado. Had the original been brown or blue? He'd quite forgotten in his rush to incinerate the offal.

In his state of deep concentration, he didn't notice the door behind him opening, nor did the sound of slippered feet disturb him. Lee had always been a small woman. She'd worn wool on purpose to avoid the rustling of muslin, silk, or God forbid chiffon. She liked to sneak, not unlike the bevy of pets—live ones—she kept at her residence. Perhaps their little faces were why she always had trouble admiring the work in front of her, though everyone said her father was a natural. What else would they have said, though? *An eccentric, more like,* she thought, unimpressed by the fox staring morosely at her as if its soul awaited rescue. She turned to the mounted bass, a little disquieted but resolved in her mission. The man must be stopped.

"Creature comforts," she said, pleased when the Colonel jumped. His startled expression quickly hardened, and he wiped his blade on a leather strip as if to remind the young socialite that she stepped into his lair, not the other way around. "As quiet as your company, I see."

"Too honored to speak, I'm sure. You would descend to me?"

"A single flight. We're hardly in the bowels."

Lee felt that the new electric bulbs were too bright, casting long shadows of tails and claws on the far wall. They did, however, give her a clear view of her opponent, fit and formidable. His hair slicked away from his face without any apparent attempt at style. Combed himself, of course, after washing his face. He smelled liked tobacco and salt.

"You've come to admire my handiwork then."

"I've come to request you stop."

The Colonel's mouth turned, a cruel edge to the look.

"And who are you to make such a demand?"

Lee looked down at the tools next to her hand, surprised at how many she could name: glover's needles, lip tuckers, tumblers, and shears. She'd spent too much time there, coming to appreciate being unsettled. Her safe, predictable world upturned. Everywhere else she went, the young Miss Roosevelt was coddled or adored, often both. She knew she was considered handsome as her mother had been, but more than that, she was fearless like her father. Unlike her father, she had rare opportunities to bare her teeth. Yet here she was, late and alone in a plain wool day dress. She selected the ear opener. Liked that the handles fit neatly in her palm.

"Who am I? A woman with your best interests at heart. A woman with the ear of a president, even."

She held up her tool at the little pun, but the Colonel didn't smile.

"A girl, surely, on that much we can agree."

"Not since last March, I'm afraid. Full-grown now, they say. Ready to make an acceptable match, et cetera."

The Colonel listened to her, but let his hands move back to the neck and the tricky business of veins. Fake, of course. The vascular system could never be saved. It wouldn't matter with a mink, but with a man? He reached for another length of copper wire.

"If you had caught me on Tuesday, perhaps. But now? I've made too much progress."

Lee glanced finally at the senator, relieved that his face didn't look familiar, though they had met. His concave torso made her cringe. How had they arrived at this moment? And how far would she go to protect her ambitions? The plan had begun—like many plans—simple enough. Her father would meet with the senator's delegation about the railroads. The politician had been encouraging squabbles about who controlled that stretch between the Great Lakes and the Pacific. He intended to embarrass the newly inaugurated President McKinley with the ensuing economic unease. In office a mere two months and the dollar was already losing ground. And this after McKinley ran on his record of saving the union from the Panic of '73. He was meant to be their protector.

"He looks like an abomination," Lee said.

The Colonel swung his substantial body toward her, his hands still gripping the wire which could—Lee was well-aware—slip easily enough around her delicate neck.

"He looks, my dear girl, like himself. A statesman, a rabble-rouser, a man cut down in his prime! Also, a son of a bitch."

"You sound like an admirer."

"How could I help but appreciate such a prize?"

"A prize? A sin against God."

"Not afraid of vengeance himself, you'll admit." The Colonel wrapped the wire once around his hand for a better grip, and Lee caught her breath. "Do you know how much a length of copper costs? Fifteen cents a pound. A bloody strong-arm move from Amalgamated. I buy in bulk, of course. Tip the delivery boys grandly. I'm beloved around here."

He took a step closer, and Lee gripped her own instrument more tightly. If he wanted a duel, he would get no argument from her, never mind the rushing noise in her head. *Not so fearless after all*, she thought idly.

"Yes, you are indeed beloved. And don't you wish to remain so? Doesn't it afford a certain flexibility in your pursuits? Leaving your domestic comforts in the dead of night for these animals. Tell me, what if the rumors should begin? You're new to this city, a stranger. Overcome by madness. By obsession. By an inability to see the line."

"The line?"

*Ah,* she had him, or nearly so.

"The line. A shot fired on the battlefield versus one in the court-house. You were always a man to know a goshawk from a vulture."

If he softened, she couldn't tell, and suddenly his hand was on her arm. She felt her flesh rise into tiny rows. Up close, he smelled less like salt and more like the earth, almost sulfuric. He squeezed, and she acted without thinking, slamming the ear opener into his exposed wrist. He cried out, but didn't let go, and she struck again, this time drawing blood, dark and persistent. He pushed her away, and Lee's small frame fell into a table, knocking over a tray of pliers.

"Enough," she shouted, her temper rising. "Do you intend to end your career thusly? Over a science experiment?"

"You will take him at your peril."

"Take him? Do you imagine I'm going to haul a murdered man into the streets of Washington? Drag him into a waiting carriage? No, you will destroy him. Tonight."

"And if I don't?"

The rushing grew louder in Lee's skull. She could hardly hear herself.

"You must know. You will be ruined."

"And yourself?"

"And myself."

It was as if a balloon deflated inside her, and silence returned. She let it, watching for any sign of rebellion. Lee didn't take her eyes off her opponent, but the Colonel looked at the senator, starting with his feet, which had been monstrously difficult to manage. The calves not as much, covered as they were in a fine pelt of hair. The knees again were something else but would look normal enough if tucked into some pants. He sucked on his hand, enjoying the sharp taste of iron as his own blood ran into his mouth.

"You're sure, Baby Lee."

"I'm sure, Father."

\* \* \*

THE TROUBLE STARTED, AS MANY troubles do, with idleness. After a bustling campaign, the Colonel found himself with more time on his hands than he'd experienced since he was a boy. He longed for his days as a Rough Rider, cringed when anyone called him Mr. Vice President. At least as governor, he'd had a few crises to manage. In Washington, he'd had exactly four days that could be deemed as work in his mind. And so, given the responsibility of a child, he retreated to his childhood interests, setting up his own space to spare his wife from the spectacle. But Lee sussed him out and began to worry what would happen if he was left too long without occupation.

At least she felt more comfortable away from the workroom, her father clearly less so. It never failed to amaze her how this soldier and explorer could turn so skittish around a flame. And together they'd produced a roaring one.

"You know them as candles, my dear. You've never seen what fire can do to flesh."

"And yet here I am, on the cusp of a new discovery."

"I'm still not sure you're right."

"I am."

She grabbed an edge of the sheet and tugged the body toward the fireplace. With only skeleton and skin, a little thread and clay, the senator seemed manageable. She could almost do this herself, if need be, fueled as she was by a desire to be more than a debutante, more than a catch. Before she pledged herself to some insipid gentleman, she wanted a White House address. And her father's peculiar hobby would not stand in her way. Another hour, and the deed would be done. She'd tolerated the progression from fowl to small mammal. She didn't even mind the bear if she didn't stare directly into its mismatched eyes. But when he brought home a human hand—to see what advancements might be made—she balked. Her concerns were dismissed as squeamishness. It's not as if he had killed the owner of the hand, merely claimed a small part of him that he would not be using anymore. But the senator? His name was in all the papers: missing.

Her father picked up a corner of the sheet, and she let herself take a deep breath. Together they moved him across the rug. Two feet from safety, the Colonel dropped his corner.

"Onward," Lee said, lowering her voice to imitate her idea of a commander, never mind that she'd only met such men in social settings where they fidgeted with their pocket watches. "Onward."

"No, wait. We're not alone."

"I don't hear anything."

But her voice shook because she did hear something. They'd drawn the curtains in the Colonel's den before hauling the specimen upstairs, but a shadow could be seen out front, pacing and accompanied by the unmistakable sound of boots on gravel. The Colonel's expression changed, a flicker of regret turning to resolve. He looked more like himself, and that should have worried Lee.

"Out," he said, pointing toward the staircase.

"Father—"

"There no reason for a Miss Roosevelt to be here in the middle of the night. There's every reason for an insomniac vice president with a predilection for zoology."

The boots stopped moving, followed by three sharp knocks. Lee turned and descended as instructed. She didn't close the door behind her, though, and stayed out of sight. She listened as her father moved the body into the small kitchen, then she listened as he returned. The Colonel opened the front door himself. He never kept staff on site, not so much worried about the talk—his interests were no great secret, at least during a more typical project—but the quiet helped his concentration. The Deputy Inspector bowed in acknowledgement, then held out his hand, which the Colonel took.

"Some blow, sir."

The Colonel looked at the wound his daughter had inflicted and smiled. Lee had always been his spitfire.

"Come in."

"Don't mind if I do. The wind's changing, sure enough, but there's still a chill at this hour."

The Deputy Inspector was a young man, or at least young for his station. A keen mind and an even better work ethic. Roundly disparaged by his colleagues for his eagerness, but he'd solved the Horseshoe Murders, which made him a minor celebrity. The Colonel respected a lawman who went out of his way for justice.

"You look in need of a drink."

The Colonel poured two neat Old Charters without asking. He let his guest take a sip first. He would let him speak first, too.

"I apologize for disturbing you at such an hour, but I saw a light and thought you might appreciate an in-person update on the investigation."

"Indeed I would. Proceed."

The Colonel settled into the seat farthest from the fire, forcing his guest to settle close to the flames.

"Quite the blaze, sir."

"As you say, there's still a chill this spring."

The Deputy Inspector surveyed his surroundings, noticing the open door to the basement stairs, seeing the indented fibers of the rug near the fireplace. Nothing or something, he noted it all.

"The senator was last seen disembarking the Virginia Midland. He left with an unknown gentleman. He's not got such a face that witnesses are much help. But his colleagues say that he was poised to introduce a bill on the rail situation."

"I've heard much the same. A shame it couldn't be found among his papers."

"May I say what troubles me?"

The man certainly looked troubled. It was too hot in the room and sweat slid down his temples. The Colonel, by contrast, seemed not to notice. He relaxed back in his chair, not bothering to feign sympathy for the senator. He'd lost more people than he could name in a night, each one hardening that muscle of sympathy inside him. Grief? Grief was life and could be fought like any other enemy.

"I'm curious to hear your thoughts."

"His clothes were recovered." If this surprised the Colonel, he didn't show it. The Deputy Inspector took a handkerchief from his pocket and wiped his brow. He placed his whiskey down and leaned forward. "Why go through the trouble of changing, only to leave the evidence behind? If you were running away, I mean."

"You think he's dead."

"I do."

"By violence."

"I do." The Deputy Inspector stood to get farther from the flames. "A first and last victim, if he's caught."

The Colonel considered his guest. The young lawman had noticed his placement near the heat and seemed to be considering what that meant, if anything. It almost impressed him, the Deputy Inspector's earnestness. But sincerity was the last thing he needed. The Colonel wished it weren't so, but his daughter had been right. What a shame.

"Would you like to see my workshop?"

The Colonel stood, gesturing toward the steps. The Deputy Inspector hesitated only a moment before making his descent. Lee had time to prepare, gripping the ear opener in both hands. She merely had to hit him. Her father, she knew, would take care of everything else.

\* \* \*

LEE TRAVELED WITH A CHAPERONE, of course, though her aunt was more of a friend these days. The two ladies joined the throng of gawkers. The lobby truly was impressive. Although she'd been to the museum before, Lee strained to see the barosaurus, admiring the impossible length of its spine, the defensive posture, positioned indefinitely to protect its young. A small child shrieked in appreciation, and Lee watched him weave closer, a hand outstretched in hopes of touching the archeological marvel. Then she hooked her arm into her aunt's and steered them toward the Hall of Vertebrate Origins. This would be her last visit for a good, long while since she'd been selected to accompany Secretary Taft on his latest diplomatic mission. It was just the sort of adventure she'd always craved, and in some ways she felt proud of the role she'd played in her father's ascension. Regrets? McKinley would never have been the equal of her father. And it's not as if she pulled the trigger herself.

They viewed the dinosaur fossils and ventured into North American birds. They passed the great egret and the king penguins. They glanced at the warblers and owls. Eventually her aunt stopped in front of the bison, their heads rising above the spectators.

"They do look lifelike," her aunt said, squeezing Lee's arm.

Lee looked at the bison, impressed by the delicate eyelashes as much as by the heavy pelts. Their horns pointed up like trumpets, as if capable of announcing their own majesty. Lee let her gaze turn to the men in pursuit, spears raised. She stared at the familiar torso, appreciating the shading below each rib. The other, though, was even more impressive, each hair on his chest curling down as if markings on a topographical map. The Deputy Inspector had been a handsome man. And her father? An eccentric, yes, but even she had to admit that her father was also something of an artist.

# THE MADISON CONSPIRACY: DOLLEY MADISON'S ZINGER
## BY CHRISTOPHER CHAMBERS

*Dedicated to Robert Ludlum*

Dolley Madison taught me to read and write. I graduated from *the apple is red*, to heresy . . .

> " . . . *and such dignity applies to the individual's right to control their life, body and limbs, their soul, and to give affection to their neighbor, spouse or child, and that itself is by divine proclamation as the New Covenant, if that is one's belief. In accord, any man or woman born in this Nation or who comes to its shores for sanctuary from want and cruelty abroad and begs the Nation's protection and care, and in return pledges fealty, are citizens of this Nation . . .*

> . . . *for indeed, the institution of slavery is, inter alia, a creature solely of mere positive law, itself carried into rather than enshrined in the Constitution, these natural rights of happiness, dignity, equal protection and due process must supervene, without exception, the positive law of States of this Union, as in no ways does the positive law declaring a human individual as property based on the colour of their skin, have any purchase within the realm of natural law. It must therefore be the duty of the Congress forthwith to put to the States the question of elimination of slavery by Amendment and by repeal*

*of all positive law giving life to the institution, and thus hold*
*that all Descendants of bound African persons be free citizens,*
*under the protection of Congress and the States, until they can*
*conduct their own affairs unimpeded and untrampled . . .*

*. . . and as such, the Anglican who proclaims, 'My means of*
*worship dictates that a Baptist may not mill his grain on my*
*stone' shall not find refuge in the First Amendment; nor may a*
*priest or pastor declare that women are apostate, and an*
*adherent of such priest or pastor thus prevents all women from*
*selling or buying produce or wares in a public market that such*
*adherent may own or operate. Thusly, "faith" is personal and*
*sacrosanct. However, 'religion' is public and outward and is*
*thus not absolute . . .*

*Now, the right of the people, as we have always referred to 'the*
*people' as collective and not the individual, to keep and bear*
*such muskets, rifles, pistols &c. and reasonable stores for*
*powder and shot, for the common defense, for duties as needed*
*for a constabulary, are well known. Yet explicit language in the*
*Constitution preventing Congress from dis-arming the people*
*had always been rejected, as seen in the proffered provisions of*
*the Massachusetts and Pennsylvania Conventions fifteen years*
*ago. In accord, Congress may advise the several States and their*
*counties, townships &c. to disband the Militia and Muster and*
*thus regulate fire-arms within their borders as to purpose or*
*number, dis-arm criminals and lunatics, and hold that*
*gunsmithing and private arsenals be made public*
*instrumentalities, for safety's sake . . . "*

Somebody, can't recall who now, once demeaned the author,
James Madison, as a withered apple-john of a man. Now he so
lay—shriveled . . . languishing . . . babbling, with little knowledge
of the ill, or triumph, he'd drafted.

Like my teacher, I was tasked with loving this poor man,
then destroying him. I was all of fifteen, few whiskers on my
lip and chin . . . and even less down below, where it itched and
ached during her lessons in the cock loft of Montpelier's great

house, in the wee hours. Itching and aching . . . as she'd be barefoot and in her bedgown, and the bedgown was but a mist of fabric over the cream and curve of her thighs, and the damn thing would fall off her smooth shoulders as she spoke arcane things at me, and made me pay attention to my letters . . . even as her plump pink breasts and rosy nipples hung bare . . . and I'd weep for what was happening in the drawers I wore to bed. Weep, because my manhood, just budding, would be torn from my body had anyone outside the great house known she was there.

"This is no time for flesh or pleasure," she'd whisper. That rocked my soul more than if had we lain together.

Poor Sukey, Dolley's body servant, she had it worse. Girls always have it worse. They are the vessels—the *teachers*—and I weep for Sukey those times when I can remember her face. "Lord, let me be their protector," I'd beg. *Naw*, said Jesus, *you are doomed to be their sapper. Prepare yourself . . .*

Wish I could say more, but Seamus Hannity's about to lay another good lick on me.

"Oy, yar cheeky naygur!" he cries as if he, not I, am the sumbitch bound to a chair at the elbows with good Maryland hemp rope. He slams a fist right into my gut and this time nothing comes out. With the first punch much of my chicken stew from supper spattered on the cell floor, there in the gaol room under the United States Courthouse on Carroll Row, F Street, in the still smoldering Federal City named for General Washington. Can't see the mess in the flickering oil lamplight, but I can smell it. Perfume compared to this Paddy's breath.

"Lissen, boyo," Hannity grunts, "I'll teach yar the meanin' o' the word, *pain*."

"I wager you can't even spell p-a-i-n. And it's illegal to teach *me* to read and write." I spit some blood to make his red face redder.

He's a big'un but I can cut him down if I wasn't lashed to the damn chair. Same odds his brethren and quite a few toothless ruddy-haired Mollies enjoyed as they rampaged out there the last two nights, all because Beverly Snow in the ole Epicurean asked them to behave.

Snow's spot, hand to God, was my refuge for oysters, blackberry pie, and rum. Freemen could eat in the same establishment as white men. Long as we were low in number, dressed well, were quiet and not obdurate.

But these Paddies were filthy, loud. Came from the Navy Yard, demanding food with nary a gold Spanish bit among them. Snow, who's aptly black as pitch, threw them out. They returned with their comrades—and lynch ropes, torches, shillelaghs, blades. Even murdered two little girls right outside Blodgett's Hotel as the rioting spread.

Dear honeys . . . they were apprenticed to their mother, Lydia, for whom I'd procured a contract at the hotel for laundering linens. Lydia'd displaced a syndicate of Mollies doing that work; I'd also helped freeman Albert DeVillers get the night soil cartage work on the block. Well, they beat Albert, burned his wagons, stole his mules. As for poor Claudia and Anna-Jean, ten and eleven years of age . . . they didn't go unavenged. Someone went and cut the throats of the Paddies who bashed their beautiful little heads in.

As I alluded, I was somewhere eating chicken stew at the time.

Sumbitch runt of a Marine, his shako high cap covering his little grimy head like a beer keg atop an apple, appeared with his company at my doorstep, under the guise of protecting we po' cowerin' culuds. With me at the point of a bayonet he said I was under arrest.

Such irony indeed. Were it not for the Militia and Marines, and gangs of ordinary peckerwood shipwrights and cordwainers who had no love for the Papist Irish, chanting all about them being "illegals" and pining for a "big beautiful wall 'round the shores," we'd all be playing lyres in Darky Heaven.

The rioters spared some bondsmen and bondswomen, however. As I was dragged into the courthouse, Seamus Hannity, his brass constable buttons popped from his girth, confessed the reason: no Irishmen had the cash to compensate slave owners. Indeed, the safest among us were those gangs of fathers, mothers and children paraded in Mr. Franklin's and Mr. Armfield's coffles, cowbells and all, in view of the Capitol or General Jackson's White House.

Enough of Snow and murder, for now. I hear the clink of a turnkey. The door swings open. The august United States Attorney for the District of Columbia now stands before me.

He looks different from when I first met him twenty years ago. Party in Georgetown he hosted, 1812, right before the war. I spent the evening in a cold downpour tending the President's brougham. But I caught a gander of this man's wispy brown curls, ramrod figure, and starched high collar. And his smirk.

Well, he's gray and fat now; the collar wants for proper laundering. Still smirking, though. Guess I'll taunt him with that li'l tune he wrote awhile back . . .

*"Oh, say can you see . . . by the ledge's early light. What's proudly I hail . . . my pipe, yonder lean-ning."*

He chuckles and bids Hannity, "Fetch and light the man's pipe."

"*Sar*? This jack'nape?"

"Do it!"

The drag's sweet. It's Upper Marlboro leaf mixed with pinch of hemp. I clench the pipe stem hard after another puff while he moves to the shadows, retrieves a document, and returns with his spectacles donned to read from it.

"Says you are 'Josiah Bourne.' Interesting name. Heard it before somewhere."

"Might have just took it when I was given my papers," I reply, blowing smoke.

"Ah, so I assume your manumission documents and free pass badge are in order?"

I nod, but then Hannity snarls, "Tha' can be t'rown in

Chesapeake Canal easy, sar, and t'is naygur sold ta New Or'lins."

"Accidents happen," he shrugs. "I must say, Bourne—this lists your age as fifty years old? You are remarkably fit."

"God lends some compensation, sir. Look at our ladies versus yours in advanced age."

He's not goaded. Rather, he motions at me with the sheet, as if daring me to snatch at it. With what, my eyelids?

"There's a record of 'J. Bourne' paying the freemen's bond to the court clerk. However, I have some sheriff's notes here. . . . 'Informant asserts that Bourne is adept at forgery: passes, deeds of manumission.' Did you provide such documents to an artful negro such as yourself, by the name of Thrush Hern, when our dear former President Jefferson gifted the property to his grandson, Mr. Randolph? Thrush has absconded north . . . "

Hannity's like a stud kicking at the paddock wall, such is his lust for beating me bloody. I just take another languid puff, shrug.

"This dossier also lists your occupation as 'private assurance.' You left Virginia per the ordinance of Eighteen-ought-three, drafted with the blessing of former President Jefferson, requiring all persons born free or manumitted who are negro or mulatto . . . or of color as defined by the Court of Appeals in *Hudgins vs. Wrights* by the Honorable Saint George Tucker, be removed from the Commonwealth or else pay a yearly surety and register to remain. Sadly, we don't have such banishment here. Too many black vagabonds, whores."

"Sir, my vocation is to be hired out to protect livelihoods and homesteads of negroes and investigate any losses thereto. Suppose I'm going to be busy . . . "

"Interesting." The smirk becomes a leer. "Because there is no such person as 'Josiah Bourne.' Then again, there has *long* been no such a person as *Paul Jennings*, either, eh?"

I keep a stone face, blow another puff into the moribund air of the cell and say, "Who?"

"Died in eighteen and fourteen, during the British attack, as one of the wagons clearing items from the president's mansion, now called the White House, careened off the Long Bridge into the swift Potomac as General Ross's invaders entered the city. Welcome back, Mr. Jennings."

I smile and grunt, "*Bourne.*"

"If you are not an apparition, you are a fraud; thus, a runaway."

Sumbitch slides another document under my gaze, and I bite down on the pipe stem so hard I fear I've cracked it.

"Magistrate's order pursuant to Section Forty-four of the D.C. Code, passed after the rampage of Nat Turner in Southampton, Virginia," he declares. "You were indicted this day for the murders of Raymond Flynn and Kelly O'Reilley. No trial. You will be hung at sunrise." He leans close, and he smells of coffee, Bay Rum toilet water, ointment for his sore bones. He whispers, "It can disappear on a zephyr's breeze . . . if you tell me where I can find Dolley Madison. The *real* Dolley Madison . . . "

"Fuck you," I spit. "*By the twilight's last gleaming . . .* "

He slaps the pipe from my mouth.

"She is counterfeit . . . *as is the painting*!" he rails.

"Sir, she's back at Montpelier, with her husband, the former President."

"No, she is retired to the Cutts' house. Unless you know different . . . "

"I don't know who lives in the Cutts' house. Nor do I know a black named Paul Jennings . . . *sir.*"

"When you were discovered," he sneers, "among the abolitionist Crandall's followers in that nest of a Colored School, General . . . I mean *President* Jackson wanted you shot. And it would have been your own fault, for you were told to stay away."

He has me by the neck. But I have him by his sack. May as well tug.

"All right sir. I tried Saint Louie but you all saw fit to confirm Missouri as a slave state in the Eighteen and Twenty Compromise, where my friend Mr. Webster and Northern men finally realized that Southern men command much real estate and electoral votes . . . but few souls."

He's breathing much harder. I fear for the man's heart.

"Why did you think it was a company of Marines that stormed the Colored School, rather than Militia or my constables? Because when you were recognized, I prevailed upon Jackson that you could be the key to tying up loose ends." He's in my face again. "Mr. Madison, for the last twenty years, has seen his faculties bounce between brilliance and vacancy. It is the highest of state secrets I say to you now. After the war, Mr. James Monroe and others had no choice but to take quiet power just as our Capitol and the White House were raised from the ashes, until Mr. Madison's term ended. I told 'Old Hickory,' in as simple language as he could ponder, that if you have suddenly resurfaced, Jennings, it means you might have knowledge of the filth who subverts our nation, using chicanery and spells to beguile good men into writing blasphemies."

I nod toward the Irish dullard. "Mr. Key, should you be saying this in his earshot? I've been hiding in plain sight for years. As for Mrs. Madison, I'd say Mrs. Cutts has been hitting the laudanum again. Her son Payne is a drunkard. Driven Montpelier to ruin . . . I hear poor President Madison doesn't even know his stepson is mortgaging the bondsfolk. *My kin.* Their blood is the ink on the note being called . . . "

O'er my sore eyes I watch, as Frances Scott Key is ungallantly screaming.

"You arrogant bastard! You *know* what's amiss! You *know* why this shakes the Republic to its core . . . and General Jackson and Vice-President Van Buren, even old Federalists such as me and Mr. Adams the younger, John Quincy—we *believe* Mrs. Cutts, Mrs. Madison's brothers, her own son! All say that the old woman is not their kin. You will confirm this. You will reveal the whereabouts of the *portrait* and what was secreted therein. Else I'll take your life, by God!"

"Then take it. Although I was once the President's slave I was still in a cage, a gilded one, and my life was not my own. I'm sure President Jefferson's Sally can so attest . . . " Before he can explode again, I cease speechifying. "*Full immunity.* Then I tell you what you want to know."

Key's beginning to pace the fetid stone floor, careful to sidestep my *vomitus.*

"For crimes not yet uncovered . . . are you daft? The only thing in play is whether or not you swing in the morning."

"You indicted a phantom. Hanging one will just render more thorny questions . . . "

Hannity senses a softening. "T'is infernal naygur kilt me mates!" he bellows.

Key stills him with a finger, sighs, "Alright. Immunity from federal prosecution for situations arising out of information you render today about the President and Mrs. Madison, and Gilbert Stuart's portrait of General Washington."

"You accused me of helping one of President Jefferson's bondsmen abscond . . . and in a few seconds you will doubtless do the same regarding Sukey and her daughter, the runaway named Helen."

He pulls up his chair, sits. "Take it or leave it, Mr. Bourne. Sorry, *Paul.*"

"Untie me first."

Such a leap of faith, for if he knows who I am, he also knows that I can break his neck surer than any rope can snap mine, and before any sumbitch can level a musket. Yet he makes Hannity cut me from my bonds, then says to him, "Constable, you may leave."

Hannity grumbles something in Gaelic, lumbers out of the cell. Key's got sand!

He says, "Start with that night, twenty years ago, after the Battle of Bladensburg . . . and the portrait."

He pulls a pad of paper and graphite pencil from his waistcoat pocket, and he's scribbling and mouthing the words, "draft . . .

immunity agreement." He tears out two scratch-laden sheets, places them on my knee in the dull pallor of the oil lamp.

"No. This goes way back to Montpelier, when I was Mr. Madison's groom . . . the day Sukey became body servant to Mrs. Madison."

"Sukey, the negress . . . " he begins, "was the so-called 'conjure woman?'"

I dip my head. Poor Sukey. "Not at first."

Sukey was just a girl who had recently budded her chest and I'd help her hang drying lines for the laundering; I'd fetch pails of water back to the great house for her. Nothing more. The gossip in both the house and quarters was that her mother, Big Helen, taught her roots and potions—*hoodoo* that kept white and negro alike away from the sick house's doctors and surgeons because doctors and surgeons and infected beds would kill you.

Mr. Madison the Elder was decent to us. He didn't beat his livestock or hunting dogs either. And though I was a buck teenager, he'd allow me to help Mr. Madison, Junior—Master Jimmy, what I called him even when he was President—mount and dismount from his favorite sorrel mare. Master Jimmy's the size of an elf. At Princeton College, those rich fellows could hop on and off a horse like Cossacks. Not Master Jimmy. Poor man, I could tote him around like he was a child, legs dangling, and yet he wasn't bashful or cross about it. Just took it as given.

That changed when the lady came. Master Jimmy was married to her out at Harewood, in the mountains. After the honeymoon she went back to Philadelphia to gather her things and her son Payne. House gossip was she was a faded woman: no husband and not a penny but what she got off men with whom she tumbled. Like Aaron *fucking* Burr . . . my poor Master Jimmy's only Princeton friend. Some friend! Passing her and her brat off on the dour boy you once teased!

So Master Jimmy was in his study, drinking lemonade sweetened with brandy. He was rattled, I recall. He loved Mr. Jefferson but he'd tell me sometimes Mr. Jefferson didn't understand that the whole of America, or the world, wasn't Virginie. And Patrick Henry—the liberty or death fellow—told him he wasn't a loyal Democrat. Those Baptists in the hills with their squirrel muskets said they were going to boycott his reelection to Congress. General Washington and Mr. Hamilton and Mr. Adams put their backs to him . . . and it hurt.

So he was locked in there, in both the room and his head, when the Madame arrived. Sukey and a bunch of us all lined up without him when she sauntered in, parasol still extended like there's damn sun and showers indoors.

And every jaw slackened when this woman floated over to me and said, all whispery, "You are Paul, boy?"

"Yes, Madame. Paul Jennings."

She looked me up and down, smiled, and with lips redder than berries set in Chinaman's porcelain said, "When the President is predisposed you will be my herald and right hand. My *Legba*."

My eyes were wider than white folks dinner plates, because *General Washington* was President. And likely Mr. Adams was going to be next, because it looked like he was going to whip any candidate Mr. Jefferson put up. I was about to remind her, but she went and touched her finger to my lips.

"Hush. That condition is temporary. Life is cruel for we widowed wives, we single mothers. Yet look at me now. Risen. As your master will rise."

Spooky, I swear. Then, she moved to Sukey. She devoured her.

"And you shall be my body servant," she said to Sukey.

As if it couldn't get any queerer, Mrs. Madison touched Sukey's chin and spoke French. But it was French with something extra. I'd heard the extra from Frenchies who ran from a different sort of head chopping than what Mr. Jefferson's friends had done in Paris: that of negroes with cane knives in Saint-Dominique, which they now called "Hayti."

This wasn't the quiet and plain Quaker lady from the Carolinas by way of Philadelphia we'd expected after the wedding. She chanted something in Sukey's ear, and the words almost knocked Big Helen to the floor. They were words no white woman should know.

"I am saved from death by *Yemoja* after her lord *Oldumare* took all whom I loved but my son, in the pestilence. *Oya* dances across the river . . . to you."

Francis Scott Key scoffs, "You expect me to believe this, Jennings?"

I nod.

"Then after all these voluptuous theatrics I supposed she threw open the doors to the President's study, went in, closed them behind her and all you heard was rutting and loveplay?"

"No. A servant brought in Payne Todd. Porky little bastard, two feet tall. Blank look in his eyes and we were told one day he'd be our master to serve. *Then* she put those thighs on little Master Jimmy, smothered his face with those breasts. Rode him proper. *Hours*."

And yet Key's not even visibly angry at that. "So," he says, "this was the beginning of the spells, the bewitching of the President that caused his . . . lapse?"

"You believe in witches, in Lucifer? Yet you can't abide something simpler—that all it takes is words and a little brewed leaf or chewed berry and flaked stone to capture the mind and steer the heart? Yes, there are conjurer women. No, witches don't exist."

"Yet, is it true there was a free colored woman—come from the French debacle on Hayti, who was your Mistress's 'apothecary' in Philadelphia—who saved Payne from the Yellowjack epidemic in ninety-three that killed Dolley Madison's first husband and other children?"

"You asking or telling? Listen, some nights the Madame would climb up to the cock loft in her robe and bedgown to fetch Sukey, whose braids'd stick out like twigs from her mobcap, and they would troop off into the night to pick mushrooms. Same things that would put to dreams every living soul when these excursions happened. Same things that, once harvested, would yield a future crop of success for Master Jimmy rising. Congress.

Secretary of State. A feather's breadth from President. Just as the Madame portended."

Key hands over a new document. I see a list of names. *Damn.* I can do it from memory.

"Aaron Burr . . . General James Wilkinson, who snitched on Aaron Burr. General Wade Hampton, butcher of the slaves who rebelled on the German Coast parishes of Louisiana . . . William Eustis, James Armstrong . . . Robert Smith . . . Patrick Henry, Elbridge Gerry . . . various parsons, priests, preachers, local drayage concerns, other planters, eh?"

"Men who fell out of the way as Mr. Madison rose to the Presidency. Men who were addled, hamstrung, made sick, made to murder their careers or murder others. Who is missing?"

"Alexander Hamilton."

"Why?"

"He loved Mr. Hamilton and it pained him that Mr. Jefferson did not."

"Have you heard of the Federalist Papers, eighty-five essays written in support of our new Constitution, forty-odd years ago? Hamilton, Mr. Madison and Mr. Jay wrote them under the pseudonym 'Publius.'"

I shrug, smiling.

"Not even the apocryphal number Eighty-Six. *A Proposal for the Maturation of the Republic,* by Publius 'Emeritus?' Do you know who Publius Emeritus is?"

"Chief Justice John Marshall?"

"Good guess, and it would be a humorous one, were the heresies in that document not so dire."

I shoot forward in my chair. He flinches and I press him, "Oh, so it's real?"

"No, Jennings," he retorts, "officially that document does not exist. We know of its . . . flavor . . . from the babbling of its supposed author—your Master Jimmy—when he's made lucid by tonic and injections. Now, start telling me facts that matter, or your deal is off!"

"The night after the defeat at Bladensburg, our party re-crossed the river to meet up with the President and what was left of General Winder's army. We stayed in Brookeville, Maryland, as Winder was to resign there and turn over command of the regulars and militia to General Sam Smith and General Stricker, which was interesting as Smith was the brother of Robert Smith, who was yet another 'barrier' to Master Jimmy, mysteriously removed. I tended to the President with donated Quaker clothing as yes, one of our wagons tipped into the river, owing to fear and a sudden gale. See, he and the Madame were supposed to rendezvous long before that, at Falls Church. The Madame, Sukey, the rest . . . they never made it. Wasn't until the night of maybe the Twenty-seventh of August that husband and wife would meet again, as the British withdrew."

His face sours into a grimace. He knows I'm playing with him.

"And it was some days after that Mr. James Monroe's agents kidnapped me, beat me, told me I would be banished, as if I never existed. That's my story, Mr. Key . . . "

"We are going to go for a ride, Jennings," Key hisses, "and settle this."

He shouts for Hannity to bring the manacles, and to call for a coach and team.

"Who's the Militiaman on duty?" he shouts.

"Corporal Enzo Giuliani, I t'ink, sar"

"Too many vowels in that name—a foreigner?"

"Uh, Ey-taly, sar."

I chuckle and correct, "No such place. There's the Kingdom of Sardinia, The Piedmonte, the Holy See and—"

"Shut yar 'ole, yar black bugger!" Hannity shouts, clapping my wrists in irons.

And those chains and manacles are jangling as the coach shimmies across the Twelfth Street plank bridge spanning the open sewer that is Tiber Creek. Whatever odor the Tiber managed that hot night was mild compared to that of the acrid smoke from the rioter's romp, polluting the night air, shrouding the stars above me. Still, I find Polaris through the haze as we ride parallel to the creek on Pennsylvania Avenue. I could jump, run. But Jesus taught me different all those years ago . . .

We turn onto H Street and Giuliani steadies the team. A hot rain now falls. Doesn't do a thing for the timber of the air, but at least the smoke's retreating.

"Must remind you of the night you 'died,'" Key scoffs as he leads me to the Cutts House. "The rain, I mean. Quenching the fire the British set. Commodore Perry the Younger, who yearns to take a flotilla to Nippon, says the Japonie have a legend of a storm that drove away the Mongols. I'd like to think the storm of that August, Eighteen and Fourteen, as our 'Divine Wind.'"

"I prayed for sunshine."

He has a key to the house and there's but two young women, both white, drawing curtains, sweeping. They avert their eyes as we ascend the stairs to a bedchamber.

I see her, laying under a quilted coverlet despite the summer night's heat. Only her head peeks up, the gray hair covered by a high-topped frilly mobcap, tied at her chin . . . her very pointed chin, filled in with a bit of pudge. Not a bead of sweat on her, while Key mops himself with his handkerchief every few seconds.

"When will my dear husband come to me, or I be sent to him?" she mewls. It's as if she's talking to me, not even noting the metal biting into my tailcoat sleeves and wrists.

"So, Ma'am, you recognize this negro?" Key inquires.

"Why yes, it's Paul."

Key sucks his teeth but then grows a smile for her and says, "Did Paul here help you slowly poison or addle the President, and dispose of a portrait of General Washington hanging in the residence, as the British soldiers, sailors, and marines marched down Rhode Island Avenue?"

"Again sir, I saved the painting," she says, pleasantly. "They lie when they say I cut it from the frame, however. I commanded Paul to break the frame . . . it was a copy Mr. Stuart made, not the orginal, you know."

She's got that part down pat. Hayseeds and gentry alike in this land repeat the folklore that she cut it out with a knife and Sukey rolled it up and tossed it in a sack.

"Y-Yes, Ma'am . . . " Key groans, and doubtless he's put this question to her before. "But I meant what was glued to the back. Sheets of paper, hand-written. Did you do that . . . or Paul, or Sukey?"

"As my husband is ill and loathe to travel to the Federal City anymore, I bid President Jackson to have a ball here, and invite those Democrats who now call themselves National Republicans or that silly name 'Whig,' to promote harmony. My dear husband wrote that political parties were injurious to the nation. Can you imagine Tennessee ruffians dancing the Allemande in the parlor here?"

"Jennings, talk to her."

"*Me*?"

I kneel on the floor, irons clanking and jangling. "Madame . . . do you recall Payne's birthday parties? Sukey made pies and we roasted chestnuts for him, there in Baltimore, at the seminary school . . . Bishop Carroll and his family had us up there many times?"

"Oh yes! My boy, born in the leap year month of February. What a joyous day to be out from my room. Fresh cold air, light . . . St. Mary's . . . I worried about him getting light, for there was so little light. Dark as when the rain came, and I was back with my dear Jimmy . . . and we drank at Wiley's Tavern as the smoke from the burning city clogged the wet sky. Drinking was all we could do to quell the horror of defeat and exile . . . "

As if a child, the old lady yawns, turns over, is dappled with sleep. I look to Key and advise, "We should go."

"What did you just do?"

"What you asked. The Madame visited Payne only *once* when he was schooled by the priests at St. Mary's in Baltimore. The bondsmen at Georgetown told me she saw the boy a total of twenty minutes that time, then left with a nun and a novice priest. They toured the church's almshouse that held lunatic women, many of whom had lost children in childbirth or to disease. Like the Madame had lost all but Payne. She took a fondness to one poor soul there. *More a sister than my own*, she'd gushed. Utterly insane, yet with beautiful brown hair, buxom form, as sweet a face as her own . . . "

He looks to the bed and mutters, "*My God . . .* "

"In twenty years, Mr. Key, you never followed up on that lead? So, shall we go?"

Sumbitch mumbles, "Come . . . come with me . . . "

We descend the stairs as if colleagues now—yet I'm the one still in irons. In the parlor, he indeed seats me in one of the fine wingback chairs I recall from the White House. He plops onto the brocaded chaise opposite me, waving off the white servant girls.

He explains that the Cutts House is where they meet. He points over his shoulder to two leather bound tomes set among the volumes in the bookcase. Their records. And who are they?

"We are called the Committee. Former President Monroe is the chair, our vice-chairs rotate. I am such now. We placed a member on Chief Justice Marshall's court, Mr. Taney of Maryland. Ex-officio members include Speaker Clay, Vice President Van Buren . . . of course President Jackson. He is a bit prickly, often a liability. Believes Mr. Biddle of the Bank and the Freemasons are a part of the enemy, along with the British East India Company and other London trading concerns. He also thinks Catholics are bad, as Catholics in the New Word have been 'mongrelized.' While Mr. Biddle has no knowledge of us, many of are indeed Masons . . . and Catholic."

"Jackson is an idiot."

"Maybe. We give him a wide berth because he's popular among the pigheaded."

"And Mr. Calhoun?"

"No. Especially since the nullification crisis over the tariffs. If the enemy doesn't tear the nation in two, Southern zealots like him will."

"Yet most of you are Southern men, but for . . . Mr. Quincy Adams, Mr. Webster?"

"Those two? We tell them what they need to know." He gives me the names of New York bankers and ship owners in their little tea party, western miners and fur traders. Then he labels the enemy of which he speaks: "'Columbiads,' as the embossed letterhead on their taunting communications carries both a cannon by that name, and the feminine symbol of America, *Columbia*, though her features are unmistakably 'mongrel,' to use Jackson's term. The letters are signed with female names. Clytemnestra, or Pocahontas or Sheba and such nonsense. The War Department uses the code 'the Squad' for them."

I nod. "When have the letters come?"

"In advance of various crises and watersheds, from the removal of the red men, to the Eighteen and Twenty Missouri mare's nest. Now they predict gold panics and Mr. Biddle's fall . . . something about Texas 'where freedom shall be false and Reconquista will spill from sunburnt lips.'" He blows out a heavy sigh then scoffs, "Their purpose is mere division and chaos, Jennings. They care not who they destroy, and they even recruit from the ranks of savages and Africans. Tecumseh, William Weatherford of the Red Stick Creeks, Osceola. Nat Turner himself."

"Abolitionists?"

His face hardens. "This is bigger even than they. Which brings us back to the woman upstairs. When do you think the Columbiads made the switch, so Dolley could make her escape?"

Alright, I'll bite.

"The last thing I saw before your 'Committee' shanghaied and banished me was the Madame and Master Jimmy *clutching* at each other, crying. True love. Master Jimmy was at Bladensburg with Mr. Monroe and they were caught up in Winder's rout. Admiral

Malcolm's fleet was bombarding Alexandria simultaneously so there was no escape to the south of the city. Worse, they were separated from General Scott's regulars. Though professionals, they were not going to stand like Spartans at Thermopylae and get wiped out as 'good men with guns' and the militias of Maryland, Virginia, Pennsylvania, and our District of Columbia rabbited!"

"The Committee saved the nation that night."

"No, sir! That honor went to Commodore Barney, his seamen and Marines. He scuttled his own flotilla at the head of the Patuxent River at Upper Marlboro and took his position at Bladensburg and I myself had handed Master Jimmy that communiqué that the flotilla was lost. He just smiled. *Took a nap.* Did you know that with Barney were dozens of negro jack tar seamen, among them Sukey's cousins, and they made the last stand on the road that saved Master Jimmy's wrinkled ass. Does your dossier say that? How about this—that I too had a cousin, a seaman loyal to *your* flag, wounded and taken prisoner? Did the Committee confirm that Sukey also had relatives fighting *alongside* the British, eh? Freed bondsmen, armed by redcoats General Ross and Admiral Cockburn and called Colonial Marines? Black men fighting for you, black men fighting against you. All cherishing the same thing: *America.* If that confuses you, then we have little else to discuss, Mr. Key!"

Unmoved, he props his filthy boots onto the chaise, "Sometime after the President and Mrs. Madison were reunited after you left Brookeville, she must have melted away. Because that, dear Jennings, is when we found that the portrait of General Washington was not spirited away for safekeeping, but among Dolley Madison's—or the facsimile's—affects. And its canvas looked to be sliced. Yet all true accounts say yes, you indeed smashed the frame; no one cut it out."

"Sumbitchin' panic, Mr. Key! We had no idea of the President's whereabouts when we received word of Barney's last stand; there were encoded courier messages intercepted from General Ross back to the Duke of Wellington himself, that he'd bring back the President and First Lady as hostages to end the war—cede the territory from the Mississippi to the Pacific and any lands seized from the crushed red men from Ft. Dearborn where the negro DuSable built the post 'Chicago,' to the Floridas. And that he'd personally *burn* Mr. Stuart's portrait of General Washington. In panics, sir, sometimes stories don't match."

He's curiously cool—even relaxed—sprawled there on that chaise.

"Cards up, Jennings; first me, then you. I don't like informants. They are snakes, yet . . . important. Our informant was a slave of Mr. Monroe's—one who knows whence his bread is buttered and is now quite wealthy in cooperation—he gave us a deposition that he witnessed Sukey 'cleaning' the portrait late in the evening when your master and President Monroe were in a war conference with Secretary of the Navy Jones, two days before Ross's force marched on the Capital. It'd been taken off the wall—meaning it could at least be removed in the frame—and yet he stopped watching because Mrs. Madison approached, in her bedclothes, and thus he didn't want his eyes recklessly focusing on a white woman. The one thing he did recall was that she carried a portfolio he'd seen the President's aide carry and something that looked like glass bottle of mucilage—with which paper can be glued to any surface. He said Mrs. Madison retreated when she saw him."

"That a fact? Think I know this man. Owns a cabaret of buck-dancers and strutters. Curious how he was given his papers, when I was given the choice of banishment or death."

"His War Department code name is 'Jeh-Hova.' Not sacrilege, more a humorous admission that his revelations and rewards have been Biblical. Jeh-Hova frequented Beverly Snow's Epicurean by the way. It was he who testified that he saw you stalking two Irishmen in the vicinity of Blodgett's Hotel the first night of the riots."

I lean forward from the chair, showing the manacles to remind him that I remain his prisoner despite his promise of immunity. "You already have your pet darky, then?"

---

"You have honor, Jennings. He does not. But he asserts that twenty years ago you and Sukey were in and out of the President's bedchamber as Mr. Madison raged in bizarre fits, and he reported the same to Mr. Monroe. Mr. Madison was screaming how he and Mr. Jefferson 'blackmailed' Mr. Hamilton into passing the Residence Act, moving the capital to the Potomac, away from the big mercantile cities. Worse, that he had the urge to write . . . something about 'write to elucidate on *right*.' Is he a liar?"

He doesn't wait for my reply. He swings his legs off the chaise as I tense-up. We stare at each other, neither flinching until the front door to the Cutts' House swings wide. It's Hannity, announcing the arrival of another man: a clerk from the courthouse. Giuliani ushers the man in; he totes a satchel and is visibly upset when he spies me sitting there in irons. Both Italian and Irish goons remain this time, posted at the open door.

"Why the delay?" Key quizzes the clerk.

"It's late, sir . . . and the curfew."

The clerk nervously lifts some scribbled notes and a pamphlet stamped from the Library of Congress out of the satchel. *Heathen & Savage Revealed Religions* . . .

"'*Legba* is from Saint-Dominique 'Vodou,'" the clerk reads, after clearing his throat many times, avoiding my gaze. " '*Eleggua-Eshu* is from 'Santería' Lucumi . . . and consequently Yoruba . . . as source for *Exu*, in Brazilian 'Quimbanda.'"

I'm watching Key's eyes narrow and his face flush red as the little white man reads on . . .

"He is . . . um . . . 'gatekeeper between realms, guide with great strength . . . associated with the image of Saint Jude, patron of lost causes who at times can work miracles to turn the tide. He is also . . . the trickster.'"

Key's now staring at me, nostrils flared as he bellows, "I had to be sure! And you never answered about Sukey's or her daughter Helen's whereabouts. You, who forges free papers . . . *you used me!*"

And now I smell Hannity looming behind my chair.

Ten seconds is all I need. *Strike like a copperhead*, I hear in my head. *Coil like a whelk's shell* . . .

. . . and I shoot up, arching my back to loop the manacle chain around Hannity's head. Twist. *Squeeze.* And see myself from above with clarity, tucking and coiling forward, Hannity hurtling over my back and shoulders, crashing into a small table by the chaise. Sending Key and the clerk to the floor like they were dolls. Me, lunging to the wall to pluck out a book with both hands . . . turning . . . kicking my chair in the path of the on-rushing Giuliani.

He's knocked to his knees but recovers just quickly enough to cock and level his musket. Anyone can crow about pulling a trigger. Doing it when the target is locking eyes with you, unafraid, is quite another thing. I'm on him and the shot hits the ceiling. Sumbitch drops the musket and scampers away, crablike and pleading.

I'm out the door, with the book tucked under one arm, hopping onto Key's coach, as me on horseback galloping away would bring more attention from these sorts than a hack or private coachman.

"*Hyah now!*" I holler as I drop the book to my feet and snap the reins. Across the bottoms into Georgetown live many negro boiler-fitters who can knock these manacles off in the ten seconds my escape took.

I slow my breathes and my heart accordingly, as I was taught, many years ago, and I guide the team gingerly, for the streets are filled with white men seeking my blood.

Yet, my mind's slipping back to the nights I was indeed taught, I was indeed conceived, quickened and born anew—as was Sukey—to our new mother Dolley's touch and voice.

" . . . we are slave and master, banker and brothel-whore, soldier and fishwife, Druid and Voodou . . . Jew, Gentile and Mohametan. But we remain shadows, until a time of great peril, where cruel and greedy men, who we shall expose, will cede this last best hope of humans on the earth to fanatics, trivial fools, criminals."

Then, the world will see all the apocryphal and apostate writings come alive, by hands of the men and women who were once wicked, made wonderful for a fleeting time. Poor Master Jimmy, if he could only see Publius Emeritus's script, glued so assiduously to the back of a painting for safekeeping.

If you are inspired by his words, there are many like me who will protect you.

If you fear his words, well . . . there are many like me . . .

# LONG LIVE LONG
BY KATE FLORA

WHEN THEY THINK YOU'RE ON your way out, unconscious, unable to hear, people speak very frankly around you. They say things they'd never say to my face, and it must be added that people are pretty darned careful what they say to me. I have worked hard to make it so. I want people afraid. In awe. Worshipful, even, were that not an affront to God. That's something I try not to do, offend God. Me and the people need Him on our side. I've often thought the other side has been recruited by the Devil. Big money. Greed. No consciences. Happy to keep people oppressed and desperate. Or indifferent. That's not how I read the Bible, and I was raised on the Good Book.

The man who was speaking now—deep-voiced, authoritative, and strangely smug—was saying things he'll wish he hadn't, should I be able to return to myself. In his opinion, that will not happen.

"There's a lot of internal damage, which we've tried to repair. But that bullet also nicked a kidney, which Robichaux, scared witless at the task of repairing an assassinated U.S. Senator, nearly missed completely."

Another voice, lower and with notes of caution, as though this man, at least, understood that the man in the bed might be listening, said, "But it was caught? The damage to the kidney? And repaired?" He had a genteel Southern Louisiana voice.

The first speaker laughed. An ugly laugh, not the gentle self-deprecation of a concerned healer. "Unfortunately, yes. Many would have been delighted if this rabble-rousing socialist had speedily gone on to meet his maker. There was already talk, at every dinner party, cocktail party, and social event that someone should shoot him. There is great joy in Louisiana tonight. Let him try to orate and dominate in heaven if he can."

There was a pause. Then the first speaker—Long had decided to call him Aristo—added, "Of course it is still touch and go, but it is leaning far more toward go." An amused snort. "I doubt that President Roosevelt has much to worry him here."

"Senator Long is renowned as a fighter," the second voice said.

Another sharp laugh. A cruel, confident laugh. "When he has troops, bodyguards, and minions to do his dirty work. Fat lot of good those bodyguards did him this time."

Long had known many men like this, here and in DC. Affluent and self-satisfied. He had taken pleasure in being an iconoclast. Being rendered so helpless here was a particular cruelty, like being staked down by Lilliputians and subject to torment. Though it verged on blasphemy, he thought of Christ on the way to his crucifixion, his stoic patience in the face of brutality and taunts. Senator Huey Long had perhaps too little Christian patience, except as was forced on him here. He listened carefully to save the voice for future reference and more particularly to learn about his fate.

Aristo said, "Recall, Nathan, that it is hard for any man to fight back when his guts are torn."

"He's a hero to a lot of people, Oren. A lot of people. They're standing out there now in the rain, singing and praying and holding up their banners. If hope and prayers do any good, he'll live to fight another day."

The loud, confident voice lowered. "It troubles me to ask this, Nathan, but are you a Long supporter?"

This was the man who was charged with his care? A man who openly wished for his death? Long silently rejoiced that the words had done what this man—Oren?—had never intended. He'd stirred up the will to fight. Fighting was perhaps what Senator Huey Long was best at. Fighting to be heard. Fighting an establishment happy to enrich itself at the expense of the little people. Fighting to achieve a political dream cherished since he was a boy. He'd read about a government of, by, and for the people. He knew from experience politicians behaved as though the words "some of" were written in front of "the people."

A wave of pain swept through him and he groaned, startling the two men chatting beside his bed like he wasn't there.

The man called Oren said, "I'll find a nurse," while the gentler man squeezed his hand and said, "Easy, Senator, easy. We're going to take care of that pain."

He wanted to reply but his voice was missing, gone along with his energy and the ability to open his eyes. He could only lie here, trapped in a body that felt foreign. An alien thing not under his command. An unresponsive lump lying on a mattress that was far from comfortable, most likely in a hospital he had built, spoken over with disdain by a doctor he might well have hired. His helplessness was terrifying.

He knew how the people he'd wrested power from hated him. Just a turnip-nosed bumpkin, a nobody from nowhere. How dare he? Oh, ah, how he'd dared!

In the distance there was a steady rising and falling surge of noise. Soothed by that mechanical hum, he went away someone dark and quiet, the place he'd been before their conversation interrupted him. He'd gone away before to recover from defeats. He meant to do it again.

He was a small boy, playing in the yard with his brothers and sisters. It was hot and he was barefoot, sifting the silky, wind-blown red dirt between his toes, and watching it puff like smoke when he wiggled them. Knowing his mother would despair but unable to help himself, pouring a bucket of water on the dirt so he and the others could wiggle their hot feet in the cool red mud. A tired family passed with a skinny, tired mule. A sagging child sat on top of the bundle on the mule, the stoic woman carrying another child sleeping on her shoulder as she trudged alongside.

His mother was doing laundry, hanging so many shirts and pants and dresses and nightshirts on the sagging line the wind shifted them like a gathering of ghosts. He was feeling the hot sun on his back, hearing the happy cries of play. Smelling the wind. He found a patch of shade and settled there with a book, knowing he wouldn't be disturbed by a mother who cherished the importance of reading.

His dream changed, as dreams do, to those years when his county, his state, his country, was plunged into despair. He was in a car driving over the meager roads in his part of Alabama, sweating and shaking hands and trying to drum up support for his election. The political machine down south firmly arrayed against him, making decisions that benefitted themselves, Standard Oil, and other corporations while the poor people, ignorant or barely educated, unable to vote because of poll taxes, languished without a voice. In his dream he roared, "I AM YOUR VOICE."

The roar echoed in his head, but no sound emerged. Their voice had been silenced.

Dammit! Regardless of what medicine said, he couldn't die. Not with so much left to be done. Not when it was clear that Roosevelt's first New Deal fell so short, wasn't reaching the little people, the small towns, the small banks, the small farmers, the small businessmen. Not doing enough to help the people who believed in him because he believed in them. News of his shooting would have reached them.

It would have reached Washington, too, where they must be dancing on their desks.

There were footsteps again. Many folks don't notice, but footsteps are individual—if you pay attention, if people want you dead and you're concerned about who comes up behind you. These were the steps of the arrogant doctor, the one who'd declared he'd die, was clearly delighted by that, and was suspicious of those who wanted to believe in what Long was doing. His inert body was swept with the chill of fear. If this man sought to hasten his demise, he was helpless to prevent it.

The man stood a long time, watching and breathing, while Long cowered within himself, waiting. Touched him hesitantly, the fingers scrabbling on his bandage.

Long managed a feeble groan.

The man sighed and his footsteps went away.

Exhausted, Long fell into a sleep so deep there were no dreams, only darkness and pain, the pain throbbing in surges like that distant thrum. He thought he felt someone take his hand, heard a soft voice, a woman's voice. He caught only the cadence and not the words but knew that Rose was with him. Then his children's voices, their soft hands gripping him, imploring him not to leave them.

Her soft hand squeezed his. Her voice spoke. Rose would keep him safe.

Long still lay inert. If ever there was a time when his enemies had all the advantages, it was now. He didn't believe he was safe here. Were his bodyguards, those faithful men he'd foolishly outstripped in his headlong rush to the next thing—unless it was a victory lap after defeating that stuffed shirt Judge Benjamin Pavy—here with him now?

They couldn't be. That arrogant doctor would never have dared to speak like that in front of his people. Why weren't they here? Was everyone so certain he would die that no protection was necessary?

He was threatened and had no way to tell them.

The possibilities terrified him. He tried to force his eyes open. They disobeyed. Tried to move his hands. Nothing. He was helpless as a newborn.

The hand squeezed his again. The voice spoke but he heard no words. He struggled with panic, trying to tell her "protect me" and the effort cascaded him back into darkness again. In that darkness he saw the gun, only a few feet away. The sweating face of the judge's son-in-law, slight, bookish, such an improbable assassin. But there it was, spears of pain crashing into him and then a confused hubbub of bodies and voices and then nothing. And now he was here.

His brain formed the words, "Don't let them near me," but nothing worked. No command reached his lips any more than it reached his limbs or his lids.

Panic choked him. He coughed. Gasped. The blackness swirled. Was this it? Was this the end? Some pissant doctor from Baton Rouge had shot him? Shot him, Huey Long? When he had so much left to do? When he *must* run against Roosevelt. Must win.

He heard voices. The doctors coming back again? Yes. There was that loud, self-important voice, and the softer one. Hadn't they just been here? Didn't they have anything else to do? He was an active mind trapped in a marble body. No way to let them know he was here. Let them speak, then. He would listen and plan.

When he recovered and was out of here, the man called Oren would regret his dismissive attitude, his cruelty to a helpless man.

The softer-voiced man was speaking, asking, "Is he Catholic? Should we have in a priest?"

An arrogant, "No. That's that damned fella from Chicago. Father Coughlin, is it? Another rabble rouser."

Rose's voice, unusually steely for such a gentle woman. "No priest. You won't need one anyway. My husband is not going to die."

He felt her squeeze his hand. Wished he could squeeze back. Wished, when he realized how much he needed her, that he'd been a better husband. There was a commotion in the room of other people arriving. The arrogant voice asking, "What is this? It is not permissible. These men cannot be here. The patient needs rest and quiet."

Rose again, certain. In control. Always there for him, tolerant of his brashness, even of his womanizing. A believer to the core. His first and most faithful supporter. Had he ever paid her back that ten dollars he'd borrowed so they could marry? His mind wanted to wander back through their years. With difficulty, he forced it back to this room, heard Rose say, "If an assassin failed once, someone might try again. These men will stay."

Relief flowed through him like honey—thick, warm, golden, and so, so sweet. His brash impetuosity had led him here, those who had faith would lead him out. He slept again, Rose's hand in his, a deeper, quieter sleep this time.

He didn't know if it was hours or days later that he began to dream of President Roosevelt, a nightmare in which he was voiceless and powerless to make himself heard. Powerless to argue for amendments, against bills that failed the regular people, to fight back against the handed-down condescension, the noblesse oblige, the big money and entrenched interests of New York and Boston on Washington. Against big oil and large-scale farms and bills that advanced their interests while leaving the ruined farmers and shuttered banks unaided and unprotected. Who would press his "Share our Wealth" program and fight for income equality? The president had grand plans, but no one who understood the desperation of those without jobs, schools, hospitals, or hope had his ear. He did not see, as Long did, the pinched faces of hungry children and the terrible shame of parents who could not provide.

He yelled. Yelled as loud as he could, and the good Lord knew that Huey Long could make himself heard. People swarmed and swirled around him like he was a ghost.

He tried harder.

Rose squeezed his hand. "Rest now, Huey," she said. "We're with you. The people are with you."

He felt the leaden shell that held him down began to lighten. Rested until the loud, arrogant voice of the man named Oren reappeared, asking everyone to leave the room so he could examine the patient.

Tried to scream "Don't go," but his voice was not yet returned.

The shuffling of feet said his bodyguards were leaving. Huey Long, the Kingfish whose favors and protection were widely sought, who had, of late, gone nowhere without those bodyguards, wanted to beg Rose not to leave him alone with this man. He couldn't trust his health and safety to one who hoped he would soon be on his way to heaven, to trouble the established powers no more. He wanted to rise up and roar, "I worked tirelessly for Roosevelt. I believed he would do the right thing. And I am left a voice, crying in the wilderness, while people still starve and die of despair, seeing their livelihood gone on the wind."

Even cased in lead, even inert as a mummy in this bed, he could still read people. This man meant him harm.

Then Rose said, "They can go. I'll stay,"

"Ma'am, you should go. You do not want to see this."

"As I said. Huey is my husband. The children are not yet grown and are still in need of a father. I am sure you're doing all in your power to bring him back to us, but I can supply something you cannot—a wife's devotion and the power of prayer. I'll stay."

Powers of speech might be beyond him, but intuition remained. He could almost feel the man's frustration at Rose's adamance. He could picture her, a smallish woman with a very straight back, those large, intelligent eyes, and a precise way of speaking. She had invoked it all. He listened for what the doctor would say.

Merely a stiff, "If you must."

The covers were lifted. He felt air on his skin and then hands that were unnecessarily rough, perhaps the most the man could get away with while a careful wife watched. A man with medical knowledge could still do harm.

He lay, tossed like a sausage in a pan as the cold, dry fingers probed, seeking to wound. Then he heard footsteps. The soft-voiced man, Nathan, entered. Greeted Rose with a respectful,

"Mrs. Long." Said quietly, again as though he knew Long was listening, "The press is asking for an update on the Senator's condition. What shall we tell them?"

One hard finger stabbed at his wound and the pain was shattering. "Tell them there is no change. The Senator lies in a coma and while we hope for the best, we fear the worst. Tell them to step up their prayers."

From the depths of his pain, Long still felt the second man approach the bed, sensing the difference between this man's warmth and the other's coolness, between the desire to harm and one to heal. A warm hand squeezed his. The soft voice said, "Come back to us, Senator."

Long felt the lead lift a little more.

A voice in the doorway said, "Mrs. Long, we have the President on the line for you."

Huey Long knew about unfounded optimism. If Rose went to take that call, he would be alone with Oren, and even if the other man remained, he would be subservient. His response, if needed, would be a verbal rather than a physical intervention. He felt the icy fear of utter helplessness again until he heard Rose say, "Please tell President Roosevelt I will be with him in a moment," as she summoned a bodyguard from the hall.

The doctor followed Rose out, his white coat hissing with frustration. Long's victories had been monumental. Now they were minute yet just as critical.

His hand was squeezed again, and footsteps departed.

His bodyguard, who had been with him since his days as governor, pulled a chair near the bed and began to talk, speaking of the tens of thousands who had gathered outside the hospital, of the sea of black umbrellas and bare heads out in the rain, the profound murmur of prayers that never ceased.

"You got to come back to us, Boss. Ain't no one anywhere who cares for the people like you do. I don't mind what some people say about you, the bad stuff, because I know why you do what you do. And I heard them doctors talking in the hall, where they didn't think I'd hear, and they were saying that you're getting better."

The bodyguard talked on, the rumble of his voice echoing the background thrum Long now recognized as the steady rumble of prayer outside. Reassured, feeling safe, and feeling the comfort of God upon him, he dropped into sleep again. Those whose plans included ensuring his death, only holding back their glee until he was in the ground, were going to be disappointed.

More of the lead lifted. He would sleep. He would heal. He would wake. And he would run against that son of a bitch Roosevelt, taking his "Share the Wealth" program to the people. Neither a communist nor a socialist, as he was sometimes called, he was an "equalist," concerned with the concentration of wealth, looking to close the vast divide between most of the people and those few who held too large a portion of the nation's wealth.

Uplifted by their prayers and protected by his own, Huey Long would live to fight another day.

His doze was interrupted by Rose's return. He heard her soft voice asking his bodyguards to take the children somewhere and get them dinner. A rumble of protest.

"I'll be with him," she said. "He'll be safe with me."

Footsteps heading away.

He heard the swish of her skirt as she sat down beside him. "I've just had a most enlightening conversation with President Roosevelt, Huey. He told me things I hadn't realized. Matters of critical importance to our country. To the people you've so long defended. Do you know what he said?"

Rose tenderly lifted his head. He felt the pillow being tugged away.

"There. That's better, isn't it? Lying flat makes it easier to breathe?"

She knew he couldn't respond. He tried to squeeze her hand.

He didn't really want to hear about her conversation with that damned Roosevelt, but Rose was speaking again.

"Roosevelt sends him best wishes for your recovery, Huey. He was very kind. And he told me something quite disturbing. About you and your plans to run against him. Something I had not thought of. He told me that your crusade for income equality has become confused with your ambitions for yourself. As I said, this was something I had not thought of . . ."

He heard her shift on her chair and lean closer, wanting to roar at her that he wasn't interested in what Roosevelt had to say. Wanted to warn her that the man, both a liar and a philanderer, would twist things about and make him—Huey Long—the bad guy, when she should know better. Rose didn't understand how these men worked. How insidious their lies could be. How smoothly a politician could talk.

He felt something land on his chest. Something light and soft.

"You know that I have always supported you, Huey. I've believed in the rightness of your cause. But President Roosevelt has explained to me the dangers of you running a presidential campaign. How it will backfire, Huey, and have the opposite result from what you intend, from what you've worked for. He told me, you see, that while he has the ability to compromise, to enact laws that he can get some business behind, get politicians from both parties behind, you don't compromise."

Her soft voice repeated, "You don't compromise."

The soft thing floated up his chest and rested, feather light, across his face. He commanded his hands to move it. They did not obey.

Rose pressed gently on the pillow as she said, "If you were to run, and Huey, you listen to no one, so you cannot see the dangers to the country, to the very people you believe you are trying to help . . ."

The pillow pressed harder. He was having trouble breathing. He gasped, but only drew in cloth and feathers.

"You know that if you can't get your party's nomination, you will run with the Share Our Wealth Party. President Roosevelt says that you and Father Coughlin are the two most dangerous men in the country. If you run," Rose said softly, "you will split the vote. And the Republicans will win. And that . . ."

The pillow pressed inexorably down. He couldn't breathe. He thrashed. He moaned. He was utterly helpless to defend himself.

"That would be a disaster for the very people you've tried so hard to help. It would destroy your legacy, how you want to be remembered. You've done much good, Huey. I know and admire that. But you would never willingly choose to step aside."

He was floating. Floating. Floating away as he heard Rose say, "For the good of everyone."

# MOTHER OF EXILES
BY S. J. ROZAN

> *Author's Note: From 1935 to 1962, Eleanor Roosevelt wrote a*
> *six-day-a-week column carried in newspapers throughout the*
> *country. "My Day" made her one of the most widely read*
> *columnists of her time. When she and Franklin were apart,*
> *they often communicated by telegram. The first three items*
> *here—an excerpt from one of Eleanor's columns, a cable from*
> *her, and the response from him—are authentic. The rest are*
> *not. But oh, if they had been!*

"My Day," by Eleanor Roosevelt, Jan. 23, 1939

Washington, Sunday—What a curious thing it is when a great musician like Mischa Elman offers the proceeds of a concert trip throughout the country to the fund for refugees, that he has to be guarded on the way to and from his first concert. What has happened to us in this country? If we study our own history we find that we have always been ready to receive the unfortunates from other countries, and though this may seem a generous gesture on our part, we have profited a thousand fold by what they have brought us.

It may be that some of these very refugees may make discoveries which will bring us increased employment. Many of them represent the best brains of the countries from which they come. They are not all of one race or religion and the wherewithal to keep them alive and get them started is being provided by such generous spirits as Mischa Elman. Must his wife and children tremble for his safety because of this gesture? He is giving concerts for the Committee for Non-Sectarian Refugee Aid. Wherever he goes I hope he will be enthusiastically supported, not only because people enjoy his music, but because they admire the extraordinary generosity which he is showing.

*Eleanor to Franklin, Feb. 22, 1939*

ARE YOU WILLING I SHOULD TALK TO SUMNER AND SAY THAT WE APPROVE PASSAGE OF CHILDS REFUGEE BILL HOPE YOU ARE HAVING GRAND TIME     MUCH LOVE ELEANOR

*Franklin to Eleanor, Feb. 22, 1939*

ALL WELL ON BOARD FINE WEATHER HERE KEEP-ING TO SCHEDULE IT IS ALL RIGHT FOR YOU TO SUPPORT CHILD REFUGEE BILL BUT IT IS BEST FOR ME TO SAY NOTHING TILL I GET BACK MUCH LOVE FDR

*Eleanor to Franklin, March 10, 1939*

SUMNER ETC WAIT FOR SUPPORTING WORD FROM YOU ON CHILD REFUGEE BILL EUROPEAN SITUATION WORSENING DAILY     MUCH LOVE ELEANOR

*Franklin to Eleanor, March 11, 1939*

BEING ADVISED I MUST WAIT ON CHILD REFUGEE BILL CANNOT SPEAK NOW     MUCH LOVE FDR

*Eleanor to Franklin, April 19, 1939*

WILL YOU SPEAK ON CHILD REFUGEE BILL SOON LOOKING HERE LIKE SUPPORT IS WEAKENING MUCH LOVE ELEANOR

*Franklin to Eleanor, April 19, 1939*

CANNOT RIGHT NOW SPEAK ON CHILD REFUGEE BILL PEOPLE ARE WORRIED FLOODGATES ETC MUST WAIT    MUCH LOVE FDR

*Eleanor to Franklin, May 20, 1939*

REPORTS OUT OF EUROPE DARK PEOPLE BEING BEATEN BEING SHOT PEOPLE ARE DYING CHILD REFUGEE BILL NEEDED NOW    MUCH LOVE ELEANOR

*Franklin to Eleanor, May 21, 1939*

HAVE CONFERRED ALL ARE AFRAID WE WILL LOSE SUPPORT FOR AID TO BRITAIN ETC ALSO UPCOMING LEND LEASE PROPOSAL WILL BE A FIGHT CANNOT SPEAK FOR CHILD REFUGEE BILL NOW    MUCH LOVE FDR

*Eleanor to Franklin, June 11, 1939*

CHILD REFUGEE BILL BEING DESTROYED IN COMMITTEE WE NEED YOU    MUCH LOVE ELEANOR

*Franklin to Eleanor, June 11, 1939*

IM SORRY ALL ARE SAYING I CANNOT SPEAK FOR THIS BILL TOO LITTLE TO GAIN TOO MUCH AT STAKE    MUCH LOVE FDR

*Eleanor to Franklin, June 26, 1939*

CHILD REFUGEE BILL HAS BEEN GUTTED WILL NOT MATTER EVEN IF PASSES PEOPLE DESPERATE SITUATION WORSENING HERR H GETTING BOLDER WHAT TO DO    MUCH LOVE ELEANOR

*Franklin to Eleanor, June 26, 1939*

APPEAL TO ICR    MUCH LOVE FDR

*Eleanor to Franklin, June 27, 1939*

HOW TO APPEAL TO ICR THEY HAVE NO FUNDS
REPORTS FROM EUROPE SAY HERR H WATCHING
US CLOSELY WANTS GERMANY QUOTE CLEANSED
END QUOTE NOT JUST JEWS ALSO CATHOLICS
ATHEISTS GYPSIES HOMOSEXUALS IF NO COUN-
TRY WILL HAVE THEM I FEAR WHAT WE CAN
EXPECT OF HIM    MUCH LOVE ELEANOR

*Franklin to Eleanor, June 27, 1939*

I UNDERSTAND SITUATION TERRIBLE AS YOU SAY
BUT MY HANDS ARE TIED    MUCH LOVE FDR

*Eleanor to Franklin, June 28, 1939*

MINE ARE NOT    MUCH LOVE ELEANOR

"MY DAY," BY ELEANOR ROOSEVELT, July 4, 1939

Washington, Tuesday—Never have I been more proud to be an American, or more proud of the President, than on this day. This anniversary of America's independence has called forth an extraordinary gesture from him, and yet one so rooted in our history as to seem straightforward and foreseeable. In ten days, which happens to be the occasion of the celebration of liberty of our dear friends the French, the President will declare by Executive Order that the words on the Statue of Liberty's pedestal have come true:

> *Not like the brazen giant of Greek fame,*
> *With conquering limbs astride from land to land;*
> *Here at our sea-washed, sunset gates shall stand*
> *A mighty woman with a torch, whose flame*
> *Is the imprisoned lightning, and her name*
> *Mother of Exiles. From her beacon-hand*
> *Glows world-wide welcome; her mild eyes command*
> *The air-bridged harbor that twin cities frame.*

*"Keep, ancient lands, your storied pomp!" cries she*
*With silent lips. "Give me your tired, your poor,*
*Your huddled masses yearning to breathe free,*
*The wretched refuse of your teeming shore.*
*Send these, the homeless, tempest-tost to me,*
*I lift my lamp beside the golden door!"*

On that day the golden doors of our country will be thrown open and the wretched refugees of Europe will begin to receive safe haven. Our quota system, a subject of much controversy, will be set in abeyance until the crisis has passed. All will be welcomed.

What is the genesis of this magnificently compassionate act? As so many know, the conference on the refugee crisis organized by President Roosevelt and held at Evian-les-Bains, France, last year resulted in the formation of the Intergovernmental Committee on Refugees. This Committee must be commended for its diligent work but it has not been able to address the emergency in Europe with the urgency the increasingly desperate situation demands. The nations of the world are under many pressures, which must not be discounted. Some, ours included, are suffering the effects of worldwide depression. Others feel the hot breath of Herr Hitler on their necks. Still, the reports out of Germany and Austria have become too horrific to be ignored. Catholics, scientists, artists, writers, atheists, liberal thinkers, Jewish people, and many others are finding themselves in grave circumstances. Human decency requires that we help.

The President is confident other nations will join us in this benevolent action. It is inconceivable that America should be the only country on earth dedicated to freedom and liberty.

And yet, if we are, so we shall be. We lift our lamp beside the golden door.

*Franklin to Eleanor, July 4, 1939*

WHAT HAVE YOU DONE    FDR

*Eleanor to Franklin, July 4, 1939*

MANY ARE BEHIND YOU ALL WILL BE WELL
MUCH LOVE ELEANOR

*Franklin to Eleanor, July 4, 1939*

BEHIND ME YOU ARE MAD I HAVE NO PLANS TO
ISSUE SUCH AN ORDER    FDR

*Eleanor to Franklin, July 4, 1939*

THE WORLD STANDS IN AWE OF YOUR LEADER-
SHIP I SAY AGAIN ALL WILL BE WELL    MUCH
LOVE ELEANOR

*Franklin to Eleanor, July 4, 1939*

WELL WHAT WILL BE WELL EVERYTHING A
WHIRLWIND I AM BEING DENOUNCED ON ALL
SIDES ISOLATIONISTS SCREAMING FATHER
COUGHLIN CALLING FOR MY HEAD    FDR

*Eleanor to Franklin, July 4, 1939*

CARDINALS O'CONNELL AND MUNDELEIN ARCH-
BISHOPS MITTY CANTWELL AND SPELLMAN TO
ISSUE STATEMENT TOMORROW ALREADY WRIT-
TEN THANKING YOU FOR SAVING CATHOLIC
LIVES ALSO THEY WILL PRESSURE POPE TO
ENDORSE THAT SHOULD DO FOR FATHER
COUGHLIN    MUCH LOVE ELEANOR

*Franklin to Eleanor, July 4, 1939*

SPELLMAN THATS A MIRACLE BUT ALREADY
WRITTEN DID YOU TELL THEM YOUR PLANS    FDR

*Eleanor to Franklin, July 4, 1939*

I TOLD THEM YOURS ASKED THEM TO STAY
SILENT ASKED FOR SUPPORT THEY WERE EAGER
MUCH LOVE ELEANOR

*Franklin to Eleanor, July 4, 1939*

THESE PLANS ARE NOT MINE GETTING CALLS FROM
FRANCE CANADA AUSTRALIA BRAZIL IRELAND
NETHERLANDS MORE ALL FEEL SANDBAGGED SAY
WE HAVE CONTRAVENED EVIAN     FDR

*Eleanor to Franklin, July 4, 1939*

EVIAN WAS GENTLEMENS AGREEMENT TO ALL
BURY HEADS IN SAME SAND THAT WILL NO LON-
GER DO MORAL HIGH GROUND WIDE ENOUGH
FOR ALL INVITE TO JOIN THEY HAVE TEN DAYS
MUCH LOVE ELEANOR

*Franklin to Eleanor, July 4, 1939*

YOU HAVE CREATED INTERNATIONAL CHAOS
FDR

*Eleanor to Franklin, July 4, 1939*

HERR H CREATED CHAOS WE AND OTHERS MUST
RESPOND     MUCH LOVE ELEANOR

*Eleanor to Franklin, July 8, 1939*

WHAT NEWS     MUCH LOVE ELEANOR

*Franklin to Eleanor, July 8, 1939*

HULL HAS NOT SLEPT IN FOUR DAYS NOR HAVE I
BRITAIN FRANCE NETHERLANDS AUSTRALIA
BOLIVIA NEW ZEALAND PERU ALL FEEL
PRESSURED INTO ALLOWING REFUGEES WILL

DEMAND VARIOUS KINDS OF SUPPORT BUT
WILL PROBABLY DO IT OTHERS DISCUSSING
POSSIBILITY YOU MUST SAY NOTHING I REPEAT
SAY NOTHING     FDR

*Eleanor to Franklin, July 8, 1939*

GOOD WORK WITH SO MANY JOINING ISOLA-
TIONISTS WILL BE DROWNED OUT ALSO RABBI
WISE IN CONTACT WITH WEALTHY JEWS ROTHS-
CHILDS ETC COMMITTEE FOR NONSECTARIAN
REFUGEE AID JOINT DISTRIBUTION COMMITTEE
CATHOLIC COMMITTEES FOR REFUGEE AID
SOCIETY OF FRIENDS MORE ALL READY TO SUP-
PORT AND SETTLE WE HAVE PROMISES REFU-
GEES WILL NOT BECOME PUBLIC CHARGES
WHEREVER THEY GO STRESS WHEREVER YOU
CAN ANNOUNCE ON FRIDAY I AM SILENT
MUCH LOVE ELEANOR

*Franklin to Eleanor, July 10, 1939*

BELGIUM DENMARK NORWAY SWEDEN CHILE
ARGENTINA ALL AGREE PALESTINE ASKING FOR
BRITISH PERMISSION REPORTS SAY POLAND
HUNGARY CZECHOSLOVAKIA LITHUANIA MUCH
HEARTENED BY REPORTS OF OUR ACTION ANTI
NAZI PARTIES STRENGTHENED HERR H BESIDE
HIMSELF     FDR

*Eleanor to Franklin, July 10, 1939*

EXCELLENT ALSO WORLD JEWISH CONGRESS
SOCIETY FOR PROTECTION OF SCIENCE
INTERNATIONAL CHRISTIAN COMMITTEE FOR
NON-ARYANS ALL PLEDGE FINANCIAL SUPPORT
MUCH LOVE ELEANOR

*Franklin to Eleanor, July 12, 1939*

SENDING RADIO STATEMENT BY COURIER PLEASE
READ AT THE EARLIEST NOT MUCH TIME FOR
CHANGES     FDR

*Eleanor to Franklin, July 13, 1939*

HAVE READ TOMORROWS STATEMENT NO
CHANGES NEEDED STRONG SILVER TONGUED
AS USUAL GRACIOUSLY PRAISES THOSE JOINING
THANKS THOSE PROVIDING SUPPORT WILL
BE LISTENING RAPTLY AT MY RADIO
MUCH LOVE ELEANOR

*Franklin to Eleanor, July 14, 1939*

ABOUT TO GO ON RADIO 26 OF 32 COUNTRIES AT
EVIAN HAVE AGREED YOU MRS ROOSEVELT ARE A
WONDER IF YOU EVER DO ANYTHING LIKE THIS
AGAIN I SHALL DIVORCE YOU     MUCH LOVE FDR

# SERVICES RENDERED
BY NIKKI DOLSON

SIX MONTHS AFTER MY FATHER had his stroke, President Reagan came to Las Vegas, ostensibly to see the strikers brandish their protest signs outside of the hotels & casinos. The real reason was that the president needed a new heart and to get that he needed to see my father, but Pop wasn't seeing anyone now. Most days he sat in front of the television watching soap operas and on weeknights, Johnny Carson lulled him to sleep.

Pop had a gift with mechanical things of any make or model, mundane or otherwise. He could shape wood into machine parts or other delicate things like snowflakes and capillaries. After a stroke which paralyzed the left side of his body, my father's old clients sought out others to fix their machines. I was equally gifted with machines though it was metal that I formed. I wanted to take over the business, but my father was hesitant. He didn't think I'd find a husband if I worked on machines like he did. At twenty-three years old, he thought I should focus on starting a family and thriving somewhere else. I was his goal line, his measuring stick, proof of his successful parenting. He refused to discuss the business with me except to let me know of the cousin with a sliver of talent who might be cajoled in taking over the business. Since he was at a city college with another year of school left, I figured I had a year to make my mark and impress my father. The jobs I found on my own were small things that didn't pay hardly anything. I knew though that if I couldn't bring in business like Pop had, he'd sell out to a mining company or a local fabricator because, really, we both knew that the cousin was never coming.

Once the business was sold, Pop would be too. Back home to Wharton, Texas to sit upon Great Aunt Emma's plastic covered couch and ask for her help. She'd give it with a heaping spoonful of distaste. Oh, how she'd look down upon him with his cane and say, "Look now, what you've become. You thought you were better than us. Ran off and married some showgirl in that vile city. I knew you'd be back." Then she'd make sure a cousin was there to help Pop in and out of the bath, that his medications were taken on time, and kill him with a kindness only found in families.

The morning Pop came to me for help, I was in the garage with a fleet of black cats all around me. Cats lounged on the hood of our car and slept in the boxes they'd soon be shipped in now that they were fitted with glass eyeballs that had cameras hidden inside. Two cats, freshly dead from the city shelter, were before me on the worktable waiting for me to coax them back to life. Eventually, they'd patrol warehouse blocks and sit high up on shelves in money rooms, watching, always watching, their tails twitching occasionally, waiting for someone to trespass. My father always frowned at the dead things I brought home and upgraded. I tried to convince him of the beauty of the animals. He wondered about their pain, if they knew what was happening. I believed they didn't hurt anymore, that death had rendered them dumb. All that was left was instinct and a little room for my talent to program them. They did not decay. They did not eat. They simply were. He always made it seem like he would never do what I did.

Pop moved carefully around the purring cats and slid his chalkboard over to me. His speech was slurred now so he didn't talk to anyone anymore, including me, but wrote on the chalkboard I'd brought him in the hospital. I stopped futzing with the cat in front of me and gave him my attention. For all his issues caused by the stroke, he still had beautiful handwriting. Sweeping curlicues on his capital letters and graceful arcs and slants to what came after.

I need you to build a heart.

I wiped off the board and slid it back. "As soon as I'm done with this order."

He wrote, Start now.

"Who's the customer?"

My father wouldn't look me in the eye. He shook his head and tapped the fingers of his good hand on the chalkboard. He was barely fifty, but he looked so much older now. His brown skin seemed faded. His hair was going gray with startling speed. He wouldn't let me shave him so he a beard which he kept in shape with tiny scissors and long hours in front of the bathroom mirror.

"Who needs a heart, Pop?"

He pushed the chalkboard, looked me in the eye and finally told me his secret. How he had been commissioned to build a heart. He believed it was for a display not for real use so while it did function like a real heart, he had exaggerated its size. He and seven others, one by one, were brought into a conference room in nondescript building just off the Strip. There he was asked if the heart worked. He said it did. A man, he'd later find out was a doctor, quizzed him about its workings. Then there was a huddle and he was congratulated and handed a check. Much later he learned that his heart had been the only working model. "I took their money and I didn't look back. I could raise you in this house and not worry about money for a long while," he said.

Pop gave me the original plans for the wooden heart he needed replaced. It had four quadrants that fit together like a puzzle box. Blood flowed in through the lower left ventricle then circulated into the upper left then diagonal into the lower right where pressure built and eventually pushed through the upper right and back out into the body. When it was new, the heart mimicked an adult human heartbeat, but it moved sluggishly now. So I built a new heart with my father's design as a guide. Smaller and more efficient, with metal gears to replace my father's wooden ones. I suppose it was vanity that made me use glass. I had to make it beautiful. I wanted Pop to see what I brought to the business, how what I could dream and build fit alongside his builds.

I knew a man who could spin glass into ethereal shapes. In this man's bed I lay beside him drawing on his chest the shape of the heart I wanted. Two unequal halves that would lock together using my father's wooden arteries. The new gears and valves would fit next to my father's delicate paper pumps.

It took eight days to build President Reagan's heart. Pop reached out just before I packed it away and ran the fingers of his good right hand against the smooth curves of the glass. He pushed it and was surprised that it was so light.

"I need to add your pumps to it but, full, it'll weigh three or four pounds at the most." He put his hand on my head and kissed my forehead.

"Beautiful," he whispered. Then he returned to his recliner in the living room.

\* \* \*

BY DAY, THE HEAT AND blinding sun dimmed the gilt edges of Caesars Palace to a muted sparkle. The heat was always oppressive. No one lingered in it long. Under the casino's canopy, where the heat was slightly more tolerable, I paid the taxi driver and was helped out of the cab by a valet. I tipped him my last five dollars. He swung open the glass doors for me and I was hit by the noise of money being lost. Most people, yanking hard on the slot arms, hoping for a line of 7s, would only leave with Vegas elbow. Casinos made you feel like you were always winning something, and that time was inconsequential. I never came to Strip. We worked for the local-focused casinos and restaurants. I fixed dishwashers. I made security suggestions. I built attack dogs that didn't care about steaks, could take a beating and still take down a burglar.

As I crossed the casino floor, I pretended I was my mother. Confident that she was more than anyone could handle and worth more than whatever was being lost on all these tables. Momma commanded these spaces. She had been a showgirl in the Folies Bergère. She wore her sparkles and feathers proudly. When she agreed to marry my father, she was convinced she could live with being a tinkerer's wife, but Pop settled into that jealousy some men can't turn away from when their wives are too beautiful. In retaliation to that beauty, he tried to squash her dreams. Told her she made pie better than she danced. That it was better that she wasn't parading nearly naked for men to ogle. Momma found another man who wanted nothing more than to see her strut in fine clothes like the showgirl she had been. She asked me to go with her but her new guy, Carmelo, wasn't looking to be a stepfather to a teenage girl and we all knew it. I was fourteen when she left. She sent letters about her travels with pictures inside of them on the French Riviera, at the Eiffel tower, Momma pointing at Big Ben. Carmelo looking like some fine fifties film star and Momma looked like Dorothy Dandridge and no matter where she went heads would turn. Ten years later and the cards and letters from fabulous faraway places still arrive. I wondered if I told her about Pop if she'd come home. I suppose that's why I'd never tell her.

I walked quickly to the bank of elevators and went to the top floor. I stepped out intent on continuing my swagger and was thrown off by a man who grabbed my arm and pulled. Another man stepped in front of me.

"Wrong floor," the one in front of me said. The other man began to shove me back into the elevator.

"Hey, I have business on this floor," I hollered.

"What business? With who?" The men looked down at me and blocked the elevator door.

"Guys move back." A blond man stepped forward and looked at me. "Nina Aldridge?" I nodded and he extended a hand and pulled me out of the elevator. "Sorry about that. You should've called from downstairs and let us know you were here." He began to walk down the long hallway toward double doors.

"I'm supposed to be here at two o'clock. It's five minutes till. Sorry I'm early?" I patted my hair and pulled at my clothes. I felt undone.

We stopped outside the doors and he looked me over. "The First Lady is waiting for you." He knocked twice and sent me in.

In the presidential suite, I sat flanked by two Secret Service men behind me and the First Lady on my left. Based on the bounce of her crossed legs, Mrs. Reagan was irritated. Her red blouse's pussybow was askew. She assessed me through a cloud of cigarette smoke while she spoke to someone on the phone. "Come on, Lee. Host the damn party. You know how we love Palm Springs." She hung up and pointed her cigarette at me.

"I'm told your father is ill."

I sat a little straighter like she was a schoolteacher I had to impress. "He had a stroke." And I swear I don't do drugs, I wanted to say.

"I'm told he's had some offers to buy his business."

"We aren't selling."

"You're his partner."

"I am."

She sighed. "Perhaps we need someone else." She stood then. Her cigarette hung from her lips and her hands smoothed her skirt. Somehow, I had disappointed her and she was done with me.

To her retreating back, I spoke quickly. "I was told he needed a new heart. How do you know that?" She kept walking. "If someone else could fix him you wouldn't have called me. We don't need the work, but my father always says to be loyal to your customers and they will be loyal to you."

At the other end of the room were double doors and here she stopped to look at me. "Come on, girl." I flinched but went anyway.

The doors opened on a mostly dark bedroom. There was a sliver of sunlight that stole in from between the curtains and fell on the former Hollywood actor turned politician. Ronald Reagan sat on the edge of the bed, unmoving, with his hands on his knees. I stood in the doorway with my bag in both hands. With each passing moment the bag grew heavier. My hands had gone sweaty and I adjusted my grip, desperate not to drop the bag and break the heart.

"Well go on, girl. Ronnie doesn't bite."

I moved closer and noticed a hum emanating from him. His eyes were open, but they didn't focus on me. The First Lady came and sat next him on the bed. She smoothed his hair. "You need a trim Ronnie," she said. His hair seemed to me to be Brylcreemed perfection.

"You love him still."

"Of course. We took vows. In sickness and in health."

"Even with him like this?"

She shrugged. "It's done now. He's the president and he has work to do. I'm so glad you're helping us." She looked up at me and smiled. "Aren't you excited? You get to touch the President of the United States of America."

"Yes." I smiled back at her. "I'm going to need a table for my instruments."

She frowned. "A table?"

"Like, maybe the coffee table in the other room? Something low is best for me."

She stood and walked out of the room saying, "Calvin, bring that there." I opened the curtains and let the light of day stream in. Las Vegas was spread out below me, blanching in the sun. I took a deep breath and turned to face the President.

The coffee table was placed in front of the bed. I had Calvin, the blond Secret Service agent who had hustled me to the suite from the elevator, remove the president's suit jacket and tie. From my bag,

I pulled my tool roll and unfolded the leather flaps revealing shining stainless steel. I donned gloves and sat on the table before the President. I unbuttoned his shirt and tried to imagine that it was Pop I was undressing, helping him change out of his Sunday church finery into his more comfortable television watching clothes. I unbuttoned the shirt to the belt line. I touched his chest and glanced at his face. It was the face of Ronald Reagan but devoid of any spark. In the center of his chest was a zip of scarred skin nine inches long. I touched it and felt a little heat. Something close to normal.

"Do you need anything else?" Calvin said.

I started to ask for whiskey but shook my head. I felt along the scar. There was a notch at the bottom. Here I pressed and I felt his rib cage move very slightly. I dug my fingers into the scar, found the edges and pulled. The chest opened along a y-shape cut. There, centered among still living lungs and other organs, sat my father's wooden heart. Dark and slick, it hummed with a rhythmic knock that was meant to be the heartbeat. The heart was always moving blood like a faucet left on, though what was moving now was a trickle instead of a torrent.

"Jesus."

I turned to look at Calvin who was standing over my shoulder, looking down in the chest cavity. He turned a shade paler and swayed.

"You okay?" I asked.

He shook himself and straightened. "The First Lady left. She's hoping you'll be done before she returns."

"How long do I have?"

"An hour, maybe two."

I saw the many arteries, both wooden and real, and deflated a little at the amount work it would take to adapt this to my glass heart.

"I won't be done. Maybe by tonight."

"I'll let her know." And he withdrew, closing the door and leaving me with the President.

In the middle of the heart was small circle. I pushed it and listened to the heart slowly wind down. I studied Reagan's face.

"Are you a good man, Mr. President?"

The eyes didn't move. I reached into my bag and removed the bundled heart. I'd wrapped it in flannel with newspaper over that. The paper made such noise in that empty room I nearly didn't hear him speak. I looked up and saw his mouth moving.

"What did you say?" I clutched the heart to my chest.

His mouth began to move again and softly his words came to me. "What is a man?"

"You're still alive in there, aren't you?"

He blinked and his eyes focused on me. The color began to drain from his face and the gears in his heart stopped. His gaze drifted back to straight ahead and unfocused.

My hands shook as I set the heart down on the table next to me. I paced the room. I went to the door and listened. My hands were tingling. I tried to slow my breathing. On the nightstand was the phone. I called home and cradled the receiver in my hands. It rang endlessly. I hung up and dialed again.

My father said, "What."

"Pop, he's not dead. He's in there."

Pop breathed heavily. "Nina, I know that."

"You could've said."

"You didn't believe."

"The animals are different."

"Are they?"

The double doors opened, and Calvin was there.

I said, "Gotta go, Pop."

"You can't use the phone," Calvin said.

"I had to talk to my father. About the heart."

Calvin saw my lie for what it was. "Just do your job." He unplugged the phone and took it with him.

I said, "I'm sorry," to what was left of the man named Ronald Reagan and then I took his heart out.

* * *

"You're not finished," Mrs. Reagan said as she entered the bedroom and closed the doors behind her.

I looked up from the president's chest. The sun had long since set. I had turned on the lights to see better. I was holding one lamp with its shade removed and its bare bulb was casting light on Reagan's lungs. I was massaging them to keep them from drying out while I removed and adjusted the wooden pieces inside of him.

"I told Calvin to let you know this was going to take a while."

"He told me." She walked over and peered in at her husband's chest cavity. I removed my hand so she could see. "God is great," she said. "We are His marvelous creations."

"What do you think He thinks of this?" I gestured at her husband.

She sat in one of the upholstered chairs on the other side of the room and lit a cigarette. "Do you know what my talent is?"

"You're an actress."

"Ha. A lesser talent to be sure." She drew deeply on her cigarette and exhaled smoke while she spoke. "My strong talent is that I can set a mean table. That's it. I have excellent wife skills."

"You have more imagination than that."

"I do," she said, delight in her voice. "Because of me, we became a political family. I set tables where a dozen conversations happened and then we were in the Governor's mansion. I make conversations happen. Sit at my dining room table and you will listen. You will be swayed."

"So you can manipulate."

"Yes, preferably with porcelain place settings." She chuckled and drew on her cigarette. "I have a friend who can see things. She thinks God is long gone. If that's true, I can't see what difference it makes."

"You're friends with a card-turner?"

"Yes. What of it? We all seek guidance."

I shook my head and bent back down to my task. "I would never want to be a politician," I mumbled.

"America sets the world on its path. Who would say no to that kind of power?" She was up now lighting a new cigarette off the old.

I said, "It seems like for every good thing the President does, there's a bad thing. And that's only what we hear about in the newspaper or from Brokaw at night."

"Ronnie and I do what must be done," she said. There was a knock at the door. It was Calvin again. "Ma'am, Mrs. Bush is here."

She looked at me. "Finish quickly, girl."

"I'm not your girl."

"One minute, Calvin." She shut the bedroom door and turned to me. I stood up. "You will be paid well for your services and then we will never have to see each other again." She advanced on me and I stepped back and back again until I hit the wall. "But if you ever talk to me that way again, no one will ever see you again. Then who will take care of your stroke-dumb father, girl? You can have enough money to never have to worry about your father. Doesn't that seem like a good choice?" She smiled revealing even white teeth. Then she spun away and left the room, leaving me in a haze of her floral perfume.

I sat back down in front of Reagan and looked at him until my hands stopped shaking. Then installed his new heart. My father's wooden arteries opened and closed for me like they were still brand new. Once attached, the heart filled with blood and spun it anew then released it into the body. Color flooded Reagan's face. He did a slow blink but still his gaze remained unfocused.

I heard raised voices. I left Reagan's body to its work restarting systems now that the blood was moving again. I went to the door and opened it a crack. Nancy Reagan stood with a lit cigarette in front of the door.

"Barbara, be sensible. We have four more years and then it'll be your turn."

"What if he doesn't win?" I saw the cloud that was Barbara Bush's white hair moving left then right in front of the First Lady.

"Of course, he'll win. Mondale can't. We have the votes."

"And if he stops working again? Be reasonable, Nan. If you step down now, we are a shoo-in. George will revere Ron. A library. A government building, whatever you want."

"No. We're done. There's a plan. Just follow it." Nancy moved away to put her cigarette in the ashtray on the end table, but Barbara blocked her and stuck her finger in her face.

"Your time is up. Ronald Reagan is dead and that thing in there is a pretender," the Second Lady said.

Mrs. Reagan slapped her. The Second Lady gasped and put a hand over the injured cheek.

"Get out," the First Lady said.

Mrs. Bush kicked off her sensible pumps and shoved Nancy Reagan into the wall. The women squared off. I opened the door a little wider. The First Lady kicked off her heels too and retied her pussybow. Then she planted a foot against the wall and launched herself at Barbara Bush. The Second Lady collided with her and the women fell into the bedroom door and crashed into the room at my feet. I fled to a corner of the room. The women rolled over and over screaming and hitting at each other. I heard seams tearing. The door at the other end of the suite banged against the wall and there was Calvin with the other Secret Service men. We all just watched. It wasn't until the president rose from the bed that I remembered where I was.

"Wait, wait," I said. I closed his chest and he began to move slowly toward the women. He shoved past me and reached down and grabbed Mrs. Bush and hoisted her backward, yanking on her arm.

"Ow. Stop it. You're hurting me," she said. The president's face was a grimace and he had eyes for no one but Nancy.

"Ronnie, honey. Let her go. Don't hurt her," the First Lady said from the floor. Her hand was outstretched toward them. Reagan paused. I thought I could faintly hear his gears whirring. Mrs. Bush gazed up at him her mouth agape. She could see the new and improved Reagan. How the newly invigorated blood was sending strength to every inch of him. This Reagan could command for years. This Reagan could be formidable.

"I'm sorry, Mr. President," she said. He yanked again on her arm. Mrs. Bush yelped and so did I. He glanced behind to see me. I was pressed against the curtains desperate to make myself small.

"Let her go, sir," Calvin had his gun drawn but it was pointing at the floor.

Mrs. Reagan stood and tucked her skirt back in as she approached the president. "See? I'm fine. And you're better. Aren't you?"

The president lowered his arm and Mrs. Bush gasped in relief. His grip released and she rolled away from them. Calvin helped her up.

"Let's practice your speech. You remember your speech?" Mrs. Reagan said. She patted his chest then began buttoning his shirt.

He straightened and smiled and gave a thumbs up to no one. Or maybe to Calvin, who was helping Mrs. Bush out of the room. "Thank you all very much. It seems we did this four years ago and let me just say, that good habits are hard to break. Just a short time ago, Walter Mondale phoned me to concede. He said the people had made their decision and therefore, we were all Americans and we'd go forward together."

"That's good, honey. Now the next part, 'Nancy and I,'" she said.

I edged around the First Couple, across the bed, and then to the coffee table. I gathered my tools up, throwing them in the bag. They hit the old wooden heart with a dull thud. Then I was out of there and down the hallway with Calvin on my heels. "Miss Aldridge."

"I saw nothing. I was never here," I said. I jabbed at the elevator call button.

He placed his hands on my shoulders turned me around to face him. "That's right you were never here. But I need that heart. You have to leave it."

I stepped away from him. "It's my father's."

"It was paid for." Another agent stepped forward and handed Calvin another bag black like my own. "Here's your money. The cash for the heart. For services rendered."

"How much is in there?"

"Two hundred thousand with a check for another three hundred thousand. If anyone asks you sold some machinery to a gypsum mine up north. I need the bag."

A half million dollars. Was what I'd done worth that much money? What if...I stopped thinking. I held out my bag for his. We swapped and the elevator arrived. The doors shut and I checked the bag. There were a great many bundled hundred-dollar bills and in an envelope, a check. Pop wouldn't need to leave. I had a future that wouldn't depend on marriage. I'd made the right choice.

I came home like a hero to Pop and showed him the money. My smile was firmly in place. "See," I said. "You don't have to worry now. I can take care of us both." Pop was happy but he didn't get better. Too afraid of becoming my burden, he fled back home to Texas and died in his sleep a year later. For all our talents, not even we can keep Death at bay for long.

All these years later, I wonder what would've happen if we hadn't had twelve years of Republican White House. If Reagan had "died" and Bush had stepped in sooner, the '88 election might have gone differently. There was talk among church folk that Shirley Chisholm might've run again. Maybe there would've been a bloodless revolution after all. A kick in our collective asses. How different the world might've been with a black president sooner in our history? Or with a woman as president even for one term.

All I know for sure is that if I had made a different decision, there would've been a heart in the White House.

# IN MOTHER WE TRUST
BY SARAH M. CHEN

January 2028
Any City in America

Karen Pence beamed at the expectant crowd as her husband, President Mike Pence, bowed his head. They stood in front of the crumbling abortion clinic, yellow crime scene tape decorating the front of it. The uniformed crusaders from the Religious Right Reformation or RRR had their batons and assault rifles ready.

"Thank you, Dear Lord, for allowing me to serve you and this great nation," her husband began. "We are all blessed today . . . "

Karen tuned her husband out. It was the same speech he always delivered at these events. Her mind wandered to the nice, cold air conditioning waiting for her in the luxury SUV.

Shouts of "Amen" shook her from her thoughts. An RRR crusader ran up with a giant pair of scissors. Her husband awkwardly snipped the yellow tape and raucous applause followed.

The RRR shepherded her and her husband away from the condemned building. Shouts of "Clear!" and "Stand Back!" filled the air. People scurried across the street.

"Fire it up!"

A deafening *boom!* The building crumpled to the ground. Concrete and debris flew in the air but thankfully nobody was hit this time. Hoots and hollers erupted.

Another clinic destroyed. Karen breathed in the acrid air, satisfaction filling her lungs.

"Fascists!"

"Puritan pigs!"

She turned to see two protestors with signs denouncing her husband. A grotesque image of Mike with the words "Pious Pence" blared out at her.

Three RRR crusaders surrounded the hooligans and shoved them to the ground. Batons slammed down on the troublemakers again and again. Blood sprayed onto the asphalt. The crowd averted their eyes, edging away from the brutal beating.

"Ready, Mother?"

She nodded to her husband. They climbed into the back of the idling SUV, Karen first. The air conditioning was just what she needed. She leaned back in the leather seat and gazed out the window. The RRR dragged the limp protestors to a waiting van.

She and Mike turned to each other and smiled.

"God has truly blessed us to lead this country and embark on this journey for Him," he said.

She patted his hand but said nothing.

God had a lot to do with it, sure, but so did she.

\* \* \*

Two years earlier
November 5, 2024
Election Day, Indianapolis, Indiana—6:40pm EST

Karen threaded her way through the restaurant as staff flew by with trays of food. They wore white baseball caps with the words "Make America Godly Again" stitched in gold: Mike's campaign slogan.

Soon the results would be called. Pennsylvania and Maine, two important swing states, had her husband far in the lead. Florida was theirs soon too.

She wasn't worried. They had God on their side.

Besides, Tim Kaine wouldn't win. And that crazy black rapper, Kanye. Running as the self-declared Birthday Party candidate. What the heck was that?

Thank God her husband listened to her about the election party. The orange fat-face wanted to host it at Mar-a-Lago, but no way was she going to spend one second in that place. Way too obnoxious for her. No, she was happy right here at Chili's in Indianapolis.

Karen joined her husband in the corner of the kitchen where he watched the election on TV. His face was unreadable.

She grabbed the remote. "Time to join your party out there." She was about to change the channel when "Breaking News" scrolled across the screen.

A female reporter at a polling place. A crowd of people behind her. A few held signs with "Calexit," a red angry slash through it. Heavy police presence.

"The video we're about to show you of a polling place in downtown L.A. went viral only hours ago."

A grainy image of a woman hurrying along a sidewalk. Skinny arms cradled a stack of voter ballots.

"How many ballots you got there? You know ballot harvesting is illegal now, right?" A male voice. "You California libtards think you can do whatever you want."

"Leave me alone." She whirled and charged at the camera. Too fast to see her face. A scuffle. The camera tilted sideways, pale blue sky, then black.

Back to the reporter. "Tensions are already high across the state with the controversial Calexit measure on the ballot. City officials are investigating the video's authenticity. Governor Elon Musk accuses the MAGAts—the fanatic right-wing organization of Trump and Pence supporters—of creating the video to wreak havoc on this critical ballot measure. The MAGAts deny any involvement."

Her husband harrumphed, frown lines creasing his forehead. "If Calexit passes, that will be a big problem. They pay 30% of federal tax revenue."

Karen shook her head. "An independent California would be a good thing. They'll self-destruct in a year. Criminal immigrants and refugees will flood their borders and take over. Gang violence will triple. Governor Musk will beg us to let California come back to the U.S."

He nodded. Looked satisfied. "You think of everything, Mother." She smiled. "I know."

\* \* \*

**BREAKING NEWS HEADLINES**
*November 6, 2024*

**REUTERS: MIKE PENCE EDGES OUT A WIN, TIM KAINE AND KANYE WEST CONCEDE**

**CNN: ELECTION FRAUD VIDEOS SATURATE SOCIAL MEDIA**
The video yesterday of ballot harvesting in Los Angeles is just one of many. Hundreds more went viral revealing nationwide election fraud. Experts say these are obvious deepfakes to taint the electoral process. However, several states found evidence of voting machine hacking. Russia denies any involvement.

**FOX NEWS: THE WHITE HOUSE CLAIMS VOTER FRAUD NATIONWIDE**
The Voter Protection Squad, led by Rudy Giuliani, reported instances of voter fraud in every state. Numerous videos surfaced revealing shocking criminal behavior at the polls!

*The president tweeted:*

The Dems LIE and cheat at the polls! Now we
have Proof! The Fake News Media doesn't even
report on this! How coMe? Because they'Re involved!
It's a Conspearasee! We must Investigate!

\* \* \*

November 12, 2024
One Week after Election Day
James Brady Press Briefing Room at the White House—
9:05am EST

Karen didn't want to be standing anywhere near the president
but here she was. She and her husband had to be a united front,
despite the huge blowout she had with him over what Trump was
planning to announce.

"Karen, it'll be a quick investigation into the election hacking," her husband had assured her last night. "It'll be over
before the end of the year. Then we can officially declare
my win and move into the White House." On her silence, he
continued. "We've got to do some kind of investigation,
don't you see? Otherwise, my presidency could be called
into question."

She had reminded her husband that Trump was terrified of
leaving the White House. He knew as soon as he did, he was going
to prison. He'd do anything to remain in office. Like release fake
videos to launch a fake investigation.

"This is the path God has chosen for us," her husband said.
"We mustn't question His will."

So here they were standing in front of the press, in front of the
entire world, accepting God's will.

"There is evidence of nationwide election fraud!" the president
said. "My attorney general here is going to handle this. It will be
the biggest investigation the Department of Justice has ever seen,
let me tell you." He looked to his AG.

The AG cleared his voice. "We're looking at every video that has surfaced to determine the source and authenticity. It will be a massive undertaking but we need to protect the integrity of our democracy. If we have to, we'll conduct another election. A do-over."

Murmurs filled the room.

Trump gestured to Rudy Giuliani who stood next to the AG. "Meanwhile, my attorney, Rudy Giuliani, as head of the Voter Protection Squad, will be assisting DOJ with the investigation."

Rudy shuffled forward. His eyes bugged out. "The Dems will be punished accordingly! It's treason to sabotage one's own election! Absolutely treasonous!" He stood at the podium, shaking his fist.

Trump nodded. "Thank you, Rudy. So meanwhile, I will remain as your president. No matter how long it takes. It could be months, years!"

Karen felt like the walls of the room squeezed together, threatening to crush her. Her head throbbed and she feared she'd have to sit down.

"I will get to the bottom of our sad election system. It will be the biggest and best election system in the world after I'm done!"

Reporters shouted questions.

"How is this not illegal to remain as our president indefinitely?"

"Do you have a timeframe?"

As usual, the president mouthed "thank you" as he stepped off the stage and walked away. Rudy and the AG followed. A reporter shouted a question.

"Mr. Vice President, how do you feel about this? As the president-elect?"

A hush fell over the room. "God will provide for those who remain faithful to Him in trying times," he said.

Another reporter shouted a question.

"So you're saying the president remaining in office despite you being the rightful successor is a trying time?"

Mike reddened. Everyone waited. "I'm a hundred percent behind the president," he said finally. He stepped back and gestured for Karen to go ahead of him. She couldn't even look at him as she stormed past.

The porn presidency would continue indefinitely. Her husband may be fine with that but not her.

* * *

November 12, 2024
Bethesda, MD—6:30pm EST

With the election over and thus her undercover mission for Governor Musk, Addison Lieu was packing her stuff to return to California when a text from Strachan came in.

> FOUND SOMETHING INTERESTING. WILL SEND LINK.

She texted him back.

> CAN'T WAIT.

Strachan:

> WORSE THAN WE THOUGHT.

After a beat.
Strachan:

> THEY KNOW WHO WE ARE.

Addison didn't like the sound of that and threw her belongings into the duffel bag with more urgency.

She'd failed her mission. She was supposed to find out who "they" were, not the other way around. The governor would be disappointed that she'd spent all this time undercover as a MAGAt sending out deepfakes and hacking into journalists' emails for nothing.

She'd assured him that she would find out who was behind the Calexit campaign tampering. Six months ago, Calexit Now, the pro-Calexit political organization, had their servers hacked. Emails and other sensitive information were leaked all over the internet.

In response, the governor had formed a special Calexit ops team and Addison, as his trustworthy fixer, became the point person and undercover op. She and the governor suspected the MAGAts were responsible—the extreme right-wing group formed in response to Trump's 2019 House impeachment—but needed proof.

Addison had spent weeks seeking the right contact. Finally landed on Strachan a.k.a. gotcha_zero through IRC, Internet Relay Chat. He was a MAGAt who dabbled in computer hacking with just the kind of hush hush job Addison a.k.a. moxie_foxie was looking for: the #destroydems campaign. The gig involved saturating social media with deepfakes, sabotaging Calexit, and hacking into servers, emails, and online profiles. Addison was in. Her mission to expose the Calexit campaign hacking operation had begun.

Soon after, she and Strachan became digital pals. Addison found out he lived in Bethesda so the governor set her up in an apartment there. That was three months ago.

Strachan wasn't the typical MAGAt based on what Addison gleaned from his texts and Slack posts. He seemed young and nerdy. He didn't have the rage or tout ridiculous conspiracies like most MAGAts. Or push the Jesus stuff on her.

When Mike Pence declared his campaign slogan as Make America Godly Again, the MAGAts became even more powerful thanks to the evangelicals and suburbanites joining their roster. The MAGAts broadened their reach and sharpened their skills. They organized, forming chapters across the nation. They went from staging protests and rallies to computer hacking and creative political fundraising.

But two weeks into the #destroydems project, Strachan and others on the IRC began to suspect their boss a.k.a. Sec_Shady wasn't a MAGAt. Why the encrypted communications through the Signal app? The payment in bitcoins? It was all very clandestine. Not MAGAt-like at all. More like Russians.

Which was why it was critical for Addison to find out what information Strachan uncovered.

She checked her phone. Still no link. She texted him again.

YOU SENDING THE LINK?

Nothing.

She scanned the apartment one last time. Red and green lights from the stacked computer equipment blinked at her. She'd wiped everything clean. Time to pay Strachan a visit.

\* \* \*

November 12, 2024
The American Family Values gala at the Sheraton
—7:05pm EST

Karen shifted uncomfortably in her heels as she and her Secret Service agent, Bill, huddled together behind a tall ficus tree by the ladies' room. She waited for the agent to say something. Maybe she'd miscalculated how loyal Bill was to her and her husband. And to God. She had taken a huge risk by approaching him for help. He could report her.

"Bill, God has blessed us with an opportunity here. We need to work together to put Mike in his rightful place in the White House." She paused. "And me."

Bill nodded. "You're absolutely right, Mrs. Pence."

Relief flooded through her. She muttered a quick prayer of thanks to God. "I think the president is making all this election fraud stuff up. Just to stay in office."

"There's a crew of us quietly mobilizing. We received good intel months ago that the president would make up some reason to remain at the White House. We just need proof."

She nodded. "Good."

"You need to get back to your seat, Mrs. Pence, before your husband thinks you've fallen in the toilet."

She shook her head. "Don't worry about him. He'll believe whatever I tell him."

"Be that as it may, we don't want to raise suspicion." He lifted his head, glanced behind her. "People will talk."

He was right. Hiding behind a ficus with her Secret Service agent could lead to all kinds of rumors. She knew she looked good in this dress so it wasn't exactly hard to imagine him being unable to control himself around her. Dragging her down the hallway to have his way with her. Tearing off her dress and . . .

"Mrs. Pence?"

She shook her head. "What?"

He gave her a strange look. "I said don't tell your husband about any of this. It's just between you and me and God."

Karen nodded. Glanced at her watch. "Dessert's about to be served."

"I'll keep you posted. Don't trust anyone."

He gestured for her to go ahead. When the coast was clear, she emerged from behind the ficus. The agent followed after a few seconds.

* * *

November 12, 2024
Bethesda, MD—7:30pm EST

Strachan lived about ten blocks from Addison. Thanks to her SpyFish app, she'd been able to pinpoint his general location by mimicking a cell phone tower. Once Addison had confirmed Strachan's neighborhood, she'd found his exact apartment thanks to friendly neighbors and a mail box.

A woman and her dog emerged from the apartment building's front gate and Addison smiled as she slipped past. She jogged up the steps to apartment 3C.

The door was unlocked. Addison peered inside before entering. The streetlamp outside cast shadows along the walls. The only other light came from the laptop sitting in the corner. Computer equipment was stacked up on a long table. The whirring of the equipment cut through the silence. She edged quietly toward the laptop and sucked in her breath.

Strachan lay face down on the desk. Blood pooled from the hole in his forehead onto the keyboard.

"Shit." She felt a twinge of sadness.

Addison scanned through his files on the computer but didn't know which one was important. Best to download them all. She stuck a flash drive in and powered up the program to create a mirror image of his hard drive. When she got back to California, she'd sift through all the data.

"C'mon, c'mon." She had to get out of there. But copying an entire hard drive took a while.

She heard a toilet flush. Addison snatched her flash drive out of the computer. Prayed it downloaded something.

A tall man in a dark suit emerged from the bathroom, drying his hands on a towel. When he saw Addison, he froze. They stared at each other. Blond crewcut. Deep set brow.

He reached for what she assumed was a gun. She grabbed the back of Strachan's chair and sent Strachan and the chair careening toward the man. He tried dodging out of the way but lost his balance. He crashed into the back wall, Strachan's body on top of him.

Addison sprinted to the front door and raced out to the hallway. She hurried down the stairs and through the gate, her shoes pounding the pavement as she ran to her car. Addison fired up the engine. As she peeled away, she caught a glimpse of the man charging out of the building. From the rearview, she saw him in the middle of the street, raising a gun, then lowering it.

She punched the gas until he was a speck in the distance.

\* \* \*

*November 13, 2024*

## BALTIMORE SUN: ONE MAGAT FOUND DEAD IN MONTGOMERY COUNTY

Montgomery County police discovered the body of a young man shot dead in his apartment. They are treating this as a homicide. The victim was a member of the powerful political right-wing group of Trump and Pence supporters, the MAGAts.

*November 14, 2024*

## CNN: SIX MAGATS FOUND DEAD IN THE TRI-STATE AREA

In the past two days, police have discovered six more execution-style homicides of MAGAts across Virginia, Maryland, and D.C. Authorities have yet to determine if they are related. It's unclear if the affiliation with the MAGAts is a factor in their deaths. Identification of the bodies has yet to be released pending notification of the next of kin.

A MAGAt rep from the local Tri-State chapter has released a statement condemning the Democrats for what they claim are hate crimes. They demand the FBI launch an investigation.

*The president tweeted:*
The Disastrous Dems are not only Cheats and Loosers but MURDERERS! The Left Wing Mob is out of control! Thoughts and prayers go to the MAGATS and their families. So sad!

\* \* \*

NOVEMBER 14, 2024
GOVERNOR ELON MUSK'S OFFICE, SACRAMENTO—8:30AM PST

Addison waited while the governor gazed out the window. Now with the string of MAGAt murders similar to Strachan's, it was clear they were dealing with something much bigger than they anticipated. At least in her mind. But the governor wasn't buying her theory.

He turned around in his chair. "You're sure it was an American?"

She nodded. "He wasn't Russian. Looked like law enforcement. FBI, detective, I don't know."

"But you only saw him for a few seconds."

"It was long enough."

"And you're sure the other dead MAGAts were all involved in #destroydems too?"

"No, I'm not sure. We don't know who these other victims are. Hopefully more information will be released." A beat. "Plus I only knew their user names. Strachan is the only one I knew personally."

He gave her an exasperated look. "You didn't get any evidence. No photos. No recordings. I can't work with just a theory."

She knew he was right. The download at Strachan's apartment didn't take. "Look, Governor, whoever hired us is killing us off one by one." She wondered if she was the only one left. "Strachan's text said they know who we are."

"Good thing your background is buried deep enough so they can't trace you here."

She could only hope. "He also texted that it was worse than we thought."

"Any guess on what that means?"

"A few of us involved in #destroydems suspected we were working for Russians."

"So what's worse than Russians?"

"The president."

"Isn't that the same thing?"

"Good point."

The governor stood up, signaling their meeting was over. "Alright. I'm headed to New Mexico tomorrow for the Mars launch of the BFD at Spaceport. You're welcome to come."

Addison brightened. Nodded.

"VP Dense and his wife will be there. The president will be helicoptering in. We've got the Southwestern chapter of the MAGAts coming as well."

"That's an interesting mix," she said. "MAGAts and SpaceX nerds."

The governor nodded. "Let's hope things go smoothly."

\* \* \*

NOVEMBER 15, 2024
SPACEPORT, TRUTH OR CONSEQUENCES, NM—4:30PM MST

Karen was not having fun. The enthusiasm around her was more annoying than contagious. She had to admit though, Spaceport was pretty impressive. Stunning views of the launch pad with the San Andreas Mountains in the background could be seen from anywhere in the terminal thanks to the floor to ceiling windows.

Not only were SpaceX groupies here, waving their rocket-shaped cheer sticks, but so were the MAGAts. From her perch up in the control room, it was a sea of red and white baseball caps down below. There were far fewer of Mike's white "Make America Godly Again" hats than the ugly red ones, which irritated Karen.

Even though it had only been three days since her clandestine meeting with Bill behind the ficus, Karen needed to talk to him about his progress. She'd been praying extra hard to God for proof of the president's wrongdoing. Or a heart attack would suffice. Time was of the essence. She and Mike should be busy preparing for their move into the White House.

Raucous cheering announced the arrival of Governor Musk. You'd think he was Jesus Christ himself, the way these people carried on. A few minutes later, the governor walked in to the control room with an entourage of suits, security, and Spaceport crew. Karen had met the governor once before. An energetic, strange man who laughed a lot at things she didn't find funny.

After exchanging meaningless pleasantries, the governor and her husband droned on about today's first manned mission to Mars and the National Space Council. The Spaceport crew spoke excitedly into headsets. The launch was in T minus 75 minutes.

"Alright, we'd like you all to head out to the launch pad soon," instructed a Spaceport employee. "We've got a stage set up where you'll address the crowd."

No way did she want to be standing out in the heat with all these space nerds and MAGAts screaming.

"I'm going to go pray for a good launch first." And a miracle. Maybe God would strike the president's helicopter down, send it plummeting into the desert. "My security will escort me back to the control room." She turned around to Bill and Ryan, the other Secret Service agent, but they were both gone.

\* \* \*

ADDISON LOOKED DOWN AT THE busy terminal from the top floor. People were jam-packed waiting for the launch.

Addison wasn't religious. Her parents had been Chinese Baptists but didn't force it on her. She believed people determined their own fate.

But once in a while, things aligned in the universe that gave her pause. Or perhaps it was all random coincidence and luck of the draw. And today was Addison's lucky day.

When the crewcut man had walked into the control room with the Vice President and Second Lady as their security, Addison immediately recognized him.

Her own government was behind the #destroydems campaign as she feared. Maybe it was just a few rogue Secret Service agents. But she doubted it.

The Secret Service agent had definitely recognized her too. They locked eyes in the control room before he snuck out. Addison had waited a bit and then followed, but now there was no sign of him.

What could she do anyway? She wasn't even carrying since this was her off day. She'd brought her tablet with her, tucked inside her jacket, but that was useless against a dirty Secret Service agent with a weapon who wanted her dead.

She contemplated alerting the governor but he had enough going on. Plus she wanted to play it out. See who else here was involved. Like maybe the other Secret Service agent. Maybe even the Pences. Although that seemed counterintuitive considering Pence won the election. Maybe the president purposely put them in the dark. He'd thrown his VP under the bus before.

Cheers erupted. The governor and VP were ushered down a red carpet outside to a stage. In the distance, Addison could make out a chopper on the horizon. The president's Marine One.

She walked past computer terminals to the elevator. Her footsteps echoed on the linoleum. While she waited, a hand grabbed her arm and something dug into her back.

"Come with me, Addison Lieu." A male voice in her ear.

She recognized the Secret Service agent.

"Shit."

"Gimme your gun."

"I don't have one."

He snorted. "Sure, you don't."

She shrugged. "Search me."

He looked around. They were near an empty corridor with several doors lining it. "C'mere." He grabbed her shoulder and dragged her toward one of the doors. The gun pointed at her head. He patted her down, lingering on her chest. "Open the door."

She pulled the handle and he shoved her inside a dark room. Her feet pounded on the tile as she regained her balance. The light flashed on revealing bulky white space suits hanging from a rack. Fishbowl helmets lined a shelf. Giant white boots and gloves were stacked underneath.

He hit her in the face. She staggered back, not prepared for it, and fell to the floor, crashing into the shelf.

"I should have known you work for the governor. The guy is such a libtard pussy. Having a chink girl doing his dirty work."

She glared at him. "And you're guarding the religious freaks. Bet that's fun. Do they make you read the Bible every night before bed?"

A phone rang. The agent reached into his jacket pocket and answered. The gun trained on Addison.

"Yeah. I got her." A smile. "No problem." He hung up. "Well I got my orders. Sorry, sweetheart." He raised his gun.

"Look, why don't you just arrest me? I can tell the president everything I know about the election tampering."

He laughed. "Ms. Lieu, the president knows more about the election tampering than you or anyone else ever will."

So Orange Oompa Loompa did have a hand in this. She knew it. "Did he order the murder of the MAGAts too?"

He pointed the gun at her head. "Catching up time is over. I don't want to miss the rocket launch. Too bad you will."

Addison stared down the muzzle. She *was* disappointed to miss the rocket launch.

The door flung open and another dark-suited man burst in. "Drop it, Ryan." Addison recognized him as Pence's other Secret Service agent.

Ryan turned around. "Stay out of this, Bill."

Addison took advantage of the momentary distraction and leapt up to her feet. She grabbed one of the helmets off the shelf and swung it around, smashing Ryan in the back of the head. He stumbled. Addison swung again. *Crack!* He fell to the floor, remained motionless. Bill straddled Ryan, yanked his hands behind his back, and handcuffed him.

"I knew he was involved." He turned to Addison. "You work for the governor?"

She nodded.

"What do you know about this fake election fraud investigation?" He stood up.

"Plenty." A beat. "And I believe the president is involved."

He nodded. "That's what we believe too."

"We?"

"FBI, CIA, Secret Service, White House aides. There are many of us. More are discretely joining our ranks." He paused. "The Pences too."

Addison raised her eyebrows. "Really?"

"Well, the Second Lady. But she's the one who counts." He paused. "We just need proof."

Addison squatted down, dug the prone agent's cell phone out of his jacket pocket. Pulled out her tablet and connected the phone. It was locked with a password. She ran a password cracking program, and once it unlocked, she checked the last caller.

The caller ID read "Sec_Shady." Bingo.

* * *

It was hotter than Hades out here. Karen saw three people faint from dehydration. Her husband was wrapping up his speech. Something about the National Space Council and this being a historic day. The sun reflected off the shiny rocket ship, blinding Karen every time she turned a certain way.

The president's green and white helicopter slowly lowered to the landing pad. Wonderful. Orange Julius Caesar was here. She wondered where Bill and Ryan were.

Applause signaled that her husband was finished with his speech. She clapped the loudest despite ignoring most of it. Governor Musk stepped up to the podium. Babbled about what an achievement this was for SpaceX. How this year was the safest time for the launch due to the critical timing of the BFD's entry into the red planet's orbit. Otherwise, they would have to wait another twenty-six months.

Karen zoned out once again.

\* \* \*

ADDISON FIRED OFF A TEXT to Sec_Shady.

CALL ME. URGENT. THE GIRL ISN'T DEAD.

Ryan groaned, twitched. Bill released a hard kick to his head. The groaning stopped.

"What are you doing?"

"Getting proof," she said.

Bill pressed his headset. "Morris, I've got a Code Red situation. We were right about Ryan. Space suit dressing room." A beat. "Copy that." He looked to Addison. "As soon as Morris arrives, we'll take it to Mrs. Pence."

Addison didn't want anything to do with the Second Lady but said nothing. The phone finally vibrated. Sec_Shady popped up on the screen. Addison went to work. She ran the SpyFish program. Hundreds of phone numbers crawled across the screen. She zeroed in on Sec_Shady's number, clicking on it. A map of the U.S. popped up. An hourglass taunted her as the program searched for the phone's GPS chip.

While she waited, she combed through Ryan's emails and texts. Found some interesting stuff.

The phone stopped ringing.

"Shit." It shut off too early. She wondered if she should text them to call back when a blue blinking dot filled the screen. Hovered above Truth or Consequences, New Mexico.

Addison looked up at Bill. Grinned. "They're here at Spaceport."

"Who's here?"

"Sec_Shady." She paused. "The last person who called this phone to make sure I was dead." She looked at Bill. "Is the president here?"

He nodded. "Marine One just landed."

She tapped a few more keys on her tablet. Downloaded data from Sec_Shady's cell phone. When it was done, she stood up. Held up Ryan's cell. "Time to make a phone call."

She'd finally get to meet Sec_Shady.

\* \* \*

KAREN TENSED AS THE PRESIDENT stepped off the helicopter. The crowd went nuts. He waved as he headed toward the stage. The president's entourage followed. Even Rudy Giuliani was there, pumping his fist like he was at a rock concert. Red and white hats were thrust in the air. Chants of "Trump! Trump!" drowned Governor Musk out.

The president approached and shook hands with her husband. Karen wanted nothing to do with his filthy hand but shook it anyway. The governor looked like he'd rather be anywhere else.

Karen spotted Bill hurrying toward the stage. Behind him was the Asian woman she recognized as one of the governor's people. They huddled briefly with the governor.

The president waved and the crowd continued chanting "Trump! Trump!"

Bill and the other woman approached Karen.

"Mrs. Pence, this is . . ." He looked at the young woman.

"Addison."

"Addison." He nodded. "She has something you might be interested in."

"Oh?" She turned to Addison. They sized each other up. The mistrust between them palpable. Why was Bill bringing one of the governor's people into this? A Calexit nut.

"She has some evidence that will bring the president down." A beat. "We need to work together on this," he said firmly.

"What do you have?" Karen asked Addison. Chants of "Trump! Trump!" echoed around them.

Addison held up a cell phone. "Evidence from the president's cell. Emails, texts, and documents. All detailing the election fraud conspiracy. Orders to kill the MAGAts. A hit list."

Karen liked the sound of that. But it seemed too good to be true. She looked to Bill. "You can verify this?"

He frowned. "We're not a hundred percent certain. But odds are this Sec_Shady person is—"

"It's him," Addison interrupted. "I know it."

"It's a gift from God, Mrs. Pence," Bill said.

Bill was right. This was the sign she'd been praying for. Addison was like an angel sent from above. Disguised as an elitist liberal but God worked in mysterious ways.

She thought of the verse from Jeremiah 29:11: *"For I know the plans I have for you,"* declares the Lord, *"plans to prosper you and not to harm you, plans to give you hope and a future."*

This was the Lord's plan for her. She nodded to Addison. "Okay. Show me."

"It's not anything until we know who the caller is." She held up the phone. "We'll expose the president as a murdering thug with one phone call."

"Okay," Karen said. She was putting all her faith in Addison but she had to trust Him. "I'll quiet the crowd. Then you call."

Addison nodded. Bill gave her a thumbs-up. Karen marched over to the podium, shoving everyone out of the way, including her husband. "Quiet, everyone!" she shouted. "Quiet!" When the cheering finally died down, she continued. "God has truly blessed us today with a miracle. To get to the bottom of this election fraud."

Murmuring. People looked at each other. Karen pointed to Addison. "This young lady, Addison, has something to share with us."

The president shoved Karen aside. Spoke into the mic. "We don't care about that election fraud stuff, right?"

The crowd jeered. Booed. Yells of "no!"

Someone ran up with another microphone, handing it to Karen. She addressed the crowd. "I'm sorry, I thought you did, Mr. President. You ordered a full investigation into it that could take years, remember? I would think you'd be interested in any evidence she had."

A few laughs. The president glared at her.

"Mr. President, this is the moment of truth. Let her tell us what she has on the election fraud." She handed Addison the mic.

Addison held up Ryan's cell. "This government agent's phone includes hundreds of texts with incriminating evidence of a conspiracy to tamper with the election using not foreign powers this time but American citizens. I have a hit list with the names of the MAGAts who were murdered." She pointed to people wearing red and white hats. "Your brothers. Your sisters. Murdered in cold blood!"

The crowd murmured. A few loud boos.

"I have proof that someone called this phone just moments ago to make sure that I was killed. Because I knew too much!"

Shouts of "Boo!" and "Shut up, bitch!" A couple people yelled, "Let her talk!"

Karen jumped up to the podium. "Don't you want to know who killed your fellow MAGAts? Your sons? Your daughters?"

She pointed to a man wearing a red MAGA hat. "Sir, don't you want to know?"

The man blinked. Another MAGAt shouted, "It's the Left Wing Mob!" A woman wearing a white MAGA hat turned to the crowd and yelled, "Shut up! My brother was killed! I want to know!"

"We want the truth!" Karen raised her fist. "Call! Call!"

After a beat, the crowd picked up the chant. "Call! Call!"

"Get out your phone, Mr. President," said Addison.

The president shrugged. "This is all a waste of time but go ahead."

Addison tapped the screen. Held it up to the microphone. Loud ringing. People looked around. Somewhere a phone went off. The Adams Family theme song.

The president smiled. "I told you it's not my phone."

Addison scanned the crowd. Saw a commotion at the end of the stage.

"He's getting away!" someone yelled. "Grab him!"

Karen pointed. "There!"

Spaceport security had Rudy Giuliani in their grasp. He struggled to free himself while a guard fished out the ringing phone from Rudy's pocket. The former mayor's eyes bugged out.

"I have nothing to do with this! This is all lies! A Left-Wing Mob conspiracy!"

"Then you won't mind us taking a look at your phone," a Spaceport security guard said.

Angry murmuring in the crowd. Some boos. Someone shouted, "Fuck you, Rudy!"

"I don't know where that phone came from!" Rudy shouted. "Someone slipped it in my pocket!"

The crowd booed. People yelled "liar!" and "murderer!"

Rudy pointed to the president. "He's the real liar! He ordered everything. The election fraud. The MAGAt murders. I've got the president on tape! Lots and lots of tapes!"

The president shook his head, held up his hands. "I have no idea what he's talking about. He's not even my attorney! I barely know the guy."

"You'll see!" Rudy shouted. "He doesn't give a shit about any of you!"

A cheer stick pelted Rudy. Then more. The crowd yelled and booed. A few yelled "Fuck you, Trump!" and "Murderer!" Karen looked around. Were a few MAGAts finally turning against Trump? Or were they SpaceX nerds? Hard to tell.

"I'll be a goddamned hero after this!" Rudy yelled as security dragged him off the stage to the terminal. Addison and Bill ran after them.

The crowd grew rowdier. A fight broke out. Then another. Full-on brawls everywhere Karen looked. Shouts of "Lock him up!" and "Murderer!" A couple cheer sticks hit the president. He held out his hands to quiet everyone. Shouted for everyone to stop but nobody listened. People yelled and shoved one another, some getting trampled. Karen wasn't sure if it was SpaceX nerds against the MAGAts or if people were just fighting with whoever they could. Total chaos.

Time to get out of here. Karen looked for her husband. Governor Musk motioned for her to get off the stage, her husband already with him.

More security arrived. Secret Service surrounded the president who by now realized things were out of control. He practically ran to the waiting helicopter. Tripped on his way up before disappearing inside.

"I was afraid of this," the governor said. "But I didn't expect it to be this bad."

Spaceport security hustled them back to the terminal. Crash! They all turned to see the crowd had surged past security and clambered up on stage, throwing equipment, destroying everything in sight.

Bang! Security shot tear gas into the crowd. Undeterred, the crowd moved on, converging onto their next target: the spaceship and launch tower.

"Oh no, the BFD," the governor cried.

Despite not caring about the Mars launch, Karen felt a stab of sympathy for the governor. But it quickly passed.

\* \* \*

*November 16, 2024*
**FOX NEWS:**

RUDY GIULIANI RELEASES NUMEROUS RECORDINGS OF PHONE CONVERSATIONS WITH THE PRESIDENT ORDERING THE HITS OF OVER A DOZEN MAGATS IN CONNECTION WITH THE ELECTION FRAUD CONSPIRACY.

**ABC BREAKING NEWS:**

MAGAT PROTESTS ARE POPPING UP NATIONWIDE, DEMANDING JUSTICE FOR THE MURDER VICTIMS.

**CNN BREAKING NEWS:**

EVIDENCE OF ELECTION CONSPIRACY
DOCUMENT FOUND IN TOP SECRET SPECIAL
CODE-WORD SERVER IN THE WHITE HOUSE.
ARRESTS WERE MADE INCLUDING THE AG, THE
ACTING DIRECTOR OF HOMELAND SECURITY,
THE ACTING DIRECTOR OF THE FBI, AND THE
ACTING DIRECTOR OF NATIONAL INTELLIGENCE.

\* \* \*

NOVEMBER 17, 2024
LIVE INTERVIEW ON NBC NEWS:

LESTER HOLT: So when you told Rudy Giuliani to
whack the MAGAts, you didn't mean kill?

THE PRESIDENT: Of course not. If Rudy thought I
meant kill, then that's his fault. It's a sad misunderstand-
ing. Very, very sad.

HOLT: But what other meaning could there be for
"whack"?

PRESIDENT: It's just a word, okay? It doesn't matter
what it means.

HOLT: Actually, it does matter—

PRESIDENT: I wanted Rudy to handle the problem...

HOLT: What problem?

PRESIDENT: ...and I knew there was no good way to do
it. But I said to myself, this election fraud conspiracy
thing, regardless of recommendations from everyone, I
had to do it this way. But it's all just a made-up story.

HOLT: No, it's not. We have several phone recordings of
you ordering Rudy to whack the MAGAts who hacked
into the election.

PRESIDENT: That's right. We have to protect our democracy. At whatever cost. It's what you [bleep] people want, right? You [bleep] liberals are never happy. First you complain Russia meddled in the election, now you say the MAGAts did it.

HOLT: Mr. President, you can't curse on national television. And according to these documents, *you're* the one who ordered the election meddling and used the MAGAts to do it. *You're* the one who told Rudy to whack the MAGAts.

PRESIDENT: I have the absolute right to do that, okay?

HOLT: No, you don't. Mr. President, you do realize this looks pretty bad for you.

PRESIDENT: No, *you* look pretty [bleep] bad, okay? Not me. I look perfect.

\* \* \*

*November 18, 2024*
**ABC NEWS:**
THE MAGATS HAVE SURROUNDED THE WHITE HOUSE DEMANDING THE PRESIDENT'S RESIGNATION.

**FOX NEWS:**
UNDER MASSIVE PRESSURE, THE PRESIDENT RESIGNS.

*December 30, 2024*
**SPACE.COM:**
THE BFD LAUNCH WAS FORCED TO CANCEL DUE TO EXCESSIVE DAMAGE FROM THE RIOTS AT SPACEPORT. THE NEXT AVAILABLE LAUNCH WINDOW IS 2027. SPACEPORT, SPACEX, GOVERNOR MUSK, AND THE ENTIRE WORLD IS DISAPPOINTED.

\* \* \*

Four years later
February 2028
The White House

"The situation at the border is getting worse," her husband said. "We captured a record number of Americans trying to cross into New California last month."

Karen put her Bible down. She huffed. "If only people realized that New California is a cesspool of sinners. They wouldn't risk their lives trying to go there."

"Should we beef up Border Patrol again?"

She nodded. "And build a higher wall. We'll get President Musk to pay for it again."

Mike cleared his throat. "Trump called again from the Canaan Penitentiary. He wants to make sure we haven't forgotten about his pardon. He misses his Twitter account." He looked at her. "What should we tell him?"

Karen smiled. "Tell him he's in our thoughts and prayers."

He nodded. "You always know what to say, Mother."

She patted his hand. "I know."

# ANDREW JACKSON BEATS DEATH
## BY ADAM LANCE GARCIA

THE FUNERAL WAS AN UNCOMFORTABLE affair, but then again, Andrew Jackson found that true of most events where the focus was on anything but himself. If that made him vain and selfish, so be it. He had liked Congressman Warren R. Davis just fine. After all, Davis had been a Jacksonian, and Jackson did not take that kind of loyalty lightly, but he had better things to do than suffer through weeping family members and throngs of voters waiting outside the Capitol hoping for a glimpse their president. Jackson raised his chin thoughtfully. No, he could suffer through that last bit well enough. The people loved him, and in Jackson's opinion, for good reason. He was, after all, a man of the people. Or so the political cartoons would have the public believe. It was best not to have his constituency believe otherwise.

He had given a speech. It was perfunctory and simple, something written by his aide that served its purpose and he had forgotten it the moment he finished speaking. If Davis's widow wept openly during his speech all the better. Now seated at the front of the assembly, Jackson rested his hands on his cane and suffered through the remainder of the funeral. He couldn't shake the feeling that he was being watched. Not by the newspapermen that filled the back seats taking notes, but by someone else. While this was a sensation to which he had become quite accustomed, there was something different today, a pressure that he could not quantify, as if someone was standing directly behind him, their hand on his shoulder. Jackson turned his gaze across the crowd and saw nothing untoward. Perhaps it was just hunger and impatience, he reasoned. He tried to ignore the sensation, took a deep breath and reminded himself that this would all be over soon.

While others made speeches lamenting the loss of Davis, Jackson did his best not to slumber, his mind often wandering. There were other matters to focus on, matters of state, matters of diplomacy within the ranks of his own Jacksonian Democrats, all of whom had greeted him today as though he were the one who had lost a beloved family member and not a political ally. This did not surprise Jackson, nor did it discomfort him. He had grown accustomed to these sorts of sycophants, indeed there was a part of him that believed he truly deserved their flattery. He was, after all, the president, and, before that, had performed deeds that many would say defined great men. And to Andrew Jackson's mind, he was most assuredly a great man. He titled his head and wondered if he would be mourned like Davis, or would it be something greater, a national affair that would cause men to weep. If Jackson were honest with himself, the image of grown men openly crying at his demise would have struck him as an impossibility. But Jackson's ego never stood in the way of logic.

If there was one undeniable fact about Andrew Jackson, it was his anger, a blazing red fury that scalded any who dared touch it. Jackson often thought of it as a fire, burning in his humors like an immortal blaze; a devil that sat on his shoulder. It would never be extinguished. More often than not, it would erupt, eating through his mind like so much kindling. Some would compartmentalize their anger, think of it as another person, a beast that could not be tamed. Jackson made no such delineation. He had contented himself with the knowledge that he would never control it, that it, his anger, would remain a constant like the sun rising in the east. There was an odd comfort in that, knowing that he would, without warning, lose all control of himself. That anger had helped him win wars, win cases, win elections.

That devil on his shoulder was why he survived.

* * *

HOURS PASSED AND THE FUNERAL was finally, thankfully, at an end.

Though his face did not betray him, Jackson was quietly elated that the service had come to an end long before the sun had set. His joints were stiff from hours seated on an ornate yet uncomfortable pew. He pushed himself up, his knees audibly popping. Jackson winced as much at the twin pains that reverberated up his legs as he did the auditory reminder of his age. There was no way of avoiding the fact that he was no longer a young man. Indeed, he was reminded of that whenever he saw his own visage in the mirror. Yet, feeling and hearing his own body rebel against him fanned the flames at his core. His jaw worked through his frustration as he marched silently out of the funeral with the other mourners.

His cane clopping against the marble floor, Jackson used the procession to eye the senators and politicians in attendance. Beyond those who had greeted him, Jackson caught sight of Anti-Jacksonians. Those whose eyes he met gave him cursory nods, and while Jackson had no love for men who spent their political careers trying to cut him off at every turn, he allowed them some respect for momentarily placing country above party.

A few members of Jackson's own Democrats made their way over to him, eager to discuss upcoming votes, legislation that was still in backroom dealings, as well as capital gossip that could serve as future currency. There was little concern of the loss Davis's vote as the number in the House sided strongly with Jackson's Democrats. If Jackson were a better man, he would have stifled such talk until after they had left the funeral, but Jackson did not become president because he was a good man. He became president to get things done, especially if doing so helped him and his allies. With each conversation Jackson found himself smiling inwardly more and more. He liked this kind of power, knowing that his whispers could move a nation.

They stepped out onto the East Portico and into the unseasonably warm January day. Jackson's overcoat felt suddenly stifling, and beads of sweat began prickling at this hair line. He reminded himself his carriage was waiting, and that very soon this whole event would be at an end.

He rounded around a column and almost crashed into a man wearing a large black hooded cloak.

"Who the devil are you?" Jackson said to the man standing before him.

"Hm?" the man sounded, looking up from his pocket watch. Where the man's face should be was a white skull. Black, eyeless sockets stared at Jackson, like twin bottomless pits that Jackson could feel himself falling into. In his left hand was a large sickle, its blade gleaming. There was a part of Jackson that felt he should panic at the sight, but that sensation was overwhelmed by a strange, comforting sensation that felt like a mother's embrace.

"I said, *who* the devil are *you*?" Jackson repeated through his teeth.

The man clapped his pocket watch closed and tucked it away. "Well, I'm not *him*, if that's any consolation . . . Though—hm." He cocked his head to the side. The man drew a large leather-bound notebook from his cloak and quickly checked the interior. "Well. I have good news and I have bad news. But, depending on how you look at it, it could be all 'good news.'"

Jackson raised his chin and stamped his cane against the ground. "Are you going to answer the question, you fool, or will I have to beat it out of you?"

The man glanced down at his robes then gestured to his bone-white visage and sickle with a skeletal hand. "Is this not enough?"

Jackson raised his cane, brandishing it like a sword. "You dare continue to mock me?" Jackson said, stepping forward, that fire in his core burning brighter and brighter. "Tell me who you are, or I shall use this to beat the life from you."

The man in the cloak sighed and shook his head. "I can see you're confused. But seeing as we are on a schedule, let me put your mind at ease and properly introduce myself." The man opened his arms and suddenly seemed to glow from within. The sky darkened, filling with clouds. The man's voice resounded from heavens, shaking Jackson to his core. "I am DEATH!"

Jackson's face screwed in a frown as his chin pressed against his throat. "No, you're not," he said, his voice betraying his doubt. "If you are Death . . . then why am I alive, aye?!" Jackson said, defiantly pounding a fist against his chest. "Why do I still breathe? Why can I feel the blood pumping through my—" Jackson stopped himself, realizing that he could not, in fact, feel blood pumping through his veins. When he struck his chest, he had not felt the familiar *thunk-THUNK* behind his ribs. But he could speak, Jackson reasoned, therefore life must still fill his humors. He began to take a deep breath but quickly realized that no air was entering his lungs.

"No!" he shouted, stamping his cane. "I refuse to believe I have passed beyond the veil! I am in prime health! I have survived wars! I am the damned President of the United States! See, here, O Death, if you truly be who you claim, I refuse to accept I have departed the mortal coil!"

Death raised his right hand and snapped his fingers, the sound like a thundercrack breaking open the sky and with it the veil that had been draped across his eyes. Like a mist burning in sunlight, Jackson saw shapes appear around him. Those shapes became shadows of men and soon they became whole and solid, familiar faces twisted in shock and surprise. And directly in front of him was a man he did not recognize, a pistol aimed squarely at Jackson's own head.

"This—" Death aimed a boney finger at a floating metal ball that had suddenly appeared inches from Jackson's face. "—is a bullet that is barreling toward your head and it was fired . . ." Death gestured to the man holding the gun. "By him."

"And who is this, eh?" Jackson snarled the name. He flicked his wrist at the man. He knew he had enemies, in the Congress and without, but he had never imagined any of his nemeses to be so bold as to arrange his murder. "One of Clay's men? Sent here to assassinate me in broad day light?!"

"Does it matter?" Death asked. "You are beyond such concerns. Mr. Jackson, this is . . . a courtesy. The space between seconds, between worlds. Typically, folks die and—" Death snapped his finger bones again "—they're on the other side, usually waiting in the line to whichever destination they're heading." Death seemed to sigh a sigh of a thousand years. "Suffice it to say, my job is simple. I am the collector, the shepherd, taking you from here," he gestured to Jackson then aimed a finger to the ground, "to there."

If Jackson understood the implication, he did not make it known to either Death or himself; his classic stubbornness blocking the truth of his ultimate fate from entering his mind. Instead, Jackson stamped his cane against the ground. "I refuse! I refuse to die."

"As one who has had the task of following your . . . *storied* career, Mr. Jackson, I do not find this surprising. Believe me, the world would be a whole lot better off if someone had put you in your place," Death said, aiming his distal phalange at Jackson as if he were a scolding teacher. "I am the Grim Reaper. Mine task is not to be nice."

Jackson cleared his throat, conceding the point. He eyed the assassin. Jackson had been near death many times before—what soldier hadn't?—but had never crossed over. "Tell me, O Death, can we bargain?" he asked, speaking in a much calmer tone, doing his level best to hide the fiery rage that continued to warm in his stomach. "Is there a way for me to prevent this ignoble death?"

Had he muscles, ligaments, and skin covering his skull, Death would be scowling. "Sorry, that's not how this works."

Jackson's eye fluttered in disbelief. Surely, he could bargain with Death, contest his appointed time. He was, after all, the President of the United States.

"Come," Death said, beckoning Jackson on.

Jackson frowned, the fire in his stomach growing suddenly dimmer. "Will it hurt?" he asked quietly, sounding suddenly like an insubordinate child realizing too late the price of his disobedience. He glanced again at his assassin, wondering for the first time why he, Jackson, had deserved to meet such an ignoble end.

"Terribly," Death replied. "The bullet is going to enter your skull, drive into your brain and about the time it hits the center of your cerebellum, you will be dead. Those will be the most excruciating moments of your life, for as long as it lasts. But, if it is any comfort you won't feel it. You are beyond the physical realm."

Jackson shook his head. "I do not understand."

Death reached out his hand. "You do not need to. Come, Mr. Jackson."

The world around Jackson clouded over and turned grey. The familiar faces of senators vanished, their silhouettes turning into shadows, and the shadows became memories. Even the assassin vanished, but his maniacal face remained etched in Jackson's mind.

Jackson glanced over at Death, who was already walking, and then turned back at where the assassin had once been standing. He grimaced, that old anger boiling over. No, he decided. He would not suffer this despicable demise. He would find a way back and make sure this man—and those who had hired him—would pay.

The only question that remained was how he would achieve that.

Jackson tapped his cane thoughtfully and followed after Death.

\* \* \*

THEIR JOURNEY WAS ONE THAT Jackson's human mind could not wholly grasp. He knew that there was locomotion, that despite no apparent change in the world around him, his feet—silent upon the seemingly nonexistent ground—were pushing him forward; that time, if there was any measure of it, was slowly moving forward. Death, ever ahead of him, did not speak to Jackson, and gave no estimation of their arrival at his final destination—though Jackson had his suspicions.

During this time, which may have been hours as easily as it may have been an eternity, Jackson devised his plan to escape the After Life. He did not have much to work with. He had no weapon, save his cane, and no sense of direction beyond the forward motion they were currently traveling.

"Tell me, O Death," Jackson called to the Reaper. "How much longer shall we travel?"

"Do not worry, Mr. Jackson," Death replied. "You shall not tire. You are beyond such trivial things as exhaustion and pain. For the time being, at least."

This last sentence struck Jackson ominously.

The soft burble of water reached Jackson's ears. At first it seemed distant, a babbling brook a mile away, but the sound grew louder quickly and at the edge of his vision Jackson saw a river take shape at the end of the impossible horizon. As they neared it, Jackson saw a figure appear into view, its hands moving up and down in slow, careful motions. Soon, Jackson realized the man was aboard a small ferry, making its way to the rocky shoreline that had appeared beneath his feet.

Death placed his hand on Jackson shoulder. "Wait here. The Ferryman will be with us shortly."

"You mean Charon?" Jackson asked, knowing the answer. He then nodded his chin at the water lapping at his feet. "And this, the River Styx."

Death's response was silence.

"This River, what is at its source?" Jackson asked.

"There is no source," Death replied. "It always was and it always will be. It runs through everything. It has no beginning; it has no end, but it only flows in one direction."

"And does it reach some other body of water, or is it also 'always?'" Death did not reply.

"Oi!" the Ferryman called when he was several feet from shore. Where Jackson had expected another wraith-like figure such as Death, the Ferryman was instead a short, slightly rotund man with a grizzled jaw and visage of indeterminate origin. "Who you got here?"

"President Andrew Jackson," Death said, gesturing to Jackson, "of the United States of America."

"President of America?!" the Ferryman replied with a barking laugh. "Blimey!"

Jackson grimaced, once again feeling the fire burn bright. He stamped his cane but held his tongue. Now was not the time to make a scene.

"Cripes," the Ferryman was saying. "You know how many of your kind we get down here? You all really like shooting each other, aye?"

"That might be in poor taste, Ferryman," Death reprimanded.

"Yeah? And why's that?"

"I was shot," Jackson said through his teeth.

The Ferryman leaned back and let out another round of barking laughs, his hands holding his stomach. "Can't never say the universe doesn't have a sense of humor. Well, I bet you're wanting to get to the other side . . ." He held out his hand expectantly.

Death turned to Jackson. "Do you have any coin for the toll?"

Jackson was about to say no—he never carried any money on his person since taking the presidency, after all why should he, when all he needed was afforded to him from the state—when he suddenly felt a weight drop into his right-hand pocket. He blinked with befuddlement as he reached into the pocket and found a large, cold coin at the bottom. Drawing it out, he discovered it to be a glimmering gold, without any marks or scratches. It appeared, for all intents and purposes, to be newly minted. Jackson couldn't make heads or tails of the head or tail. He could see the images that had been stamped into them, but his mind couldn't coalesce them into any understanding. Without a word Jackson dropped it into the Ferryman's extended hand, the coin ringing as it passed through the air. The Ferryman's fingers curled around the coin one-by-one until he held it in his fist. He smiled a wolfish grin, tapped his cap, and gestured for Jackson and Death to climb aboard. Jackson did so without a word, a growing sense of panic mixing with the anger that continued to blaze inside him.

"How much further?" he asked once he was seated.

Death tilted back his head as if gazing to the sky. "Not long now."

"Don't worry, Mister Jackson," the Ferryman began pleasantly. "I've ferried countless souls across the River. I'll get you were you're going in—" He cut himself short when he caught Death shaking his head. The Ferryman cleared his throat and shuffled awkwardly to pick up his oar. "Ah . . . Well. We'll get you there sure enough."

"What is on the far shore?"

"The End," Death replied.

Jackson's lips firmed into a line. "Yes," he said, his voice tight. "I had deduced that, O Death, but what is there? What is *the End*? Describe it so my human mind can understand."

Death cocked his head, his black, empty eye sockets considered Jackson with curiosity. Did the specter know what Jackson planned? Did he see what he would do once the opportunity arose? Death then looked to the distant shore, as if he were looking for the words to describe what he saw.

"The shore is different for each soul," Death replied after a time. "Some see what they read in their books of faith, others see what they lived wishing were true, others see their dreams, but many see their nightmares."

Jackson felt a shiver race down his spine. "Many?"

Death skeletal visage was inscrutable. "Kindness is harder than cruelty. Cruelty is easy. One man has land, the other needs it, so the second kills the first. Simple. Two men sharing the land, splitting the fruits of the land and their labor, that is hard. Many choose cruelty. Too few choose kindness."

Jackson scoffed. "And what if the second man purchases the land? What then, aye? The first man lives, he now has currency to do with what he wishes, and the second owns the land and owes the first nothing more."

Death looked away. "Cruelty is easy," he repeated and said no more.

The Ferryman pushed off from the shore and the boat listed into the river. Jackson leaned over the edge to peer into the murky depths. He couldn't see the riverbed, but he had been in deeper bodies of water before. The current seemed strong yet swimmable. Jackson licked his lips eagerly. He could swim it, yes. For how long remained to be seen, but he was certain he could not let Death and the Ferryman take him to the far shore. The question now was when the right time would be to make his escape. He did not want to wait until they were halfway across the river, that would only assure his demise—doubly so as he was already, for the time being, deceased.

It was now or never, Jackson decided. Without preamble, Jackson threw himself overboard, gripping his cane. The River's water was icy and bit at Jackson's skin. Jackson tried to keep his head above the surface, but his clothes quickly drank in water and pulled him down. His free hand flailed, reaching for the disappearing surface as he sank to the bottom of the River. Desperate, he tried pull himself free of his increasingly heavy coat to no avail. Panic stabbed at Jackson's mind. The water was black as obsidian and grew impossibly darker as he sank further down, the Riverbed seemingly miles below him. Were it not for the faint sensations of gravity and water moving over his body Jackson would have believed himself suspended in space. There was no fear of drowning, only the dread that he may spend eternity lost to the current.

It was only when he felt something grab hold of his coat that Jackson realized the full consequence of his decision. At first believing it to be some branch or rocky protrudent on the Riverbed, Jackson tried to use his cane to wrench himself free. But his efforts aided little, and whatever had caught hold of him was now pulling him down further. Twisting his body, Jackson saw what had grabbed him and he, were he able, would have screamed in terror.

Holding him down was what looked like a young woman, eyes and mouth stretched beyond human limits in abject horror and desperation. Jackson could almost hear her wordless screams, her pleas for release. He understood, somehow, that she wasn't trying to bring him down, but rather, pull herself out. In a panic, Jackson brought his cane down upon her slender, pale white, shimmering fingers, failing as before to loosen her grip. He then felt something else grab hold of the other end of his coat. Turning to the source, Jackson saw another pale white horror, grasping for release. The entire Riverbed was filled with these luminous, panicking figures, all them reaching out, screaming for release that would never come.

Jackson knew that if they were to pull him down, he would be trapped alongside them for eternity, lost in a nightmarish limbo beneath these black waters. Seeing no other choice, Jackson let go of his cane and began to struggle out of his coat. The weight of it was immense, its waterlogged fibers clinging to his person. With each second he struggled he could feel the wraiths below him pull him closer to the Riverbed. Were his heart still beating it would have thundered in his ears. No coherent thoughts passed through his mind as the red light of panic seemed to envelope his whole person.

Jackson's right hand slipped through the cuff of his coat and it was enough for him to wriggle his shoulder free. Twisting and turning his body, Jackson was able to free himself like a crustacean shedding its shell. Suddenly feeling a hundred pounds lighter, Jackson began to swim toward the surface, the subtle, terrifying glow of the beings filling the Riverbed his only guide as to what was up or down.

He did not know how long he had been swimming when his head finally breached the surface. He gasped, not out of need for air but from sheer panic. Treading water, Jackson tried to make sense of his surroundings. There was no sign of Death or the Ferryman, nor could he see any sign of either shore. The current, invisible and powerful, had pulled him far downstream. He had no way of knowing how far, but where the River had once been a placid, mirrored surface, there was now turbulence and whitewater. Jackson could feel himself being pulled with the current, the roar of rushing water growing louder in his ears. Struggling to stay above the waterline, Jackson could barely see a few feet ahead of him and did not see the sharp end to the approaching horizon. Not until the deafening thunder of the waterfall surrounded him did Jackson realize what was about to happen.

Jackson tried to swim in the other direction, but it was no use, and seconds later he was tumbling over the edge of the waterfall into the infinite night.

\* \* \*

SOMEONE WAS HUMMING OFF-TUNE.

Jackson's eyes creaked open and saw a red sky above him, like the edge of a flame. Rolling over onto his side, Jackson realized he was on a rocky lake shore, the stones hot beneath his palms.

"Where am I?" Jackson said aloud.

"You are here," the humming voice replied.

Jackson turned to find a small, impish man seated on a small nearby boulder. The man smiled, a long, thin smile that seemed to encompass his entire face. He was wearing a simple tunic and pants, looking more a child than a man.

"Who are you?" Jackson asked as he weakly sat up onto his knees.

The other man smiled. "Who are you?" the man repeated back.

"I am Andrew Jackson," he replied, exhausted and weak. "President of the United States."

The smiling man frowned expressively and cocked his head in thought. "That so? Hm. We wondered when you were going to show up here. I see you went for a swim." The man pressed his tongue into his cheek. "How was that?"

"Where am I?" Jackson asked again, ignoring the man's comment.

The man shrugged. "The End."

A scream welled up in Jackson's chest. He tried to push it down, to remain calm, but the anger at his core burned too bright. After all he suffered to escape his fate, he still had failed. He howled to the red sky and slammed his fist against the ground. "No! NO! I refuse to die by the bullet of a coward!"

"Is that so?" the smiling man hummed. He stepped off his boulder, stuffed his hands into his pockets and strolled over to Jackson. "And what would you do to prevent such an occurrence?"

"The Reaper shall find me on this shore and take me from my destiny." Jackson shook his head and fell back onto his rump. "I fear I have done all I can."

The man tutted. "Seems like all you did was go for a swim."

"How dare you, sir!" Jackson shot back.

The man held up his hands. "I mean no offense, sir," his voice filled with laughter. "I just mean to say there are still options for you, should you desire a reprieve from your circumstance."

Jackson furrowed his brow and gave the smiling man a sidelong glance. "What do you mean?"

The smiling man held out his hands but said nothing.

Jackson made his way to his feet, his legs weak from untold time in the afterlife. "You still have not," he grunted, "told me your name."

The smiling man shrugged. He knelt down, picked a stone off the ground and skipped it across the River. Jackson could not count how many times the stone raced over the water before it finally sank beneath the surface.

"The name of the man who killed you is Richard Lawrence," the smiling man said at length, his gaze ever on the river.

Jackson frowned. "I do not know that name."

"No, of course you wouldn't." The smiling man turned back to Jackson. "Tell me, what would you do to Mr. Lawrence should you return to the mortal realm?"

Jackson considered the question. "I would kill him," he replied. "And I would destroy all those who were a part of his conspiracy."

The smiling man's grin broadened. "No room for forgiveness?"

"None," Jackson replied firmly.

"Even if I were to tell that he was mad, that he murdered you for no reason other than the disease that had overtaken his mind?"

Jackson had no response.

"No, I thought not." He hummed with what sounded like laughter. "You do not disappoint, Mr. Jackson, even your silence speaks volumes. Do you know where you are?"

Jackson knew the answer but could not speak it. Instead he shook his head, hoping that denial would make his fears unfounded. It only made the smiling man laugh more.

"I do not know why you should be so surprised, Mr. Jackson. With so much death on your hands, one could not expect to arrive anywhere else but here."

"But I am a good Christian man," Jackson whispered, the only defense he could muster.

"Mm? You believe so?" the smiling man replied. "You believe the color of your skin determines your supremacy over others. How many innocents died because of the simple crime of being born on land you wanted? How many children are born into slavery because of your actions? 'Good Christian man?'" The man laughed. "You belong here more than anyone else."

"What can I do?" Jackson asked in a whimper. "What can I do to avoid this fate?"

The smiling man shrugged. "Mr. Jackson, what would you say if I offered you your life back? For a few years at least."

The thought of returning to the land of the living sent a shiver of relief down his spine. It was only when he considered the offer that Jackson frowned. "And what would you ask in return? My soul?"

The smiling man's lips were thin yet broad. "No, Mr. Jackson. What I want is you to be the man you always were for a little bit longer, and all will be equal."

Jackson shook his head. "I do . . . I do not understand."

The man brushed his hand through Jackson's damp hair. "I don't need you to."

Jackson licked his lips. "Very well."

The smiling man clapped. "Excellent."

The world the around Jackson began to grow brighter, as if the sun were rising. "But wait. Please, I don't understand, why would you give me my life back without asking anything in return?"

"Because, Mr. Jackson," the smiling man said, his voice growing distant, "you were always ending up here."

Before the light overtook him, Jackson thought he saw the smiling man sprout large, black wings. Laughter was all he could hear.

* * *

ANDREW JACKSON ROUNDED THE COLUMN of the Capitol East Portico and came upon a man with a pistol aimed directly at his head. Jackson fell back a step in shock, a sense of strange unreality unseating him. For a moment, two visions of his future presented themselves before his eyes. One ended with him dead on the floor and the other—he blinked. The memories of his journey vanishing before he could even try to remember them. The faces of Death, the Ferryman, and the smiling man, evaporating like dew in the early morning sun. All he saw now was the assassin's pistol . . .

. . . Which misfired.

Jackson heard shouts of panic and shock, but before he could react, the assassin drew a second pistol, pulled back the hammer, pulled the trigger and . . .

. . . misfired.

"No!" the assassin shouted.

Jackson did not wait another second and struck the assassin with his cane. The assassin's head kicked back, blood spurting from his nose. The man's useless pistols tumbled from his hands, clattering to the marble ground. The scarlet sight ignited Jackson's rage, and he unleashed it with another strike of his cane. The handle hit the assassin's temple, knocking the man off his feet and onto the ground. Jackson was upon him instantly, viciously beating the man with abandon.

There were further cries of shock and panic, and in the corner of his eye, Jackson caught sight of Representative David Crockett rushing toward them. But Jackson ignored them, ignored the cries for him to stop, the people trying to pull him back. It didn't matter, Jackson would continue to beat the man until he was dead, or, short of that, until every bone in the man's body was broken. There was a devil on Jackson's shoulder eking him on and he would listen to it until he couldn't.

After all, Jackson knew where he was going.

# OLD PHARAOH
## BY DANNY GARDNER

THE MISSOURI FALL NIGHT BROUGHT with it the fullest, most watchful moon. In the cold wind, Sister Kathy looked out upon the mountain bluffs. She felt a chill upon her walnut skin, well beyond the gusts unsettling her bones. The quiet of the Railroad always brought a strange clarity to her thoughts, although she dare not take advantage of the stillness. She covered herself with her cloak and trudged on, hoping against hope those she transported on freedom's invisible tracks would be safe, and not recaptured and dragged back to bondage. Sister Kathy's charge was the living lost souls yearning to be free of anyone's grip, be it the Red, the White, or the Green. Those World-Lost. Those caught Between. Kathy knew too well of the keeper of those who fall by the wayside. It was he she searched for, in between the endless trees. She knew he'd be out there, providing his vile, evil succor to those lured into his comforts.

She knew that she owed him.

She checked the tree line at the clearing, where she had been trained to watch for those seeking the Railroad's last mile. She had also been trained to watch for the evil that lay just beyond, in those Missouri woods so close to Illinois freedom. She watched for the living, those she would not allow her wicked, dead kin to claim.

She heard slithering sounds through the vegetation, reached into the pouch she stole from the big house, and found her bundle of sage. She lit it with the business end of her torch and waved it in front of herself, whispering something that may have pleased a god from the Once Before. She looked past her own nose, without really focusing, and could see the faces of those lost in the Green. Those the Railroad could not save. She listened to their faint whimpers of discomfort and requests for warmth.

"Come in the trees," they whispered. "Play with us."

She shuddered, for that meant her father was in the woods, and Papa only ever arrived for his grim sacrifices. Kathy, who was no one's sister, carried the harshest burden of all for her master, and keeper, out in those same woods where she, herself, was born a forbidden child of fate. One child, born of the Red, and the Black, and the White. Three tribes, two torn between their gods and the power of the Green, and one, the Black, who endeavored to be left alone by both. Kathy knew what hid in those woods. Something frightening enough to make a soul abandon its yearning. Something that would make a bad child of the Black, or the White, or the Red remain on the plantation.

"I'm cold," one tiny voice said. "Keep me warm, sister."

"I ain't your sister," Kathy said.

"It's dark." Tiny eyes of burning coal illuminated a small, dark face. "I can't see."

In the shadows between trees, tiny eyes blinked away burning orange tears. Kathy watched the tree line for the sign. Burning embers, behind pale lips which burped smoke with each lie.

"Are you my sister?" One asked, as it extended a grim finger out past the oak near which Kathy walked too close. It burned her hand. She snatched back, waved the sage, and a little boy appeared.

"Why can't I come?"

"You don't need freedom," Sister said. "You're already free."

"I don't feel free," the dead thing said, its voice as hollow as its eyes.

"You're dead," Sister Kathy said, before she turned toward another moonlit clearing, the only place she'd be safe in those dark, crowded, woods. The dead thing reached out to her again. Shadows with orange eyes gathered on the other side of the trees. She withdrew with a gasp.

"Then why does it hurt, Sister?"

"I'm not your damned sister!"

Kathy drew her cloak over her face as the dead children gathered around her, one by one; as their forms appeared, with no shadows. Each spirit bore its scars.

"Papa says family is the most important thing."

"He ain't your Papa," Sister Kathy said. "He's only mine."

She waved the sage in front of her, and her dark siblings screeched and retreated into the trees. She backed away from them, into the moonlit clearing, which was the only way she'd be safe. But this ensured her Grim Pappy would be finding her, and soon.

\* \* \*

JAY HAD ONLY SEEN ABRAHAM Lincoln once, when he was barnstorming through the prairie—riding the rails, as he was then, sitting in the caboose, confidently providing leadership and power without balance. His crime was attempting to weaken the Confederacy with appeals to better, whiter angels. The shit-stain of abolitionism was full-smear across the consciousness of the white man in the North. Lincoln's poison campaign was weakening the South, the same as it had weakened his family: from within, which is why Jay picked Missouri to strike. He'd be most vulnerable just outside his own home state. The moonlight was perfect. The tree cover in the mountains gave him a solid perch. The Missouri Mountain Pass station was the only rest point. The train would have to stop.

Jay contributed the oratory of the production, understudying for Midnight Jeffries, the Cherokee who, again, played Othello. Jay studied hard to get off book before the southern leg of the tour, but no matter. Their undertaking was for the good of the nation, and needed by the confederacy of states, in order to manifest change for the white race in the assault against his ability to do for self, and family, and nation. In order to inflict the worst economic violence on the South, Lincoln, a rumored half-breed Cherokee, meant to free the black, and for the enslaved to meet white men eye to eye. It would be the final judgment. Lincoln had to be stopped.

"Dammit, Jay-dubya. You told me it'd be a stop off."

Toby Winthrop, acting company dandy, stepped through the trees in his powder-blue southern getup. Jay hated the fop, but he was the local, and in with the League. Jay meant to return his family to the prominence they enjoyed in New England before Abraham Lincoln's sedition shifted their fortunes, and he needed the dandy to rise in the fraternal ranks.

"We're not stopping, you bumpkin," John said, keeping his invective under his breath. "We can bag him tonight."

Toby was in from the git, as was Eldritch, a slave from his parents' stables. His line had been bred to hunt those woods for his masters across four plantations and two generations. They'd get close enough to the coon-loving president to strike a blow for freedom, for sure.

"Maybe everyone should be quiet," said Midnight Jeffries, the Cherokee wandering man, the shaman, who was with them since Baltimore, and who drew large crowds who weren't convinced a savage could be educated. He was noted amongst the company as a sell-out's sellout. Through every production, he scurrilously carried on about the shame and indignity suffered by the Red, who seceded with the South at the promise of statehood, but somehow came up short in the land exchange. He was arrogant, and eager to please a fawning crowd of festering simps, so long as they allowed him to make tribute to his onerous gods and goddesses. In tirades during rehearsals, he'd sing of the disappearance of the white man, although his appearance at the back door of the Civilized Tribes never made it into the lyrics. He wouldn't take his eyes off the woods.

"The moon is just right."

"Shut up, Midnight," John said, turning up his floppy hat after it was pushed into his face by overhanging branches atop the bluff. "No one believes that horse shit."

He had heard the stories as well, from the old Indian who rolled tobacco out by Elkhead Pass. The one with the long burn marks on his arms. He said Jack Scratch preferred to suckle wayward orphans left stricken in loss and dismay.

"He eats the tears of children who don't listen, you know?"

"Midnight," Toby said, with a skeptical snicker.

"Elders said, white boys who didn't listen, made the tastiest tears."

"We've all had just about enough of your savage tales, Midnight," Simon said.

All were hired by the actor Simon O'Finnegan, on loan from the Royal Theatre, to carry out his mission to inspire the troops with narrative, as they did since the Battle of Carthage, on behalf of the international faction of the League of the White Circle, or whatever it was in French, as they had funded the current company. After the War of 1812, the French held all the money, and Franco-America wanted Illinois to be free for slaves to find new, chosen masters. Simon was old, and spooky, and smelled of rich folks who hung around too long. Of course he would find no titillation in tales of horror meant to frighten mannish little boys and girls from getting too close to the colored slaves and letting them out of their chains in the middle of the night.

Midnight stared out into the trees. "They say children see him first. He lures them into the trees."

"Who?"

"The Whiskey Man," Midnight said.

"I said I had enough of this shit." Jay held up a bandaged and bloodied hand. "Show me your commitment."

Slowly, everyone did, save Eldritch, who said nothing, but didn't stop watching the trees.

"We took a blood oath. Lincoln is our prisoner, and tonight. Now, who's on first watch?" Toby struck a match to light a smoke. John put his hand over it.

"Dip snuff," he said.

Toby snatched away and snickered. "You're yellow."

Jay pointed to the mountain bluff, and the train tracks, and the teams of well-dressed guards at the train station down below.

"Unless you want the Pinkertons upon us."

Jay took a pocket watch out of his vest.

"We have three hours."

"If the train is on time," Toby said.

"We pose as the greeting choir, nab him, and get away on horseback with Eldritch leading the train through the woods into Missouri. Are the horses in place?"

"Slave," Toby said. "Have the horses ready."

Eldritch nodded, silently, and never stopped watching the trees.

"I'm curious," Simon said. "How ever did you get out here, in this dreadful climate, to sully yourselves with as grim a task as a kidnapping."

"Mother had me trained in opera," Toby said. "Lincoln loves opera."

* * *

THE CHEROKEE AND THE COLORED slave often mixed in the ways slaves were forced to with their earthly masters, despite their strict rules against half-blood children of tainted union. The Cherokee watched the white man's miscegenation with his own slave property, which was wanton, and destructive in its lust, and knew better. They came from a Red tribe that enjoyed conquest, and its price, long before the White did. They knew what you love eventually strangles you, therefore making half-slave, half-Cherokee babies was the undoing they avoided.

Still, the half-man they allowed amongst them, he who was of the Red, and the Black, and the White, was useful. He was older and understood prophecy, both in the language of the Great Spirits of the Green, and the White's Holy Bible. He used both to make his land grow. He spoke of the faith of the White, and knew of the Black's knowledge of the Green. He knew White medicine, which cured the diseases that came from their gold and blankets. The colored Cherokee could speak many Native and white tongues. He read books. He was useful, as a slave should be.

The half-man had means, and land, and was oh, so very knowledgeable, so once his loneliness was upon him, the tribe afforded him a woman, barren, fallow, and expected to be useless. In this, there was no risk of more half-breeds like him.

Kathy was only seven when they discovered her in those woods, in the same light that presided over her forbidden birth. She remembered seeing him burn to death under watchful moonlight, as they covered him in coal tar and the feathers of dead things. She remembered screaming out to her Papa, as those Cherokee stood over him, chanting, and unknowingly consecrating him in their evil. Seeing them burn him, out there, in moonlight's ever-present gaze, she told herself she only imagined the colored balls of light that rose up from the Green.

Kathy watched him fall down dead, but then mix in with the moss of those woods, and then the creeping things, and the souls of the dead out on the Underground Railroad. She watched her Papa rise, dead, as one living, and in control of the Green. Covered in bubbling coal tar, spitting ash and embers, he howled in that moonlight, casting hot fire over his attackers. One received a face full of hot tar as Papa vomited all over him.

"Excuse me, boss," Papa would say that evil night. "Can't handle my liquor."

Her mother, who was to join her pap in the tarring and feathering, instead hurled herself off the Missouri mountains, screaming, for her Cherokee culture taught her to recognize evil. She didn't hit the rocks before grabbing Kathy by the arm, intent upon casting her vile progeny over the rocks first. That was before the Green rose up and took Kathy back. Vines, and branches bound Kathy, as did her blood. The Green wrapped around her legs. It did no such thing for her mother.

He sucked their attackers' souls from them like marrow, leaving Kathy to watch as her daddy went down a man and rose as a foul thing wandering the Railroad. Something that was Red, and Black, and White enough to hold the woods that lie where the Missouri boot heel touched Illinois.

"They always want to come between a fella and his chirrens," Papa said, belching hot ash and tar. He reached down at one of his kneeling attackers. He was wearing a top hat. He begged in Cherokee for his life.

"Y'all wouldn't let me learn the lingo, I'm afraid," Papa said. "Allow me to divest you of your finery."

Papa reached for him with tarred and feathered talons and claimed the top hat for himself. Kathy watched her father's jaw unhinge, twice, before vomiting hot tar all over him. He burst into flames. Papa laughed and found a jug of whiskey his attackers enjoyed while raping his wife. He offered his screaming victim some before his charred body finally fell down into the Green. Papa donned the top hat and danced a tarred, feathery jig as he enjoyed the bourbon. Once the flames finished burning, left behind was a small, eyeless child. Smoke rose from the holes in his face, where eyes and a nose once were.

"So dark out here," Papa said. "So cold, for a little orphan."

Kathy, seven years old, saw her daddy, laughing and howling, take the spirit of that dead Cherokee boy up into his arms.

"Come meet your brother, baby," he said, fixing his coal-black eyes, with no pupils, upon his own flesh and blood. Kathy ran through to a clearing in the Missouri woods, where the moonlight was so bright she wouldn't need a torch, and kept on running, right into the arms of slavers who found her fair skin and long hair appealing. She allowed them to take her, for she knew something worse was in the woods. Something that called out to her. Something that smelled distinctly of corn mash, and distillates, and spirits of the grain.

\* \* \*

KATHY WAS TEN. HER EYES rolled in the back of her head. Her throat seized as if she were under garrote. She was in her pap's dark grip.

"Speak your lessons, child," Papa said, except he looked like he did before the Green changed him.

"One of the Red will free the Black." She couldn't stop herself from speaking.

"What next, child?"

"One of the Black will claim the White."

"Like ink on snow, tiny terror," Whiskey said, and he extended a smoking hand to her face, caressing her cheek, leaving ash along the line of her tiny, but brave jaw.

"I don't want to play any longer, Papa."

"Bring it on home, baby."

Kathy couldn't move. She couldn't do anything but say the words as her dead mama played the banjo.

"The Black will return to Black and the Red returns to Red."

"Red returns to Red! You hear, Mother?" Papa Whiskey coughed up more ash and soot. He was taller. "Everyone takes their own bad chirrens and goes home."

"The White must return to the snow," Kathy said, now coughing smoke, and embers. "The White must return to the cold."

"Papa," Dead Broken Mother said. "What's snow?"

"Where nothin' grow. Where no fool 'cept a white fool willing to go. Go where the Sun don't allow 'em, kill us all to remain, 'cuz that White don't want to flow back into the earth, where it must begin again, and again, and again, and again . . . "

Papa Whiskey pointed to the train tracks near the Missouri mountain pass. His talons had returned.

"The Red will free the Black," Kathy said compulsively, burping hot tar.

"The Red is on that train," Dead Mama said. "The Red is on that train."

Papa kept dancing, now in his festering form, as his dead wife played. He turned his coal eyes toward Kathy, his one true flesh and blood. He ran his talons across her mouth, touching the bubbling tar that escaped her tortured body.

"You get it hot enough," he said. "I'll go gather the feathers."

"The White, they come, to claim the Green."

"Yes, child." Papa pointed over to a tree. It had a white circle with a cross on it.

* * *

Sister Kathy's visions always grew stronger out on the Railroad, that ran through the richest part of the Green. Once Harriet tapped her on the shoulder, her sight grew stronger. Others figured she was lying about her visions, and hearing the voice of God as she took up her mission, but Sister Kathy knew there must have been a God who wanted the Black to cross the Green on the Railroad, for she knew the Devil of the Green existed, and it is God which makes the Devil plague Her most wanton and unbridled children. As she rose and gathered her pack, Sister Kathy felt the rustling air.

"What have you brought me, daughter?"

The smell of spent whiskey mash returned. Kathy shuddered as she reached a hand forward, her prize for him in her mitt: a pickaninny doll, with black yarn for hair, rosy cheeks and lips, and wide eyes.

"Bring it to me," it said. Kathy felt the warmth of his presence, that sickening warmth borne of the searing rage that created him. "Don't keep Papa waiting, now. You know what I need."

She ran forward, Kathy did, and as that moonlight hit her, she tossed that pickaninny toward a clump of trees, two of which bore painted white circles on the bark, with a cross inside each.

"Yes," he said, as he touched it. "A white boy child lost this one. Fresh, and slick with tears. Give me more."

"No," she said.

A shadow hissed. The smell of sulphur hit the air, followed by the reek of spent, rotten whiskey. The sound of a vile burp left the shadow hiding within the clump of trees. It stuck its face out of the shadows as it followed her movements. He pressed himself against the trees made impenetrable by the insignia painted on the bark. The demon belched smoke with each word.

"I'm your daddy," it said. "You do what I say."

"Don't say that," Kathy said. "Ain't no chirrens out here. Only orphans."

"Not you," it said, and a long arm reached past the trees. "Now, give it here."

"No," Kathy said, as she snatched back just far enough to reach the tree line.

"I said I need more, goddamn you, stupid, ornery girl child."

A long, black, charred, bubbling hand and gleaming, black talons nearly found her flesh. The hand was at the end of a finely coated arm, covered with the feathers of dead things that once flew high in the sky. Out it stepped around the trees, seeking a clearing that was free of the white sigil which abated its way. Faster and faster it moved, through the thicket, and the dead foliage, as animals in its wake lay dead from fright. It found purchase in a clearing of moonlight, far from the shadow hater's reach. When it spoke, it burped ash and embers, which burned her skin. But Kathy did not move, no, not once, although she was afraid. It tipped its top hat to her, also covered in feathers. Its skin crackled in the moonlight. Wounds bubbled and hissed with each stretch of the being's anguished sinew.

"Daughter," it said, and smiled, burping up more ash. Smoke steadily emanated from its gullet.

"I said, you need to stop calling me that," Kathy said, and she threatened her kin with more toys of woe. He hissed.

"I hunger for the Green, child," it said. "You made me assurances."

Sister Kathy took another pickaninny doll out her bag. "I need you to do something for me."

"Why would I? What did you ever do, save deny I'm your father?"

"I got what you need here," Sister Kathy said. "I need something, too."

The being hissed as it found its flask, took a sip of whiskey which smelled rotten, and belched ash.

"I need you."

"For?"

"To help the president."

Papa Whiskey laughed, and he spilled hell's foul brew into his flaming gullet. "There's no helping him, or the Black, which you foolishly think you can save."

"Yet and still, you my daddy, and we have an arrangement, so if you want these white boy toys, you'll help me."

Papa Whiskey roared, and tar and feathers flew from him. "I can let you have one of your siblings."

"They ain't no kin to me," Sister Kathy said.

"I'm your pappy," Whiskey said, barking foulness in her face. "I'm the one what decides who's kin. Give me what I need, and I'll let you have your little sister. The one with the singing voice."

Papa chuckled. Fissures in his skin opened. Foul steam and soot escaped. Kathy took off the skin bag and threw it at the being's feet. He picked it up with his talons, sniffed the skin.

"Negro," he said. "From the rooter to the tooter, my, the White gets full value from his slaves."

"Daddy!" Kathy held her torch at him. "Watch your mouth!"

"Made you call me daddy," Papa Whiskey said, and he winked an evil eye her way.

He laughed as he opened the bag, found all the stolen white child toys, and laid them out in the moonlight. Soon, things of abominable description found their way into the clearing. Each took one of their adopted parent's toys, casting him as the grim, drunken Saint Nick of the Missouri backwoods. The non-children shrieked as they retook to the shadows between the trees, the guard rails along the human flesh train that was freedom. Papa Whiskey doffed his feathery, tarred top hat, winked, and then stepped aside as a normal-seeming pickaninny was formed of the doll Kathy first tossed him.

"Bring her back unharmed, now, child," he said. "Silly thing won't be so entertaining. She only knows one tune."

"Hi, Sissy," the child with orange eyes said.

"I ain't your sister."

Kathy shivered as the child grew actual human eyes in the sockets where the hot coals once burned. Sister Kathy threw up her guts in that clearing before they moved on. It was time to take up their grim mission.

\* \* \*

THE WHITE CIRCLE, WITH THE cross inside, hovered in the air above her. She reached for it, for she knew it meant the difference between the Deadfree and the Allfree. She remembered hearing her mother whisper it in her own trances at night. Deadfree. Allfree. She reached for the circle, and cross, hoping to pull herself from the Red, the Black, the White, but most importantly, the Green, which is what controlled all. She kept jumping for the white circle, and its cross, for she could smell the mash, and the sulphur, and the hot tar, as she heard rustling from just beyond the trees.

\* \* \*

SISTER KATHY ROSE FROM THE moonlight. Her seizures were returning, and stronger than before. That meant she was close to fulfilling her task. She realized it was because her father had claimed more orphans from the Underground Railroad. She was failing in her duty. He was getting stronger.

"What were you singing about, Sis?"

Although there was no change in the moonlight, or the foliage they used to cover their escape, Sister Kathy watched as shadows with no master hovered near the trees. Kathy stepped toward a clearing, while her moonlit shadow stayed right in the spot she left.

"Sissy—"

"As long as you take the form of a child, you will mind me. Do not call me your kin. You got no kin. You Deadfree, hear?"

Kathy produced her sage but realized her torch went out. She next felt the pain in her head. Fiery fingertips pushed through her eyes into the back of her skull. As the demon child followed behind her, she winced as she walked, and tried to ignore that four dead squirrels fell into the mossy dirt below. She could hear, inside of her own head, Papa Whiskey laughing. He was pleased with his charge. She despised being the living older sister of every foster child of Sam Hain.

"You're his real daughter," the spirit said. "He says you don't mind him."

"I have my own life, damn him."

"He said you're mean because you only help the living on the Railroad."

"The living's the onliest ones need the Railroad," Sister Kathy said. "Mind your business, imp."

"You should mind Papa," the spirit child said. "He has to do a lot to provide for us."

"Don't you tell me about my daddy. Papa Whiskey is just like the spirit in the bottle. Made from the Black, by the White, to poison the Red, and take the Green. If you don't have Papa Whiskey's money, you owe him a favor, and he especially likes favors from chirrens who are stuck somewhere in Between."

The demon laughed. "You sound like us. I can't wait until

you come to live with us, in the trees. Papa wants all his children together."

"I said shut your evil mouth," Kathy said.

She saw them, up ahead, same as Harriet said. A costumed group, mixed of race, stood on the precipice of costing enslaved Americans their freedom. Tubman's premonitions never lied, damn her. Kathy wished she hadn't spoken up. She was no volunteer. It would be a special assignment, damn the abolitionists. The Confederacy meant to stop Abraham Lincoln, once and for all, from freeing the slaves by taking him at the train junction between Illinois and Missouri. The Underground Railroad needed a guard. Someone to protect the lost and weary who suffered on the route to freedom. The president born of the Red, who would free the Black, was in danger.

She thought of the entity she watched grow from the twisted desires of the Green, the same as it watched her grow and come of age imprisoned on the Railroad. Herself a ghost of a sort, born to a spirit that was already free, and therefore she'd be neither slave, nor freed. She remembered the white circles with the crosses on the trees. It seemed to be the same power in the other sigils of the White, which they used to control the Green. When she made the deal with her devil, her daddy, she bargained the tears of the privileged, carried upon their stolen toys, which were always moistened by the spittle of whining little boys, in exchange for help from the shadows. Papa would give Sister Kathy whatever she needed to be free, and help the living be free, but the dead, and their tears, would be Papa's. That was the deal. She pondered learning the sigils of the White. If it could keep her daddy at bay, perhaps she could, herself, finally be free.

She heard horses in the distance.

"What is that, sis?"

"It's them."

The demon thing was nice enough to appear kind to her Sister. It hugged her around her neck, singeing her flesh. Its breath smelled of sulphur.

"Should I go sing them a song, sis?"

"Save me the one named Booth," Kathy said. "I want to know his secrets."

"I love secrets."

The bad kid from hell walked through the trees that lay next to the mountain pass on a precipice where, not but a few hundred feet below, the Red who would free the Black from the White was to be kidnapped.

\* \* \*

BOOTH CHECKED HIS POCKET WATCH. "It's time."

"He's not due to leave until ten-thirty," Simon said. "We take him from the other side of the state line, in Illinois. That fulfills the prophecy."

"And I said," Wilkes said, drawing his side arm and pointing it at Simon. "He's to be kidnapped and brought to Mississippi to stand trial for economic sedition against the commonwealth."

"You were a shit actor, Booth," Simon said. "And you're a shit patrician. You don't pay the bills here. The league does. Stand aside. Arms at the ready. We take him as he hits his homeland. For Valhalla."

"For the white circle," all said, except Eldritch, who noticed the rustling of the trees.

"Get the horses, boy," Toby said, and he took a swipe at their slave with a crop. The horses jumped, and whined, and bucked. Eldritch made no eye contact.

"Go down," a child said, "Moses."

Tiny footsteps appeared out of the trees. Little orange-lit mouths singing a sweet song of freedom.

"Way down in Egypt's land."

Soon the children were joined by older lads and lassies, who ambled forward along the dead ground cover in the Missouri mountain range, their mouths burping tar, and soot, and ash, and they sung along, their eyes like coals burning in a furnace, in hell.

"Go down," they said, linking hands, "Moses."

One reached out to Toby, brushing past his delicate hand, burning it with hot tar from its talons. "Sing with us."

"Yes," another demon child said. "You're an orphan, too."

"Orphans make the best actors," one of the imps spoke aloud, as they closed their hellish circle, hand in hand, around the group, ever more ghosts entering the clearing from the shadows. The Railroad had all the lost souls they could ever need.

"He made all pharaohs understand," one shouted.

"Let my people go!"

"Yes the lord said: go down, Moses"

"Let my people go."

"Way down in Egypt land."

"Let my people go."

On, they sang, in full rhythm, clapping, and testifying along with each other. That's when Toby's face began to catch fire.

"Tell all pharaohs to—"

"Let my people go!"

Simon tried crawling away, but the Underground Children had him, and they enjoyed vomiting hot tar all over him. Papa Whiskey's special child took up the charge, and belted out soulfully, far beyond the age of her living illusion.

"Thus spoke the Lord, bold Moses said, if not I'll smite your firstborn's dead, what did the Lord say to mean old pharaoh?"

"Let my people go!"

Each child put a hand upon a kidnapper, caught fire, and burned every human, horse, and devil to a crisp. Their howling was finally overcome by their feast, as they consumed the tarred and feathered flesh of every human in the grove, save their Sister Kathy and John Wilkes Booth, Abraham Lincoln's would-be kidnapper.

"Look at me, scum," Sister Kathy said. "Horrors worse than this lie along the Underground Railroad. Tell me what you know about the League."

"You can't make me talk," Booth said.

"I don't have to."

Kathy pointed to the tree line. The children, who finished consuming Booth's accomplices, left behind their carrion and took back to the trees. A top-hatted, tarred, and feathered man stepped forward, doffing his cap.

"My, my," Papa Whiskey said. "So many unattended chirrens."

The spirits of the Railroad turned aside and allowed the child forms of Simon, Eldritch, Toby, and Pearl to join them holding hands. Their eyes were orange. Their mouths looked like candled hen eggs. Each began crying, looking for their parents. The smell of sulphur, coal tar, and spent whiskey mash filled the air. Papa chuckled.

"That's it," Papa said. "Help your new siblings."

He turned his attention to John Wilkes Booth. "Such a lonely boy."

A tarred and taloned finger reached out to touch him, but Booth held up a crucifix inside a circle white, the whitest Kathy had ever seen. Her father howled.

"Alabaster," Booth said. "The league knows of your evil. You've done nothing here today but ensure Abraham Lincoln dies after I show the world he's in allegiance with dark forces in his effort to end the South."

"So dramatic," Whiskey said. "My babies will enjoy your company."

Booth shoved his hand into his coat pocket, pulled it out, and threw white salt at Whiskey. His skin cracked and bubbled as he screamed. Booth whispered incantations under his breath before pointing at Sister Kathy.

"Now, the league knows you, as well. And Harriet Tubman. We will respond in kind."

Booth kept the crucifix high in front of him as he grabbed one of the horses Eldritch kept for Toby. Sister Kathy pulled her revolver and began firing at John Wilkes Booth, but he reached the mountain pass where neither bullets nor shadowy spirits would meet their target. The children all laughed, taunted Booth to his back, or asked if they could find another playmate.

"Come now," Papa said. "Gather your new siblings."

Sister Kathy watched the tree line as her father, Papa Whiskey, disappeared beyond the shadows, taking the souls of abandoned and orphaned children lost on the Rails with him, now joined by those who wouldn't slip away as John Wilkes Booth had, he who didn't share with his fellow white folks the magic of the White.

Kathy looked away as Papa reached out to her, extending a talon.

"I'll miss you, child."

Kathy turned to see Papa holding the spirit of a boy, seemingly native in extraction. He was pretty. He wore his native dress. He didn't speak, only sat in Papa Whiskey's arms taking a swig of his jug.

"Chip off the old block," the vile spirit said, and he tipped his top hat to his only begotten daughter. "Nothing like the real thing, tho'. Come back and see me, darling. Bring me more goodies for your brothers and sisters, now."

Sister Kathy wouldn't speak. She pulled her hood over her face, hitched up her pack, and took back to the clearing, making certain to avoid the trees, unless she intended to visit upon her dark, adopted siblings and their dark daddy.

Her charges were the lost and weary, and living, out on the Underground, where she was born and watched evil consume all she knew. She feared nothing, save the Green, that thing everyone wished to possess, for she knew what lay beyond its trees. Grim, undead judges waiting to convict those who failed to cover their own cartage on through that precious Last Mile. The Underground Railroad knew those who truly wanted freedom from those who professed it, but secretly despised it. For them, there was always room in Papa Whiskey's tribe for the World Lost. Those who learned to love the Between. Orphans made the best actors, it was said, and yet, on the Railroad, actors made the best orphans, as the tribe of kidnapping thespians, who learned out in the Missouri woods, under that watchful moon, that it was better to be cold, or hot, but never, ever, lukewarm, for that wouldn't be enough heat for Papa Whiskey's many children.

A foul, whiskey-scented whistle blew. A dark, tar covered horse arrived, lead out to the clearing by Eldritch, now a burning-eyed child.

"Can't have you out here raggedy," Papa Whiskey said. "Until next time, daughter. Don't forget toys for your brothers and sisters."

"They're not my—"

"I know, I know," Whiskey said, chuckling, smoke rising from his rotting throat. "Sassy."

Whiskey pulled her toward him in his foul talons. His face changed back to normal, same as when he was just her happy, fun, bright pap. He gave her a kiss she didn't fully turn away from.

"You get it from me."

Shadows flew from Whiskey's sinister form and took to the trees. Papa Whiskey doffed his top hat and joined his undead brood. Kathy pulled her cloak over her body, covered her head, mounted her daddy's dark steed, and rode it through the Missouri Mountain Pass as she watched Abraham Lincoln greet voters at the train station, within spitting distance of the Green, and the Railroad, and vile things trapped in Between.

# THE CAMELOT COMPLEX
BY ALEX SEGURA

SERGEANT GUARDIAN SARAH GUNNER AWOKE with a start.

She felt the same sinking feeling she got whenever she took on one of these missions. The disorientation. The nausea. The feeling of displacement that she could only liken to that ancient word—what was it? "Jet lag." Yes. That was it. That sense of not being fully there.

At least they'd placed her properly—off to the side, away from the crowds lining the streets. The air was crisp and felt clean, unlike the air she was used to back home, which was often inhaled through a mask's protective filters. No, this was direct. It felt good. Pure.

She stood up hesitantly, getting used to her body and surroundings. She checked her clothes. It appeared to be a police uniform of some sort. She smiled. Larcen was good at this stuff, she knew. But on cases like this, he went the extra mile. She checked the badge: POLICE—DALLAS TEXAS. She checked her wrist—people kept time with watches on their wrists, she reminded herself—and let out a quick gasp as she did the quick formula that allowed her to figure out what time it was here, in 1963.

\* \* \*

12:15PM.

SHE WALKED OUT OF THE alley and entered another world. Men, women, and children were crowding the sidewalks and into the streets, waiting. Some waved signs. Excitement and energy crackled in the air. She heard someone nearby mutter, "He's coming, his motorcade is almost here."

She had to hustle. If she saw his car, it'd be too late. She scanned the Dallas skyline and found the building easily. It was getting there that would be problematic.

"Could've dropped me with more time, Larcen," she muttered to herself as she shoved and moved through the crowd. The uniform gave her more leeway—people in this time tended to defer to the police—but not much. Everyone was on some primal high, as if waiting to touch the hand of God. *Pretty close*, she thought.

She saw her reflection in a nearby store window and almost froze. It was her; she could see her dark eyes, brown hair and pale complexion. But the attire and demeanor were off. When these trips happened, you were yourself, but you weren't. It was disconcerting, to say the least. It felt like you were driving a rental instead of your own body. She crossed the street, the large Warehouse building looming behind her. Her shoulders brushed up against another man. He apologized quickly, not stopping, a long bag slung over his broad shoulder. She looked at him. At first glance, the uniform screamed "police," but something stuck with her—the uniform didn't match hers. It seemed off—slightly worn and not pressed, the colors muted—like a costume. His badge, too, wasn't right. A five-pointed star, the kind of badge you'd see kids wearing as costumes in past centuries. Well, now, if she was being technical. It was bright, too, as if made with aluminum foil, reflecting the strong Dallas sun.

She shrugged it off. There was no time. When she turned around again, the man was gone.

"Your friend was in a hurry!" a woman said, scurrying past Sarah. She was carrying a large, bulky camera. A Polaroid? She hadn't prepped enough.

"Never seen him before," Sarah said, without hesitating. She flinched. Contact was frowned upon. "In and out," Larcen said. Don't talk to anyone, don't look at anyone, don't leave a fucking footprint if you can help it.

"Now, how is that possible?" the woman said as she wheeled around, her eyes on Sarah now, squinting as if trying to get a better look at her.

She was young, Sarah noticed, with plain, pleasant features. She wore a conservative, embroidered dress and seemed energetic and enthusiastic. She smiled and extended her free hand.

"I'm so sorry, officer, that was rude, it's just, well," she said, hesitating. "You don't often see a woman in uniform, is all. I mean, well, I know we've had lady police officers and all, but . . ."

She sighed. Sarah took her hand, despite knowing how badly she was fucking this up now.

"My name's Mary Moorman," the woman said. "I'm just excited, is all. I've never seen the president, or his wife. She's so darn pretty. I feel like a kid on the first day of school!"

Sarah looked at her watch: 12:20pm.

"Nothing to worry about, ma'am," Sarah said with a nod. "Have a great day."

Mary Moorman nodded, as if she wanted to say something more but thought better of it. *Shit*, Sarah thought. Larcen had been clear about this. What was it he always said? "Time travel is like tossing a rock into a lake—no matter how or what you do, it'll cause ripples. The trick is to be gentle and light, so the ripples are minimal."

*So much for that*, she thought.

Sarah made it to the other side of the street and nodded to a fellow officer as she entered the Book Depository. The bulk of the crowd was in front of the building's main entrance, mesmerized by what was to come down the street in a few minutes. *If they only knew.*

She noticed a man shoving a final piece of sandwich into his mouth as he stepped out of the building.

"Lee around?" she asked.

"Lee?" the man asked. "Oswald, you mean? That freak?"

Sarah nodded. She was kicking herself, but she couldn't think of a faster way to get to where she needed to go. *Damn the ripples for now.*

"Up on six, f'r all I know," the man said. "We were all just havin' some lunch before this motorcade thing, but Lee was too busy, asked if we could send the elevator back up for him when we was done horsing around, but I'm not sure if anyone did. Anyways, he should still be up on six, doing whatever his strange self wants to be doing right now."

Sarah nodded and moved past the burly, lethargic man. She'd done more than enough talking for the day.

* * *

12:23PM.

SARAH TOOK THE STAIRS. No time to wait for an elevator. She was fit. Toned. She didn't start breathing heavily until the fifth flight of stairs and by then she knew she was short on time. She heard the roar of the crowd, even through the old Texas Book Depository's thick walls. She was running late, and her being late could impact much more than her own private schedule when it came to Dallas, Texas. And Lee Harvey Oswald. And John Fitzgerald Kennedy.

She was breathing heavily now. The weight of her mission crystallizing in her mind. Why had she agreed to this? Larcen had been clear. They were going rogue. They were trying to fix what couldn't be fixed in their time anymore. Civil action was dead. Free speech a joke. The planet an overheated, festering carnival where all people cared about was how many heart-taps they got on the way to their stations and whether their personal filtering units were in working order. The cities were split, with sweeping, beautiful aerial edifices crowding the skies and dank, dingy, rat-infested ghettos at the bottom, where once, centuries before, people walked and talked and loved.

"We gotta do something, Sarah," Larcen had said, slamming his fist onto his terminal for what felt like the hundredth time that night. "What happened to hope? To belief in something greater? To serving your country?"

"Country?" Sarah had asked. The term was archaic. The idea of a "United States of America" felt more like a fable and less like the past. Like a novel idea that had been worn into the ground, distorted and crushed into a fine powder, then snorted up by a vile, boil-infested monster. Country? What country?

"You know what I mean," Larcen said.

It was in those moments that Sarah was reminded why she loved him—that spark in a droning sea of nothing, that desire to do *something* in an era of expectation and disinterest. People didn't work anymore. People didn't fight for things. People didn't love or believe or dream. There were the rich ones above, who sat in their simula-spaces, hypno-helmets on, gourmet feeders plugged into their arms, and muscle stimulation suits coating their mottled, almost translucent skin. Down below were the scragglers, the desperate and hungry, the sunsick and burnt, clawing and scraping and scrounging for any bit of life—water, food, anything. And then there were Larcen and Sarah. The Guardians. Members of a wide-ranging force that, if Sarah was being honest, did one thing: kept the rich ones safe and the scragglers at bay. A middle class by default, the Guardians made just enough to survive. Were given homes and lives that resembled the stuff of legend but didn't quite add up. Their bosses were distant and muted, but emotional and prone to tantrums. Their targets were pathetic. Once human. Barely alive.

The idea had come to Larcen one night, as he made the

rounds of the Science Hive, near the Capitol Collective of Tubes. There were no scientists left. No thinkers. Society relied on the reheated brains of dead geniuses and luminaries to try and keep the engine running a bit longer. Interested parties could communicate with a simulated amalgamation of the world's great minds, smooshed together to help keep a world on life support. Part of Larcen's job was to ensure this Hive, this last bastion of free thought that was now squeezed through a filter of laziness and disinterest, remained pure.

"We can do it," Larcen had said that night. "The Hive told me so. They can send you back."

\* \* \*

"You know it's forbidden to use time travel to alter history," Sarah had said. "To preserve and protect, yes, but never like this."

"Preserve what, Sarah?" Larcen spat, his eyes wide and desperate. "We're barely holding on. One wrong move and we'll be sent down into the abyss, where we'll burn to ash and be erased from history. And we don't even get to determine the rules. If we happen to upset one of the lazy ones, one of the globs of flesh sucking out what little resources this planet has left, we're as good as dead."

Sarah didn't respond.

"But I've figured it out," Larcen continued. "I've tracked the moment where . . . well, where everything went to hell."

The moment was upon them now, she realized. She was moments away from the single episode that would send us, as a society, hurtling into the abyss—and Sarah couldn't find Lee Harvey Oswald.

She turned left and scrolled through her mind, trying to remember the map she'd glossed over on their way to The Hive last night—or was it three hundred years from now? She was dizzy. The effects of the jump still throttling her brain, leaving her disconcerted and lost, like walking through a pool of clear sludge. She knew she was moving, she knew what was happening, but she couldn't control her actions as fast as she wanted to. Her reflexes were shot.

*There he is*, she thought, her mind's voice sounding distant and sloth-like.

"Stop!" she heard herself yell. She saw her arm shoot out, a 20th century gun in her hand. "Don't do it!"

Oswald turned around, a look of complete shock on his face, the rifle resting on his shoulder.

\* \* \*

12:28PM.

"No, no," he said. His voice was soft, nebbish-like. He sounded like a rodent made human. He was fearful and confused, his movements jittery and hesitant. This had not been in the cards, he surely thought, this was not part of the plan.

"Drop the gun," she said, but Oswald wasn't listening—his entire expression had changed. From confused and sheepish to focused and in control, as if a switch had been flipped.

"No, must complete—"

She didn't hesitate. Larcen hadn't slung her back into this world, this year, this time, to stop and ponder. She had to act. She wanted to see a better world. She wanted to help Larcen do something. Hell, for anyone to do something. To live. To strive for a better world.

The bullet blasted into Oswald's face, shattering his nose and tearing through his skull. Brain matter and fragments splattered on the wall behind him, flecks of bone and organ peppered the stacks of boxes that surrounded Oswald's little private gun-nest.

His gangly, awkward body flopped back onto itself, what was left of his head making a hollow *scrushlk* sound. Sarah felt herself recalibrate. Felt her mind clear. The roar of the crowd had surely drowned out the bullet, she thought. Now, all she had to do was watch President Kennedy's motorcade make—

Gunshots. Rifle shots.

Sarah stepped toward the window and tried to follow the sound. She saw the familiar visuals and felt her heart clench—the car swerving, the pink-coated Jackie Kennedy huddled over her husband. The screams of fear and panic.

But then, something different. Movement. The President reaching over and clutching his wife. Pulling her down with him. His body trying to shield her. The blood on his head—there was blood—seemed gruesome, but not nearly as bad as she remembered seeing in that footage so long ago. *The only brain matter flying around is Oswald's,* she thought as she looked closer, this time through Oswald's rifle sight. Kennedy was alive. The president survived. She'd done it.

But those gunshots—someone else had been gunning for Kennedy. *No matter,* she thought as she tapped the area above her heart. The failsafe. The get home button. She could only use it once. It was her exit. Once she tapped it, she'd be pulled back home, win or lose. But Oswald was dead, Kennedy was safe. She won. Right?

Nothing. Was she stuck here?

Sarah cursed under her breath. She had to get out of here, fast. Find time to regroup, to think about what to do next. Her eyes scanned Oswald's broken, bloodied, and lifeless body. But what about this mess?

Then she heard the footsteps. Four pairs. Had to be police. She had to move fast.

She repositioned Oswald's body and dropped her gun near his left hand. She remembered he was left-handed, at least. She grabbed his rifle and stood hastily. The footsteps were growing louder. She gave the room one last scan. It'd have to do.

Then she was gone.

\* \* \*

*From The Dallas Morning News, November 23, 1963.*

**KENNEDY NEARLY SLAIN ON DALLAS STREET**

*President dodges assassination attempt, rushed to hospital with minor injuries*

*Mafia Associate Taken into Custody*

*Pro-Communist Commits Suicide Near Shooting Scene*

President John F. Kennedy and Governor John Connally were both injured in a daring assassination attempt on the president's motorcade as it wound through Dealey Plaza in Dallas yesterday afternoon. The sniper, who'd set up on the northwest side of the plaza, was first spotted by local resident Mary Moorman, who'd been taking shots of the motorcade and surrounding areas with her Polaroid camera.

The shooter, identified as Johnny Roselli, a mob associate tied to the Chicago crime organization, was apprehended at the scene. Dallas Police are investigating Roselli's motive, and alleged ties to not only organized crime, but the Central Intelligence Agency's efforts to topple Fidel Castro's communist regime in Cuba.

\* \* \*

NOVEMBER 24, 1963.

SARAH WATCHED THE WESTERN UNION building on Main Street. It was 11 in the morning. She sipped her cold coffee and waited as the burly man filled out a wire transfer form. She watched as he and a small dachshund dog exited the building. She crossed the street. She was wearing nondescript clothing now. She couldn't pass as a cop anymore. Too risky. The exit button still wasn't working, but that might repair itself. Time travel had a way of doing that. Of trying to regain consistency even after drastic changes. But this was a big change, she knew. The ripples would be huge.

She was a few paces behind the man when she pulled out the gun. A Colt Cobra she'd managed to get her hands on the night before, as she'd mapped out what to do next. The police were holding Roselli and transferring him shortly. The timeline was trying to reconstruct itself.

The burly man turned around quickly, faster than Sarah had expected for such a swarthy, pudgy figure. He saw the gun immediately, but it was too late. She fired three shots. Two into his stomach, another in his head. Jack Ruby collapsed, muttering something about just doing his job. Paying his debts.

The shots had been loud. People turned and noticed. Some screamed. There was no way Sarah could get away. Had it been worth it?

She tapped the button.

# THE EVENT THAT DIDN'T HAPPEN
## BY TRAVIS RICHARDSON

NOVEMBER 2000

AL GORE WON THE 2000 election in Florida by the slimmest of margins in spite of Republican interference, defeating George W. Bush to become the 43rd president. World events as we know them changed forever.

JANUARY 2001

MONTHS LATER, GORE HAD HIS inauguration on the Capitol steps. Meanwhile in Las Vegas, 33-year-old Mohamed Atta sat at a table with colleagues he called friends in spite of them being non-Egyptians. They were bound by something stronger than geographic rivalry. A belief united to the point that it almost transcended their collective faith. That one thing, an emotion so pure and true, gave him a reason to live, and it had to be the same for them. They were united in a singular vision of destroying the United States of America.

Since coming to America in the summer of 2000, Atta had been disgusted by the decadence that this most vile of countries produced. Thank Allah he was strong enough not to succumb to evil.

His colleague, the plump Marwan al-Shehhi, said something, but it was hard to hear over the thumping music blasting through the sound system. A catchy tune, sure, but those with pure hearts should never tolerate secular music.

"Where did Ziad go?"

"He's getting a lap dance," Atta shouted as he watched whirling flesh on the stage and tried to keep from ejaculating a second time. If it weren't for the wet spot on his crotch, he might've been enjoying some hedonistic pleasure himself. His fourth colleague, Nawaf al-Hazmi, was getting his third dance. Perhaps God gave him this quick-fire burden so he wouldn't be lured into temptation. Or maybe he should bring a second pair of pants and underwear to future tactical meetings.

"This decadence is disgusting," al-Shehhi said, not letting his eyes leave the breasts of an undulating redhead.

"I completely agree. They shake their naked bodies forgetting it's a gift from God that should only be preserved for a husband."

The caress of a feminine hand sent electric bolts through Atta (and his little Atta).

"Hey, honey," an otherworldly voice purred in his ear. "Want a private dance?"

"I, uh . . . uh . . . ah."

The wet spot on his crotch doubled.

"Looks like you're taken care of." The brunette's hand slid off Atta's diminutive shoulder and drifted to al-Shehhi. "How about you, sexy? Wanna take me for a ride?"

Al-Shehhi's glasses fogged up. "Yes, madam. Right now. Please."

The 23-year-old stood, banging his erection on the table. Drinks splashed.

"Oh my," the stripper said.

"I'm okay," he muttered.

The woman led al-Shehhi by the hand to a private section of the club. Her G-string-exposed bottom swayed hypnotically. Atta sipped his rum and Coke, fuming with jealousy. The drink tasted sweet enough that one could hardly call it alcohol, and, since the bar had a two-drink minimum, he couldn't refuse. One must follow rules.

Today's outing reminded Atta of his time as a graduate student slumming in Hamburg's redlight district. How many prostitutes did he pay for sex? Several. And how many times had he pre-maturely ejaculated before his pants were off? Almost the same amount. The hookers always pocketed the money, the transaction complete in spite of his pleas for the remaining twenty-nine minutes he paid for. Shame reddened his face. He desperately wanted to kill. Kill sexy women. Kill Western women. Kill Westerners. Kill Americans.

FEBRUARY

TWO WEEKS INTO HIS PRESIDENCY, Gore held a meeting with the National Coordinator for Security, Infrastructure Protection and Counter-Terrorism, Richard Clarke. Although Reagan had appointed him in the State Department, the feisty 51-year-old spoke about threats to America without a political agenda. That is why President Clinton promoted him and Gore kept him in the same role.

Clarke had written a couple disturbing memos about a future attack coming from Al-Qaeda. As Vice President a few months earlier, Gore was familiar with the terror organization and the fanatical financier Osama bin Laden—two threats that shouldn't be ignored.

When Clarke walked into the Oval Office, Gore rose to greet his white-haired colleague. "Good to see you, Dick."

"Wonderful to see you in this new capacity, sir."

"Take a seat, please." The President pointed to the couch. "I'm sure you didn't come here to congratulate me, right?"

"No, sir." Clarke sat, placing a folder on the coffee table. "I take it that you've read the security memos I sent."

"I did. Scary as hell. How accurate is the intel?"

Clarke leaned forward, his eyes blazing. "Eighty percent minimum. Maybe as high as ninety percent, sir."

"Hmm." Gore leaned back. "That seems mighty high for a theoretical event."

"I'd love for this to be a theory and not the real deal with an explosion at the end. But the intelligence agencies have concluded that Al-Qaeda and bin Laden are brewin' something big."

Gore shook his head. These Islamic terrorists, led by a wealthy Arab, were so hell-bent on blowing up US foreign assets in the Middle East and Africa. "Another embassy, I assume? Or is it a destroyer? I'll put 'em both on high alert."

"Neither. We're pretty certain this is going to be a highly coordinated attack *inside* the US."

Gore's heart froze. "How are they going to do that?"

Clarke sighed. "We don't know."

"What do you need then?"

"A task force and the authority to make agencies cooperate."

Gore stood. "Put a task force together with all the relevant agencies and if anybody gives you flack, let me know."

Clarke shook his hand. "Thank you, sir."

MAY

ATTA HAD A CRISIS ON his hands. Ziad Jarrah was uncertain about continuing on this sacred mission. The trained pilot asked if he could stay on the ground and provide logistical support.

"Are you kidding? Kahlid Sheikh Mohammad has been paying us for months. Bin Laden picked you along with al-Shehhi and me to carry out this mission. It's God's will. We cannot fail Him."

"Your entire life," al-Shehhi said, putting a hand on his comrade's shoulder, "has been building to this moment."

Jarrah shook his head. "That doesn't make sense."

"What do you mean?" Atta swallowed back fear. What if he didn't have the answers like bin Laden or the clerics in Afghanistan gave for martyrdom?

"Does it make sense that I took calculus in Hamburg so I could fly a plane into a building years later?"

"Yes," Atta and al-Shehhi both answered.

"That's like a saying a middle-aged man who gets hit by car worked his entire life just to get run over. Why did he have a job in the first place when he could have stepped into traffic as a boy? The result's the same."

Atta and al-Shehhi looked at each other.

"It's God's will," Atta said. "We never question it."

Atta realized the "God's will" argument was the answer most clerics gave. Don't question God. End of argument.

Jarrah rubbed his forehead. "Was it God's will that I ate rocky road ice cream last night?"

"It wasn't," al-Shehhi said. "It's a sin to indulge in Western delights."

"You had ice cream too," Jarrah said, pointing.

Al-Shehhi crossed his arms. "Yes, but my scoop wasn't rocky road—a purely western creation. I had pistachio to remind me of my work in Afghanistan and what I must do to destroy the infidels. I'm justified in eating ice cream."

"Ice cream is a Western creation!"

"Actually, it's attributed to ancient Persia during the Achaemenid Empire," Atta said.

Both men turned to Atta.

"But they are Shiites," Jarrah said.

"And it was jahiliyyah, before the Prophet," al-Shehhi said.

Atta sighed. "The eating of ice cream shall be forbidden from now on."

His colleagues dropped their heads as sadness blanketed the room.

Jarrah cleared his throat. "While I agree to never eat ice cream, I need to think . . . and pray about continuing this mission."

He walked towards his room.

"It's not a mission, it's jihad," al-Shehhi shouted.

Jarrah slammed his door.

Atta looked at al-Shehhi. "Will he stay with us or should I find a replacement?"

"I don't know. Hopefully he'll see God's will."

Atta rubbed his temples. "I'll call Moussaoui. Make sure he's trained and ready."

"Zacarias Moussaoui? He's an idiot. He flunked basic flight school in Oklahoma after how many months? Did he even fly for a minute solo?"

Atta shook his head. "Since Ramzi can't make it through immigration, Moussaoui is our only hope to seize four planes. I'll get more money wired. There's a school in Minnesota I can send him to."

## JUNE

CLARKE'S TASK FORCE, COMPOSED OF acronymed agencies including the FBI, CIA, INS (Immigration and Naturalization Service), and FAA (Federal Aviation Administration) were present. The first two meetings, while informative, broke down with the FBI and CIA shouting at each other for hiding information.

Frances Bikowsky of the CIA's Bin Laden unit (aka Alec Station) and John O'Neill of the FBI's New York field office were both great at their jobs and understood the threat of Al-Qaeda, but they hated and mistrusted each other.

During the third meeting, an INS representative said that her office noticed a slight uptick in flight school enrollees from nations known for Al-Qaeda recruits.

O'Neill shot up from his chair. "Flight school."

"That's what she said," Bikowsky said without irony.

"No, Saudis coming over here and taking flying lessons. It makes sense now."

Clarke's mind raced. "They obviously want to hijack planes and fly them some place." Although he realized it didn't go with the rhetoric about the streets flowing with blood.

"That's my thought too," O'Neill said.

"Where would they fly to?" the FAA representative asked.

Clarke rubbed his chin. "I don't know details, but if they take an international flight, they could try to a West African country. Maybe an old Soviet base in one of Stans."

"But where's the promised bloodshed?" Bikowsky asked.

"They'll plant bombs," O'Neill said, still standing. "They love to blow things up."

"You don't need be a pilot to plant bombs," Bikowsky said.

"Unless . . . " Clarke trailed off.

"What?" O'Neill asked.

"That's not their plan."

"What do you mean?" Bikowsky asked.

"Egyptian Air nine-ninety. The flight that left JFK going to Cairo. The co-pilot yelled *Tawkalt ala Allah* before nose-diving the plane into the Atlantic."

"What is Tawkalt ala Allah?" the FAA representative asked.

"I rely on God." Bikowsky said with a snarl.

"NTSB says it was suicide because the pilot was going to get fired for sexual misconduct, but thirty-three military officers were on board. And the Egyptian government twisted like a pretzel denying that an Egyptian would kill another in spite of the evidence." Clarke shook his head.

"Deniability from a nervous government," Bikowsky said.

"We'll need to send investigators out to interview foreign flying students."

"I can handle the New York area," O'Neill said, "but you'll need to go to Director Freeh to go nationwide. He'll give you some pushback."

Clarke nodded. Louis Freeh was not a bad man, just ineffective as director. Overly cautious to the point of being comatose.

"I'll see what I can do." Clarke turned to Bikowsky. "Can you check with embassies to see how many students came over here to be pilots?"

"Sure," she said, looking away.

Clarke made mental note that Bikowsky was hiding something.

JULY

ATTA FLEW TO ST. PAUL to meet with Moussaoui. The French national of Moroccan descent had been driven from Norman, Oklahoma to Minneapolis, Minnesota by a colleague since nobody trusted Moussaoui behind the wheel of a car. The squat and jumpy man couldn't stop thanking Atta for giving him another shot at becoming a martyr.

"I will not fail you on this most holy of missions, brother. I promise, with God's strength, to bring the sword of death against the infidels."

"Just get your instrument training done first. I have to be certain you can handle a Boeing seven-forty-seven." He handed the French National a packet stuffed with hundred-dollar bills. "Your hotel is paid for the next two months. Use this money to pay for lessons and nothing else except for food. Got that? Anything else will be a violation of God's will."

"I understand, brother."

He nodded his head so fervently that Atta wondered if he might dislocate his neck. What a fool he'd been burdened with. No way would Moussaoui be able to walk through security, not to mention a cockpit. He prayed God would provide a better solution.

AUGUST 15

"WAIT, WHAT?"

"Do the cockpit doors have locks?" Moussaoui asked.

The Pan Am flight instructor looked at this peculiar flight student who still couldn't figure out how to read the altitude on an altimeter, even after two weeks of testing and previous training from another flight school.

"Why would a cockpit need to have locks on the door?"

"I don't know," Moussaoui said with a dopey-eyed look and a shrug. "But do they have security by the door?"

"Like a bouncer?"

"Sure. Like that."

"If you count a stewardess, sure."

A smile spread across Moussaoui's lips. Hijacking a plane was going to be super easy. He just needed to learn how to fly the crazy machines.

\* \* \*

THREE HOURS LATER THE FLIGHT instructor called the Minneapolis FBI. He was routed to a field agent and told the agent about the suspicious questions Moussaoui had been asking.

"Can you spell his name?" the agent asked.

A crosscheck on a database system brought up an expired visa. Enough to detain him. He scheduled a meeting with his boss that afternoon.

AUGUST 16

IN THE EVENING, TWO FBI and two INS agents waited outside the hotel for Moussaoui to emerge for his flight class. Stepping into the humid air with a friend, they gave no fight. Moussaoui clamped down with wild-eyed bafflement, only saying that he would not allow agents to search his hotel room. The friend was more generous allowing them to search his car and room. Agents and analysts cataloged several items including a laptop and cell phone.

Later Moussaoui sat in an interrogation room saying very little.

"What do we do now?" the arresting agent asked her supervisor.

"Nothing. Let's wait to hear what Quantico says. We need a FISA if we're going to open his computer or phone."

AUGUST 18

ATTA STOOD FROM HIS PRAYER mat, his stomach rolling in knots. He had been to Spain to meet with Khalid Sheikh Mohammed and other hijacking participants. Jarrah finally saw the light and would fly the fourth plane, which was great since Moussaoui wound up in jail. He had monthly meetings in Vegas with Khalid al-Mihdhar, a Saudi who was organizing a fourth team. He had flown to New Jersey and oriented the arriving Saudi muscle that would help overpower the flight crews so their pilots could fly without interruptions. Now he was back in Florida. He had planned to pick up another Saudi in Orlando, but the muscle was held for acting suspicious. At least this guy was mostly clueless. Moussaoui, on the other hand, knew things . . .

Atta rubbed his forehead, having banged it on the floor while doing his prayers. He hoped the idiot wouldn't say anything incriminating and that the FBI wouldn't go through his emails. Would Moussaoui have even password protected his computer? Please God, don't let them find out.

## AUGUST 31

THE PRESIDENT SUMMONED CLARKE TO the Oval Office. Gore sat behind the desk looking perturbed.

"What's going on with the terrorist investigation? I understand from the memos that something is going to happen soon."

"We still don't know who or when."

"What's holding you up?"

Clarke threw his hands in the air. "Everybody. Everything. CIA's bin Laden unit."

"Alec Station, right?"

"Yes, sir. I get the feeling they aren't sharing information with me or the FBI."

"Aren't FBI agents assigned there?"

"Yes, but they can't report to their supervisors without CIA clearance."

"Are they being blocked?"

"That's my understanding. Reporting without CIA clearance could be a ticket to prison."

Gore rubbed his chin. "Sounds like I need to go over there."

"Alec Station?"

"Why not?"

"Well, people come to you, not . . . "

"I should be where the intelligence is analyzed by analysts, not an agency chief who manages thousands of people."

"When do you want to go?"

"Tomorrow."

"But they're in New York City—"

"Is this issue urgent?"

"Yes, sir."

"Then tomorrow it is. I'll have my people clear my slate."

## September 1

Manhattan nearly came to a standstill as the president visited the World Trade Center. CIA Director George Tenet flipped out when he learned President Gore was going to Alec Station.

"It's a secret site. Everybody will know where it's at now," the Director shouted on the phone to Clarke.

"It's in the World Trade Center," Clarke responded.

"It's one of the smaller buildings though. Nobody knows we're CIA. People think they're bankers."

"So, the president is checking local businesses. But we definitely don't want you there, because that would really tip off the media on what's happening."

Clarke hung up before Tenet could respond.

When President Gore walked through the doors with his Secret Security officers and Clarke, the receptionist asked for security clearance.

"Really?" Gore said.

"I'm sorry Mr. President," she said, blushing. "Go on back."

All thirty agents and analysts came out of their offices or cubicles to see the president.

"Is everybody here?" Gore asked.

The slack-jawed employees nodded their heads.

"Thank you for letting me into your private offices. I am here today because we have a dire situation and we need answers."

Several eyes darted over to Bikowsky.

"What is it that you need to know, Mr. President?"

"Are there any terrorists right now in the United States that you are aware of?"

Bikowsky blushed.

"Can you answer me, Ms. . . . "

"Ms. Bikowsky," she said, shaking the president's hand. "I need to ask my supervisor."

"I'm your ultimate supervisor, Ms. Bikowsky."

Clarke had a pen and paper ready.

"Khalid al-Mihdhar and Nawaf al-Hazmi are two Saudis involved in al-Qeada that are here some place."

"Where?"

"They were in Los Angeles and then San Diego. They enrolled in a flying school, but . . . we lost them after that."

"And you didn't tell the FBI? Anybody? Once they step foot on US soil, your job is over."

"We were tracking them, sir. We didn't want them getting arrested and having the FBI do a prosecution that nobody knows about for two to three years."

"But these guys are dangerous."

"And so is bin Laden. But he's not traveling to the US, is he? He's the big fish. They could lead us back to him."

Gore turned to Clarke. "Did you get the names?"

"Yes, sir."

"Anybody else we need to know about?" the President asked.

She shook her head. "But something big's about to happen."

"Keep monitoring the situation and let us know anything else. Not your supervisor or the director, us. Got it?"

"Yes, sir."

"That goes for the rest of you too."

The members of the unit nodded and said "Yes, sir." With that Gore marched out of the office.

SEPTEMBER 2

THE SAN DIEGO FBI FIELD office had been working to trace the two terrorists down. Agent Stephen Buehler went over to the Sorbi Flying Club at a small runway near Interstate 15.

He asked a flight instructor about al-Mihdhar and al-Hazmi.

"Yeah, I remember the two of them," the instructor said. "Horrible English. They wanted to fly Boeings. Tried to bribe me when they couldn't pass the basic written exam." He shook his head in disgust.

"Know any place we could find them?" Buehler asked.

He scratched his chin. "There's a mosque around here that I think they went to. I'll ask around."

An hour later Buehler met with an imam from Masjid Ar-Ribat Al-Islami. "The young men from Saudi Arabia were here. They grew close to our previous imam, Anwar al-Awlaki."

"Where did al-Awlaki go?"

"The Washington, DC area. I think he provides spiritual services for students at Georgetown."

Buehler called in his findings. Ended up that al-Awlaki was the imam at George Washington University. He'd also been arrested a few times for soliciting prostitutes in the San Diego area. The call went over to Quantico, and was forwarded to Clarke.

"Stake out his house," Clarke said on the phone to FBI director Freeh.

"He's well connected," Freeh said. "We can't have this blow up in our face."

"I don't care. He's close to al-Qaeda. He's also a john, so I don't think he's as holy as he pretends."

The director sighed, but the President had sent out a directive to all intelligence agencies giving Richard Clarke full authority to make decisions.

## SEPTEMBER 3

REPORTS CAME BACK FROM AGENTS that several people were visiting al-Awlaki's house in Fall's Church, Virginia. Photos were taken. Clarke called a meeting with Bikowsky and Freeh along with a few other agency representatives.

Bikowsky thumbed through the photos, stopping at one set. "That one with the mustache is Mihdhar."

"The one that looks like Oates from Hall and Oates?" Clarke asked.

She nodded. "Let's raid the place."

"It's not enough to get a court order. We need a positive identification," Freeh said.

"See?" Bikowsky said. "This is why we don't work with you guys."

"Or," Clarke said, "We can put al-Awlaki in a compromising position."

"Like what?" Bikowsky asked.

"Let's set up a sting," Clarke said. "That way he'll have to talk to us or we'll let people know about his extracurricular activities."

## SEPTEMBER 7

AL-AWLAKI WALKED INTO A DC hotel and took an elevator to the sixth floor. He looked around. Not like any of his members would be in a seedy joint like this, but you couldn't be too certain. He tapped lightly on the door. A woman in purple lingerie opened it.

"Come on inside," she said with a sideways smile.

He followed her, shutting the door.

"What would you like today, cutie?"

"What do you offer?"

"Everything. You just have to pay for it."

The tall, gaunt imam with round-spectacled glasses licked his lips in anticipation.

"How much does a rimjob and unprotected sex cost?"

"Unprotected?"

"Yes." He stroked his beard.

"That'll cost you extra. Let's say five hundred."

He shoved his hand inside his pants pocket and pulled out five hundred-dollar bills. She slid the money in her bra.

"Take your clothes off and get comfortable. I'll be back."

She blew him a kiss and strutted into the bathroom. In a matter of seconds, al-Awlaki stripped off his clothes and started to rub himself in anticipation.

The adjoining room door opened and al-Awlaki couldn't understand why men in dark jackets rushed in. What was happening?

Then the truth dawned on him. He grabbed a shirt, covering his holiest of regions.

"This is entrapment. This is religious persecution!"

"I bet your congregants would be interested in knowing where you spend their money," an FBI agent responded.

"They'll never believe you."

"Maybe, but we have video of you asking for a rimjob. Isn't that kind of sodomy forbidden by the Quran?"

The imam's mouth hinged open. This was definitely not a good position to be in.

"What do you want?"

"Tell me about two guys you know. Hazmi and Mihdhar."

Al-Awlaki pursed his lips and looked away. He couldn't give them up, could he? Not days before they were going to do something spectacular in the name of Allah. But then again, if he held out and they achieved success, wouldn't he be tried as an accomplice? It was hard to bargain with his dick in his hand.

"What do you want with them?"

"We need to talk to them."

"If I get you to them, can we, uh, forget this particular incident?"

The imam gave a sheepish smile to the agents.

SEPTEMBER 8

AT NINE IN THE MORNING, an undercover agent spotted five Middle-Eastern men enter a Gold's Gym in Greenbelt, Maryland.

Thirty minutes later, FBI agents entered the gym, walking up to the men as they lifted barbells.

"FBI. Hands up," an agent shouted, as his colleagues drew their pistols.

Raising his hands, Mihdhar dropped a 30 pound weight on Hazmi's foot.

\* \* \*

ALTHOUGH THE WEIGHTLIFTERS WEREN'T TALKING, the FAA confirmed they all had purchased tickets for American Flight 77 for September 11. One of the men, Hani Hanjour, was a certified pilot from Saudi Arabia. A search of Mihdhar's car revealed a flight manual for a 757 and flight paths to the Pentagon. Their hotel rooms had more material including box cutters and correspondence in Arabic. Since none of the agents knew Arabic, the documents were boxed up and sent to FBI agent Ali Soufan in New York, one of eight agents who knew Arabic.

The task force in DC gathered for a post-operations analysis and a quick celebration.

"We still need to be vigilant," Clarke warned. "Al-Qaeda might have another cell around."

SEPTEMBER 9

AT THREE IN THE MORNING, Clarke's cell phone rang, almost giving him a heart attack.

"Mr. Clarke, FBI agent Ali Soufan. I was given your personal number and told to call you whenever I finish my analysis."

"That is correct. I've heard great things about you. Tell me what you know."

"Examining all of the documents, there is more than one hijacking team planning to hit American targets with planes on Tuesday morning."

"Are you certain?"

"Dead certain."

"How many teams?"

"It looks like there are three more."

"What are the targets?"

"Two planes to hit each of the twin towers. One to hit the Pentagon and the other to hit the US Capitol. They're flying out of Newark, Boston, and DC."

"Do you know who they are?"

"Somebody named Atta is leading this attack."

"Atta what?"

"I don't know. A shot in the dark would be Mohamed."

"Of course."

"Most of the notes have either Atta's name or the assholes arrested at the gym. Although there's a note about Moussaoui replacing Jarrah for the Capitol job."

Clarke wrote everything down and hung up. There'd be no more sleep tonight. He'd call the FAA to look for any tickets in the names of Jarrah, Atta, and Moussaoui as well as the Treasury department to see if anybody with those names had made recent purchases.

* * *

ATTA WOKE UP AND BEGAN his morning prayers in the Milner Hotel in Boston. Two days to go until he could finally strike a dagger in the heart of the American monster. Everybody had their tickets. They knew their targets and their assigned jobs. They needed to say their prayers, stay calm, and follow through on September 11. He would meet with his team today, go over the plan one more time, and then pray some more.

* * *

THE FAA DISCOVERED A ZIAD Jarrah who had purchased tickets to United 93 from New Jersey to San Francisco. The Treasury Department found a charge under his name at the Newark Airport Marriott hotel. An Atta was found to have charged a room in a Boston hotel. The FBI put squads together in each city to capture the terrorists. Working with hotel management, the agents established associates of their primary targets. The teams would raid each hotel simultaneously in the morning so the terrorists wouldn't be able to alert the others.

SEPTEMBER 10

CLARKE AND HIS TEAM SAT in the situation room around a speakerphone waiting to hear the results. He began pacing.

The Newark team called first.

"We've apprehended four terrorists, including Jarrah," the agent-in-charge said.

The group cheered.

"How are they reacting?" Clarke asked.

"Two fought. One hid. And Jarrah started crying."

"What do you mean crying?" Clarke asked.

"I think he's relieved. He's been muttering in Arabic, but I heard him say 'Thank God' in English."

Boston called two minutes later.

"Good news and bad news," the agent-in-charge said.

Everybody in the room took a deep breath.

"Okay, what's the good?" Clarke said.

"We apprehended five suspected terrorists. They've got tickets and flight manuals, but Atta left early this morning."

Clarke hit his palm on the table. "Shit. Wasn't anybody watching the lobby?"

"I'm not sure how, but he disappeared. I'm sorry."

\* \* \*

ATTA HAD PICKED UP SAUDI bruiser Abdulaziz al-Omari at the Park Inn Hotel north of Boston early in the morning. They drove for two hours up to South Portland, Maine where they checked into a Comfort Inn. The two were solemn, hardly speaking a word. The quiet remained as they dined on a double crust supreme at Pizza

Hut. Their last dinner before heaven, if that was God's will. Atta liked this silence. Why couldn't the other days of his life have been more like this instead of the nonstop chatter and noise he encountered on his recent travels? Please let heaven be like this.

Atta got a call from overseas while he and Omari were walking back to their hotel with bellies full of pizza.

"Jarrah and al-Shehhi got arrested."

Atta's bowels clenched. "That leaves only me. I can take out one of the towers."

"You should. Virgins will be waiting for you in heaven."

Atta hung up, trying not to think about an eternity of future humiliations.

Later that night, Atta prayed, reciting Quran verses until he fell asleep on his mat. Five hours later, he woke, still prostrate. He went into the shower with a plastic razor. Turning on the water, he lathered himself with soap. He began shaving his chest, taking off the hard wiry hairs. Next his armpits followed by his legs. He went over his back as best he could. Finally, he needed to remove his pubic hair. Sighing, he shaved the dark tufts away, revealing his bumps of shame. A virus he caught in Hamburg. A secret nobody knew about except for a doctor who had prescribed medication. Atta wanted to kill the man for the knowledge he possessed. Luckily for Dr. Heinrich, that never happened.

Out of the shower, Atta bathed himself in cologne. Nobody would prepare his body for burial, not when he'd be incinerated in a jet explosion. That was wonderful. Nobody would know his secret. Only God, himself, and oh yeah, that infidel German doctor. A pang of fear hit Atta. He hoped that patient-client confidentiality agreements continued after a person died. He didn't want this martyrdom to be tarnished by a loudmouth Westerner.

## SEPTEMBER 11

ATTA KNOCKED ON OMARI'S DOOR at four-thirty in the morning. The bleary-eyed muscle rubbed his eyes.

"Is it time?"

"Did you shave your body? Put on cologne?"

"Yes shave. No cologne yet. Give me ten minutes."

"Five."

He nodded and walked into the bathroom. Atta stepped back in the hallway next to his suitcase. How had Omari been able to sleep? He had a wife and kid too. Such an amazing sacrifice. He looked at his watch. Plenty of time. The other three hijackers would board with him on the flight in Boston. Should he call them again? No need to put his people on edge. He'd see them in the waiting room.

Omari opened the door. His hair was wet and his body reeked of Polo cologne.

"Did you use the whole bottle?" Atta asked.

Omari shrugged. "Did somebody else want to use it?"

Atta drove to the South Portland Jetport with the windows down. While proper Muslims anoint their dead with perfume before burial, this was ridiculous.

He parked in a lot nearest the airport. $60 a day. Good luck getting payment on that bill, infidels.

At 5:40am, they walked into the airport carrying attaché cases. Atta's had maps with the coordinates to New York City, photocopies of a 747 manual, and the Quran.

"Mohammed Atta," a voice shouted from behind.

He turned. Two men in suits with two uniformed police officers stood fifteen feet away. Oh no. Turning back he spotted two police officers next to the metal detector.

"Run, brother," Omari shouted, swinging his attaché case and tackling three of the four lawmen.

Atta took off sprinting to a door with "Do Not Enter" printed across it. He hit the push bar at full speed. A loud siren wailed as he ran on to the tarmac, dodging a passing baggage cart. The cart driver swerved and bags flew off the cars, knocking down two pursuing officers. Running down the middle of the airfield, Atta realized the jets were impossible to get into from the ground. Besides, no pushback-tug operator would help a hijacker back out a commercial jet. What was he going to do? He could not fail on this holy mission.

The sun broke through the horizon, and Atta spotted a bright yellow plane glowing in the distance. It was like a vision from heaven. An avenue of escape like the Prophet's hegira from Mecca to Medina. Closing the distance, he saw a lone operator going through his pre-flight checklist. Atta wondered if the plane, an unmistakable Piper Cub, was too small to carry out his mission. Could it even break the tower's window?

A man holding a gun chased after him. He needed to have faith, not questions. God would see him through.

As the pilot started climbing into the cockpit, Atta clocked him over the head. The man dropped to the tarmac. Atta climbed in, tossing his attaché in the back passenger seat. A key hung from the ignition. He turned the engine over. The propeller spun rapidly. God is great. The door to the Cub flew open. A pasty, out-of-breath agent pointed a pistol at Atta.

"FBI. You're under arrest—"

The Egyptian smiled and released the brake. The plane took off, causing the agent to fall. The gun fired, a bullet fracturing the windshield. More agents and police ran towards Atta, but the Piper had too much speed. It just needed to gain altitude before the runway ended. This plane was odd: only a stick poked up by Atta's crotch and his feet controlled the steering. He'd read about these planes before, but never flown one.

The wheels bounced off the pavement and onto the grass. The Fore River lay ahead. Atta closed his eyes and prayed as he pulled on the stick between his legs. The flaps went down and the plane rose. The wheels skimmed the top leaves of trees. His mission, while compromised, wasn't over. God was still with him.

\* \* \*

CLARKE PACED IN THE SITUATION ROOM, furious. "What do you mean Atta got away?"

"I'm sorry," FBI director Freeh answered. "Omari took our men by surprise. He knocked some of the agents down, and then a luggage cart . . . "

The director faded under Clarke's sharp glare.

"Where's Atta now?"

"He hijacked a small two-seat plane. A Piper Cub."

"What are you guys, the Keystone cops?" Clarke turned to the Air Force general. "I want jets scrambled to follow this plane. I'd like to have him taken alive if possible, but if he gets too close to a high density population center, shoot him down."

"I'm on it."

"Do we know where he's at right now?" Clarke asked the FAA representative.

"He is flying really low, mostly under the radar outside of a blip here and there. He's definitely headed south. That much is for sure."

"Can we call him? Try to talk him down?"

"It's my understanding this plane doesn't have a radio. It has mostly original equipment besides an automatic starter."

"What is the range of a Piper Cub?"

An aide typed on her laptop. "Two-hundred-and-twenty-five miles."

"How far is DC from there?"

*Click-click-click.* "Five-hundred-and-thirty-nine miles."

"How far is New York from there?"

*Click-click-click.* "Two-hundred-sixty–eight miles."

"So that would leave Boston as a target, right?"

"An improvised target," Bikowsky said.

"Let's scramble the jets there too," Clarke said.

The general nodded.

\* \* \*

ATTA PUTTERED ALONG IN THIS strange aircraft, keeping his altitude below 100 feet, hoping to avoid radar detection. He could barely see over the dashboard and the basic gauges felt pre-historic. He had trained for months on Boeing jets and now he had this little yellow machine from the 1940s. Crazy world. He reached over his seat to the back and grabbed his attaché.

Unzipping it, he brought out a map and studied it. According to the old-fashioned compass, he was heading south, which was great. He'd been over the ocean for quite a while and needed to head more southwest. He didn't know how long it took to get to New York or if he had the fuel to get there, but there seemed to be a wind beneath his wings like the hand of God, propelling him forward.

\* \* \*

FOUR F-16 JETS ARMED WITH sidewinder missiles flew around the city of Boston.

"Where is he?" Clarke shouted.

"He might've crashed into the ocean," Freeh said.

Clarke considered that. "No. Not unless we had him cornered. He believes he's going to escape and might be trying to hit New York."

"That's impossible," Bikowsy said.

The FAA rep cleared her throat. "Um, there's a strong southern headwind."

"What does that mean?" Clarke asked.

"He's saving fuel and might have enough to make it to New York."

"I'll tell O'Neill and the Army to keep their eyes open."

\* \* \*

ATTA KEPT PRAYING AND STAYING low. The flying contraption had no gas gauge that he could see, so he had no idea how much fuel was left. According to his map—which was hard to unfold in such a small area—he should be coming up on New York Harbor any time. He had flown through a section of Rhode Island and then into Long Island Sound. Finally he saw New York City with all of the ugly, insufferable Western architecture. He couldn't wait to destroy the most obnoxious structure of all.

Somehow in fantasizing the destruction, he got lost. Trying to keep low with so many tall buildings, he mistook the East River for the Hudson and had been flying around Brooklyn trying to find the World Trade Center.

He turned west and, flying past Governor's Island, he finally spotted the evil towers. "Allah Akbar," he shouted. Destiny at last.

To his left stood the Statue of Liberty and he considered how much more realistically he could damage the statue than a 100-story building. But he promised Khalid that he'd take down the Trade Center, so that's what he'd do.

Straightening the plane, he flew into the wind. Gaining altitude, he aimed his yellow machine at the south tower, planning to smash into the upper two-thirds of the building.

\* \* \*

RETIRED FBI AGENT AND NOW head of security at the World Trade Center, John O'Neill, stood on top of Tower One with a cigar in his mouth. The day was a crystal clear enough to see a puny yellow plane puttering up the harbor towards him.

"That's the best you got, bin Laden? Ya piece of shit."

An Army Sergeant with a Stringer missile company stood beside him.

"Get ready," the sergeant called to his men.

"Target in sight, sir," a soler said, holding the missile-rocket launcher.

Two Apache helicopters flew overhead at top speed, the vibrations of their motors shaking the roof.

"God-dangit," the sergeant said. "Hold fire."

The sergeant looked so mad, O'Neill thought he might throw his beret off the tower.

\* \* \*

ATTA SAW THE TWO HELICOPTERS racing toward him and laughed.

"You can't stop me. I've got God. You've got the Devil," Atta shouted. "You're pathetic!"

Then the engine began to sputter.

"Oh no, no. Please no. Not now. Please God."

The plane began a descent.

\* \* \*

FROM ATOP OF THE TOWER, O'Neill watched the yellow plane splash into the harbor twenty yards from the shore. He laughed and handed out cigars to the soldiers.

"Looks like your Towers are safe, even without the Army," the sergeant said.

O'Neill shook his head. "Nah. They're never safe until Osama bin Laden's dead."

"Who?" a soldier asked as he accepted a light.

"The biggest threat to American safety since the Soviet Union."

"One guy?"

"Yep, one guy and a religion he's twisted to get people to kill themselves."

"Sounds like a short-lived movement to me."

O'Neill puffed on his cigar. "You'd think."

\* \* \*

ATTA POPPED OPEN THE CABIN door. Freezing water filled the cabin. Should he sink with the plane or escape and kill infidels by hand? He still had his Swiss Army knife. Maybe slash a few throats before they killed him. As he pushed himself out of the cockpit, his pant leg caught on the stick. He splashed to the surface, taking a gulp of air. But the sinking plane pulled him down. He struggled, but could not free his leg. Unable to hold his breath, salty, polluted water filled Atta's mouth.

He heard a splash and felt hands around his waist, but passed out before he figured out what was happening.

* * *

ATTA OPENED UP HIS EYES and coughed up seawater from his lungs. A man, inches away from his mouth jerked back.

"He's breathing!"

Wait, did that man have his mouth on his? More water surged out of Atta's lungs and he wanted to die. No, no. He was not a homosexual. More coughing. Through tear-streaked eyes he looked at the crowd of people around him, many with cameras taking photos. Several pointed at his crotch and laughed. That was when he realized he was naked below the waist.

## SEPTEMBER 13

PRESIDENT GORE HANDED CLARKE A glass of cognac.

"The Saudi embassy is officially upset that we've arrested so many of their citizens, but I've received word they're thrilled we caught them."

"That's to be expected. More face-saving."

"On the domestic front, Rush Limbaugh and his echo chamber are saying this whole thing was a boondoggle," Gore said with a smirk.

"Doesn't he know we saved thousands of American lives?" Clarke asked incredulously.

"He doesn't care. It's all about tearing down my name, regardless of the cost. Party over country, hands down."

"Reminds me of terrorists we've encountered. Unhinged nihilistic fanaticism."

Gore nodded. "Leveraging fanaticism for power. All you need is faith, not facts."

"Let's hope nobody that narcissistic ever wins the presidency."

"Hear! Hear!"

They clinked glasses.

# BUT ONE LIFE TO GIVE
## BY PETER CARLAFTES

I'M ABOUT TO MEET MY hero in the flesh. Me—Beau Brainer. Waiting to pass through White House security. Soon to be face-to-face with President Donald J. Trump. I'd come oh-so-close twice before he won the election. Back in '01 with the mint deal and then my audition for Season Five of *The Apprentice*. Destined both times for major success but somehow the fates turned against me. Need I say—now, with Spot Juan Dot Com, the third time will positively be a charm . . .

A tall, pale guard sealed in dark green camos beckoned me forth, commanding, "Please remove your keys, wallet, cell, and place them in the orange bowl then put your belt and jacket into the plastic bin, Sir." To which I quickly complied. He signaled me through the scanner.

"Halt!" he barked—left hand up, right hand edging toward the holstered gun at his hip and, before I could pass, asked, pointing, "What's that thing wrapped there around your neck, Sir?"

"Uhm," I fluttered, somewhat embarrassed. "It's just a soft brace. I was injured in Mexico not too long ago. It's made out of some kind of pliable plastic. Shouldn't set anything off. At least it hasn't. I mean, not in any airport."

The guard stared me down and then waved me on through. No alarm sounded.

The second guard, seated behind the screen, watched my items pass without incident, and when they arrived where I stood intact the first guard leveled his left arm, directing, "Please pick up your belongings and situate yourself on that black marble bench under the portrait of Jared and Ivanka, Sir. We'll take you in shortly."

As I made my way over to the bench, slipping my suit coat back on, the first guard spoke quietly into his headset, "Another guy with a cast. When was the last one? . . . Right—the knee brace. So is this like the same thing? . . . Absolutely. No problem." The first guard gave a thumbs up to the second one.

I sat under the very life-like portrait of the second couple and made sure I had turned off my cell phone.

---

*(from a command post across the Potomac in Virginia)*

*COMMAND: O.B-Wan, Command. Do you read me?*

*(from a different location in Washington)*

*O.B-WAN: Loud and clear.*

*COMMAND: The bull is in the China Shop.*

*O.B-WAN: Copy. We're listening. Over.*

---

I have been a huge fan of Donald Trump since first reading *The Art of The Deal* back in high school. I was most impressed with how he was able to put deals together with his cocky attitude at a time when New York City was bankrupt in the late 70s. He had laid all the groundwork for many hotels and of course Trump Tower which sprang up from an outright never-gonna-happen. After reading his book I decided—THIS IS WHAT I WANT TO DO IN LIFE: MAKE DEALS; AND FROM THOSE DEALS: MAKE MONEY.

Insomuch that, when the opportunity arose, I took a job with a roommate from Penn's (yes, *that* Penn) family business the day I graduated in the Spring of 2001.

Their company had such a great relationship with a food-processing plant and packaging company in Taiwan at the time who was ready to manufacture the product then customize the wrappers. COMP–LE–MINTS was the product's name and the plan was to have these tasty little morsels laid out on every pillow in eight million hotel rooms around the globe. It's truly hard to fathom how much profit can be generated with a product of this caliber placed everywhere. Consider the Gideon Bible. We had tested the market base for a managed, intentional experience and the numbers were astronomical. In the U.S., we had three different colored packages (red, white, and blue) and each mint was color-coded to three words (ON: red, THE: white, HOUSE: blue) so when a service employee cleaned the room, three mints were laid out on each pillow with those words in order—ON THE HOUSE. Super positive reaction. And we could arrange colors for any country's flag in the world. And the words or the saying could easily change languages. Take France. While the flag colors were the same, the three segments could read—the French equivalent. Europe, Asia, etc. After Hilton showed remarkable interest in mid-August, I scheduled a meeting with the Trump Organization for late September which I heard the Donald himself had placed at the top of his list.

After 9/11, the hospitality industry tanked, so I began a new career as an Assistant VP to the COO of a Fortune 500 in Chicago listed number nine by *Forbes*, but this position only lessened the odds of my ever getting close to Trump. Three years of the grind passed before another amazing project fell into my lap. And I didn't want to just meet Donald Trump. I wanted to impress him.

I had met Trump a handful of times. He signed a book or something like a kitchen magnet with his face embossed, nodded his head, and off one went as if touched by an angel at this or that guest appearance. He even answered a letter I wrote him after reading *The Art of the Deal* in 10th grade though I doubt very much he'd remember. I knew his letter by heart though:

*"Dear Beau, Unusual name. You should think about changing it to something more acceptable if you really want to make it in this world. Anyhow—it's great to hear you love my book. I have a feeling you'll go far. Especially if you change your name. Truly, Donald J. Trump—*

Still have it framed above my desk at the office. And I guess he was right. His analysis inspired me to work all that much harder without changing my name.

The next time I almost had the future president's ear was in the summer of 2005. A fantastic opportunity came along that I couldn't refuse. I cashed in my corporate perch at the ripe young age of 25 and put in with a thriving entrepreneur by the name of Carl Frandee in Sarasota, Florida. The product was can't lose.

Fifteen years ago, Climate Change was not the dire be-all end-all it has manifested into today. Our product was an applicably-suited alternative hypothesis to the whole idea of Climate Change. The product was an impulse-counter liquid called One Degree. That was it. One Degree. And what One Degree did was lower the body temperature one degree from 98.6 to 97.6—or thereabouts. And the ripple effect for this was plain and simple: If five billion people ingested a One Degree per diem, the Earth's surface temperature would be lowered by five billion degrees. And that would only benefit all the inhabitants of our third rock from the sun. Sure, there were detractors, but for every jeer of *Snake Oil!* there were four *Changed My Life's*.

The numbers were staggering. Capital was pouring into our venture. And since my hero was at the top of his game with a hit TV show, I felt my concurrent success worthy of taking another stab at seeing him. I put in an application and was soon accepted to audition for *The Apprentice* in June.

There were many haters of One Degree. Their main pushback was that the internal temperature of Earth's denizens had zero to do with global warming, but no one could really argue against a figure like five billion degrees. We needed no FDA approval. Unfortunately, luck was not on my side. Carl Frandee absconded with all of the company's funds in mid-April. Twenty-eight million dollars to be exact. They said follow the money. There was none to follow. Frandee disappeared without a trace. This must've been his true calling because the authorities never found him. I was under investigation for eight months which is why I lost my chance to appear on the show. What a setback! I could've made billions. Instead—Frandee vanished to what may have been a Micronesian atoll or some completely cloistered spot in the Caymans. And I had to return to the corporate grind.

*"BRAINER!"* screamed the first guard.

I sprang up out of my reverie. "Yes!"

He smiled walking towards me, "How's the neck?"

"Uh . . ." his question threw me. "Kind of sore. Why?"

"Because we care about our guests," he answered politely. "Turn right and go through that door and then straight ahead across the lobby till you reach the reception desk. They're almost ready."

"For what?" I asked.

"For *you*," he beamed, pointing. I gestured at the doorway. The guard slowly nodded and when I stepped into the lobby I heard him whisper, "Godspeed."

---

```
COMMAND: The fox is in the henhouse.

O.B-WAN: Affirmative. Let's hope he doesn't
run off to fire someone again.

COMMAND: Very unlikely. There's nobody left.

O.B-WAN: Good point. Over.
```

---

Crossing the West Wing lobby of the White House, I knew this deal was already done. I'd spent the last twelve years of my life managing a consulting platform for start-ups called MEGA. We opened doors for some of the most innovative tech firms in the country, placed their top-of-house, and put them on creative paths to prosperity. My first major client was Airbnb. That was in 2009. Not an easy year to raise capital with the new administration treading water. My portfolio reads like a *Who's Who* of digital success. But when those two kids from Texas came to me six months ago with a wireframe for Spot Juan Dot Com, I instantly knew this was my ticket to ride.

I caught a glimpse to my left of the curly blonde's enormous bust behind the desk and, uncontrollably mouthed the words *Oh My God*, approaching her radiance.

"You must be Beau Brainer," she said through a smile.

"I am indeed!" I playfully responded.

"My name is Valkyrie. I'll be your liaison until they call you in."

She must've been late 20s—maybe early 30s. I couldn't take my eyes off her lightly-curved breasts pressed inside a metallic-blue tunic. She seemed to understand all at once.

"Stare all you want," Valkyrie granted. "Everyone else does. That's why I'm here!"

"I'm really sorry, I—uh . . ."

"This is the first day of spring," Valkyrie flirted, adding, "Don't you have a girlfriend?"

I said, "Well, actually I do. Her name's Alicia. Haven't seen her since we got back from Mexico two weeks ago. We went down to celebrate my setting up this meeting with the President."

"Where did you go?" she asked.

"Cancun. I met her only a few months ago at a New Year's Eve party. I'd been so wrapped up with this pitch, it was nice to get away and just relax for a bit."

"Sounds perfect," soothed Valkyrie. "Have a seat on the settee to my left. I heard that Vice President Pence is already inside with the President, so it shouldn't be much longer."

```
COMMAND: The kids are in the candy store.

O.B-WAN: Release the resin-marker.

COMMAND: Affirmative.

O.B-WAN: Every second counts now. Over.
```

When I sat, Valkyrie looked at my neck brace and asked, "What happened to you?"

I told her that I'd had a parasailing mishap down in Cancun. "It's funny, but I don't remember one second of agreeing to parasail or even parasailing at all for that matter. This was on our third day there. We'd been drinking a little. Not much. A few shots of tequila—nowhere near blackout drunk. And the next thing I know I'm in a bed at the American hospital where a doctor is wrapping my neck with this thing. Alicia said I must've had some kind of allergic reaction to the alcohol or something because I was hellbent on parasailing and it sure seemed like I understood the instructions for lift-off, but when it came time to lift-off—I took a step back instead of forward and jammed my neck against the side of the floating square dock and did some damage. Luckily there were knowledgeable people there to get me untangled and to the hospital. And the doctor was adamant that I do not remove the soft brace for one month or else. There was no way I was going to miss another meeting with my hero."

"How does it feel?" Valkyrie asked.

"A little sore," I answered. "And now it's starting to feel a bit warm. I almost cut this damn brace off today. I was worried about first impressions."

"Don't," she blushed. "You made a great one on me!"

Worked like a charm.

She asked, "Where'd you get the name Beau?"

"Funny you should ask . . ." I sat down on the bench and continued, "My parents were at the movies in the winter of 1979 and that was the first time I kicked my mother's belly. And when she looked up at the screen there was the actor Beau Bridges in the movie *Norma Rae*. So I was named Beau for that reason. Had I been a girl my name would've been Sally since Sally Field was the star of the film."

"That's such a sweet story!" Valkyrie cooed.

"Where did you get the name Valkyrie?"

"Because I *am* a Valkyrie," she answered.

"Haha!" I started laughing when the desk phone rang once and Valkyrie pushed speaker.

"Yes, Mr. President?" She asked.

"Who is this?" the inimitable voice thrust.

"My name's Valkyrie!"

"What color is your hair?" Trump asked.

Valkyrie told him blond.

"Good," he allowed. "I told them to only hire blonds. And what size—you know, what size is your bra?"

"38D, Mr. President."

There was a short silence.

Trump asked, "Is my man out there with this Juan thing?"

"Yes, sir. He's very eager to see you."

"Well, tell him that I'm sitting here with Mike and that Mitch and Lindz are on their way, so as soon as they get here we're gonna bring him right in. Okay?" Trump said.

"Yes, sir," agreed Valkyrie.

He added, "Thanks." More silence. "I told them 38 was unacceptable . . ."

Valkyrie turned off speaker and explained, "They should be ready for you shortly."

I had to get my game face on now. Trump, Pence, McConnell, and Graham. They'd be eating out of my hand in no time. My plan was win/win for the entire administration and the US of A. My soft brace was hot and strange to the touch.

---

COMMAND: The boys are back in town.

O.B-WAN: What's the Thermalyte reading?

COMMAND: All systems go!

O.B-WAN: This is bigger than Geronimo with
Seal Team Six.

COMMAND: Copy that!

O.B-WAN: We're going high. Over.

---

"What's this Juan thing the President spoke of?" Valkyrie asked.

"A game changer!" I answered, adding, "No. A *world* changer. There's approximately 2,000 miles of U.S./Mexican border. Right?"

Valkyrie nodded.

"Well. On Spot Juan Dot Com every U.S. citizen can sign up to be daily border control agents by logging on to the satellite surveillance platform where every chosen agent is assigned a random quarter mile sector to surveil for a two-hour shift. And if there is any illegal activity, the agent reports this immediately and the nearest border checkpoint will spring into action."

Valkyrie asked, "So you basically sign up to turn in your fellow man?"

"Exactly!" I agreed. "It cuts right to the core of the human condition. We can keep our country safe with minimal expense above initial outlay and operating costs. Spot Juan Dot Com will save the government billions. And our labor cost is zero. See. Like I said, there are approximately 2,000 miles of U.S./Mexican border and each mile is broken up into quarters—so that makes 8,000 sectors. Then there are twelve two-hour shifts per day, that twelve times eight for a total of 96,000 shifts per day. Plus you need another 96,000 completely random back up agents to make sure the first shift doesn't try to use their power to abet the enemy. So say 200,000 Americans per day protecting our southern border. What could be more patriotic?"

"I guess you're right," Valkyrie admitted, "But isn't "Juan" just a bit of a slur?"

"Not in the least," I jumped. "J.U.A.N. stands for Joint Undesirable Alien Neutralization. Believe me—we've thought this thing out. And we could enhance the program by allotting tax credit to those who complete X amount of exemplary service. Even put their Social Security into a higher-yield market. The possibilities are endless. And it's win/win for everyone!"

"Might even monetize the system eventually," she suggested.

"Absolutely! Every American would be honored to serve."

"I probably shouldn't tell you this," Valkyrie began, "But, about two months ago another man like yourself came to meet the President with a similar proposition. I think his had a wall built out of lasers at the border. Impossible to penetrate. Well. He also had a similar accident on jet skis in Bermuda or somewhere like that. Wore a knee brace. Sat right where you are but the president had to go wine and dine half the Senate."

"Were you here at the time?"

"No," she answered. "He had his own Valkyrie. And his own Alicia!"

"Now what's that supposed to mean? I mean, earlier you said *you* were a Valkyrie—"

The intercom buzzed and she put it on speaker.

"Send in Brainer," ordered Trump.

"Right away, Mr. President," she replied.

There was another short silence and Trump's voice continued, "What do you mean they can impeach me again on a different charge? Whatever happened to Double Jeopardy?"

Then what sounded like Senator McConnell's voice chimed in, "Double Jeopardy doesn't apply to impeachment, Donny. Not to worry either way. They can't touch you in the Senate."

Valkyrie clicked off the speaker and told me, "Straight down this hall. Second door to your right."

I quickly stood up, cleared my throat, and adjusted my red tie. My neck was burning.

Valkyrie asked, "Do you really like Trump?"

"I don't have to like him," I answered. "I admire his acumen. We are a nation of consumers. And Trump's greatest strength is his ability to consume." I winked, passing her desk, "If I pull off this deal, I'll be one of the richest men on the planet."

"You'll be well remembered," she whispered as I made my way off down the hall.

---

COMMAND: Device ready for detonation.

O.B-WAN: I'm almost feeling sorry for the guy.

COMMAND: Why? He's the perfect patsy.

O.B-WAN: He got us into Trump's spin zone.

COMMAND: Our team in Mexico did their job.

O.B-WAN: All systems go. Over.

---

Kellyanne Conway quickly crossed paths with me, talking on her cell phone. "I'm telling you, George," she explained, "It's like way worse than the Ides of March. Everybody knows! Well I'm gonna need a job, George."

I turned back and watched Kellyanne disappear around the corner and noticed Valkyrie pulling up the sleeves of a colorful metallic silver coat. She blew a kiss and ran off in the same direction as Kellyanne. My armpits were soaked.

I'd always heard about how disruptive life was inside the walls of Trump's White House but had no idea things would be quite so crazy. Didn't bother me in the least. I was here to put over a very worthy deal for everyone.

---

COMMAND: Spot Juan Dot Com is an exceptional idea, Sir.

O.B-WAN: We could always run it by Nancy.

COMMAND: That's right. He won't, uh . . . It's your idea now!

O.B-WAN: We could use it as leverage to register voters.

COMMAND: Perhaps you could run again, Sir?

O.B-WAN: Not unless we get rid of the 22nd Amendment.

COMMAND: We're taking our country back.

O.B-WAN: Godspeed . . .

---

I arrived at the open doorway of the Oval Office. The view looked like a lead story on Fox. There stood Trump behind his desk with a welcoming smile and right hand held out for the taking while his left was a big thumbs up. Pence flanked his right side, with McConnell flanking his left, and Graham to Pence's right. I made a beeline for Donald Trump's outstretched hand.

---

. . . Over.

---

# ABOUT THE CONTRIBUTORS

ERIC BEETNER *(Bush Jr.)* is the author of 23 novels and zero happy endings. The award nominations are plentiful, the wins less so. His story is about a fictional article in the Constitution, but, man, he wishes it were real. Also, this marks the first time he's used "fisticuffs" in a story, but it won't be the last.

PETER CARLAFTES *(Trump)* has edited three noir anthologies and published a total of eight mystery/noir collections, including the Anthony Award-winning *The Obama Inheritance*, which is the companion piece to *The Faking of the President*. The next milestone he's waiting for is #46.

CHRISTOPHER CHAMBERS *(Madison)* is the author of numerous novels (including the forthcoming Three Rooms Press release, *Scavenger*), as well as short stories, pulp novellas and graphic novels of dubious quality yet like many a POTUS has conned the public into accolades. He spends his free time warping young minds at Georgetown University two miles from the White House.

SARAH M. CHEN *(Pence)* has published numerous short stories and her noir novella was an Anthony finalist and IPPY Award-winner. She's held various jobs like private investigator assistant, studio script reader, indie bookseller, and bartender. The one job she'd never take on is POTUS and not just because she's Canadian.

ANGEL LUIS COLÓN *(Eisenhower)* is the Derringer and Anthony Award nominated writer of five books including his latest novel *Hell Chose Me.* In his down time, he edits anthologies and produces the writer interview podcast, *the bastard title.* While he doesn't believe in anything as patently ridiculous as squirrels taking over the world, he's not that surprised to see the White House filled with a bunch of nuts.

S. A. COSBY *(Bush Sr.)* is an award-winning writer from southeastern Virginia who doesn't believe in conspiracy theories . . . he believes in conspiracy facts!

NIKKI DOLSON *(Reagan)* is a Derringer-nominated writer and the author of two books. She lives in Las Vegas where pirates and feathered people roam, where a door to New York is just down the street from a door that leads to Paris and where, if you're lucky, you might see subtle magic at a convenience store or hear about a government official with a clockwork heart.

MARY ANNA EVANS *(Wilson)* is the author of the Faye Longchamp archaeological mysteries. She is also an assistant professor of professional writing at the University of Oklahoma, where she teaches impressionable young people how to get paid for telling big, whopping lies in print for all to see. Mary Anna has never personally infiltrated the White House and upset the world order, but she has ideas about how one could do it.

KATE FLORA *(FDR/Huey Long)* is an Edgar, Anthony, Agatha, and Derringer finalist who leans toward the dark side. Twenty-two books and a lotta stories into this career, the chicken farmer's daughter from Maine fell in love with Huey Long's populist support for the little people and small business and income inequality. She's sorry about what she did to him.

ADAM LANCE GARCIA'S *(Jackson)* first novel, *The Land of Nowhere*, was written entirely in crayon and remains unfinished to this day. However, Adam is currently completing the final chapter of his *Green Lama: Legacy* series and beginning the third volume of his graphic novel, *Sons of Fire*. In addition to print work, he is a writer and producer of the audio drama podcast *Radio Room*. When not writing or photographing his cats, Adam works as a video producer in Manhattan.

DANNY GARDNER *(Lincoln)* is a screenwriter, comedian, and three-time award-nominated writer of *A Negro and an Ofay*. He believes life is too short, and far too fragile, to not express ourselves truly.

ALISON GAYLIN *(Nixon)* is the Edgar Award-winning author of 11 books. A former reporter for a supermarket tabloid, she enjoys writing about people doing despicable things. While the events in her story are mostly fictitious, she does believe that Las Vegas is a magical place, where pretty much anything can happen.

GREG HERREN *(Buchanan)* is the award-winning author of over thirty novels and fifty short stories. He enjoys researching James Buchanan because it reminds him that things could, in fact, be worse.

GARY PHILLIPS *(Clinton)* must keep writing to forestall his appointment at the crossroads. All those Jack Kirby-drawn Marvel comic books and original *Twilight Zones* he devoured as a kid have shaped his work as much as jobs delivering dog cages, printing shampoo labels, or running a political action committee. Turns out is everything is through the looking glass, baby.

TRAVIS RICHARDSON *(Gore)* has been a finalist for the Anthony, Macavity, and Derringer short story awards. He is the author of two novellas and a short story collection, *Bloodshot and Bruised.* He often wonders what would have happened and where America and the world would be today if the outcome of the 2000 election had reflected the true will of Florida voters (and the country).

S. J. ROZAN *(FDR)* is a best-selling award-winning immigrant-loving patriarchy-smashing fellow-traveling red-diaper baby from the Bronx. www.sjrozan.net

ALEX SEGURA *(JFK)* is the twice Anthony Award-nominated author of the Pete Fernandez Miami Mystery series, comic books like *The Black Ghost* and *The Archies,* and the *Lethal Lit* podcast from iHeart Radio. He's been obsessed with the Kennedy assassination since as far back as he can remember and wishes he could time travel himself to figure out just what the hell happened.

ABBY L. VANDIVER *(LBJ)* is a *USA Today* and *Wall Street Journal* best-selling author of some 25, give or take, novels and short stories. A former lawyer, she now writes about murderers instead of looking to defend them. She has penned a few stories with characters that hail from Texas, however, this is the first one she thinks might be true. Born and raised in the city that sits on one of the few rivers that caught fire and where the music that rocks and rolls was named and is now housed, she often has a hard time remembering to be politically correct.

ERICA WRIGHT'S *(T. Roosevelt)* latest novel is *Famous in Cedarville,* and her latest poetry collection is *All the Bayou Stories End with Drowned.* She has yet to take up taxidermy but is a frequent visitor to natural history museums.

# RECENT AND FORTHCOMING BOOKS FROM THREE ROOMS PRESS

## FICTION

Rishab Borah
*The Door to Inferna*

Meagan Brothers
*Weird Girl and What's His Name*

Christopher Chambers
*Scavenger*

Ron Dakron
*Hello Devilfish!*

Robert Duncan
*Loudmouth*

Michael T. Fournier
*Hidden Wheel*
*Swing State*

William Least Heat-Moon
*Celestial Mechanics*

Aimee Herman
*Everything Grows*

Eamon Loingsigh
*Light of the Diddicoy*
*Exile on Bridge Street*

John Marshall
*The Greenfather*

Aram Saroyan
*Still Night in L.A.*

Richard Vetere
*The Writers Afterlife*
*Champagne and Cocaine*

Julia Watts
*Quiver*

## MEMOIR & BIOGRAPHY

Nassrine Azimi and Michel Wasserman
*Last Boat to Yokohama: The Life and
Legacy of Beate Sirota Gordon*

William S. Burroughs & Allen Ginsberg
*Don't Hide the Madness:
William S. Burroughs in Conversation
with Allen Ginsberg*
edited by Steven Taylor

James Carr
*BAD: The Autobiography of
James Carr*

Richard Katrovas
*Raising Girls in Bohemia:
Meditations of an American Father*

Judith Malina
*Full Moon Stages:
Personal Notes from
50 Years of The Living Theatre*

Phil Marcade
*Punk Avenue: Inside the New York City
Underground, 1972–1982*

Alvin Orloff
*Disasterama! Adventures in the Queer
Underground 1977–1997*

Nicca Ray
*Ray by Ray: A Daughter's Take
on the Legend of Nicholas Ray*

Stephen Spotte
*My Watery Self:
Memoirs of a Marine Scientist*

## PHOTOGRAPHY-MEMOIR

Mike Watt
*On & Off Bass*

## SHORT STORY ANTHOLOGIES

### SINGLE AUTHOR

*The Alien Archives: Stories*
by Robert Silverberg

*First-Person Singularities: Stories*
by Robert Silverberg
with an introduction by John Scalzi

*Tales from the Eternal Café: Stories*
by Janet Hamill, with an introduction
by Patti Smith

*Time and Time Again:
Sixteen Trips in Time*
by Robert Silverberg

### MULTI-AUTHOR

*Crime + Music: Twenty Stories
of Music-Themed Noir*
edited by Jim Fusilli

*Dark City Lights: New York Stories*
edited by Lawrence Block

*The Faking of the President: Twenty
Stories of White House Noir*
edited by Peter Carlaftes

*Florida Happens:
Bouchercon 2018 Anthology*
edited by Greg Herren

*Have a NYC I, II & III:
New York Short Stories;*
edited by Peter Carlaftes
& Kat Georges

*Songs of My Selfie:
An Anthology of Millennial Stories*
edited by Constance Renfrow

*The Obama Inheritance:
15 Stories of Conspiracy Noir*
edited by Gary Phillips

*This Way to the End Times:
Classic and New Stories of
the Apocalypse*
edited by Robert Silverberg

## MIXED MEDIA

John S. Paul
*Sign Language: A Painter's Notebook*
(photography, poetry and prose)

## FILM & PLAYS

Israel Horovitz
*My Old Lady: Complete Stage Play
and Screenplay with an Essay on
Adaptation*

Peter Carlaftes
*Triumph For Rent (3 Plays)*
*Teatrophy (3 More Plays)*

Kat Georges
*Three Somebodies: Plays about
Notorious Dissidents*

## DADA

*Maintenant: A Journal of
Contemporary Dada Writing & Art*
(Annual, since 2008)

## TRANSLATIONS

Thomas Bernhard
*On Earth and in Hell*
(poems of Thomas Bernhard
with English translations by
Peter Waugh)

Patrizia Gattaceca
*Isula d'Anima / Soul Island*
(poems by the author
in Corsican with English
translations)

César Vallejo | Gerard Malanga
*Malanga Chasing Vallejo*
(selected poems of César Vallejo
with English translations
and additional notes by
Gerard Malanga)

George Wallace
*EOS: Abductor of Men*
(selected poems in Greek & English)

## ESSAYS

*Womentality: Thirteen Empowering Stories
by Everyday Women Who Said Goodbye to
the Workplace and Hello to Their Lives*
edited by Erin Wildermuth

## HUMOR

Peter Carlaftes
*A Year on Facebook*

## POETRY COLLECTIONS

Hala Alyan
*Atrium*

Peter Carlaftes
*DrunkYard Dog*
*I Fold with the Hand I Was Dealt*

Thomas Fucaloro
*It Starts from the Belly and Blooms*
*Inheriting Craziness is Like
a Soft Halo of Light*

Kat Georges
*Our Lady of the Hunger*

Robert Gibbons
*Close to the Tree*

Israel Horovitz
*Heaven and Other Poems*

David Lawton
*Sharp Blue Stream*

Jane LeCroy
*Signature Play*

Philip Meersman
*This is Belgian Chocolate*

Jane Ormerod
*Recreational Vehicles on Fire*
*Welcome to the Museum of Cattle*

Lisa Panepinto
*On This Borrowed Bike*

George Wallace
*Poppin' Johnny*

Three Rooms Press | New York, NY | Current Catalog: www.threeroomspress.com
Three Rooms Press books are distributed by PGW/Ingram: www.pgw.com